Charmed

JAYNE ANN KRENTZ

writing as

JAYNE CASTLE
JULIE BEARD
LORI FOSTER
EILEEN WILKS

BERKLEY BOOKS, NEW YORK

CHARMED

A Berkley Book / published by arrangement with
the authors

PRINTING HISTORY
Berkley edition / October 1999

The Penguin Putnam Inc. World Wide Web site address is
http://www.penguinputnam.com

ISBN: 0-425-17129-9

PRINTED IN THE UNITED STATES OF AMERICA

10 9 8 7 6 5 4 3 2 1

Contents

Charmed

BRIDAL JITTERS

JAYNE CASTLE

One

Harmony: Cadence City, two hundred years after the closing of the Curtain

"So, is it true what they say about ghost-hunters?" Adeline Delmore leaned close and lowered her voice as she helped herself to another orange-frosted cookie. "Are they really *amazing* in bed after they've zapped a ghost? I've heard the sex is unbelievable right after a burn."

The question caught Virginia Burch just as she took a sip of the sparkling wine punch. She coughed and sputtered. Heat infused her cheeks. Unfortunately, she reflected glumly, bright pink was not her best color, especially on her face. She glanced wildly around to make sure no one else had overheard Adeline's outrageous question.

The offices of Gage & Burch were crowded with friends and colleagues, some of whom she could not recognize because, even though they were here to celebrate her engagement, most wore masks and costumes. It was Halloween week, after all; otherwise known here in Cadence as party-till-you-drop week. She wondered if the fact that her friends had chosen to throw a surprise engagement party with a Halloween theme was a bad omen. Not that she needed any more to warn her that her forthcoming marriage was probably a huge mistake.

Luckily someone had cranked up the volume of the music. The throbbing beat of a rez-rock song created a blanket of white noise that effectively shrouded conversations. As far as she could tell, no one had overheard Adeline's question about the sexual habits of ghost-hunters.

"Uh," Virginia said. To buy herself some time, she groped for a napkin decorated with a cartoon picture of a woman in a pointy black hat and a cape, riding a broomstick. "Uh, well—"

"I've heard the stories," Adeline continued, eyes gleaming. "And if you'll recall, I dated that good-looking hunter for a while. The one with the blue eyes and the curly black hair. I can't remember his name."

"Brett." It was hard to keep up with Adeline's ever-changing list of boyfriends, Virginia thought. But Brett had been memorable mostly because he had been a swaggering braggart. Of course, a lot of ghost-hunters were swaggering braggarts.

But not Sam. Whatever else he was, he was not a typical hunter.

She glanced across the room to where her new combination fiancé/business partner stood talking with one of the guests. Sam Gage didn't have to do any bragging, she thought wistfully. You knew just by looking at him that he could take care of himself and any ghost that happened along.

She was pretty sure he'd be terrific in bed, too, but she was beginning to think she might never find out the truth of that for herself.

"Oh, yeah, right," Adeline said. "Brett. That was his name. At any rate, he made some very interesting claims and promises. Ghost-hunters are not exactly shy when it comes to telling you about their sexual prowess. But our relationship didn't last long enough for me to run an experiment. Anyhow, I'm curious. I realize it's none of my business—"

"No, it's not."

"But I *am* your very best friend in the entire world," Adeline reminded her. "If you can't tell me, who can you tell?"

Virginia cleared her throat and decided to be honest. "Sorry, I'm not in a position to answer your question."

Adeline looked dumbfounded. "You're not? But you're going to marry Sam Gage. He's a hunter. This is your engagement party."

"Oddly enough, it looks more like a Halloween party to me."

"Okay, okay, so we decided to give it a theme. All the best parties have themes. I read it in last month's issue of *Harmonic Home & Garden*."

"I can't believe *Harmonic Home & Garden* told you that Halloween is considered an appropriate theme for an engagement party."

"Personally, I thought it was kind of original." Adeline looked across the crowded room to where Sam stood. A speculative light glittered in her deceptively innocent eyes. "Are you telling me that you two haven't done it yet? How weird."

"Adeline, I explained that Sam and I intend to apply for a two-year marriage-of-convenience license, not a covenant license."

"So what? That doesn't mean you aren't going to sleep together, does it?" Adeline broke off abruptly, eyes widening. *"Does it?"*

"This is business." Virginia swallowed. "I told you that."

Adeline looked skeptical. "One hundred percent business?"

"Yes."

"No fooling around at all?"

Virginia fought to quell the panic that had been nibbling at her for the past few days. "Like I said, it's a business arrangement."

Adeline groaned. "I don't believe it. You and Sam are a perfect couple."

Virginia paused, her plastic cup of punch halfway to her mouth. "What ever gave you that idea?"

"Are you kidding? You and Sam were made for each other. You've got so much in common."

"Such as?"

Adeline's brow climbed. "Well, for openers, you're both repressed, obsessive workaholics. Neither one of you seems to know how to have fun."

"Thanks a lot."

Adeline chuckled. "Should have seen the looks on your faces when you walked into the office this evening."

"We weren't expecting a party, Adeline."

"Yeah, I know." Adeline smiled smugly. "It was a surprise party. And it worked, didn't it?"

Virginia thought about the way her stomach had clenched when she had opened the door a short time earlier and been greeted with shrieks of *"Surprise."*

"It worked," she mumbled into her punch. "I was definitely surprised."

Adeline gave her an admonishing frown. "A lot of people went to a lot of effort to pull this off. Do me a favor: Try to look like you're having a good time, okay? Sam is taking it in stride."

Sam could take anything in stride, Virginia thought morosely, even an unanticipated engagement party. She caught a glimpse of him through the forest of black and orange balloons that dangled from the ceiling. He was still talking to the earnest-looking man in glasses.

Even surrounded by bobbing cardboard goblins, plastic jack-o'-lanterns and several yards of black and orange crepe paper, he looked, as he invariably did, completely at ease, totally in control.

He was a powerful dissonance-energy para-resonator—a ghost-hunter—but, thankfully, he did not go in for the long-haired, supermacho, khaki-and-leather look favored by most hunters. Tonight he was dressed in a black T-shirt, black trousers, and a tan jacket that fit well across his broad shoulders. He wore his resonating amber in a simple, gold ring rather than set in a massive belt buckle or a flashy pendant.

There was a relaxed air about him. The graceful languor of a natural-born predator at ease between kills emanated from him in psychic waves. Virginia could feel the disturbing energy all the way across the room. No one else seemed to be particularly aware of that aura—both dangerous and deeply sensual—that enveloped him, but it stirred all the tiny hairs on the nape of her neck.

Another twinge of panic zapped through her, unsettling both her physical and paranormal senses. The combined assault on her awareness made her shiver. The anxiety attacks were getting worse, she thought. Every time she contemplated marriage to Sam, she felt the small, high-rez shocks of trepidation.

What had she done?

She had agreed to marry Sam Gage; that was what she had done. Granted, it was only a two-year marriage-of-convenience. Nevertheless, she was going to be legally tied to him for two full years.

What had she done?

She forced herself to take a couple of deep breaths. When that did not block the tide of uneasiness that was doing such strange things to her insides, she tried another sip of the wine punch.

Just a marriage-of-convenience. They were common enough. It would end in two years unless she and Sam elected to renew it for another two-year period. There would be no reason to do that, she assured herself; no excuse to convert the MC into a more formal and far more binding covenant marriage.

Adeline was right; she had to project a little more good-natured enthusiasm here, Virginia told herself. She had agreed to the MC, after all. It was a terrific business move. And she certainly could not blame her friends for throwing a party. They meant well. And she was genuinely fond of most of them.

She was surrounded with a representative sprinkling of the professional and not-so-professional types involved in the many legitimate and not-so-legitimate businesses that had grown up around the excavation of the Dead City of Old Cadence. There were a number of academics from the university who were in the process of building distinguished careers studying the alien ruins. There were also several contract and freelance para-archaeologists, such as herself, and a few of Sam's ghost-hunter buddies who provided security to the excavation teams. In addition, there was a colorful assortment of gallery owners, hustlers, and ruin rats who worked the fringes of the trade in alien artifacts.

It was a mixed lot, to say the least, but they were all bound by their mutual interest in making their livings from the exploration and excavation of the ruins left by the long-vanished Harmonics.

It should have been a cheerful occasion, but she could feel the panic nibbling at her stomach.

"Sorry, Adeline. I guess I'm not in a party mood tonight."

"Fake it," Adeline said with a stern look.

Virginia gave her a reluctant smile. "Yes, ma'am."

"That's better." Adeline searched her face more closely. "What's the matter? I thought you were excited about this arrangement. Why the cold feet?"

"I'm not getting cold feet."

"Yes, you are. This is your old pal, Adeline, remember? I

know you better than anyone else. You've been getting increasingly short-tempered and high-strung for the past two weeks.''

Virginia glared at her and picked up the punch ladle. ''I've been a little busy lately, okay? I just finished the Henderson job yesterday, and Sam and I signed our first joint client this morning. We start work on the project tomorrow. On top of everything else, my family is hassling me about this MC, even though I've explained a hundred times that it's just a business deal.''

''Your family is still convinced that Sam is just taking advantage of you?''

''That's their official position.'' Virginia ladled more punch into her cup. ''But the truth is, they want me to settle down in a covenant marriage with Duncan.''

Adeline shrugged. ''Can't blame them. Duncan is a great catch. Good family, good connections. Nice guy.''

''Duncan and I are friends, but it will never amount to more than that.'' Virginia dropped the ladle back into the bowl and took a hefty swallow of the punch. ''Duncan and I both know it, even if our families don't.''

''You mean you don't love him, and he doesn't love you.''

''Yes. That's exactly what I mean.''

Adeline raised her brows. ''So, instead of a nice, safe marriage to good ol' Duncan, you're going to take a flyer on a two-year MC with a man you hardly know and who is a ghost-hunter to boot. Gee, can't imagine why the family is upset about that decision. Nope. Can't think of a single reason why your relatives would have a problem with your plans.''

Virginia gave her a speaking glance. ''It's business.''

Adeline assumed an infuriating all-knowing expression. ''Know what I think?''

''What?''

''I think you've got a radical case of nerves. Bridal jitters, as my aunt Sally would say.''

"That's ridiculous. Why would I be nervous?"

"Excellent question."

"This is just a business deal." Virginia suspected that she was beginning to sound desperate. She tried to temper her tone. She wanted to sound calm and cool. As calm and cool as Sam had sounded when he had presented her with the proposition three weeks ago.

"This section of the Old Quarter is slated for gentrification within the next couple of years," he had explained. "Investors and developers are already starting to nose around. This house is going to be worth a fortune soon. But in the meantime, I've got to find a way to hang on to it."

She gazed at her new landlord in genuine alarm. She had rented her office and her upstairs apartment from him less than two months ago. She had found the old house at the end of a long, fruitless day spent tracking down the addresses of virtually every affordable rental in the Old Quarter of Cadence City. It had not been an advertised rental, but she had decided to make inquiries after noting the small sign on the door, which read Dead City Security, Sam Gage, Prop.

Her intent had been to ask the unknown Mr. Gage, who was clearly a small businessperson like herself, if he was aware of any suitable space in the neighborhood. The choicest rentals, she had learned, were frequently obtained by word of mouth rather than through the want ads.

Her initial impression of Sam Gage, the owner and sole employee of Dead City Security, was that he was not what one expected in a ghost-hunter who had set up shop as a security consultant. She had found him in his office, ankles propped on his desk, deep into the current issue of the *Journal of Para-Archaeology*. Heavy reading for a ghost-hunter, she thought. Most of the ones she knew preferred *Sex-Starved Psychic Playmates* and *Naked Amazon Maidens of the Alien Catacombs*.

Before the end of the conversation, Gage had offered her

an office on the first floor and an apartment on the second. She had fallen in love with both spaces the moment she had seen them. She was beginning to think that she had fallen in love with her new landlord at approximately the same time, but that was another issue altogether, one she did not want to confront.

"Hang on to it?" she repeated warily. "Is there a problem?"

"Just the usual. Taxes, upkeep, repairs." He spread the fingers of his amber-ringed hand in a gesture that encompassed all the trials and tribulations of home ownership. "This house was built right after the Era of Discord. That makes it over a hundred and fifty years old. It was built to last, so it's sound, but it needs a lot of work."

"I see." She looked around at the elegant molding, gleaming wooden floors, and uniquely framed windows.

The place was perfect for her one-person consulting business. The location, only two short blocks from the great, green quartz wall that surrounded the Dead City, was ideal. Her work required frequent trips both above ground and deep into the catacombs of the ancient alien ruins. From here, she could walk to her job site, which meant she would not have the expense of a car.

She cleared her throat uneasily. "Are you thinking of raising the rent already? Because, if so, I'd like to remind you that I do have a one-year lease."

He braced his hands on the top of her desk and leaned slightly forward. His amber-colored eyes were steady and intent. "No, I'm not going to raise your rent. I've got a proposition for you. If things work out the way I think they will, we'll both make a killing."

His idea had been a straightforward business arrangement. A marriage-of-convenience and a merger of her consulting business with his Dead City Security. He'd painted a dazzling picture. Operating as a single entity, Gage & Burch Consulting, they would double their resources overnight. Together, they would be able to compete for larger, more lucrative clients. The increased revenue would go into maintenance. The MC would ensure that they paid lower taxes. When the house was sold to developers in two years, they would share equally in the profits. A win-win situation.

All she had to do was find a way to be as cold-blooded about the arrangement as Sam. Unfortunately, the closer they drew to the date of the wedding, the less certain she was that such a thing was possible.

"I told you," Virginia said to Adeline. "Sam wants to hang on to this house until some developer is willing to pay big bucks for it. He offered to cut me in on the profits. It's a terrific business opportunity for me." Who was she trying to convince? She wondered.

Adeline reached for a piece of neon-orange candy. "Maybe the fact that it's just a business deal is part of the problem. Maybe that's not what you want."

No, Virginia thought. It most definitely was not what she wanted. Late this afternoon, after a long walk and a cup of coffee in the lonely little park at the end of the street, she had finally forced herself to face that fact. She was in love with Sam, but all he wanted from her was her signature on a contract. Marriage, especially a marriage-of-convenience, would be hell. The frustration factor alone would probably drive her to the nearest para-psych ward within a month. She was almost sure now that she could not go through with the arrangement.

But she had not yet figured out how to tell Sam.

She had planned to get things out in the open tonight. Then she had opened the door of the office and walked straight into the engagement party.

She could hardly bring up the subject now in the midst of a party. She would wait until morning. Tomorrow would be soon enough to tell him that she was having second thoughts.

She felt a guilty sense of relief at having made the decision to put off the inevitable for another few hours.

She was getting cold feet. He could feel the chill clear across the room. Every time he caught her eye, she averted her gaze or started up an earnest conversation with whoever happened to be standing nearby.

The last of the guests finally departed shortly after midnight. Sam closed the door behind the laggard and turned to see Virginia sinking down into the chair behind her desk. His bride-to-be looked both relieved and exhausted. She also looked cross. But then, lately she frequently looked tense and irritable. Bridal jitters. The odd thing was that the more anxious she got, the calmer and more certain he became.

She leaned back in the chair and closed her eyes. "Thought they'd never go."

"They meant well," he said.

"I know." She rested her head against the back of her chair. "But they don't understand."

"Sure they do. We're getting married. People like to celebrate marriages. Even MCs."

"I don't see why."

"Because there is a streak of the romantic buried somewhere inside most people," he explained patiently. "Deep down, everyone hopes that marriages-of-convenience will morph into the real thing."

"That's a highly unrealistic expectation. Statistically speaking, most MCs end on the first or second renewal date unless someone makes a mistake and gets pregnant." She paused meaningfully. "And there is absolutely no excuse for that kind of mistake."

"Right. No excuse."

Few mistakes of that sort were made because the First Generation colonists who had settled Harmony had crafted very strict legislation covering marriage and family. The more liberal social policies of Earth had been abandoned when the energy Curtain that had served as a gate between worlds had unexpectedly closed, stranding the settlers. The founders, desperate to provide a social structure that would ensure the survival of the colony, had opted for stern laws. But in their wisdom, the First Generation planners had also understood that harsh rules that did not take human weaknesses into account would ultimately fail. Failure of the social structure of the tiny band of desperate settlers would mean catastrophe.

In an effort to deal with basic human foibles, the founders had provided the socially and legally sanctioned marriages-of-convenience to cover many of the traditional and less-than-romantic reasons that drove people into wedlock: family pressure, business, or simple passion. Couples who elected to have children were expected to file for the more formal covenant marriage.

The muted warble and twang of a high-rez rock guitar sounded from the street. Sam crossed the office to the window, made a space between the blinds, and studied the night-shrouded sidewalk.

The Old Quarter teemed with revelers tonight. The heavy river fog that had cloaked Cadence nightly for the past several days had deterred no one. People dressed as witches, goblins, and ghosts—the fairytale sort, not the very real remnants of dangerous alien energy known as *unstable dissonance energy manifestations*—drifted in and out of the mists. Orange lights came and went eerily in the shadows. As Sam watched, a grinning jack-o'-lantern appeared out the gloom. Someone shrieked in pretended fright. Raucous laughter echoed in the night.

This was Halloween eve, and the noise level was already high. Tomorrow night, Halloween night, would be bedlam. Half of Cadence would flock to the Old Quarter to party. There was no place in town quite as atmospheric at Halloween as the seedy districts adjacent to the ancient walls of the Dead City.

In this part of town, ambient psi energy leaked continuously through tiny, often invisible cracks in the emerald-colored stones. It seeped up from the endless miles of green quartz tunnels and corridors beneath the pavement. The little currents and eddies of energy were part of the lure of the Old Quarters of all the cities on Harmony that had been built near the sites of ancient ruins. Tourists and locals alike loved the creepy sensations, especially at this time of year.

Maybe there was something to the theory that the flickers of psychic and para energy were stronger at this time of year, Sam thought. Ever since he had been a kid running loose on the streets, it had always seemed to him that he was more aware of the traces of ancient alien psi energy at Halloween. Tonight was no exception. The not-quite-human trickles of power that leaked out of the Dead City felt very strong. The stuff whispered through his mind, making him deeply aware of the unseen paranormal world that hovered just beyond the range of the physical senses. The surge in power levels that he detected were probably nothing more than the result of his overactive imagination, he thought. The same imagination that had conjured up the brilliant idea of talking Virginia into a marriage-of-convenience.

In hindsight, all he could say was that it had seemed like a good idea at the time.

Behind him, Virginia yawned. "We'd better get some sleep. Mac Ewert will be expecting us early tomorrow morning. He's anxious to get his excavation site cleared so that he can get his team back on the job. He made a big point of reminding me of how much money he's losing with every day of lost work."

"You're right. We need some sleep. Don't want to doze off in front of Gage & Burch's first client." Sam turned away from the window. "I'll see you to your door."

For a few seconds, the tension in her eyes retreated. She gave him a familiar, laughing smile, the kind of smile she had bestowed on him frequently until he had asked her to merge her business with his and file for an MC. At the sight of the glowing look, he felt his whole body tighten. The desire he had worked so hard to conceal for the past two months heated his blood. With every passing hour it was getting harder to quash the rush of sexual anticipation that stirred him whenever he was near Virginia.

By the time his nonwedding night arrived, he would be a basket case.

What the *hell* had he been thinking? A marriage-of-convenience in which he slept on the third floor while Virginia slept on the second floor was going to make him certifiably crazy.

She rose from the chair and stretched. "I thought it was my turn to see you to your door."

"Want to flip a coin?"

"Okay, but this time let's try one of my mine. I don't trust that one that you like to use. It always comes up heads." She dug a quarter out of her pocket. "Call it."

"Heads." He moved toward her.

She flipped the coin into the air. He caught it before it struck the polished surface of her desk.

"Heads," he said without bothering to look at it.

She wrinkled her nose. "You're in luck. I'm too tired to argue."

At the door of the office, she paused to switch off the lights. He followed her out into the front hall and locked up. Together, they climbed the elaborately carved central staircase to the second floor and went down the corridor to the small suite of rooms she used as an apartment.

She opened her door, stepped inside, and swung around to face him through the narrow opening. Her green-and-gold eyes were big and deep in the shadows. He could feel the tingle of awareness in his paranormal senses and knew that he was responding to her on the psychic plane as well as on the physical level. Sensual psi energy shimmered disturbingly in the small space that separated them. Couldn't she sense it? He wondered. Was she really oblivious to the attraction between them?

The wariness in her eyes made him uneasy. With each passing day, she appeared to be growing more restless. His fears of being driven crazy by sexual frustration were submerged beneath a new concern: What if she changed her mind? What if she canceled the MC?

Stay focused, he told himself. *This will work.* It had to work.

"Good night," he said as casually as he could manage. He forced himself to take a step back. What he really wanted to do was pick her up and carry her through the small living room, straight into her bedroom. "I'll see you in the morning."

She hesitated. "Sam?"

"Yeah?" He realized that he had stopped breathing.

She sighed. "Never mind. It's not important. Good night."

Very gently, she closed the door in his face.

He reminded himself to breathe.

Two

He did not sleep well that night. It was not the noise from the crowds in the street or the whispers of Dead City psi energy that kept him awake. It was the realization that Virginia was getting ready to tell him that she did not want to go through with the marriage. He knew it as surely as he knew that when she called off the engagement, his world was going to become as bleak and gray as the tide of fog that had boiled up out of the river.

He rolled out of bed at dawn, shaved, showered, and dressed for the meeting with Ewert. He was still mulling over various means of convincing Virginia that the MC was a terrific idea when he went downstairs to collect the morning edition of the *Cadence Star*. He opened the front door and was greeted by a wall of gray mist. The fog was so thick that it had blotted out the early-morning sun, creating an artificial twilight that looked as if it would last all day.

Perfect Halloween weather.

He shrugged off the fog. It would not affect today's job. He and Virginia would be working underground in the catacombs. Down below in the endless miles of glowing green corridors, there was no day or night.

He saw the small package on the step just as he started to reach for the newspaper. A faint hiss of all-too-familiar psi energy whispered through his para senses in silent warning.

"Damn." Hell of a way to start the day.

He crouched on his heels to get a closer look at the square object wrapped in brown paper. It was addressed to Gage & Burch Consulting. There was no return address. He did not pick it up.

"Something wrong, Sam?" Virginia called out from half-way down the stairs.

"An unscheduled delivery." He did not take his eyes off the package.

"What is it?"

"I think you'd better take a look at this. If I'm right, it falls into your area of expertise, not mine."

She descended the rest of the stairs quickly and hurried across the wide front hall to the door. She came to a halt beside him and looked at the package.

She pursed her lips thoughtfully. "Uh-oh."

"I hate it when you use that professional jargon." He glanced at her. "What do you think?"

"The same thing you're thinking, I imagine. It's an illusion trap. I can feel the energy pattern. Someone left us a nasty little trick. I'll bet it was some idiot who had one too many bottles of Green Ruin to drink last night. Probably thought it would be a great Halloween prank."

"I think he'll change his mind when I find him," Sam said softly.

Virginia glanced at him, frowning slightly. "Don't worry, it's just a small trap."

"Can you de-rez it?"

"Does amber resonate? Of course I can de-rez it. But I'm

not going to do it out here on the front step. Let's take it into the kitchen.''

She reached down and scooped up the box with a nonchalance that made Sam wince. He followed her into the big kitchen at the back of the house and watched her set the box down on the scarred counter.

''You might want to stand back a little,'' she said as she clipped the string. ''Just in case.''

''We're partners, remember?'' He moved closer to the counter.

She smiled as she began to unwrap the package. ''Yes, but you've never seen me work. I wouldn't blame you for being a tad cautious. Even small, simple illusion traps can be very unpleasant if they aren't untangled properly.''

''I've spent a lot of time underground and I've worked with some clumsy tanglers. I've caught the flashback from an accidentally sprung trap more than once.''

''Well, there won't be any flashback this time. You have my personal guarantee.''

Her cool, professional arrogance amused him. He watched her peel away the brown paper. A small cardboard box was revealed. With a good deal more caution than she had exercised a moment ago, she raised the lid and gazed inside.

''Well, well, well,'' she murmured. She sounded as cheerful as if she had just received a bouquet of flowers.

Personally, he could think of a number of other things he would rather find on his doorstep first thing in the morning besides an illusion trap. But if the challenge of de-rezzing it lifted Virginia's spirits and gave her something else to think about besides calling off their marriage, he might be willing to overlook the prank.

''What is it?'' he asked.

''A very nice piece.'' She angled the box to allow him a closer look at the object inside. ''A little unguent jar. Museum quality. Not spectacular, but quite excellent. It would bring a good price in a gallery. I can't imagine anyone in his right mind wasting it just to play a vicious Halloween trick.''

Sam eyed the small green quartz jar. It was elegantly rounded in a shape that was not quite comfortable for a human hand. The top was carved in an airy, fanciful design similar to many he had seen in the course of his career. The art and sculpture left behind by the long-vanished Harmonics always reminded him of the Old Earth poet Goethe's description of architecture: *frozen music.*

"You're right," he said. "It's not unique, but it's definitely valuable. Whoever our prankster is, he must be a wealthy collector if he could afford to use an artifact worth a couple of grand just to pull off a Halloween stunt."

An illusion trap had to be anchored to an artifact or to old green quartz from the ruins.

"Probably too drunk to realize what he was doing." Virginia carefully lifted the top of the jar and peered into the dark interior. "Okay, here we go. It's a simple pattern. This won't take long."

"Easy for you to say." He looked down into the shadows inside the little unguent jar. The darkness there was not normal. There was a dense quality to it, the only visible warning of the tiny trap. In the eerie glow of the green catacombs of the Dead City it was all too easy for a member of an excavation team to mistake illusion dark for ordinary shadow, but here in the brightly lit kitchen, the difference was obvious to the trained eye.

Obvious, but no less dangerous.

He had seen other tanglers work, but this was the first time he had watched Virginia in action. She'd only had a handful of clients during the time she had been renting office space from him, and she had dealt with them on her own.

He felt psi energy spark and shiver in the air. Very high-rez. He was impressed. She was as powerful as her academic credentials claimed.

Technically speaking, she was an ephemeral-energy para-resonator; a tangler in common parlance. With the aid of the specially tuned amber that she wore in her earrings, she could focus her particular type of paranormal energy in a way that allowed her to neutralize the vicious and sometimes deadly illusion traps. The wicked snares were one of the hazards of para-archaeological work in the alien ruins. The vast majority of tanglers became para-archaeologists. It was one of two natural career paths, the second being the illegal antiquities market.

An illusion trap was tricky. Once tripped, it released a web of ephemeral psi energy in an alien nightmare that enveloped the mind of the unlucky person who had triggered it. No two traps produced the same harrowing visions. Some were simple to de-rez, especially the really old ones. But in later Harmonic traps, the energy had been woven into complex patterns that defied all but the most skilled tanglers.

No one who had ever survived the experience of being caught in an illusion trap's web could ever fully describe the nightmares. Sam had sensed enough on the occasions when he had been zapped with some of the flashback energy from a poorly sprung trap to know that the visions were composed of unimaginable colors and a vertigo-inspiring darkness. The experts claimed that the nightmares lasted only a few minutes before the human brain sought refuge in unconsciousness. The resulting coma, however, could last for hours or days. When the victim eventually awakened, he or she invariably suffered an amnesia that cloaked most memories of the event. Some never recovered completely. They tended to end up in the para-psych wards of mental institutions. Others were so traumatized they could never work underground again.

No one knew why the Harmonics had booby trapped their underground catacombs. Whoever their enemies had been, they were as long gone as those who had set snares for them.

"Got it," Virginia said with soft satisfaction. She took a

breath and looked up from the jar. "Didn't even heat up my amber. It's clean."

"Nice job." He picked up the jar and turned it in his hands, examining it from every angle. The fizz of malign energy that had warned him of the trap had ceased. The trap could be reset by a skilled tangler, but unless that was done, the unguent jar was safe to handle.

He looked down into the interior. The unnatural, viscous shadow was gone. In its place was the ordinary darkness one expected to find in the interior of any small vessel. There was also something else inside the little jar. He pulled out a square of folded paper.

Virginia frowned. "It looks like a note."

"Yes, it does, doesn't it? Maybe our prankster wants to brag. Thoughtful of him to provide a clue." He unfolded the paper and read aloud the single sentence typed on it. " 'Happy Halloween. The ghosts and goblins are real in the catacombs this week. Stay out. This will be your only warning.' "

"What in the world?"

"Not real original," Sam remarked.

Virginia snatched the paper from his hand. "Let me see that." Her brows drew together in a stern line as she read it silently. Then she looked at him. "What do you think this is all about?"

"I think," Sam said, "that one of Mac Ewert's competitors doesn't want us to go to work for him. Wouldn't be the first time a rival has tried to scare off another team's consultants."

"Huh." She dropped the note into the trash. "Obviously whoever sent this doesn't realize who they're dealing with. The firm of Gage & Burch doesn't get scared off *that* easily."

Sam saw the gutsy determination in her eyes and smiled. For some reason he suddenly felt a lot more optimistic about his marriage prospects than he had when he had come downstairs earlier.

• • •

"Damndest thing I've ever seen." Mac Ewert ran a blunt-fingered hand through his thinning gray hair. "I've heard of waterfalls, but I've been mapping catacombs for twenty years, and this is the first one I've ever run into."

"They're rare," Sam agreed. "But I think we can handle it for you."

Virginia felt her jaw drop. She barely managed to conceal her shock. She was amazed by Sam's casual response to Ewert's announcement. They were going to have to de-rez a *waterfall?* She almost groaned aloud. Of all the bad luck. This was just what they did not need for their first time out as the new firm of Gage & Burch; a nearly impossible assignment. She was the one who had taken the call yesterday morning from Mac. He had certainly not mentioned anything about a waterfall.

She reminded herself that waterfalls fell into Sam's area of expertise. She had to admire him for projecting an image of professional confidence, but she seriously doubted that he'd had any experience with waterfalls. Few people had.

She had read about them, of course. They were described in the textbooks as unique cascades of unstable dissonance-energy manifestations—ghosts—that could block entire corridors. Unlike most UDEMs, they did not drift aimlessly through the underground tunnels of the Dead City. Instead, they were anchored in one place, forming impenetrable walls of seething psi energy that could fry anyone dumb enough to get too close. Little was known about them because so few had been discovered. Those that had been found had been de-rezzed by teams of very expensive, highly specialized experts, not by small-time security consultants. Sam would be on his own with this one. Her name was now on the newly repainted door of the office, but that didn't mean she could help him with the waterfall. This was a job for a ghost-hunter. A really, really good ghost-hunter. All she could do was cheer him on.

Ewert gave Sam a look of mingled desperation and aggressive demand. "Think you can handle it, Gage? This project is already running behind schedule. I've had one delay after another in the tunnels during the past month. I can't afford any more."

"I'll take a look," Sam said. "I can give you a firm answer as soon as I examine it."

Ewert planted his hands on his desk and glanced at the khaki-and-leather clad man who lounged against the wall. "Leon, here, doesn't think any single hunter can deactivate it. He tells me I'm going to have to contract with the guild for a team of specialists. Trouble is, my budget won't stretch that far."

"It's big," Leon drawled. "More ghost energy than I've ever seen in one place and I've been working underground for damn near fifteen years."

Virginia glanced at him. Leon Drummond was the Ewert team's ghost-hunter. He was working on a standard guild contract. He had made it clear that he resented having a private consultant brought in to handle the waterfall problem.

Leon was everything that gave ghost-hunters a bad name, as far as Virginia was concerned. He was arrogant, macho, ill-mannered, and he had poor taste in clothes. His oversized belt buckle was studded with so much amber that if he ever fell into the river, she was pretty sure that he would sink like a stone.

"Like I said, I can give you an answer after I've had a look at the waterfall," Sam said calmly.

"Suit yourself," Leon muttered.

Ewert leaned wearily back in his chair. "Leon will take you to the site. I can't allow anyone else into that corridor until the waterfall is cleared. Too dangerous. For God's sake, don't do anything stupid. If you and Miss Burch can't handle it, just say so. My insurance won't cover any lawsuits."

Sam nodded as he got to his feet. "We'll keep that in mind. Ready, Virginia?"

If nothing else, this was going to be interesting, she thought. Not many people got an opportunity to see a real ghost-energy waterfall. In spite of her misgivings, anticipation rose within her.

"Ready," she said.

With a shrug, Leon managed to straighten himself away from the office wall. He turned and sauntered out through the door without a word. Sam and Virginia followed him outside to where the utility vehicle waited.

The eerie green glow given off by the emerald-hued quartz that lined the alien catacombs always had the same effect on Virginia: It sent a tiny chill of dread and wonder down her spine. The sensation was not a thrill of fear exactly; more a deep, elemental response to that which was not human. She had grown up in the very shadow of the ancient ruins, and she had been aware of her own psychic response to the peculiar energy that resonated within its walls since childhood. But she did not think that she would ever be entirely comfortable in the mysterious tunnels. Some part of her would always feel like an intruder here.

No one knew what the ancient Harmonics had looked like. No pictures or records of physical descriptions had ever been found. None of the art that had survived depicted the vanished beings who had created it. No one could even guess why Harmony's original inhabitants had built these endless miles of catacombs, most of which had never been charted. But one thing was certain: The business of exploring, mapping, and excavating relics from the ruins was big. And the competition could be fierce.

Virginia sat next to Sam on the second bench of the small, open-sided utility truck. Leon Drummond took the wheel, piloting the vehicle through the maze of intersecting corridors with the aid of an amber-rez locator. He had remained sullenly silent since leaving Ewert's office.

Sam had not had much to say, either. Virginia studied him out of the corner of her eye. He was playing it cool, she thought. But, then, Sam always played it cool. If he had any doubts about confronting a dangerous waterfall of unstable dissonant energy, he did not allow them to show.

Virginia wanted to ask him why he had not mentioned the illusion trap they had found on their doorstep that morning to Mac Ewert, but she was not about to bring up the subject in front of Leon Drummond.

There was another, more personal matter that she had not yet gotten around to this morning, either, she reminded herself: marriage. She had promised herself that she would tell Sam about her growing doubts, but then had come the business of the illusion trap, and after that they'd had to hurry in order to make the meeting with Ewert.

What with one thing and another, she had found excuses not to deal with the issue of their marriage.

She glanced at the glowing green maw of an intersecting corridor as Leon drove past. There was a warning sign posted at the entrance. Keep Out. Unmapped Zone. Sort of like her engagement, she thought. Another little chill went through her, but this time it had nothing to do with the alien catacombs. She would talk to Sam this evening, she promised herself. Right after they had finished this consulting project.

She could not put it off another day. Her nerves couldn't take the stress.

She studied the quartz walls as the utility truck traveled along the corridor. The endless green stone passages were interrupted here and there by small, slightly less than human-sized openings that, she knew from experience, led to chambers. Most of the rooms and anterooms discovered in the underground regions of the ancient city were small, but some vast, exotic spaces had been found. Explorers had untrapped chambers so large and elegantly proportioned that many para-archaeologists assumed they had been used for ceremonial functions or royal tombs. But they could just as easily have been employed as underground aircraft hangers for all anyone knew.

Twenty minutes later, Leon slowed the cab and turned into the entrance of a branching tunnel. Virginia caught a glimpse of another warning sign. Keep Out: UDEM Ahead.

Leon brought the cab to a halt and finally deigned to speak. "The waterfall is down that corridor on the right."

The announcement was unnecessary. The pulsing, acid-green light of the unnaturally large concentration of ghost energy was already visible. It throbbed at the entrance of the corridor. Virginia gazed at it, amazed. She had never seen that much ghost light in one place in her entire career. She could only guess at the size of the UDEM itself. It was still out of sight around the corner.

Beside her, Sam moved. He got out of the cab and walked toward the entrance of the branching corridor. His hard face was etched in lines of concentration and keen anticipation. He was looking forward to this, Virginia thought. Well, what else had she expected? He was a ghost-hunter, after all, and this was undoubtedly the most dangerous, most challenging energy specter he had ever been called upon to de-rez. She would probably be feeling the same excitement if they were confronting a particularly complex illusion trap.

Sam paused at the entrance of the tunnel. He glanced back at her over his shoulder "Wait here. I'm going to take a closer look."

Leon draped his arms on the steering wheel and watched Sam disappear around the corner into the pulsing green light. "This won't take long. Once he sees the size of that thing, he'll be back. He'd have to be a fool to try to tackle that sucker on his own."

Virginia did not like his tone. The last thing she wanted to do was wait here with Leon.

"I'm going with him." She hopped lightly down from the truck.

Leon scowled. "Are you a hunter, too?"

"No, I'm a tangler."

"This ain't no job for a tangler," Leon said. "That's a ghost in there, not some wimpy little illusion trap."

Virginia ignored him. She went quickly toward the tunnel entrance. When she rounded the corner, she was nearly blinded by the fierce, oddly cold glare. She narrowed her eyes against the intense glow and saw Sam. He was silhouetted in front of a cascading wall of pure green energy: the waterfall.

It was an astonishing sight. Light tumbled, swirled, and flowed in oceanlike waves that poured in an endlessly circulating fountain from ceiling to floor and back again. The wall of churning energy blocked the entire corridor, which was narrower than most. The interior dimensions were much smaller than those of the outer tunnel where Leon Drummond waited in the truck.

For some reason, the silence of the waterfall struck Virginia as strange, even though she had seen enough ghosts in her time to know that there was rarely much noise associated with them. A few pops and crackles and the occasional hiss of the ice-cold energy constituted the usual range of the sound effects.

"It really does look like a waterfall," she exclaimed as she went forward to join Sam. "You'd almost expect to see a river or a pool of psi energy forming at the bottom."

Sam frowned at her. "I thought I told you to wait in the truck."

"Not a chance." She gazed at the tumbling green waves. "We're a team, remember?"

"This isn't illusion energy."

"Right. You're the expert on this stuff. I'll just supervise." He hesitated. "I've always worked alone."

"Not anymore." She turned toward him. "It was your idea to merge our businesses, remember?"

He gave her an odd look. "Yeah. I remember."

She turned back to the cascades of green fire. "Well? What's your professional opinion, Mr. Ghost-Hunter? Can you handle it?"

Sam did not answer immediately, but his eyes gleamed in the reflected glow. His mouth curved slightly.

"Does amber resonate?" he asked with just a hint of old-fashioned ghost-hunter arrogance. "Yeah, I can handle it. But I'll have to de-rezz it one section at a time."

"Why?"

"Because it's not really one large ghost. It's composed of a number of smaller UDEMs that have been linked to create the waterfall effect."

"Aha. That makes sense. Whoever did this also figured out how to anchor it in place, too, like an illusion trap. I've never heard of a ghost that didn't just drift aimlessly."

Sam moved a little closer to the waterfall. "It's old. Very, very old. Probably been here for eons."

"I can believe it." Virginia shivered. "I'm sure the ancients knew a lot of Halloween tricks that we humans will uncover the hard way."

"Might as well get to work." Sam walked slowly across the width of the tunnel, as though measuring the breadth of the waterfall. He came to a halt at one side.

Virginia felt the invisible rush of human psi energy. A lot of it. She had seen Sam work before but never on a project that demanded so much para-talent. She took a respectful step back, not wanting to get in his way or disturb his concentration. De-rezzing this monster ghost was going to take a great deal of focused psi power.

Silence hummed for a few minutes.

Waterfall light flared, glinting off Sam's strong cheekbones. The green glare transformed the hard planes and angles of his face into an eerie, menacing mask. He gazed, seemingly riveted by the waterfall.

It was probably because he was concentrating so intently on the job at hand that she was the one who heard the high-pitched whine of the utility truck's engine first. She glanced back over her shoulder, surprised to see that Leon had braved the corridor, after all.

The small truck barreled toward where she stood with Sam in front of the waterfall. It was moving quickly; too quickly. She put up a hand to warn Leon to halt.

Then she realized that Leon was not at the wheel. No one was in the open-sided truck. Someone had rezzed the engine, slammed it into gear, and sent it hurtling down the narrow corridor toward Sam and her. It was a tight fit. Assuming the vehicle continued to travel in a straight line, there would be only a foot of clearance on either side. With a sickening sensation in the pit of her stomach, she realized that even if they could flatten themselves into that small space, it would do them no good. When the truck slammed into the energy waterfall, there would be an explosion. The flashback of ghost energy would crash over them. If they survived the experience, the tide of raw alien energy would fry their brains. She and Sam would not be able to do much more than sit in front of a rez-screen watching sitcoms twenty-four hours a day for the rest of their lives.

If they survived. And that was a very big if.

"Sam."

He swung around, taking in the situation in a single glance.

"Sonofabitch." He scooped her up in his arms. "Hang on. Tight."

She wanted to argue, but there didn't seem to be much point. There was no place to run. She wrapped her arms around his neck and buried her face against his chest, filling her senses with the scent of him one last time. If they were going to go, she couldn't think of anyone she would rather go with than Sam.

"I love you," she whispered into his shirt.

But she knew that he had not heard her. For one thing, the utility truck was almost upon them now. The fully rezzed engine was screaming too loudly to make even normal levels of conversation possible.

The second thing that made a dramatic farewell impossible was that Sam was projecting an enormous amount of psi energy. She could feel it enveloping her as he held her tightly against his chest. So much power required the use of all of his internal resources, both physical and paranormal. The last thing he could do at that moment was pay attention to what she had muttered into his shirt. It was a wonder he had the strength to hold her in his arms.

She heard the whine of the swiftly advancing truck, felt Sam tighten his arms fiercely around her, and then, impossibly, she was suddenly aware of being surrounded by a rushing sea of alien energy. Ghost energy.

She realized that Sam had chosen to escape the utility truck by leaping through the waterfall with her in his arms.

The acid-green waterfall washed over her in a giant wave. She braced herself for the searing mind burn but, incredibly, the energy did not touch her. She could feel the weight of it pressing on her from all sides, sensed the raw power that seethed in the cascade, *but it did not touch her.* It was as if she was protected by an invisible envelope.

The world whirled on its axis. She felt a jarring thud that took her breath. She heard Sam grunt and then she felt the cool green quartz beneath her. She realized that they had both landed on the floor of the corridor—on the other side of the waterfall.

Sam rolled with her in his arms, carrying her to the edge of the tunnel. They came up hard against the quartz wall.

Sam released her and got to his feet. He swung around to

face the cascade of green energy. Dazed, Virginia sat up slowly, pushing hair out of her eyes. She stared at the waterfall. Sam had carried her through that mass of alien energy. Without a scratch.

Unless, of course, this was how you felt after your brain got fried. Maybe her mind hadn't yet assimilated the fact of its own destruction. Perhaps a lifetime of sitcoms still awaited her. Heaven help her, maybe she would actually enjoy them.

Before she could mention that awful possibility to Sam, she heard the explosion on the other side of the UDEM waterfall. She knew what had happened because she had seen similar events, albeit on a far smaller scale. The utility truck had slammed into the energy wall and been bounced back like a rubber ball. The inevitable blast that accompanied the meeting of an immovable object and an unstoppable vehicle had taken place at the point of impact on the other side of the waterfall.

Here on the back side of the energy cascade, it was business as usual. There was no backwash of energy.

A stunning silence descended. Nothing broke it except the occasional hiss and crackle produced by the tumbling fountain of ghost energy.

"You did it." Virginia tore her gaze off the waterfall and looked at Sam. "You got us through it in one piece. How in the name of Old Earth did you manage it?"

"I didn't try to de-rez the whole damn waterfall. Just neutralized a section big enough to allow us to pass through for about thirty seconds." He spoke absently, as if his thoughts were on something else that was far more important. "Couldn't hold it any longer than that. At least not while I—" He broke off.

"You mean, you couldn't de-rez it for more than a few seconds and carry me through it at the same time," she said. "You don't have to spell it out. I know how much psi power that little leap through the waterfall must have cost you. I must have felt as heavy as that damn truck in your arms."

His brows rose. "A gentleman never calls attention to a lady's weight."

"I appreciate that." She frowned. "You must have melted your amber."

He glanced at his ring. "Yeah, it's fused. I've got a backup chunk, but I won't be able to use it for a while."

She looked around warily. The section of corridor in which they stood looked very much like the section on the other side of the waterfall. The same pale, luminous green glow infused the impermeable quartz. Here and there she caught the telltale trace of illusion shadow that marked the concealed door to a hidden room or antechamber. The dizzying maze of intersecting tunnels stretched out ahead as far as she could see.

The difference between this section of the catacombs and those on the other side of the waterfall, of course, was that this sector had not yet been officially mapped. The safest way out would be to go back through the waterfall, but that would not be possible until Sam had recovered from the aftereffects of melting amber. Besides, Leon Drummond might be waiting on the other side.

She checked her earrings. "My amber is still good. At least we won't lose our sense of direction."

Underground, the only thing that kept you oriented was tuned amber. Without it, the endless miles of eerie quartz tunnels became a hopelessly impenetrable labyrinth, even with a locator.

"Drummond tried to kill us," Sam said without inflection. "My guess is he's our Halloween trickster."

"The one who left that trap on our doorstep last night?"

"Yeah. Someone must be paying him very well to sabotage Ewert's map team. The guild frowns on that sort of thing. Bad public relations."

"Especially now when the guild is trying so hard to build a good public image." Virginia scrambled awkwardly to her feet. She glanced down, half-expecting to find scorch marks on her trousers. She saw nothing but a few new wrinkles. She looked up again. "Sam, you must be exhausted."

"Not yet. The afterburn is still kicking in. The buzz will last for about an hour. Then I'm going to have to crash for at least two or three hours. No way to beat it."

She nodded. The syndrome was well-known. Ghost-hunters who expended large amounts of psi energy needed time to recover.

Sam studied the corridors that branched off in different directions behind her. "We need to find a place where we can hole up for a while. In an hour I'm going to be asleep, like it or not."

She glanced around. "Why can't we just stay here? No one else is going to come through that waterfall."

"Probably not," Sam agreed. "But that's not what's got me worried."

"Well? What is worrying you? Aside from the fact that Drummond just tried to nail us?"

"It occurs to me that whoever hired Leon Drummond to keep Mac Ewert from making any progress in this corridor may be working illegally on *this* side of the waterfall."

Virginia widened her eyes as understanding hit her. "Yes, of course. An illegal excavation project on this side would explain a lot. But if you're right, we could run into Drummond's pals any minute."

"I'd say that's a definite risk." He started toward her. "Come on, we've got to find a place to hide until I can sleep off the afterburn."

"There are bound to be some chambers or rooms we can duck into for a few hours," she said. "All we have to do is pick one that doesn't look like it's been charted yet. Odds are no one will find us during the next few hours. Heck, I doubt if anyone will even come looking for us. Drummond must think we're dead. He'll no doubt report that we got reckless, got ourselves fried by that waterfall, and that the firm of Gage & Burch is out of business.''

"True. He can't have any way of knowing that we survived. All the same, I don't want to take any more chances than necessary." Sam looked at her. "We haven't got a lot of time."

The prowling urgency in him worried her. She opened her mouth to say something reassuring, but the words got caught in her throat. He was only a short distance away now. For the first time since they had come through the waterfall, she got a close look at his eyes. What she saw there stilled her breath for a few seconds.

Hot, intense, brilliant; sexual desire, elemental and dangerously compelling, blazed in his eyes. His gaze literally glittered with what, in any other circumstances, she might have mistaken for the first evidence that he felt a degree of genuine passion for her.

Adeline's question came back to her in an uncomfortable rush. *"So, is it true what they say about ghost-hunters? Are they really amazing in bed after they've zapped a ghost? I've heard the sex is unbelievable right after a burn."*

What she saw in Sam now, she realized, was no more than the aftereffects of a massive expenditure of ghost-hunter psi talent. Chemically speaking, it was the result of a combination of testosterone, adrenaline, and the potent biological cocktail his paranormal powers had dumped into his bloodstream.

Nothing personal, she reminded herself. He wasn't attracted to her, per se. It just happened that he was rezzed for sex, and she was the only female in sight. Anything in skirts would probably do just fine for him at that moment.

"Uh, Sam? Are you okay?"

"No." He went past her, heading for the first branching corridor. "Let's get moving."

Three

He was freaking her out. He knew it, but there wasn't much he could do about it. Hanging on to his self-control required every shred of what little willpower he could muster. Getting them both safely through the waterfall had required more power than he'd ever used in his life; more than he'd known he possessed. He did not intend to tell Virginia the truth: that it had been damned close. They had made it, but in the process he'd poured so much psychic wattage through his amber that he'd destroyed the resonating properties of the precision-tuned stone. Melting amber meant you'd pushed the envelope. There was always a price to pay.

He'd experienced the sexual buzz that often occurred after a major burn before. In the past, he'd always felt fully in control of the predictable arousal. But this time things were different. It wasn't just that the burn had been bigger; the real problem was that this time, he was alone with Virginia, the woman he'd been lusting after for nearly two months.

He was in the grip of a feverish desire that was all the worse because he had worked so hard to suppress and conceal it.

All right, so he had a major hard-on. Just a few rampaging hormones. So what? He wasn't a kid. He could control himself. He *had* to control himself. If he lost it now, he would probably terrify her and turn her against him forever. Any chance he had with her would go up in smoke.

He tried to concentrate on moving ahead down the corridor, searching the walls for the barest hint of illusion energy that would indicate a hidden chamber they could use. All of the rooms that had ever been discovered in the corridors had been found sealed with illusion traps. If they could find a sealed room that looked as if no one else had ever de-rezzed the trap that guarded it, Virginia could unseal it, and they could hide inside for a few hours.

Simple. All he had to do was concentrate and not think about the fact that she was only a few inches away.

"Sam, you're shivering." Virginia touched his forehead with gentle, questing fingers. "Good heavens, you're burning up. You must be running a temperature. Is this normal?"

"Damn it, *don't touch me.*" He closed his eyes briefly and drew a deep breath. Great. Now he was snapping at her. "We'll both be sorry if you do."

She frowned; not with fear or trepidation but with a concern that horrified him. If she started in with the sweet, nurturing stuff, he was doomed.

"This can't be normal," she insisted. "I think that burn must have made you ill."

"Trust me, it's normal," he said through set teeth. "A little intense, but normal."

He could not screw up and lose control. Not now. It was crucial that he did not scare her to death. Because maybe, just maybe, he really had heard her say "I love you" in those few seconds before he carried her through the waterfall.

"Slow down, Sam, I can't keep up with you."

He realized that he was loping down the corridor as he

raked the walls for telltale signs of illusion dark. "Sorry." He forced himself to slow somewhat.

"It's okay. Let me worry about finding a trapped chamber. We're back into my field of expertise now." She moved out ahead of him. "I think I see something up ahead. Yes, I can feel it."

He tried but he did not pick up the psychic tang of illusion dark. "I don't feel a damn thing."

"Probably because your para-senses are temporarily over-rezzed. But I'm sure there's something up there." She broke into a quick trot. "Positive. And it's big. A big trap usually indicates a large chamber. Maybe we'll luck out and find a palace. They always have lots of little antechambers around them. Plenty of places to hide."

He hoped she was right. Beneath the clawing surge of sexual need and the rush of the burn buzz, he thought he could detect the first warnings of the crash that would soon follow. He could not afford to collapse here in the open corridor. Not when there was a possibility that Leon Drummond's cohorts might be in the neighborhood. He had to stay on his feet long enough to make sure Virginia was safe.

He followed her around a bend and saw that she had come to a halt in front of what, at first glance, appeared to be a section of green quartz wall. But there was something not quite right about the center portion. He peered more closely, blinking to clear his jumpy vision. The wall wavered slightly before it came back into focus. Illusion dark.

"Big," he muttered.

"Yes. Very unusual. Also very, very old."

The thoughtful, decidedly academic tone of her voice worried him. The last thing they could afford to do was waste time while she analyzed the trap from a professional point of view.

"You can write it up for an article in the *Journal of Para-*

Archaeology when this is over," he said roughly. "Right now, we need to get into the space behind it."

She gave him a disgruntled look. "I know. Give me a minute here, though. There's something different about this trap."

A new wave of concern washed through him, rezzing up the already fizzing effects of the afterburn just as it had started to fade. "Can you handle it? Because if not, we've got to find another—"

"I can handle it," she assured him. "It's just . . . different, that's all. I can't explain—" She broke off. "Never mind."

She went to work untangling the trap that barred the door. Restlessly, he watched the corridor in both directions while she de-rezzed the entrance.

"Got it," Virginia whispered softly.

There was a disturbing note in her voice, but he did not have time to question her about it. He swung around and saw that there was now an opening in the green wall. Virginia had already moved through it.

He followed her quickly, surprised that he had to give his eyes a moment to adjust to the shadowy interior of the chamber. His first impression was of a vast space filled with green-drenched shadows. His surroundings glowed, just as the tunnel did, but the light emitted by the quartz was much weaker and much dimmer in here. The effect was an emerald twilight.

The only thing he could tell for certain was that this chamber was large, much bigger than any of the others he had ever seen. In the gloom he could not make out the far walls or the ceiling. The space was filled with a number of structures of various sizes, all fashioned of the familiar green quartz. They were packed closely together and piled on top of each other, forming what looked like miniature city blocks crammed with a number of small apartments. The blocks were separated by narrow, twisting lanes.

He started toward the nearest of the apartments, asssessing it as a potential hideout. He saw a narrow opening. It looked large enough to provide access to the interior of the building but small enough to be protected by a single man armed with a mag-rez gun.

Perfect.

"Hang on while I reset the trap," Virginia said behind him.

He paced restlessly while she worked. In a matter of seconds, illusion shadow once more obscured the entrance of the chamber.

"It won't deceive a trained tangler," she said as she turned back to face him, "but it might go unnoticed by a hunter or an excavation team worker, especially if he or she is in a hurry."

"With luck, there's no one out there looking for us."

"But you don't want to depend on luck, do you?"

"No." He scanned the dim chamber. "What the hell is this place?"

"Who knows?" She walked slowly toward him, searching the narrow canyons between the apartment-like structures. "I've never seen anything quite like it. Maybe it was a zoo. All those little cubicles and small rooms might have once been cages for animals."

"Maybe. Could just as easily have been a storage locker facility or an office park or a prison."

"We'll probably never know."

He came to a halt in front of the nearest apartment structure. It appeared to be several stories high. He could see many rows of neatly marked openings on the side.

"There must be a hundred little rooms in there," he said. "We can use one of them."

"Sam?" Virginia sounded uneasy again. "Are you thinking of hiding inside that particular building?"

"Uh-huh. Is it trapped?"

She went closer to examine the nearest entrance.

"Yes," she said.

He frowned. "Well? Can you untangle it?"

"Yes," she said again very evenly.

He waited for a few seconds, but he did not sense any psi energy. She was staring at the trapped entrance, but she wasn't working.

"What the hell's wrong?" he asked. "It's not like we've got all day here."

She turned slowly to face him. In the green twilight her eyes were more shadowed than the interior of the cubicle.

"Not this one," she said. "Let's try another one."

He started to argue and then reminded himself that when it came to traps, she was the pro. "All right, pick another one, but hurry."

She was already moving down the narrow lane between two looming structures. He paced behind her, controlling his temper when she passed up three more trapped entrances. Silently he willed her to make her choice so that he could get on with the task of rigging up some sort of defense that would protect her while he slept off the afterburn.

She turned at an intersection and went down another lane. Just when he was ready to take charge and make the choice for her, she came to a halt.

"Here," she said. She sounded relieved. "This one is okay. We can go inside."

"About time," he growled. "Do what you have to do."

She glanced at him. "No problem. There's no trap at this entrance."

"Damn." He took a closer look. The doorway she had chosen looked more elaborate than the others. It was wider, more ornately carved. It was taller, too. He shook his head. If push came to shove, it would not be as easy to defend. He turned away, scanning the ranks of darkly glowing openings in the green walls.

"No good," he said brusquely. "Pick one with a trap that you can reset after we're inside. It will give us an extra level of protection."

"This is the only one I've seen that feels okay."

He scowled. "What the hell do you mean, it feels okay?"

"Just what I said. This one is okay." Stubborn determination gleamed in her eyes. "This is my area of expertise, and I'm telling you that this will be a safer place to hide than any of the other possibilities that I've seen so far."

"But it's not even trapped."

"There's something wrong about those traps on the other entrances," she said. "I could untangle them, but I don't think that I should."

"You don't think you *should?*" He wanted to shake her. Didn't she realize he was trying to protect her? "What kind of a reason is that? If we get cornered in this chamber by a couple of hunters trying to protect an illegal excavation site, we're going to need all the help we can get. I want a doorway that's well-trapped."

She wrapped her arms around herself and looked at him with unshakable conviction. "We can't go into any of those other rooms. Trust me on this, Sam. This is the only chamber I've seen yet that feels safe."

He hesitated. "Safe?"

"Yes." She unhugged herself and touched his cheek. She dropped her hand immediately when he flinched. "Sam, we've got to get you inside. You're in bad shape. You're scaring me."

"Just don't touch me," he warned. "Not until I've slept this off."

"Don't be ridiculous. How can it hurt if I touch you? Sam, you're not yourself. If you've got an ounce of sense, you'll admit that you're in no condition to be in charge of the firm of Gage & Burch at the moment."

She was right, but he did not want to admit it. Another wave of shivering swept over him. "Find a trapped room."

"We don't have time to keep looking. You need sleep."

"In a while. Not just yet."

"I'm officially declaring myself the boss of this partnership, at least for now. And I say you need sleep. Come with me."

She reached out without warning. Her hand closed around his arm, sending a tide of sensation screaming through his senses. This time he knew he was lost. The raging hunger roared past the last of his defenses. A great shudder of need wracked him. He no longer possessed the will to resist.

When she tugged him gently toward the doorway, he lurched once and then stumbled after her. At that moment he would have followed her anywhere; straight into hell, if that was where she wished to lead him.

She seemed oblivious to the storm that had him in its grip. She drew him through the untrapped doorway into a wide, softly lit room. He was vaguely aware of a tall piece of statuary in the center of the space. It soared toward the ceiling, delicately carved in the familiar airy, abstract designs the Harmonics had favored. There was a shallow pool beneath it. Emerald streams of sparkling energy poured gently from the top of the ornately designed quartz. The gentle waves bounced and splashed in the pool.

"A fountain," Virginia breathed in wonder. "I've never seen anything like it. Never even *heard* of anything like it. Maybe this place was some sort of park, or maybe it was a garden in some wealthy Harmonic home. But why all the little tiny rooms in that warren outside?"

"Maybe the neighborhood went bad. Turned into a slum." Sam shook his head, unable to concentrate on the fountain or any of the other questions she had brought up. All of his over-rezzed senses were riveted on her.

"This way," she said.

He did not reply. He knew that he was so far gone now, that if he tried to speak, nothing coherent would come from his throat. He stared longingly at the back of her head as she urged him through an interior doorway. She had a beautifully shaped head, he decided. And the color of her hair, a warm reddish brown, was perfect. The urge to pull her down onto the hard quartz floor and cover her body with his own was nearly overwhelming. He prayed that he would crash into deep sleep before he succumbed to the torrent of desire that was pulsing through him.

Inside the smaller antechamber, Virginia paused. "This will do, I think. You can sleep it off here."

He caught a glimpse of some large chests arranged around the room, saw a green staircase in the corner, but all he could think of was Virginia. He closed his eyes to shut out the sight of her. The attempt to banish her vision from his senses did not work. The scent of her hit him like a narcotic.

Crash, he thought. *Just crash, and this will all be over.* Then he remembered something else; something he had to do first. He reached into his boot and removed the slender little mag-rez gun. He held it out to her.

"Take this. If anyone comes through the door of this chamber before I wake up, use it."

She looked at the gun and then raised startled eyes to his. "Since when did you start carrying a mag-rez?"

"Since I ran into my first ruin rat on my very first consulting assignment," he said brusquely. "I nearly got myself killed. After that, I started carrying one. I also carry a flashlight, even though no one's ever found a darkened tunnel, and extra tuned amber. Call me superstitious. Do you know how to use this?"

"No, of course not," she said primly. "Instruction in the use of mag-rez weapons is not included in the curriculum of the department of archaeology at the university. Probably because it's illegal to carry one underground."

He gritted his teeth and pointed at the weapon. "This is the safety. Disengage it before you use it. When you want to fire, just point it in the general direction of that doorway and squeeze the trigger. Don't worry about aiming. This thing will stun a man regardless of where you hit him.''

She looked dubious. ''Do you really think I'll need it?''

''I can't think clearly at all right now,'' he said flatly. ''So just take it and promise me you'll use it if necessary.''

''Okay.'' Gingerly she took it from his hand.

He looked around for a place to lie down. But he was still humming with afterburn sizzle and the sexual energy continued to wash through him. It would be a few more minutes before he could take refuge in sleep. He closed his eyes, fighting back raw need. When he raised his lashes, he saw that Virginia was watching him with intense concern.

''Sam?''

''I want you.''

She blinked but she did not draw back.

''Sorry,'' he muttered. He wiped his damp forehead with the back of his sleeve. ''Can't help it.''

''I know.'' There was no fear in her eyes, but there was something else; something that could have been sad resignation. ''It's all right. I understand about the effects of the afterburn.''

''The hell with the afterburn.'' Unable to keep his hands off her any longer, he gripped her shoulders. ''I've wanted you since the day you walked through my front door.''

She stared at him with what could only have been amazement. ''You have?''

He groaned, pulled her hard against his chest, and tilted her chin. ''More than I've ever wanted anything or anyone else in my life.''

He kissed her before she could respond. He had to kiss her. Just one kiss, he promised himself. Drain off a little of the sexual charge. By the time it was over, surely the crash would have overtaken him. It had to hit soon. Any second now. Then he would escape into the merciful oblivion of sleep before he did anything else real stupid.

As a plan, it seemed simple and straightforward. Then again, he might have been hallucinating by now, he thought.

But however brilliant the scheme seemed, he knew as soon as he took her mouth that something was going horribly, wonderfully, terrifyingly wrong. Virginia put her arms around his neck and kissed him back.

"Oh, *Sam.*"

"Oh, *shit.*"

Her response was the last straw. He cradled her face in his hands and drank hungrily from her lips as if he could consume the essence of her vibrant spirit. She moaned softly and tightened her grip on his neck. He could feel the swell of her breasts beneath the sturdy twill of her shirt. The inside of her mouth was warm and welcoming, just as he had imagined.

For the first time he feared that the crash would overcome him before he could finish what he had started. A whole new sense of urgency slammed through him.

Not daring to raise his mouth from hers for fear that he might somehow lose her, he started to undress her. It was not an easy task. His hands were shaking so badly that he could barely manage the buttons.

He felt her fingers slide beneath the waistband of his trousers, gliding up beneath the hem of his shirt. Her palms flattened against his chest, and he thought he would go through the roof. He realized that she was shivering now, too.

"Sam, are you sure you're not ill?"

"I'm okay." He struggled with her shirt.

"I was so afraid that you—"

"Nothing to be afraid of." He managed to wrench his mouth from hers long enough to kiss her throat. "I swear it. You don't have to be afraid of me. I won't hurt you. I could never hurt you."

"I know. That wasn't what I meant."

He finished fumbling with the last of the buttons that closed her shirt. He peeled the garment off her shoulders and hurled it aside. Then he heard himself utter a thick, husky groan. He could feel her firm little nipples pressing against the sleek fabric of her bra.

She was working on his belt now. The sweet torture was almost beyond endurance. Every time her fingers brushed against his skin he thought he would explode.

He dragged the straps of her bra down her arms, freeing her breasts. He leaned his hot forehead against her cool brow and looked at the taut, peaked curves.

"You are so beautiful," he muttered, awed.

She gave him a smile laced with infinite mystery. "No, but you're making me feel beautiful."

He lacked the patience to argue. She was beautiful; the most beautiful, most desirable woman he had ever seen in his life. He knew that, even if she did not.

He scooped her up in his arms, intending to lower her to the floor. Out of the corner of his eye, he saw a wide chest carved of quartz. It would not be any softer than the floor, but at least it looked vaguely like a bed.

He carried Virginia to the hard couch and put her down on it. She lay back on the emerald stone, her hair spilling around her head, her eyes glowing with desire, and watched him with great expectation as he unbuckled his belt.

Her expression nearly finished him.

He yanked impatiently at his clothing. The cocktail in his bloodstream made him clumsy and awkward. But when he finally lowered himself onto the chest and pulled Virginia into his arms, he had never felt better in his life.

Nothing had ever been this good.

He slid one leg between hers and dampened his fingers in her liquid heat.

She gasped, trembled, and closed her eyes. She slid her palm down his chest, across his belly, and lower. He felt her fingers close around him and thought his heart might stop.

"Sam."

Another wave of need thundered through him. "No, don't touch me like that. I won't be able—"

"It's all right."

"Stop saying that." He came down on top of her. Her green-gold eyes were luminous with desire. "Virginia, this isn't the way I wanted to do this, but I can't wait. Not this time."

"It's all right," she said. She opened her legs for him, drew up her knees, and wrapped her arms around him. "Really."

"Hold me." It was half plea, half demand. "Promise me you won't let go."

"Never."

He squeezed his eyes shut against the riptide of need that was threatening to sweep him out into a dark sea. She shifted a little beneath him, and the glide of her silken skin against him nearly ended the matter right then and there.

He plunged deep, sinking recklessly, exultantly into the snug, tight channel of her body. He felt the initial resistance and then she closed around him. She cried out and clung to him, fighting him for the embrace.

He rocked violently against her, driving himself to the hilt with every thrust, needing to forge a bond that would hold long after this encounter.

The climax hit him. Simultaneously he thought he felt Virginia convulse beneath him, but he could not be certain. He barely had time to register a sensation so intense that it could not truly be described as pleasure. But it was not pain, either. Something else, he thought vaguely, something infinitely more important.

There was no time to analyze the incredible feeling. Hard on its heels came the crash. He could only marvel that it had not struck sooner.

He collapsed on top of her, aware that he was trapping her against the quartz chest with his weight. But there was nothing he could do about it. The deep, dreamless sleep took him.

Four

It felt as if one of the ancient stone corridors had caved in on top of her. Sam was no lightweight to begin with and, as she quickly discovered, he seemed to be built mostly of muscle and bone. There was no softness in him and there was none beneath her.

Talk about being between a rock and a hard place, Virginia thought.

She took a deep breath, braced her hands on Sam's chest, and heaved upward with all of her strength. She managed to gain some wiggle room and, with another strong shove, she was finally able to slide out from underneath his inert body.

She sat up and got cautiously to her feet. There was something wrong with her knees. They were not quite steady. A tremor went through her. She had to grab hold of the edge of the chest to get her balance. *For the record, Adeline, everything you've ever heard about sex with a ghost-hunter in the midst of an afterburn is true.*

Or maybe this was just the result of sex with Sam, she thought cheerfully. She didn't have an extensive amount of experience to call upon when it came to this kind of thing, but it didn't take a lot of experimentation to know what she'd just shared with Sam had been very special. At least she no longer entertained any doubts as to whether or not there were fires of passion burning somewhere inside Sam.

They were there, all right. Enough to set a whole forest ablaze.

Of course, his response to her could have been ignited simply by the legendary ghost-hunter buzz, she reminded herself. Her euphoric spirits sank as suddenly as they had risen. Anything in skirts might have had the same impact on him at that particular moment.

Reality returned with a jarring thud. With a sigh, she steadied herself and glanced around the gloom-filled room. The carved stone chest on which Sam slept was one of several in the chamber. There were also a variety of vases and urns set in softly glowing alcoves. The drenching shadows created a solemn but surprisingly tranquil effect. Perhaps this had once been a meditation room in a Harmonic home. Assuming the Harmonics had meditated.

Questions, questions.

She dressed quickly and picked up the little mag-rez gun. She checked the safety as Sam had demonstrated and then shoved it into her belt.

She glanced uncertainly at Sam. He certainly looked magnificent stretched out stark naked on the stone chest, and she knew he was not cold because the temperature in the catacombs was always the same, comfortable and dry, day and night, year in, year out. But the sight of him was more than a little distracting. The muscled, well-defined contours of his chest and shoulders sent a pleasant little shiver through her.

Their lovemaking had been fast and furious. There had been no time for her to indulge herself in an exploration of his body. She had been intensely aware of the thick, heavy size and weight of his erection, but she had not really *seen* him. Now, she could not stop gazing at him. He fascinated her, she thought. She had wanted to stroke him and touch him for weeks, but this was the first opportunity she'd had to satisfy her longing.

She examined the fierce planes of his face, relishing the determined angle of his jaw and the pleasing, masculine shape of his ears. His dark hair was seductively ruffled where she had run her fingers through it earlier. With his eyes closed he was all hard edges and tough, sleek male. But when his eyes were open you saw the intelligence and the self-control that defined his nature.

When Sam loved, she thought, his emotions would be as steady and as enduring as the glow of Harmonic quartz.

Unable to resist the temptation, she reached out very carefully and slowly closed her hand around the top of his muscled thigh. He was hard and warm beneath her fingers. She drew her palm slowly down to his knee, savoring the feel of him.

Sam shuddered and mumbled something in his sleep. Startled, she snatched her hand away and stepped back. But when he did not awaken, she reached out once more.

This time she traced a path upward toward his chest, curling her fingers in the crisp hair there. He shifted slightly, but she knew from the steadiness of his breathing that he was still sound asleep. A part of him was stirring, she noticed. She stared at his penis, fascinated to see that it appeared to be swelling in length and width once more. Apparently, the deep sleep of afterburn did not shut down all systems.

There was probably a law against looking at him like this, she thought. If there wasn't, there should have been. It was entirely too much fun.

On the other hand, she was going to marry him soon. Surely that gave her some rights.

"Enough with the voyeuristic fun and games," she muttered. "You're supposed to be standing guard."

She picked up Sam's discarded clothing and covered his torso with his shirt. Then she folded his trousers and placed them neatly beneath his head to serve as a pillow. She was already starting to feel quite wifely, she thought, amused.

With a last glance at him, she turned and walked out into the fountain room. The green energy continued to flow and splash in the small pool. It had no doubt been doing so for several thousand years.

She braced one hand on the thick edge of the doorway and looked around with professional interest. This room had the same somber, curiously reflective feel as the smaller antechamber in which Sam slept. She could not explain, even to herself, why these spaces felt safe while the countless little cubicles outside did not.

She took her hand off the wall and made her way across the fountain room to the outer door. She gazed into the narrow aisle that separated this block of cells from the one across the way and listened intently with both her physical and para senses.

Nothing. No indication that the unusual trap that guarded the main entrance to this weird complex had been breached. No voices or footsteps echoed on the paths that intersected the ranks of cubicle-laced buildings. She detected nothing that indicated that anyone who might be looking for them had discovered the zoo chamber.

She waited quietly in the fountain room for a while longer, uncomfortably aware of the weight of the mag-rez gun on her hip. Gradually, boredom set in. Professional curiosity followed closely on its heels. Whatever this place was, it constituted a spectacular new find. She had a degree in para-archaeology, and she was diligent about keeping up with the research on the subject. She was quite certain that nothing remotely resembling this nest of tiny, illusion-trapped cubicles had ever been written up in the academic literature.

She stepped cautiously out into the shadowy lane, visions of an article in the *Journal of Para-Archaeology* with her name on it as author dancing in her head. That kind of publicity would do wonders for the reputation of the new firm of Gage & Burch.

She walked slowly along the gloom-filled path and paused in front of the first of the small cells that lined the little alley. She examined the dense shadow that glinted just at the edge of her vision. The human eye could detect the stuff that the Harmonics had used to weave their dangerous snares, but it could not focus directly on the nearly invisible psi energy.

She crouched down, concentrating with her para senses, and probed the pattern. As she had concluded earlier, there was nothing particularly complex about the design. She could undo it easily enough. But the sense of wrongness was deeply disturbing. Everything within her resisted the notion of untangling the trap.

With a shock, it occurred to her that perhaps it was not the trap itself that was dangerous. Maybe the true threat existed— or had once existed—*inside* the little room. Perhaps the trap was just a warning.

Maybe this place had once been a Harmonic hotel and all of these little traps were nothing more than ordinary Do Not Disturb signs hung on doorknobs to keep the maid from entering unexpectedly.

She contemplated that possibility for a moment and then returned to her zoo theory. She liked it much better. The traps might have functioned as fences to keep dangerous creatures locked inside or to keep curious visitors from getting too close to the beasts inside the cages.

She straightened and walked a few more feet to examine some of the other illusion-darkened entrances. Every single one of them gave off the same clear psychic warnings.

After a while, she returned to the fountain room. A quick check on Sam showed that he was still totally out of it.

She sat down on a glowing quartz bench facing the untrapped doorway and took the mag-rez gun out of her belt.

She wondered how long Sam would sleep.

• • •

Sam came awake with a sense of urgency, as if someone had just yelled *fire*. He sat up quickly, memory returning in a heated rush. But there was nothing to indicate that the situation had changed while he had slept off the worst effects of the afterburn. If any of Leon Drummond's pals had burst through the doorway, he would have awakened with his hands and feet bound in duct tape, if he had awakened at all.

Relief swept through him. Something soft slid off his chest and fell to the floor. He looked down and saw his shirt. Virginia must have covered him with it after he had nodded off, which had been right after he had taken her with all the finesse of a specter-cat in full rut.

Virginia. He briefly closed his eyes as the images cascaded through him, burning more intensely than ghost fire. For a few seconds he savored them. Then reality closed in. He knew that his recollection of her passionate response might be nothing more than an illusion concocted by his singed senses; some sort of weird para-psych rationalization for what he had done to her.

Yet he could still feel the softness of the skin on the insides of her thighs and the damp, clinging clasp of her body. Just remembering made his insides tighten all over again.

He had wanted her more than he had ever thought it possible to want any woman. But no more so because of the buzz from the afterburn. The truth was, he had been wanting her just as badly for weeks. The only difference was that two hours ago he had lost control.

The flash of relief he had experienced after waking evaporated. In its place was a bottomless pool of dread. He had to face the grim truth: After weeks of being so cautious, so careful, there was a damn good chance that he had destroyed the glowing future he had worked so hard to build.

He had no one to blame but himself.

Virginia had had a bad case of bridal jitters before they

embarked on this venture. After what he had done to her here in this room, she no doubt despised him. It would be a miracle if he hadn't scared the living daylights out of her. She was probably making plans this very minute not only to call off their marriage but their business partnership as well.

He picked up his shirt and got to his feet. Anger washed through him. He was furious with himself. The loss of control had been inexcusable. He could only pray that he had not hurt her.

How long had he been out? He glanced at his watch. Two hours. Long enough to restore some but not all of his depleted psi energy. He needed more sleep to function at full capacity but he could manage with what he had regained during the nap.

He grabbed his trousers and pulled them on. The only thing he could do to make amends to Virginia was to get her safely back to the surface.

A shadow moved in the doorway that separated the antechamber from the fountain room. Not illusion-shadow, but it might as well have been, given the hopelessness of his situation.

"Sam." Virginia hovered anxiously in the doorway. "You're awake. Everything okay?"

"Good enough." He realized with a jolt that he did not want to meet her eyes. He did not want to see the accusation and the wariness that he knew he would find there. "Nothing new outside?"

"We're still alone in this place. I'm beginning to think I was right when I suggested it might have once been a zoo. Something about the nature of the traps makes me think they were set to keep visitors away from whatever used to live in all these little apartments or cages."

"Whoever or whatever once lived in the cells is long gone." He reached for his boots. He did not remember removing them. His jaw tightened. "Got the mag-rez?"

"Right here." She took a few steps into the room to hand it to him. "Sam, are you really okay?"

"Don't worry, I'll be able to get us out of here." He took the narrow little gun from her and shoved it back into his belt. "There's probably another exit around here somewhere, but I think our best bet is to go back out the way we came."

She halted. "Back through the waterfall?"

"Yeah. It's the last thing Drummond would expect. Especially after all this time has passed. By now he'll have reported us officially missing, probably killed by an explosion of dissonance energy. I doubt if we'll find him hanging around on the other side waiting for us. But just in case, I'll have the mag-rez in my hand when we go through the waterfall."

"All right. Whatever you think best. You're the expert on ghost-energy."

He glanced down and realized that he was dressed. He could find no more excuses for avoiding her eyes. Time to act like a man. He turned slowly around to face her. "Virginia—"

"Sam—"

They both broke off, staring at each other. In the gloom it was impossible for him to read the expression in her eyes. If she was frightened of him, she was hiding it well, he thought.

He braced himself and tried again. "I'm sorry for what happened," he said evenly. "I don't know what else to say. I could promise you that it won't ever happen again, but I don't know if I can keep that promise."

She did not pretend to misunderstand. "I see."

He drew a deep breath. "I realize that you're probably having second thoughts about our business arrangement as well as our marriage. I don't blame you. I've been doing some thinking about it, too."

"You have?"

He glanced around the tranquil little room. "This is not the time or place to talk about how we're going to terminate our business futures."

"No, it's not." There was an unsettling, flat note in her voice.

"Yeah, well, let's save that conversation for later." He started toward the door, aware that even in the depths of the disaster, he was still trying to buy himself some time. The odds were strongly against him coming up with a way to talk her into going through with the marriage after what had happened, but he could not give up without a fight.

She looked at him as he went past her. "Sam, do you really regret what happened?"

"Hell, yes, I regret it." He planted one hand against the green stone doorway and turned to face her. "Making love to you was the last thing I wanted to do."

She stiffened. "I realize that you were rezzed up because of the afterburn."

"That was no excuse."

"Just tell me one thing. Would anything in skirts have worked for you two hours ago?"

He frowned at her trousers. "You aren't wearing skirts."

She narrowed her eyes. "That was a figure of speech."

"It's never smart to use figures of speech when you're talking to a hunter who's still recovering from an afterburn. We tend to be literal, even on our good days."

"For heaven's sake, this is no time for wisecracks. We're talking about our future."

"I thought we just got through deciding to talk about it later." He took his hand off the wall and stalked into the fountain room.

"Damn it," she called out behind him, "don't you dare walk out on me when I'm talking to you. Come back here, Sam Gage."

"What the hell do you want from me?" He felt his temper ignite. "I said I'm sorry. I don't usually lose control, not even during an afterburn. But things got out of hand this time."

She swept out her palm to indicate the quartz chest on

which they had made love. "Didn't what happened in here mean *anything* to you?"

"Of course it did. It meant I screwed up everything. But what's done is done."

She raised her chin, eyes glittering with anger. "Would you undo it if you could?"

"Didn't I just get through saying that I—" He broke off abruptly. There was no point lying about it. The damage was done. He set his back teeth. "I wish it had happened under other circumstances. I wish I had done things differently. I wish I hadn't scared the hell out of you."

"But you aren't really, truly sorry that you made love to me?"

He hesitated. "Well—"

"Just say it."

He felt cornered. Despair, anger, and frustration boiled together, a dangerous stew spiced with emotions he knew he did not handle well. "You want the truth? The truth is what I said to you just before I tossed you down onto that damned stone chest. The truth is that I've been wanting to make love to you since the first day I saw you."

A short, intense silence gripped the chamber.

Virginia's brows bristled in a ferocious scowl. "Good. Because that's pretty much how I've felt from the first moment I saw you, too."

He felt as if he'd just been struck by lightning. For a few seconds he was too stunned to do anything more than stare at her. "It is?

"Yes." She glared at him. "But you seemed so distant and cool. So businesslike. You kept talking about how many new clients we would attract working as a team. You went on and on about how much money we'd both make once we sold the house to developers."

He finally managed to unfreeze himself. He took a step toward her. "I never wanted to sell the house in the first place.

I came up with the idea because I thought it would be a good way to talk you into a marriage-of-convenience. I figured if I—'' He stopped. ''Hell, I don't know what I was thinking.''

She cleared her throat. ''We're both adults. We're single. There's no reason we can't simply admit that we're attracted to each other. Marriages-of-convenience are designed for just this sort of situation.''

''A legal, socially acceptable, two-year affair.''

''Exactly.'' She shrugged. ''If it's just passion, it will probably burn itself out in that length of time.''

''Yeah. Sure.'' Never in a million years. How could he possibly let go of her in two years? Better not to go there in the first place if he knew that he would eventually lose her. But how could he not take what she offered, given the lonely alternative. ''Virginia—''

''That's what you wanted, wasn't it? That was the deal. A two-year MC.'' She smiled a little too brightly. ''And I agreed.''

She was acting weird, and it made him more uneasy than ever. What the hell was the matter with him? He had gotten exactly what he'd asked for, what he'd wished for when he'd concocted the plan in the first place.

''You know, you were right when you said that this was not the time or place to discuss this sort of thing,'' Virginia said briskly. ''We'd better get going.''

He moved toward her. ''Is sex all you want out of this?''

''Isn't that what you want out of it?''

''Sex is good. Great.'' Anger pulsed in him. ''I can work with sex.''

Her face tightened in renewed concern. ''You know, you really don't look normal yet, Sam. You could still be suffering from afterburn. Maybe you'd better get some more sleep before we attempt to go back through that waterfall.''

''You're right about one thing. I'm not feeling real normal.''

Her eyes widened as he closed the distance between them. "Now hold on just one damn minute. If you think we're going to have sex every time you claim to be in the throes of an afterburn buzz, you can think again. I'll admit it's interesting, but—"

She stopped talking abruptly when he caught her wrists and pinned her to the wall.

"You just got through telling me that you were in this deal for the sex," he reminded her.

"I've got nothing against sex." Her voice was tight with anger. "But the next time we do it, I want to make sure it's for real. Not just the result of a bad burn buzz. Don't you get it?"

"No." He leaned in closer. "Explain it to me in short words."

"I want to be sure it's me you want. I want to be absolutely certain that not just any female would do."

"Trust me, no one else will do."

There was a short, tense silence. Then she cleared her throat and wriggled her fingers in his grasp. "In that case, stop acting like some macho jerk hunter."

He kept her wrists anchored against the wall. "But I am a macho jerk hunter."

"No, you are not," she muttered, seriously disgruntled now. "Stop talking like that."

"You've as good as said I behaved like a macho jerk hunter a couple of hours ago when I made love to you just before I crashed. What happens the next time we get into this kind of situation? Am I going to have to listen to a lot of accusations about how anything in skirts would do? When it's over, will I have to explain that I knew it was you I was having sex with?"

"Just because I wanted to be sure you knew it was me—"

"Believe me. I knew it was you. Just like I know it's you now."

He kissed her, hard and deliberately, letting her feel the frustration and temper she had aroused in him, letting her know that this time he knew full well that she was the woman he had pinned against the glowing quartz wall.

She went rigid. Despair knifed through him.

"Virginia." He released her wrists and caught her head between his hands. "Damn it, Virginia. I want you so much."

She gave a muffled cry and threw her arms around his neck, kissing him feverishly. "I didn't mean to call you a stupid, macho jerk hunter."

"Don't worry about it." Relief surged through him. "Sometimes I am a macho jerk hunter."

"No." She clenched her fingers in his hair. "Never. I knew from the first day that you weren't a macho jerk hunter."

"Yeah?" He took her tender earlobe between his teeth and nibbled hungrily. "What was your first clue?"

"You were reading the *Journal of Para-Archaeology* instead of the latest issue of *Sex-Starved Psychic Playmates*."

"Lucky for me my subscription ran out three months ago," he said very fervently against her throat. "I never got around to renewing it."

She laughed softly. Her head tipped back against his arm. "Oh, Sam, do you really think this will work?"

"We'll make it work." Two years. He had two full years to make it work. He touched the edge of his tongue to the soft skin beneath the collar of her shirt.

She stiffened.

"Sam?"

"It's okay. Even without the skirts, I'm positive I'm dealing with the right lady here."

"No, wait." She planted her palms against his shoulders and pushed him away from her.

He stilled, aware that something was wrong. "What is it?"

"Psi energy. I can feel it. Someone is trying to take down the big trap at the entrance to this zoo."

"Drummond's friends. So they did come looking, after all." The charge of sexual anticipation that had been arcing through him instantly transmuted itself into another kind of high-rez buzz.

"Wait here." He turned and went swiftly across the fountain room. He halted in the outer doorway and listened intently. Sound carried underground. So did the feel of psi energy.

He heard voices reverberating in the distance. They came from the vicinity of the entrance to the vast zoo chamber.

". . . waste of time. Don't care what Drummond says. No way the S.O.B. coulda made it through that waterfall with the little lady tangler. No small-time security guy could be that good. Even if he was that good and even if he did make it through with her, he'd have one hell of an afterburn. He'll be wasted for at least another hour or two."

"We're working for Fairbanks, not Drummond. He said not to take any chances, and he's the one paying us. The orders were to check out every possibility in this damned corridor, so that's what we're gonna do. Now, shut up and untangle this trap."

"Okay, okay. Give me a minute. It's a big sucker."

Sam left the doorway and went to where Virginia stood waiting.

"Let's go." He took her arm.

"Where?"

"Up." He took her arm and started toward the emerald staircase. "It's easier to hunt when you've got the high ground."

"Whatever you say."

She followed him up the narrow, twisting steps to the next level. He saw the gloom-shrouded entrance to another chamber similar to the one below. An energy fountain cascaded silently in the center. Several more ornately carved chests were arranged in an artful manner around the room.

But the thing that interested him the most was the narrow window. He hesitated before he crossed the threshold and glanced at Virginia.

"Trapped?"

She shook her head, frowning intently. "No. This room is clear. Maybe this was the zoo's souvenir shop."

"Or the visitors' room in the prison." He went to the window, braced one hand on the wide ledge, and looked down into the lane. "This will work. If they bother to search this far, I'll have a clear shot."

". . . Got it. We're in."

"Shit. What the hell is this place? Look at all those little rooms. Some kinda cheap hotel, d'ya think?"

Virginia stirred hesitantly in the doorway. Then she walked slowly into the room, careful to keep a respectful distance from the energy fountain. "I don't like this."

"Don't worry. I've got a hunch that once they get a good look at all these little cubicles and realize how long it will take to search this place, they'll figure out something else to do. If they do get this far, I can handle them."

"I know that." She folded her arms very tightly beneath her breasts. "Sam, I'm afraid that tangler will try to de-rez some of the traps."

He sank deeper into the gloom and watched the lane. "So?"

"I told you, I don't think they should be touched. If he starts fooling around with some of them, looking for us—"

She broke off.

He gazed at her. "You're really worried about the nature of the those illusion traps, aren't you?"

"Yes." Her mouth tightened. "I told you, there's something very, very strange about them. One way or another, they all seem to spell out Do Not Disturb in great big capital letters.

"Whatever didn't want to be disturbed is long gone, Virginia."

"I know, but it just doesn't *feel* right."

He shrugged. "Maybe that tangler down there will come to the same conclusion, and he and his hunter pal will leave us in peace."

". . . Gonna take a couple of hours to go through this place room by room. Must be hundreds of little cubicles in here. And they're all trapped, I'm telling you."

"If they got this far, neither one of 'em would be in great shape. Gage will have crashed, and the tangler will be scared out of her wits. I'll bet they would have picked one of these little cubbyholes near the entrance. Start working, man. I'd rather find the bastard before he recovers from the crash. Easier to handle that way."

"Uh, Drake, I don't like the looks of these traps."

"I don't give a damn how they look to you. Start takin' 'em apart."

"There's something real weird—"

"Shut up and get to work, Chaz. Unless you wanna explain things to Fairbanks."

"Sure. Okay. I'm workin' on it."

"Oh, damn," Virginia whispered. "He's going to do it."

Sam took his eyes off the lane long enough to look at her. The stark alarm in her voice worried him. She was scared, he thought. Genuinely, thoroughly, deep-down scared.

"What is it with you and these traps?" he started to ask.

"*Sam.*" Her eyes widened in sudden alarm. "Get down. Now."

"Take it easy, honey, I've got to keep watch—"

"He's got it. He's undone the first trap. I can feel it."

"It's okay—"

"No, it's not okay." She flew toward him across the room and seized his arm. "Get away from the window."

Automatically, he started to resist the tug of her fingers. But the urgency in her was not to be ignored. He reminded himself that traps fell into her area of expertise. They were partners. He had to respect her instincts.

He allowed himself to be drawn away from the window. She pulled him deeper into the room.

"Down," she whispered, dragging him down behind a large quartz chest. "Hurry."

He crouched beside her, the mag-rez gun in hand. "I hope you know what the hell you're doing."

Before she could respond, an inhuman shriek of mingled rage and despair rent the gloom of the alien zoo. It echoed endlessly off the walls. Sam froze, his hand tightening convulsively around the gun. Beside him, Virginia shuddered.

"What in the name of Old Earth . . . ?" Sam whispered.

A very human shout went up, a high, keening cry of terror.

"There's something in there."

Chaz, the tangler, Sam thought.

". . . Get outa here . . ."

Another alien scream rose, joining the crescendoing wail of the first. And then a torrent of screeches, shrieks, howls, and dreadful cries arose. There was a hellishly mournful quality to the unnatural sounds, as though whatever had once inhabited the small cells had been aroused from their centuries-deep sleep to protest the disturbance. The cacophony of otherworldly cries drowned out the screams of Chaz and Drake.

The vast zoo room began to darken. The green gloom seemed to thicken and grow dense. Sam followed Virginia's gaze. They both looked out the narrow window. It was like looking into the depths of an alien sea.

"Dear heaven." Virginia said in amazement.

He knew what was going through her mind. There was no such thing as night and day in the ruins. The glow of the quartz was always steady. True, there had been more than the usual number of shadows in the zoo chamber, but there had been light, and it had remained at a constant level.

Until now.

Only the chamber in which they crouched remained luminous.

Jagged shards of green lightning flashed outside the narrow opening, shattering the heavy darkness that enveloped the zoo. The alien shrieks grew louder.

More lightning sizzled. As Sam watched, an acid-hued bolt of energy illuminated some thing that floated in midair outside the window. He caught a glimpse of a green phantom so gossamer thin and transparent that he could see straight through it to the opposite wall. As he watched, another specter joined the first.

"UDEMs," Virginia whispered. "When Chaz untangled the trap he must have disturbed some."

"Whatever the hell those two things are, they aren't standard-issue energy ghosts." Sam probed cautiously, feeling for the telltale trace of psi energy emitted by normal unstable dissonance energy manifestations. What he picked up with his para senses felt wrong. He cut off the probe immediately. He did not want to draw the attention of the strange specters.

"If they're not UDEMs, what are they?" she asked very softly.

"They're energy ghosts of some kind but not like any I've ever dealt with. Look at the way they move."

"As if—" Virginia hesitated. "As if they're headed somewhere."

"Yeah. Right toward Chaz and Drake."

"But that's impossible."

"Uh-huh."

She was right, of course. UDEMs were not sentient beings. They certainly weren't the ghosts of long-dead aliens, although more than one or two hucksters and con men had tried to convince the gullible of that over the years.

Technically speaking, UDEMS were nothing more than

balls of residual psi energy left behind by whatever had once powered Harmonic technology. The only reason they were called ghosts was because they tended to drift through the ancient corridors like ghosts.

Green lightning zigzagged through the misty darkness outside the window. More ghosts drifted past the opening, streaming toward the entrance of the zoo chamber.

"Damn," Sam said. "What the devil is going on out there?"

"I don't know, but I can tell you that this is Chaz's fault," Virginia said grimly. "He set them off. I knew there was something strange about those traps."

The hideous wails continued to rise and fall in the unnatural night.

"Sounds like a reunion of lost souls," Virginia whispered. "I can't even hear Chaz and Drake now. Wonder what's happened to them?"

"Maybe we don't want to know."

"Maybe you're right."

Virginia huddled close, but Sam noticed that she was careful not to impede his gun hand. Not that the mag-rez would be effective against whatever was out there, he thought. If one of the things changed course and drifted through the window, their only hope would be his psi-talent.

More lightning sparked violently. Again and again it shattered the night. But there was no accompanying roll of thunder, Sam noticed. For some reason that only made the energy flashes seem all the more bizarre.

"It's like there's a storm going on out there," Virginia muttered.

"Maybe that's exactly what it is," Sam said, thinking about it. "An energy storm triggered by the untangling of the first trap."

"But to what purpose?"

"Who knows? We're talking about the Harmonics here. No one has a clue about why they did anything. If the place was a zoo or a prison, it's possible those in charge installed some unusual security measures. Maybe we're witnessing some kind of system meant to round up the escapees."   •

"*Sam.*" Virginia touched his arm, her eyes fixed on the window. "Look."

"I see it."

One of the phantoms had halted in front of the opening. Sam told himself that it was just a mindless UDEM, but it was all too easy to imagine that it was peering into this room as if it sensed prey.

He readied himself, not wanting to use psi energy unless there was no alternative, because he could not be sure that his talent would work against this stuff.

The ghost hovered. The brightest portion of it was at least three feet in length, but its aura flared out in a much wider band of acid green.

It drifted through the window.

"Damn."

Beside him, Virginia sucked in a deep breath, but she said nothing.

Decision time, Sam thought. He could either try to prod it back out the window or he could attempt to clobber it. He opted for the gentle nudge.

He sent out a pulse of psi-talent, gently summoning energy from the quartz walls, ceiling, and floor. A small ball of glowing green fire took shape in the center of the room. He propelled it gently toward the intruder.

The strange UDEM that had drifted through the window paused as though confused. Then, to Sam's enormous relief, it retreated from the smaller ghost.

It wafted back out through the window and disappeared in the wake of the school of phantoms roaming through the streets of the zoo.

Virginia exhaled on a long, soft sigh. "Nice. Very nice."

He could almost taste his own relief. For the first time, he realized that his shirt was stuck to his back. "Don't ever say I don't know how to show a lady a fun time on Halloween."

"A lot of hunters would have tried to blast it to smithereens," she said very seriously. "For some reason, I don't think that tactic would have worked."

"No," he said, "I don't think it would have."

The storm crackled and blazed. An endless parade of desolate-sounding specters and phantoms flitted past the window.

The tempest seemed to rage for hours, but when at last it began to abate, Sam looked at his watch. He was startled to see that only twenty-three minutes had passed.

"I think it's ending," Virginia said.

Gradually, the unholy wails receded. The flashes of lightning grew pale, then ceased altogether. As if some invisible hand had flipped a switch, the familiar green glow seeped back into the atmosphere. The strange darkness retreated into the pooling shadows from which it had come.

"Must have seemed like an eternity to Chaz and Drake," Virginia whispered.

"It may have turned out to be just that."

"Are you saying you don't think they survived it?"

"I don't know what was going on out there, but whatever it was, they were caught out in the open." Sam smiled slightly. "Thanks to you, we were safe in this room."

He got cautiously to his feet and went to the window. When he looked out he saw that everything looked very much as it had just before the tempest had been triggered.

Virginia stood slowly behind the chest. "Now what?"

"Now we get the heck out of here before someone else sets off another storm." He moved swiftly back toward her. "Ready?"

"If you're waiting for me, you're backing up."

They found Chaz and Drake lying on the floor near the main gate into the zoo. It was obvious that the two desperate men had tried to flee back through it, but something had caused the illusion trap there to reset itself. The energy storm had caught up with the pair before Chaz could untangle the trap a second time.

Virginia hesitated and then went down beside one of the men and checked for a pulse. She looked up in surprise. "He's unconscious, but alive."

"Same here." Sam rifled through the pockets of the man dressed in leather and khaki until he found a guild license and an amber-powered grid locator. "This is all we need. The locator shows three exits in this sector. We won't have to go back through the waterfall, after all."

"What are you going to do with that man's guild license?"

"I'll give it to Mercer Wyatt. He can take it from there." Sam got to his feet. "The guild polices its own."

Virginia gave him an odd look. "You're, uh, friends with the head of Hunter's Guild?"

"Let's just say that Wyatt and I have a nodding acquaintance. He owes me a couple of favors." Sam studied the illusion trap that guarded the exit. "Go ahead and de-rez it. I'll drag these two out of here. We'll leave them in the corridor. Wyatt can send one of his staff to clean up this mess."

Five

"We were worried sick." Adeline helped herself to a leftover black-and-orange cupcake from the plate on Virginia's desk. "First we hear that you and Sam have gone missing in the corridors; a report which, I hasten to add, none of your buddies believed for one tiny minute, because we all know how good you and Sam are; and then we learn that the two of you got zapped by some sort of massive ghost called a waterfall."

"The waterfall part was for real." Virginia rocked back in her chair and took a sip of hot, spiced cider. "But, as you can see, neither of us got zapped."

She peered at her watch, wondering what was keeping Sam. After talking to the police, he had gone to meet with Mercer Wyatt. She had not liked that. It was no secret in Cadence City that Wyatt ran the guild as though it was his own, private fiefdom. A lot of folks, including an editorial writer on the *Cadence Star* considered him no more than one or two steps removed from being a gangster. But she could not argue with the fact that if you were a ghost-hunter, you had to form some sort of business relationship with the guild. She had not asked

Sam just what kind of terms he had worked out with Wyatt. She was not sure she wanted to know.

"So what, exactly, was going on down there in the tunnels?" Adeline asked around a mouthful of cupcake.

"A band of ruin rats headed by a recently fired employee of the University Museum named Fairbanks uncovered a hole-in-the-wall just beneath the museum's basement. They were using it to siphon off some of the museum's holdings. Stuff that had been in storage for years, which might not have been missed for years. If Mac Ewert hadn't accidentally stumbled onto that waterfall and asked us to help him de-rez it, the rats probably would never have been caught."

Holes-in-the-wall were not uncommon. They usually took the form of tiny cracks and fissures through which little more than ambient psi energy could squeeze. But some of the openings in the thick quartz walls and underground corridors were large enough for a man to crawl through. A few were even bigger: eons-old stairwells and empty shafts that no longer ascended anywhere. It was one of those that Fairbanks, a powerful tangler, had discovered while laboring in the basement of the huge museum.

Adeline gazed at her with the look of a professional inquisitor. "What now?"

Virginia shrugged. "The cops take it from here. Last I heard, they'd picked up everyone involved except Leon Drummond. But I doubt if he'll escape. Not with the guild looking for him as well as the police."

"I wasn't talking about your big case. I know the firm of Gage & Burch has closed it. Probably be all over the evening news." Adeline selected a black-and-orange petit four. "I meant what happens now with you and Sam?"

Virginia took another sip of hot cider and contemplated the heavy mist that drifted in the street outside the office window.

She thought about the passion that had exploded between them in the little fountain chamber.

"Good question," she said quietly.

The narrow streets and twisted lanes of the Old Quarter were thick with fog, but that did not deter the throngs of hobgoblins, ghosts, witches, and assorted monsters who had come to the district to celebrate Halloween.

Virginia walked out of the little corner restaurant with Sam at her side shortly after ten. She could feel the stray pulses of psi energy that leaked from the ruins. They seemed stronger than usual tonight. Maybe it was true that the Dead City was more alive at Halloween than at other times. She was aware of constant little frissons across her para senses. Some just tickled; some were more disturbing. But she could not be sure that all of them were caused by ambient Harmonic energy. She knew that some of the ripples were attributable to Sam, who seemed blithely oblivious to the new level of awareness that pulsed between them.

When he had suggested dinner together earlier, she had been sure that he wanted to talk about their future. But the only thing that had been discussed over a bottle of wine and a leisurely meal of tapenade-tossed cheese ravioli and good bread had been their case.

She did not want to hear another word about their case. She was heartily sick and tired of discussing their case.

Sam paused on the restaurant step and eyed the tide of costumed celebrants that flooded the street.

"I don't know about you, but I've had enough of ghosts and goblins for a while," he said. "What do you say we take a shortcut home and drink a private toast to the successful finale of Gage & Burch's first case?"

Home. To talk some more about their stupid case. Virginia steeled herself. "Sam, we need to talk about us."

"I know," he said.

She was so surprised by his casual agreement that she was momentarily speechless. His mouth curved slightly as he took her arm and steered her along a side street, away from the crowds of revelers.

She shoved her gloved hands into the pockets of her coat and slanted him a sidelong glance. His expression was as enigmatic as ever, but she sensed something going on beneath the surface.

She had come to know him better than she had realized during these past few weeks. And much of what she now knew for certain verified her initial impression. Her instincts had been right that first day. The cool, self-contained veneer was a cover for the deep passions, the unyielding determination, and the rock-solid strength that was at the core of this man. If Sam Gage gave you his word of honor, you could take it to the bank.

If Sam Gage ever said he loved you, you could depend on that love forever.

Commitments like that were dangerous things. Sam probably knew that better than anyone else, she thought. Maybe that was why he was so cautious about making them in the first place.

She decided to take the plunge.

"Sam, about our marriage—"

"I don't want an MC," he said bluntly.

That brought her to an abrupt halt in the middle of the sidewalk. She stopped and swung around to face him. "You've changed your mind?"

"Yes." He watched her with unreadable eyes. "It won't work. I can't handle it."

Despair jolted through her. "You can't handle it? But you're the one who suggested it in the first place."

"It was a mistake. I think I knew it all along, but after what happened in the ruins, I'm sure of it."

"I see." She did not know what to say. This was not how

she had anticipated the conversation would end. "I thought that after what had happened, you might feel differently, but I didn't realize—"

"A marriage-of-convenience will drive me crazy," he interrupted. "I don't want—"

He broke off suddenly as a goblin-masked figure in a long black coat stepped out of the shadows. Light gleamed wickedly on a mag-rez gun.

"I'd say trick or treat," Leon Drummond growled behind the hideous mask. "But you haven't got a choice. You're going to get the trick, whether you want it or not."

Virginia caught her breath. Drummond ignored her. She could see the baleful glitter of his eyes through the holes in the mask. His attention was focused on Sam.

"I'm surprised you're still hanging around, Drummond," Sam said. "Wyatt's got men out looking for you."

"You sonofabitch, you screwed up everything," Leon hissed. "We were nearly finished. Two more days and we would have shut down the operation with no one the wiser. The museum wouldn't have missed the pieces we took until the next full audit. But Ewert had to call you in, and you ruined the whole damned project."

"What can I say?" Sam smiled coldly. "It's what I do."

"Well, it's gonna be the last damned thing you do." Drummond raised the mag-rez gun. "Nobody messes with Leon Drummond and gets away with it. Especially not some two-bit private detective."

Leon was concentrating so fiercely that he never even noticed the ball of green energy that was forming rapidly behind him. Virginia was impressed. Not every hunter could summon a ghost outside the Dead City, let alone control it.

The energy ghost flared and pulsed, gathering strength as Leon continued with his tirade.

"Wyatt's security people are watching my house, thanks to you. I can't even get to my car. They're covering the airport, too. I'll have to use the tunnels to get out of Cadence."

"Risky," Sam said, sounding mildly interested. "Not many people get far in the tunnels once they get beyond the mapped sectors. Unpleasant way to go, all alone in a maze filled with traps and ghosts and who knows what else. They say that even if someone survives the experience, he isn't real sane afterward."

"I'll make it." Leon's hand tightened on the mag-rez. "But I'm gonna make sure you pay for what you did first."

The ball of ghost fire was quite large now. The energy aura pulsed outward abruptly, enveloping Leon Drummond. He jerked wildly when the fringes of the green field touched him. His hair stood on end. His mouth parted on a silent scream. The mag-rez fell from his hand and clattered on the pavement.

A few seconds later, Drummond collapsed, unconscious, beside his weapon.

Virginia exhaled slowly. "You really are good, partner."

Sam gave Drummond a dismissive nod and turned back to her.

"Where were we?" he asked.

She swallowed and managed to drag her eyes away from the still and silent Drummond. "I, uh, think we were discussing the fact that you no longer want to get married."

He frowned. "I didn't say that. I said I didn't want a marriage-of-convenience."

"Oh." Her heart was suddenly weightless. "You did say that you were kind of literal on your good days."

"I thought an MC would give you time to get used to the idea of a real marriage," he said with an air of dogged determination. "But I don't think I could take it, knowing that you were just trying me on for size."

"Size? But there's nothing wrong with your size. I already know that you fit. Perfectly."

"I want a commitment. I want kids. I want to know you'll

be there ten, twenty, forty years from now. I don't want to play house with you. I want a home."

"Oh, Sam, that's what I want, too." She threw herself against him so hard that it was a wonder he did not go down. "Why didn't you say something sooner?"

He caught her close and wrapped his arms around her. "I was afraid I'd scare you off," he said into her hair. "I came up with the deal on the house and the MC plan as a way to make sure I could hold on to you until I could convince you to fall in love with me."

"I fell in love with you the day I rented the office and the apartment."

"Why the hell didn't you say so? Look at all the time we've wasted."

She raised her head and smiled. "How was I to know that you had fallen in love with me? You never said anything. You were always so cool, so controlled. I was beginning to wonder if you ever got excited about anything."

His eyes gleamed. "You want excitement? Let's go home. I guarantee I'll come up with something exciting."

She hesitated, pointing down at Drummond. "What about him?"

Sam groaned. "I guess I'd better make sure Mercer Wyatt sends someone out to collect him. If I leave him here, he's liable to wake up later and make a nuisance of himself."

"Call Wyatt," Virginia smiled, aware of the happiness blossoming deep inside. "I can wait."

Six

The reception following the lengthy, formal covenant wedding service was held in the downstairs offices of Gage & Burch. Virginia's beaming father and brothers toasted the bride and groom so many times that her mother had to call a cab to take them home. Adeline performed brilliantly as a bridal attendant. Mercer Wyatt created a small stir when he showed up with a gift for the newlyweds—a fine, museum-quality Harmonic vase that had to be worth several thousand dollars. Virginia made a mental note to ask Sam the precise nature of the favors he had done for the head of the guild.

When it was all over, Sam insisted on carrying Virginia up the stairs and through the doorway of the darkened bedroom. The long sweep of her white satin skirts cascaded over his arm. Her veil was a gossamer cloud that clung to his sleeve.

He put her down on the wide bed in a tumble of satin and silk and went to the dresser. She curled up against the bedpost and watched him remove his cuff links. He took off his white shirt and then he removed the bottle of champagne from the ice bucket that sat on a stand.

The cork made the appropriately cheerful sound when it

came out of the bottle. Sam poured two glasses full of bubbling champagne and carried them both back across the room to the bed. He handed one to Virginia.

"To us," he said softly.

"To us." She smiled.

They did not take their eyes off each other as they drank the toast to their future. When Virginia had drained her glass, Sam took it from her and put it down beside his on the nightstand.

She saw the steady glow of love and happiness in his eyes when he turned back to her. She knew that he saw the same expression mirrored in her own gaze.

She slid off the bed and got to her feet. He reached out to lift the veil from her hair. She turned her back to him. He kissed the nape of her neck and went to work on the tiny buttons that secured her gown.

A thrill of pleasure went through her when the bodice of the dress fell to her waist. Sam put his arms around her from behind and cupped her breasts. His thumbs grazed across her nipples. He bent his head and kissed the side of her throat.

"I love you," he said.

She leaned back against him, savoring the warm, sleek feel of his bare chest. "I love you."

A moment later, the frothy gown cascaded into a pool at her feet. He unbuckled his belt. When she turned around, she found him ready for her, his hard body fiercely aroused. He picked her up again and settled her against the pillows. She reached for him with a kind of hunger she had never known.

He crushed her into the soft bedding, his mouth hot and deeply sensual on her skin. All of her senses opened at his touch, the paranormal ones as well as the physical. Effervescent, invisible psi energy hummed in the air that surrounded them. She knew it came from both of them, sparked by their passion and fueled by their pleasure.

Sam took his time with the lovemaking, crafting a slow,

sensual dance. She felt his mouth on her breasts, his teeth light and tantalizing on her taut nipples. She kissed his shoulder, using her own teeth in ways that made him murmur husky, sexy threats.

When, eventually, he did retaliate, she wanted to scream with delight. But she made no sound because he had stolen her very breath.

He parted her legs, settled himself between them, and forged slowly, deeply into her. She sank her nails into the hard contours of his muscled back and gloried in the full, heavy heat of his erection.

He eased himself partway out of her channel and then pressed forward again. The intense, impossibly stretched sensation was almost too much. She lifted herself against him, silently demanding that he move more quickly.

But he only laughed softly in the darkness and whispered wicked things that exacerbated the sensual torment.

Finally she could not stand it any longer. She pushed against his chest. His eyes gleamed as he allowed himself to be rolled onto his back.

She came down on top of him, fitting herself to him, kissing his chest and his throat, riding him with a wild abandon that carried them both into the heart of pure ecstasy.

A long time later, she came awake, aware that Sam was not asleep. She stirred and stretched and drew her toes up along his leg.

"Something wrong?" she asked.

"No." His arm tightened around her. "I was just thinking about that place where we hid out while I recovered from the burn."

"The zoo?"

"The more I think about it, the more I think that maybe it wasn't a zoo."

She shrugged. "A down-market apartment complex or a

cheap hotel. Maybe a prison, as you suggested. I doubt if anyone will ever know for certain, even when the experts get through untangling all the traps.''

''True, but there is one explanation for the chamber that we overlooked. It fits with everything we experienced while we were in it, and it explains a lot.''

She propped herself on her elbow and looked down at him. ''What's that?''

''Maybe what we stumbled into was a Harmonic graveyard.''

For a moment she could not believe she had heard him correctly. And then the implications hit her. Her mouth went dry.

''You think it was a *cemetery?*''

''That would account for all the small chambers,'' he said seriously.

''Graves and crypts.'' She shuddered. ''Good grief. Now that you mention it—''

''It would also account for the weird feeling you got from the traps that guarded the cubicles. Maybe they were set as warnings against disturbing the dead.''

''But that fountain room and the little antechamber off of it,'' she interrupted quickly. ''Why wasn't it trapped?''

''Probably because it wasn't an actual grave site. It may have been a meditation chamber or a viewing room. Or it could have been the place where the caskets were displayed for sale, for all we know.''

''Aaargh.'' She flopped back on the pillow. ''Do you think we really spent Halloween in an alien graveyard?''

''I think there's a good chance that we did, yes.''

She stared at the ceiling. ''Kind of boggles the mind.'' Abruptly she sat up amid the sheets. ''But what about that strange energy storm that Chaz triggered when he untangled one of the traps? And those things that we saw drifting past the window. You don't suppose they were—" She broke off, unable to put the thought into words.

Sam smiled slightly. "Real ghosts?"

"No." She shook her head violently. "I absolutely refuse to believe that. The only ghosts are unstable dissonance energy manifestations. UDEMs. Composed of ambient psi energy. There is no such thing as real ghosts."

"Whatever you say." He threaded his fingers through her hair. "Who am I to argue with an expert such as yourself?"

"Definitely not real ghosts," she reiterated very forcefully. Then she frowned. "But about that antechamber off the fountain room."

"What about it?"

"If it was a funeral room or some sort of viewing chamber, then that big chest where we . . . where we—"

"Where we made love for the first time?"

"It must have been a—"

Sam grinned. "Yeah, I think it might have been a casket or a sarcophagus."

She swallowed. "We did it on top of a casket? Our first time together took place in an alien funeral parlor? On top of a *coffin?*"

"I'm pretty sure it was empty," Sam said. "There was no trap, remember?"

"That's not the point. What am I supposed to tell our grandchildren when they ask us about our first real romantic date? That you took me to an alien cemetery and made wild, passionate love to me on top of a *sarcophagus?*"

Sam roared with laughter and eased her onto her back. He lowered himself until he covered her body with his own. Then he braced his arms on either side of her head and looked down at her with eyes that gleamed with sensual amusement.

"Maybe we ought to make it our own, private Halloween tradition," he suggested. "We could hunt up a new alien graveyard every year."

"Don't even *think* about it."

He smiled slowly. "Then what do you say we get busy on creating some children so that one day we'll have those grand-children you mentioned a minute ago."

"At last, a truly brilliant idea." She wrapped her arms around his neck and urged his mouth down to hers.

He kissed her until she stopped thinking about Halloween and graveyards and alien sarcophagi; until she could think of nothing else except their love and the future that they would build together.

MAN IN THE MIRROR

JULIE BEARD

For Bob Everson
Writer, friend, and cousin

One

"Thank heavens this day is over," Katie Montgomery said, heading down the platform toward the commuter train that would take her home from work.

This had, without a doubt, been the unluckiest day of her life. And now the weather was taking a turn for the worse, abruptly ending a beautiful Indian summer day. A full moon was clouding over, and a cold wind whistled along the street, rustling leaves and biting through her coat.

"Perfect weather for a bizarre Halloween day," she muttered as she hoisted her purse over her shoulder and pulled up her collar.

She continued on toward the northbound train that had just pulled into the station but stopped abruptly at the sound of a bellowing crack of thunder. *Bam!* She jumped nearly out of her skin, her heart pounding in her chest. She looked threateningly up at the sky.

"Don't you dare! I have no umbrella."

But the sky did not listen. There was another crack of thunder, then a deluge of water began to fall as if someone had turned on a giant shower. In an instant her hair was drenched and matted to her cheeks. Hurrying toward the train, she stepped into a heated car, took off her coat, and sank down onto a window seat with a heavy sigh.

"What else is going to happen before this day is over?"

"Halloween," a voice croaked in reply from the seat behind, as if that explained everything. Then came a soft cackle of laughter, and the unmistakable odor of whiskey.

Katie turned and smiled politely at what was almost certainly a homeless woman. "Yes, I know. Halloween on a Wednesday doesn't seem quite right, does it? Lots of folks left work early to take their kids out trick-or-treating."

That was all the invitation the old woman needed. Her eyes lit up, she picked up her garbage bag of belongings, and sat down next to Katie, nudging her closer to the window. Katie realized the woman reeked not only of whiskey but of clothing that hadn't been washed in years.

"Kind of spooky," the old woman said, her broad smile exposing nearly toothless gums.

She was dressed in filthy clothes and battered tennis shoes, her gray hair was matted in knots, and her nose sported a wart. She looked like a witch, but Katie knew she was just one of the many bag ladies that comb the city streets for food and shelter.

"I said kinda spooky, isn't it?"

"Yes." Katie didn't want to be rude, but she didn't want to get into a long conversation either, so she turned her gaze out the window.

"What's wrong with you?"

Katie turned in surprise to regard the forthright stranger. With amazingly perceptive eyes, the old woman seemed to see through her veneer of competence.

"Well, nothing's wrong with me. And I'm not a superstitious person, but some bizarre things happened today."

"Walk under a ladder?" the old lady asked, nodding as if she already knew the answer.

Katie frowned at her. "Why, yes, I did. How did you know? I walked under a ladder and the painter above spilled paint on my new shoes."

"Trip on a crack?" the bag lady asked as she pulled out a bruised apple and polished it on her tattered sleeve.

"Yes," Katie said, again amazed by her perceptiveness. "Yes, I tripped on a crack at work and sent a tray of petri dishes crashing to the floor. I work as a medical researcher and I . . ."

She let her words fall away. Why was she telling this stranger so much about herself? Was it merely because a bag lady wouldn't be passing it on to anyone Katie knew?

"See any black cats?" the old woman prodded.

"No," Katie said, smiling with relief. "That's one superstition I didn't have to worry about today."

"Well, watch out for mirrors," the old woman said ominously and bit into her crunchy apple.

"Yes," Katie said distractedly, halfheartedly filing away the warning.

What a silly conversation. Her father, who was a surgeon, had taught her to rely on logic and judgment, not superstition. Katie wouldn't even be thinking of old wives' tales if her life hadn't taken such a drastic turn for the worse recently. Dropping out of medical school last spring and breaking off an engagement had been a double-whammy from which she hadn't yet recovered.

Willing herself to think of happier things, she looked out the window, watching as the city skyline gave way to the autumn leaves that lined the tracks leading into the suburbs. The sun was sinking fast and with it memories of the day's eerie events. The rhythmic sound of the train's metal wheels lulled her into an easy daydream until the train horn blared.

Katie gasped at the sound and clutched her chest.

"Just a horn, missy," the bag lady said, her voice needling

with uncanny insight. "Don't like the sound of train horns, do ya?"

"They always catch me off guard."

Katie left it at that. This stranger didn't need to know why she always jumped in terror at the unexpected blare of a train horn. Two years ago, she was waiting for a train in an underground station when a swarm of students on a field trip filled the already crowded platform. A shove from behind sent Katie over the edge, knocking her onto the tracks. Though not seriously injured, she was dazed by the fall and couldn't get her bearings.

As the horn of an oncoming express train blared in the tunnel, horrified onlookers started screaming at Katie to get up. Just as she saw the glare of the train's light brightening the dark tunnel, a Good Samaritan jumped down onto the tracks and yanked her into his arms, lifting her up to the other anxious commuters. He climbed to safety himself just moments before the train barreled by with a deafening rumble.

Keith Herrod had been her knight in shining armor; handsome, well-to-do, and obviously chivalrous. They'd started dating that very day and became engaged a short time later. Last month—just six months before their wedding—Keith ended the engagement. Katie would have been heartbroken if she hadn't been responsible for the breakup. Unable to stop herself, she'd pushed Keith away in subtle ways almost from the start. She'd cared for him, and Lord knows she was certainly grateful to him, but there had been something wrong with their relationship.

Perhaps it was the overwhelming sense that she owed him her life that burdened her. How could she repay such a debt? Or perhaps it was his lack of understanding when she'd dropped out of medical school unexpectedly just months before her internship was to begin. Still, she wondered, if she couldn't love someone as perfect and heroic as Keith, who could she love?

"He wasn't the one," the bag lady said, carefully wrapping up her apple core in a used tissue, dropping it into her garbage bag, then dusting her hands off as contentedly as if she'd just consumed a gourmet meal.

Katie turned her head slowly and stared hard at her. "What did you say?"

"I said he wasn't the one. It wasn't meant to be. You'll know the right one when you see him. He'll be wearing the sign of the dragon." She raised a gnarled finger in the air. "Mark my words!"

"But I didn't say anything. I was just thinking about Keith." Katie's voice began to rise. "How could you know what I was thinking? I—"

Suddenly the rear door that connected their car to the next whooshed open, giving Katie another start. The conductor marched through, stopping at the old crone's side.

"Come on, Crazy Clara," he said, grabbing her by the arm. "I heard you'd sneaked on the train. But I'm not gonna let you sleep here tonight. You can get off at the next stop and stay at Hope Mission. Get yourself a hot cup of soup and a clean bed."

"All right, all right," the old woman groused. She clutched her bag of belongings to her tattered coat. "I'll get off. Just let me be till the next stop. I'm not a criminal, you know."

"Come on, Clara, I know better than to let you be. We'll be playing musical chairs all night if I don't keep you by my side. Come ride with me up front."

The old woman nodded in resignation, then glanced at Katie with an embarrassed smile. Katie felt a pang of sympathy as she watched Clara reluctantly rise and scuffle along behind the conductor toward the engine car.

Then she recalled Clara's words and shivered. *"He wasn't the one. You'll know him when you see him. He'll be wearing the sign of the dragon."*

Two

Downtown Addison was a cozy village dotted with stately old homes, clustered with trees whose leaves, at this time of year, turned to brilliant shades of copper, russet, and yellow. Addison had once been a small but bustling metropolis for local farmers with a turn-of-the-century grid of storefronts that once housed such necessities as a general store and a milliner's shop, and later a single gas pump on a front porch and a five-and-dime.

But with the pernicious spread of Wal-Marts and big grocery chains in surrounding suburbs, the village had been forced to change. Now it was trendy, serving a different purpose to the folks who commuted here for a respite from the city's hustle-bustle.

The general store was now a needlepoint shop. The five-and-dime had been taken over by a posh florist, and an old feed store was now a bebop coffee house, a funky alternative to Starbucks.

Katie stopped there every night for a latte on her way home, just as she routinely visited British Isles Antiques. The shop was located in the Victorian-style two-story brownstone building that stretched half of the block from Oak Street to Maple. Katie's apartment was located on the corner, just above the antique store.

The shop was owned by Lillian Bloodsworth, a sixty-year-old British expatriate who spoke the Queen's English with charm and gentle effervescence. She was passionate about British furniture in a proper English way and enjoyed regaling Katie with the history that accompanied each piece she brought into her store. With Katie's family in California, Lillian had become like a mother to her, and she couldn't wait to tell her about the day's weird mishaps.

"Oh, Katie love, good to see you," Lillian said, looking up at the sound of the bell that always jingled when the door opened. "I have to close up the shop early and wanted to make sure you were home safe and sound before I left."

"I'm a big girl, Lil. I'll be twenty-nine next month, as a matter of fact. You don't have to worry about me."

"Well, it's Halloween, and I didn't want you to catch your death of a chill in that sudden downpour. I see you didn't have an umbrella."

Katie laughed and swiped her fingers back through her wilted hair. "How could you tell?"

"I just don't want anything bad to happen to you."

"The only bad thing that will happen to me is if nobody rings my apartment for candy and I end up eating an entire bag of miniature chocolate bars by myself."

Lillian gave a melodic laugh. "Save some for me. I must hurry now. I have to pick up Stan at the airport."

"Your son is here in the U.S.? How exciting!"

Katie took off her coat. It was still damp, so she placed it on a wall hook, careful not to brush it against a nearby Queen Anne chair. She breathed in the comforting odor of musty antiques that cluttered the store and smiled lovingly at Lillian as she bustled behind her counter, bifocals dangling on the tip of her button-sized nose.

"Yes, Stan is here from England!" Lillian's lapis lazuli blue eyes sparkled with pride. "He came over unexpectedly on an important business trip to New York. He's flying into Addison from the Big Apple tonight. I was afraid I'd miss you if you didn't get home soon. I have something for you."

When Katie said nothing, Lillian gave her a quizzical look and frowned. "What is it, dear? You look as if you've lost your best friend."

"I do?" Katie shrugged and turned away, nonchalantly smoothing a hand over a perfectly polished Chippendale table. If she let Lillian look into her soul, they'd both be here until midnight. "I'm fine, Lil. It's just been a weird Halloween, in more ways than one. But don't worry about me. You've got to get to the airport."

"Nonsense. I can take a few moments for a good friend."

Katie shrugged again and plopped down in an overstuffed chair that dated back to the 1940s. A plume of dust rose and tickled her nose.

"I don't know what's bothering me. I had the strangest experience on the train. This bag lady sat down next to me."

"Begging for money?" Lillian gave her a sympathetic smile.

"No. That would've been fine. I would have gladly given her some money if she'd asked. In fact, I wish she had. Instead she . . . she read my mind somehow. I know it sounds crazy, but I was thinking about Keith and the engagement and she said . . . she said he wasn't the one."

"Well, we all know that, my dear." Lillian said this matter-of-factly as she sorted through receipts behind the counter.

"But how could a stranger know?"

"She was probably just talking to herself and said something that coincidentally made sense. She was probably drunk."

"I thought so, too, at first. But she was too . . . perceptive . . . to be drunk."

"Then just blame it on Woden's Curse."

Katie let out a laugh. "Woden's Curse? What's that?"

Lillian looked at Katie over the rims of her half-moon glasses. "Don't laugh. You know my family dates back to the days of Celtic Britain. Apparently one of my Briton ancestors outsmarted some very short-tempered Saxon invaders. Being pagans, the Saxons called on the god Woden, cursing future generations for centuries to come."

"So I take it Woden's Curse strikes every Halloween."

"Not precisely." Lillian took off her glasses and let them dangle from the chain around her neck. "Only when Halloween falls on a Wednesday."

Katie's amused skepticism deepened. "Go on. I'm intrigued. Why Wednesday?"

"Because Wednesday was named after Woden, or Odin as he was sometimes called. Thursday, incidentally, was named after Thor."

"I see." Katie tried to downplay her burgeoning smile.

"So whenever Halloween falls on Wednesday, I blame every mishap on Woden. Take this, for example."

She rounded the counter and went to the door, pointing to a crack in one of the antique lead panes of glass. "Do you know how much this will cost to replace?"

Katie rose and joined her at the door. The merciless wind seeped through the cracked glass with a biting chill. Two trick-or-treaters dressed as Ninjas walked by, laughing as they peeled open candy bars.

"It cracked sometime this afternoon, probably when I went out for a bite to eat."

"And you blame it on Woden?" Katie's voice was rife with skepticism.

"Of course. Woden loves to shatter and break glass."

Katie frowned with worry. "I suspect this window was broken by pumpkin smashers who got an early start, Lillian, not the pagan god of the Saxons. Hopefully, they got their jollies and won't be back."

"Pumpkin smashers?" She turned to Katie with a blank look.

"You know, teens who run amok on Halloween night. They throw eggs and smash pumpkins, sometimes even windows, depending on whether they're hoodlums in the making or just troublemaker wanna-bes."

"Oh, I see, one of those phenomenons of American culture."

Katie chuckled. "Something like that. You know, Lil, America is full of oddities. Rich kids who dress like poor kids to be cool, talk shows that entice people to confess their deepest secrets to the entire world, young women who become engaged to the perfect catch and then sabotage the relationship just months before the marriage."

"Now, now," Lillian said, giving her a hug. Katie welcomed the warm embrace and breathed in Lillian's sweet rose perfume. "I was right. There is something wrong. You're sad. It will take time to get over Keith, my dear."

"I wish that were the case," Katie said wryly, pulling away. They both naturally sank onto the blue embroidered settee where they'd shared many cups of tea. "I don't think I ever really loved Keith. I just loved the idea of being in love. We went to all the right parties and socialized with all the right people. But already I can hardly remember their names. What is it going to take, Lillian, for me to really fall for someone?"

The older woman sighed as she considered the dilemma. "Every heart has a unique lock, Katie. Each one takes a special key. Didn't you say you almost married another fellow who helped you and your family after a hurricane or something of that nature?"

Katie nodded soberly. "Yes. Michael helped us from a hotel that had collapsed in a hurricane during a Florida vacation.

He and I had a summer fling that became serious very quickly. But again, the relationship fizzled out when I lost interest.''

"Hmmm. Both Michael and Keith rescued you in dramatic fashion. Perhaps it's time you stopped playing the damsel in distress and rescued someone yourself. Isn't that what got you interested in medicine? Saving people?''

Lillian was right, but Katie didn't want to talk about medicine right now. It was too painful to think about how easily she had quit her lifelong dream to become a doctor after the death of a single patient.

"I guess I've been too good at playing the damsel in distress," Katie admitted. "Truth is, I don't know what role I should be playing. I just wish I knew what my purpose in life was.''

"Dear," Lillian said in her gentle, no-nonsense manner, "we all need to give as well as receive. If all you do is take from others, after a while you feel unworthy. Giving to others is good for the soul.''

"I guess the question is, am I strong enough to save anyone else?''

"I don't think there's any question of that, my dear. You just have to recognize your own strength. Maybe then you'll be ready for Mr. Right." Suddenly Lillian looked at her watch. "Oh, my! I must hurry. Be a dear and take that mirror upstairs.''

She rose and grabbed her jacket from a coat tree, pointing to an enormous and ornate freestanding oval antique mirror Katie hadn't yet noticed in the clutter of antiques. "My room of mirrors is filled to overflowing. I've been meaning to give you that one for months. It's a family heirloom, and I'd like you to have it.''

Katie whistled in awe, then examined it more closely. It had to be worth five hundred dollars at least. "Oh, Lillian, it's beautiful. But shouldn't Stan have it?''

"What do men need with mirrors? My son has a whole

house full of family heirlooms in Cornwall. He'll never miss it, believe me. Consider it an early birthday present."

"I'd love to have it, but I insist on paying full price."

"I won't hear of it."

"Then half price."

"Not a penny, do you hear? Can you manage getting it up the stairs?"

"I'll ask my neighbor's teenage son. He'd do anything for a fin. I'll tell him to be *very* careful. I don't want to break it. But I don't know why I'm worried. You'd simply blame it on Woden's Curse."

Katie expected a laugh, but when she turned to look at her friend, Lillian was zipping up her parka, gazing into space with a mischievous look burning in her eyes.

"What is it, Lil? You look like you're plotting a murder."

"I was just remembering something my grandmother used to tell me." She tapped a forefinger on her upper lip and put her other hand on her hip. "An old wives' tale. She said that if a young woman peels an apple in front of a mirror on Halloween night, she will see the man she is going to marry reflected in the glass."

A frown gathered on Katie's forehead as she remembered the bag lady's ominous warning: Watch out for mirrors. A chill skittered down her spine. "Not another superstition. I've decided to stay away from mirrors today. I've had enough bad things happen already. If it breaks, I'll have seven years' bad luck. I'll come back for it tomorrow."

"Nonsense, my dear, that's a silly superstition."

Katie exhaled a laughing breath. "But your idea isn't?"

Lillian's lips curled gently at the corners. "Katie, have some fun. You can't take love too seriously, or it will never come your way. You need to make light of it. Dream about your fantasy man; then you'll know what you really want in a partner. But whatever you do, don't worry about it. Love usually comes when you're looking the other way."

"So you *really* want me to peel an apple in front of this mirror?"

Lillian nodded mischievously and hurried to her desk. "Here's an apple I didn't have time to eat." She dropped it in one of the pockets of Katie's beige cardigan sweater. "Now, not another word. Do it for me. That will be your payment for the mirror."

Katie sighed. "Very well, but only for you, Lillian. And only if you *swear* you'll never tell a soul."

Lillian smiled. "Scout's honor, as you Americans would say."

Three

Katie's apartment was old style: hardwood floors, thick plaster walls with too many layers of paint, cast-iron radiators in every room that clicked and hissed when dragged into service by low temperatures. In short, it had character and charm. Katie loved the feel of the place. She loved things old-fashioned. It was one of the bonds she shared with Lillian. The moment they'd met, Lillian and Katie had known they would be close friends. Soul mates, even, despite their age difference.

Only a rare friend would give you an incredible mirror like this, Katie thought as she sat in front of it an hour later. The teen next door had put it down in the living room, and Katie sat before it now with a paring knife in hand. She pulled the apple out of her pocket and turned it over in her hands.

"I can't believe I'm doing this," she muttered to herself as she began to peel the fruit. She briefly thought of lighting a candle but refused to give the wives' tale that much pomp and ceremony. "At least I can honestly tell Lillian I fulfilled her request. Small price to pay for a gorgeous mirror."

After a few juicy peels of apple skin curled above the knife and tumbled to the floor, Katie looked into the glass. She saw nothing but her own reflection, shoulder-length hair a wheat-colored blond cut fashionably blunt and all one length, parted on the side. Her face was formed with delicate bones—a small nose and gently lilting lips, the kind of features you might see in a Cezanne painting on the faces of puffy-skirted ladies bearing parasols.

Katie's eyes were two sparkling peridots, green and wide. Innocent, one might say. Maybe that's why men were always coming to the rescue.

"Ow!" she muttered when the blade nicked her thumb. She should be paying more attention to the knife, she realized as she examined her injury. No blood. She turned her focus back to the apple. "Let's get this over with."

Just a few more twists of the knife and she would have fulfilled her promise to Lillian. As she worked, she listened to the wind whistling through the living room window. She usually kept it cracked open for fresh air, even in winter, but tonight the air was more than cold. It was downright pernicious.

The wind rattled the window in its casement, and autumn leaves rustled tempestuously on the pavement two stories below. More rain began to pelt the glass with hypnotic little thuds.

Katie hurried on with her task. The last peel gave way with a muted, fleshy cutting sound. Just as the skin hit the floor, she looked up into the mirror.

She frowned. Someone was frowning back at her. Two desperate eyes, not her own. Then a face took form. A deeply tanned and furrowed brow, stained with blood. A straight, strong nose; three days' growth of beard. A man.

"Katherine!" he gasped.

She sucked in a quivering breath. Her whispered name chilled her to the marrow. She shivered, as if he'd grabbed her arms and had given her a violent shake.

"Katherine, help me!" he cried. Then he was gone, as if the silver mirror had swallowed him up.

"Oh, my God!" she whispered in the silence that followed. Then she shivered violently from head to toe. "Oh, my God. Who on earth . . . ?"

She reached out and touched the glass, not quite believing her eyes. "It couldn't be! I'm imagining it. Am I that desperate? No! I *did* see someone. W-who are you?"

But there was no time for answers. A deafening clap of thunder burst, seemingly just outside her window, and lightning flashed for what seemed an eternity. When the sky turned dark again, Katie realized the lights had just blown. She let out a shaky breath, willing herself not to run from the darkened apartment in terror.

The room was utterly black, save for the cloudy moonlight filtering through the window. She shut her eyes and swallowed a great lump of terror lodged in her throat. She wasn't alone. She could sense it. Someone . . . *something* . . . was waiting for her in the mirror. She could feel his desperate need as if she were cradling it in her arms.

With her pulse pounding in her ears, she forced her eyes open. Knowing it could be hours before the lights came back on, Katie tried to decide what to do. She had to think logically. But, no. Logic and reason had made her life hollow. This was a time to follow her heart. To believe the absurd. She *had* seen someone. Someone who was hurt. Someone who was asking for her help.

Moved by a terrific urge to see the face again, she leapt up and went to the kitchen, fumbling in her junk drawer for matches. Finding them, she dashed back to the chair and lit the candle on a nearby table. In the sputtering yellow light of the flame, she returned to the dark kitchen and yanked open the fridge. Two Red Delicious apples sat in the shadows of the second shelf. She grabbed them and hurried back to the chair.

Hands trembling this time, she popped the knife edge

through the skin of the smallest apple and tugged at the cold flesh. This was crazy and she knew it. If anyone else saw her, they'd think she'd gone mad. But she didn't care. She had to see him again. In a few brief moments she'd felt a connection with him stronger than she'd ever experienced before. *Hurry! Hurry. He might go away.* It didn't occur to her that she had lost all reason. Her gaze darted intensely from the blade up to the mirror and back again. His words rang in her ears. *"Katherine, help me!"*

Disappointment hovered as she approached the end of her task. What if he didn't reappear? What if it had all been her imagination? She didn't want it to be. There had been something so desperate, so real about the image. She wanted to help him. And she wanted to know who he was. Where had he come from? How did he know her name?

When she reached the last strip of skin, she peeled it carefully and watched as it fell to the floor, seemingly in slow motion. When it hit, she looked up. Her eyes dilated. Her heart began to pound. There he was! She wasn't imagining him. She could see more this time. There were bloodied swords crashing behind him. He turned and looked at her, his eyes begging her.

"Come, Katherine! I need you."

Just then a sword raised over his head and came down hard. She heard his grunt of pain.

"No!" Katie cried out, leaping to the edge of her seat. "Don't hurt him!"

Suddenly, a powerful breeze burst through the window and the candle guttered out.

"Damn it!" she cried, glaring at the smoking wick in frustration. When she looked at the mirror again, even in mere moonlight, she could see that he was gone.

"No, come back!" she called, her anxiety spilling out in a rush. "Who are you? What do you want me to do? I can't help you if I can't see you. Come back!"

There was no answer. And she knew there would be none, unless she peeled another apple. The last apple. She fumbled for it in the moonlight, glancing at her illuminated digital watch. It was one minute and fifteen seconds after seven. There was plenty of time before midnight. She had to see him one more time. She'd run out and buy another bag of apples if she had to. He needed her, and she desperately wanted to help him. But where was he? What kind of man would be having a sword fight?

These questions faded as she concentrated on her task. *Show yourself to me, please!* she thought over and over, willing him to return, until the last peel fell. And there he was.

His eyes burrowed into her like drills penetrating her deepest subconscious. This time his face was calm. *I know you,* he seemed to be thinking. *I know you as no one ever has. I want you. I will have you.*

"Come to me," he commanded.

She rose without a shred of resistance and reached out as if she'd been waiting all her life for this very task. When she touched the man in the mirror, to her surprise the glass was malleable, like gelatin. Her hand plunged through, and she felt a cold emptiness, then the warmth of contact. *She was touching him.* Yes! She grasped his fingers as if for life. A hand with rough, strong fingers grabbed hers in return.

"*Come!*" a deep, male voice whispered.

As if in a trance, she did not resist when he tugged at her. In one fluid motion, she leaned forward, and through the mirror she went.

Four

Whatever happened, it happened in an instant. The hand that pulled her through suddenly turned into a slender, cone-shaped stone. It was cold and wet, and her fingers instinctively recoiled. She looked around and saw nothing but blackness. Cool underground air seeped through her sweater, and she shivered. She heard springy plunks of water dripping into a still pool and realized with a pang of terror that she was in a cave. What she'd been clutching was a stalactite. Suddenly hyperaware, she heard the rustle of bats hanging along the stone roof. She had to get out of here!

"Hello?" she called out, her voice thin and tense. "Anybody here?"

"Out here!"

It was *his* voice. Relief and excitement flushed her skin with warmth. She was finally going to see him in the flesh. She started forward, then realized she didn't know which way to go.

"Where are you?" she cried out. "I can't see a thing."

"Just follow the sound of my voice."

He called to her a few more times, and she inched forward

slowly, touching the ground with her toes before each step to make sure she didn't stumble or fall into a pool of water. Running a hand along the moist stone wall, she soon saw a glimmer of light and hurried toward it.

"Are you there?" she called out, and as soon as she had said it, she saw a body lying at the mouth of the cave. She rushed forward and stopped when she reached him, blinking against the glaring sunshine. At last focusing on his long, strong body, she swallowed thickly.

"Oh, my God," she whispered, staggered by what she saw. She didn't know what stunned her more, the uniqueness of his bloody injuries or his stunning beauty, which was evident even though his face was marred with dirt and dried blood.

His cheeks were high and ruddy, his forehead prominent and tanned, his nose elegant and romanesque, and his chin was marked with a distinctive cleft. His brown hair, matted with blood, flowed down to his shoulders. Wings of gray hair fanned out at his temples, adding drama and distinction to his already powerful presence. She did not know the color of his eyes because they were closed and did not open, even when she knelt at his side. With a deep and instant compassion warming her heart, she touched his shoulder.

"Are you all right?"

No answer. Obviously, he was not all right, but there was something almost unreal about his injuries. It probably seemed that way because she'd never seen anyone come into the emergency room with sword wounds. Why had he been fighting with such an archaic weapon? And where the devil were they? She looked around, recognizing nothing. The last thing she remembered was stepping through the mirror. Was she dreaming? No, she thought, squeezing his shoulder. She wasn't imagining this handsome stranger. She wasn't touching a ghost or an apparition.

She licked her lips and tried again. "Can you tell me who you are? Or at least tell me where you hurt."

He didn't move. In fact, he was deathly still. *Oh, Lord, was she too late?* Had she failed yet another patient? Had he died in the last few seconds it took for her to reach him? A wave of vertigo bowled her over. She dropped her head to her bent knees and hugged herself, breaking out in a cold sweat.

"Ohhh," he groaned.

She bolted upright just in time to see his eyelids twitch. He was alive. She had to get herself together. This was no time for panic or despair. She leaned over him and gripped his shirt—actually, it was some kind of old-fashioned leather tunic that covered his chest. "I'm going to help you. Try to stay with me here."

When he merely groaned, she gripped one of his massive wrists to take his pulse. It was weak but steady. As he roused back to consciousness, his eyes fluttered open and focused on her with piercing blue. He looked startled, as if *she* were a ghost. Then a smile spread slowly on his gorgeous, wide lips and his pulse beat stronger.

"It is *you!*" he said in a hoarse baritone. "He said you would come. But I did not quite believe him until now."

The certainty that resonated in his voice sent a shiver down her spine. "Who? *Who* said I was coming? How did he know? I myself only decided to come just minutes ago, when I stepped through my mirr—"

She stopped mid-sentence, realizing how absurd her story would sound. No matter how she got here, he was lucky she'd come when she did, or he would have died alone. She didn't even know if this was real or if she had somehow lost her mind. But it felt real, and she knew one thing. No one should have to die alone.

"I'm here now," she whispered, seeing in the depth of his eyes the instant connection and deep need that had compelled her through the mirror. "I want to help you. But you must tell me your name."

She reached out and stroked his forehead, feeling much

more for him than would a doctor for a patient. She felt as if she were soothing an old and dear friend, but one she'd suddenly discovered she cared for on a much deeper level.

"I'm Tristan," he said. "Tristan of Ilchester."

She frowned. "What an unusual name. Is Ilchester your family name?"

"No. It is the town where I grew up."

"Tristan of Ilchester." She blinked rapidly several times. Something was niggling at her mind. She'd heard names like that before, but only in history books. Her frown deepened. "Is that where we are? In Ilchester?"

But the answer to this and many other questions would have to wait, for his eyes closed again. Moments later, he muttered something incoherently and twisted his head from side to side. He was obviously delirious.

"You're very sick, Tristan of Ilchester. You must have an infection," she whispered as she stroked her fingers down his cheek, where the beginning of a beard bristled at her touch. "I need to get you to a hospital."

But where on earth would she find one? They were obviously in the middle of nowhere. He'd apparently been fighting on horseback. His powerful steed grazed leisurely a hundred yards away in the shade of a giant oak tree. Tristan had managed to unsaddle his mount before collapsing. Was it possible she'd somehow been propelled through the mirror to some backward country where people still fought with swords and horses instead of guns and tanks? Someplace like the Balkans or the former Soviet Union?

Their location certainly seemed foreign. The hills that sloped sharply around them were dotted with caves. They definitely weren't in Addison. The air was too pure, the grass too green. It was as if all her life she'd been looking through dirty glasses and suddenly they'd been wiped clean. Was it possible that her mirror had been some kind of window to another place or even another time? The very idea was so fantastic it made her weave with nausea.

She forced her thoughts back to practical matters. Wherever she was, she had to help Tristan. Since they were apparently far from civilization, getting him to a hospital would not be an option. She would have to dust off her medical knowledge and recall the skills she'd practiced in her last semester at school.

She studied the blood encrusted on Tristan's head where a sword had grazed him. A scab was already forming. But she'd seen him struck in that very place not more than a few minutes ago! It happened just before she'd stepped through the mirror, at seven o'clock on Halloween night. Seven-oh-one and fifteen seconds, to be precise.

She glanced down at her wrist, then blinked hard. It was now seven-oh-one and twenty four seconds. According to her watch, only nine seconds had passed since she'd traveled through the mirror. It had felt more like fifteen minutes. Either her watch was running out of power, or time here wasn't what it seemed. Perhaps minutes in her world equaled hours in this place beyond the mirror, in this parallel universe, or twilight zone, or whatever it was.

"What difference does the time make?" she said, irritated with herself. He could be dying. She had to help him somehow.

She quickly scanned the rest of his muscle-bound body for other injuries. His right arm was badly cut at the wrist, but it was a clean wound that had not harmed the tendons or muscles. That would heal in time. The apparent source of his infection was his right leg. A sword had slashed through his leather boot. She quickly unfastened it.

"This may hurt, so bear with me," she said, but he gave no reply. Gingerly, she tugged off the boot and cringed when she saw what lay beneath it: an angry wound, mottled with blood and bruises and the telltale white of a life-threatening infection. Her heart sank. He needed more than she could offer him. He needed medicine.

"I'm sorry," she said sadly. "I thought I could help you, but I can't."

"Yes, you can," he answered unexpectedly.

Startled, she looked at his face and found him watching her again with his penetrating blue eyes. He was conscious.

"What did you say?"

"I said you *can* help me. Do not give up so easily."

"I'm *not* giving up. I'm just being realistic. You still haven't told me where we are, but it's obviously in the middle of nowhere. Your leg is badly infected and without a miracle it will spread to your whole body and you'll—" She stopped and swallowed the word *die*. "I need medicine to help you. Or do you think I'm a magician?"

Despite his pain, he chuckled softly at her ironic question. "No, I do not. But Merlin does, or he wouldn't have brought you here."

She frowned as the name registered. *"Merlin?* You mean Merlin the magician?" That niggling sensation tickled her memories again as the pieces of a very unlikely scenario began—against all odds—to fall into place. "Tristan, you say the name Merlin as if you were utterly serious."

"I am," he replied without a hint of mockery.

Her heart began to hammer in her chest. This couldn't be happening. "You called me by name earlier. Do you know who I am?"

"Yes. You're Lady Katherine of Addison."

Her jaw dropped. "How did you—?"

"Merlin told me."

She began to tremble all over. *"Where are we?"*

"We're in Dumnonia, of course."

"Dumnonia." She repeated the word, calling it from her dusty memory. She'd been a lifelong Anglophile and had read much about England from its earliest incarnations. It had been

Katie's one incongruity. She was a logical science major who reveled in the mystical lore and legends of Great Britain. Finally the word registered.

"Dumnonia," she said to herself, her arms breaking out in gooseflesh. "Dumnonia is what they called Cornwall during the Dark Ages. During the time of King Arthur and . . ." she looked down at him in disbelief, ". . . and Merlin!"

Five

"Oh, good Lord!"

She struggled for a breath of air as her skin turned cold, then hot, then cold again. She staggered to a stand and ran both hands through her hair, her mind reeling at what was now an obvious—though still incredible—realization.

"I've . . . traveled . . . back . . . in . . . time!" she said slowly and emphatically to herself. "There can be no other explanation!"

She ran a few feet from the matted earth at the mouth of the cave to the grass that stretched up and down the sloping hills as far as the eye could see. She bent down on one knee and ran her hands through the soft, moist blades. "This is England. That's why the grass is so green. And the air is so pure because this is—what, the sixth century?"

She turned back to him and found him regarding her as if she'd gone mad. She laughed giddily, then took in a quivery breath as she steadied her nerves. "Bear with me, Tristan. I know I must sound like a loon. But . . . Oh, God, this is incredible! What year would this be? I'm sure you don't think in terms of centuries. But this has to be somewhere around the year five hundred. That's why there's no pollution to cloud the sky.''

''No *what?*''

''Pollution. It comes from fossil fuel. It's—'' She halted. He wouldn't know anything about fossils. Or fuel. Or cars or airplanes or anything that she took for granted. Suddenly she was aware of a rich, sweet smell. She breathed deeper, and turned around, hugging herself. ''I can smell daffodils in the air! And heaven knows what other kinds of flowers you have. Everything is so fresh!''

She excitedly returned to his side and knelt down. ''Tristan, I don't want to upset you. But you look like you're feeling better. Are you?''

He nodded.

''You're not as flushed as you were before.'' She took his pulse again and felt his forehead. ''Yes, your heart is beating stronger. The fever has subsided for the moment. I think I can tell you without disturbing you too much. Let me explain from the beginning. I've ... I've come from another century. Another country. In my time, this place is called Cornwall. Only in history books written about the Dark Ages is it called Dumnonia.''

''The dark ages?'' he repeated sardonically. ''And so it will be if we don't conquer the Saxons.''

''The Saxons?'' She touched his sleeve. ''Yes, I recall something about them! I remember reading about how they invaded England after the Romans gave up their occupation during the fall of the Roman Empire. So you must be a Briton. You come from one of many kingdoms that date back to the Celts. Is that right?''

He nodded and tried to prop himself up on one elbow but wasn't strong enough. He pointed to his leather saddle. ''Would you please?''

''Of course.'' She retrieved it and placed it under his head. That way he could see her as he continued his explanation.

"After the Romans left our country," he began, "we lost our central authority and our petty Briton kings began to war with one another. Now we face the conquering Saxons and must unify or risk being taken over once again."

He took a deep breath and continued.

"Arthur's Uncle Ambrosius and his father Uther Pendragon united the warring Britons, each in their own turn claiming the mantle of High King. But it wasn't until Arthur pulled the sword from the stone that the other petty kings truly put aside their discord and recognized Arthur as the salvation of Britain. He is the first High King who has a true chance to reign in peace. He is a great man and a dear friend."

"A-Arthur?" she said, stuttering with excitement over the word. She inched closer so she could burrow her gaze into his eyes, searching for a glimmer of a jest. "You're not joking, are you? Did you say Arthur is your friend?"

"Yes."

"How exciting! What is he like?"

He grinned at her, not quite believing she could be so ignorant. "Have you not heard any ballads around the fire of a night, tales of Arthur's heroism? Why are you so full of questions about commonplace matters?"

Truth to tell, he had many questions for her as well. He had never seen any woman quite like her. She bore herself with the dignity and grace of a queen, and yet she dressed like a peasant. A *male* peasant at that. She wore loose leggings instead of a long gown, and some sort of woven garment that hung on her like a sack. Still, he managed to make out the curves of her very feminine form beneath her peasantlike garb.

"Well, you may have appeared in the cave by magic," he said, "and you may be talking of things that make no sense to me, but you are not a witch. I can see that much by the innocent light in your beryl-colored eyes. Your lips are no more brazen than a rosebud, clearly incapable of chanting a curse."

And I long to kiss them, he thought as he regarded her simple, elegant demeanor. He had waited for a woman like Katherine all his life. The advantage of never having found one was that he recognized her as *the one* instantly, for all his dreaming and waiting for her. He sighed with a sense of peace deeper than he had ever known.

"Merlin told me you would come. He saw a vision of you in his crystal cave. But he did not tell me how beautiful you were."

Their eyes locked, and she felt that overwhelming warmth in her heart again. If she didn't know better, she would think it was love at first sight. Then his words registered and she sobered.

"If Merlin had a vision of me, perhaps he had something to do with my arrival. But I thought it was the mirror that brought me here."

When Tristan frowned questioningly, she explained. "You see . . . I was given a mirror. A glass with silver painted on the back. A looking glass, you'd probably call it. It was given to me by a woman whose ancestors date back to your time. I saw your reflection and I . . . I reached out and felt your hand. Then I felt you pull me through the glass."

"I felt your hand as well. In a dream," he murmured, and nodded encouragingly as she began to make more sense. "Your mirror may have been the vehicle of your . . . your time travel, as you call it. But I daresay Merlin had something to do with it."

She stared at him a long moment. "Doesn't any of this shock you? Aren't you the least bit skeptical about my story?"

He quirked his brows. "Why should I be?"

She shrugged in resignation. "Well, I suppose if you believe in Merlin's magic, what I'm saying must sound commonplace." She decided to toss out a theory equally fantastic in her own mind. "Perhaps my sudden arrival here can be blamed on Woden's Curse."

"Woden?" He gave a derisive snort of laughter. "That pagan god has no power over you, my lady. He is a useless idol whose name will soon vanish from the tongues of superstitious men."

If Tristan himself didn't worship pagan gods, what exactly did he believe in? Her eyes widened slowly as she considered another possibility. "Oh, good Lord, you're not a *Druid,* are you? Do you worship trees?"

He barked out a deep, rich laugh, his white teeth flashing, then he groaned from the pain it caused him. "Do you not make any jests, I pray you. It is too painful. Like King Arthur, I am a believer in the one true God."

"You mean Christ?"

"Yes. Arthur says believing in one god alone will help unite our kingdom in victory over invaders who believe in many gods."

"Is Merlin a Christian then?"

He frowned as his mind sorted through Merlin's enigmatic nature. "I think not. Some say he draws his powers from the gods and goddesses of old. Whatever his religion, when Arthur's next battle comes, I'll be glad to have Merlin on our side, be he Christian or no. He told me you would come. So I am not surprised to learn you are from another world."

"If Merlin is that powerful," she said, "then perhaps he will see you in one of his visions and realize you're injured! He can send help."

"No," Tristan answered ruefully. "Merlin is in Gaul with Arthur. He won't be thinking of me now. He has more important matters to tend to."

She sighed, once again coming back to the realization that she would have to save him herself. Apparently she'd given up on medicine too soon.

"Tristan, I'm not a licensed doctor, but I do have some medical skills. I'm going to clean your wound. It will be painful, but I can't help that."

He nodded his understanding.

"I'll need a knife, and it has to be sterile."

"Sterile? What is that?"

"Something doctors won't know about until the next millennium. I'll explain later. What I need to do is start a fire."

"There's a knife in my scabbard at my waist. And a flint in my saddlebags."

"Good! Oh, and I need some sort of container to heat water. The bandages for your leg will have to be boiled. I'll use my teddy for material."

He frowned. "A what?"

She blushed. "A teddy. It's sort of . . . an undertunic, I guess you'd call it. An undershirt."

He nodded, gallantly letting the subject go, though a hint of a teasing grin tugged at the corners of his mouth.

"When you start the fire," he said, "fashion some kind of torch. Use a stick and go in the cave. You'll find a pot there."

She cringed at the prospect of returning to the cave. He gave her arm a reassuring squeeze.

"Do not fear. If you veer to the left at the entrance you will see a dwelling there. This is one of Merlin's caves. He has cooking utensils inside. There are no bats in his private quarters." He chuckled with irony. "And to think I made it this far but collapsed before I could get inside. I knew this would be a safe haven from the Saxons."

He shut his eyes and exhaled a weary breath.

"You're tired," she said. "Try to rest while I get ready."

He followed her advice and fell asleep immediately. She watched him slumber a moment, still not quite believing she was really here in the Dark Ages. Not quite believing how much she wanted to save him. That desire burned in her belly like a fierce flame, one so intense that her fear of losing another patient paled in comparison.

Getting to work, Katie started a fire and retrieved the pot. By the time she was done with her preparations, she had a much greater appreciation of the conveniences of modern medicine. She'd give anything for a pair of rubber gloves and alcohol.

When everything was laid out, she shook Tristan, trying to wake him. She wanted him to be prepared for the pain. To her surprise, when he stirred, before she could even say a word, he reached out and pulled her close, enveloping her in his arms. She resisted at first, freezing up, but his warmth thawed her in an instant. Feeling an incredible well of intimacy, she wrapped her arms around his neck, resting her cheek against his. He was her only anchor in this strange world, where a woman had little chance of surviving without the protection of a man.

Nothing less than tenderness flowed between them: the bond felt by a healer and her patient, the mutual need of two people who must depend on each other for survival, the deep attraction of a man and a woman who feel an instant connection for reasons that cannot and need not be explained.

"I don't want to hurt you," she whispered, inhaling the scent of wood smoke and leather that clung to his skin. She nestled her cheek to his, relishing his warmth, wondering how she was unquestionably drawn to his embrace, and why it felt so right.

"You won't hurt me. Not in any way that matters." He put his hands to her cheeks and held her face in his line of sight. He looked at her—looked through her—then drew her lips to his, giving her a kiss that they both knew might well be their one and only. If she couldn't cure him, he might not make it through the night. Laden with such understanding, the kiss was tender and thoroughly breathtaking.

At length he drew back and said, "Do your best."

She blinked back tears. "I will."

By the time it was over and she had tucked the last bandage in place, the sun had set and Katie was grateful for the fire.

She sank back on her knees, finally releasing the tension that had gripped her for the last hour. Treating his leg had brought back painful memories of the girl who had died in her care. But no matter how insecure those memories made Katie feel, they hadn't detracted from her determination to make Tristan better. Perhaps it was because she suspected that saving Tristan had been the very reason for her incredible voyage back in time.

"Your wound was badly infected," she said, stroking his forehead, brushing aside a wisp of gray from his damp temple. She spoke softly, her tone reflecting her tender feelings for him. "I had to cut away more tissue than I cared to. I . . . I've never seen any patient endure that kind of pain without so much as a whimper."

Though his brow was still furrowed with the imprint of that pain, he gave her a lopsided grin. "Pain is my friend. It reminds me I'm still alive."

"I'll tell that to my HMO patients who complain about lack of service."

"Your patients? I thought you said you were not a doctor."

"I would have become one soon if I hadn't dropped out of medical school."

Disapproval lined his forehead with a frown. "Why did you quit?"

"Well," she began, clearing her throat, "I let a patient die. It was my shift in the ER. That's the emergency room, where they take care of people who need immediate help. There'd been a terrible accident involving two buses filled with students. Bloodied children flooded the emergency room. The staff was overwhelmed, and there was no one to supervise my work. I took charge of a girl. Amanda was her name. Six years old. Her leg was . . . seriously damaged. My . . . my hands were shaking so bad I . . . I didn't work fast enough to stop the bleeding. She went into cardiac arrest. I . . ."

She covered her face with her hands, the guilt washing over her as it had a thousand times before.

He said nothing, but she felt his empathy. His silence was a soothing balm. She lowered her hands and found him regarding her with incredible softness for a man so strong.

"You did not let her die," he said.

"But I didn't keep her alive."

"You are not God."

"But I could have worked faster."

"And she might have reached you sooner," he reasoned.

That was what the dean had told her when he'd tried to talk Katie out of taking a leave of absence from school. He said she'd done the best that she could, but the child had arrived at the hospital too late.

Somehow hearing this argument from Tristan—a warrior who knew much about fighting but likely very little about medicine—meant so much more. He barely understood the circumstances, but he grasped the underlying concept. She had been expecting herself to wield the power of God. Odd, though she could talk about this with a stranger, she hadn't even told her family about it. She just told them she'd lost interest in medicine. How could she tell her father—a world-renowned surgeon—that she hadn't even been able to keep her hands steady?

"All you can ever do is try," Tristan said. "As you did with me."

She sighed with relief, as if a terrible weight had finally been lifted from her shoulders. "You're right. I tried my best with you, and so far so good. But I'm not done torturing you yet. I've cleaned the wound, and I hope the infection will subside. However, if it goes into your bloodstream, if it becomes systemic in nature, nothing short of a heavy dose of antibiotics will save you."

"I don't even know what anti . . . antibi . . ."

"Antibiotics."

"I do not know what that is."

She sighed, suddenly discouraged by the odds stacked up against her. "No, of course not. It's a medicine that hasn't been invented yet in your time. I need something that does the same thing, or close to it. What would you normally do for a wound that won't heal?"

"I'd go to a doctor or a wisewoman for a poultice."

"Hmmmm. Probably a bandage treated with herbs. Where is the nearest doctor?"

"Camelot." He shook his head. "We cannot leave here until I'm strong enough to fight my way out. The Saxon warriors who injured me will be waiting for me at Willow Pass, and that is the only passageway leading to freedom."

"But you won't regain your strength unless we go where you can get medicine." They were silent a moment as she mulled over this conundrum. "I wonder what Merlin would do if he were here. Lord, I can't believe I'm talking about Merlin as if he were a medical specialist working in a hospital down the road. I still can hardly believe I'm really here."

"Merlin would use his herbs to help me. He is a powerful healer as well as a magician."

"He has herbs?" Katie met his gaze and held it as an idea kindled. "Are they here?"

"Yes, he keeps them in all his hideaways. I don't know the names of them, but they are potent."

She scrambled to her feet and pulled the torch from the fire, feeling her first true glimmer of hope. "Don't go anywhere."

He smiled sardonically. "Would that I could. Where are you going?"

"Back into Merlin's cave. And somehow I'll find the right combination of herbs to heal your leg once and for all!"

Six

In Merlin's cave Katie found what she was hoping for—and much more. There were rows of small casks containing every herb imaginable. Though she'd studied homeopathy for a semester in school, she didn't recognize many of the dried plants. They probably didn't grow in the United States. And many others had doubtless been lost to antiquity and were no longer available even in England in the twentieth century.

Without instructions on how to use the herbs, all Katie could do was experiment, and she did so with fervent dedication for two days. She boiled leaves and stewed plant stems, soaking poultices, steeping decoctions, straining physiques, and brewing tinctures, praying all the while she wouldn't create any lethal combinations or dosages.

Tristan watched her in amazement and admiration, valiantly drinking down with gusto any strange concoctions she contrived. Katie admired his tenacity and quiet fortitude, and she cherished his obvious trust in her abilities. In turn, as she plied her skills with increasing confidence, her contentment with and faith in herself grew as well.

To her surprise, her newfound joy fostered her ability to

love Tristan. She'd tried so hard at love before, but with him, here in this strange and wonderful place where she was forced to rely on her own instincts, love came naturally.

How could she do anything but love a man so gentle and yet so strong? She learned much about her man in the mirror as she tried to heal him. They shared stories of their disparate lives, each amazing the other with tales of wonder, of vastly different customs and strange inventions. He tried, in vain, to describe the thrill of victory in battle, and she tried futilely to describe an airplane, giving up in the end and pointing with a sigh of frustration to a bird flying overhead.

At night they huddled together for warmth, modestly at first, then eagerly. Their affection was not based on lust, for he was still not in full vigor. Instead, their growing love sprang from a deep and fundamental sense of caring. The attraction was there, but the desire to make the other whole, to nurture, to lift the other up, was paramount.

In the end, their time together, her experimentations, their shared stories, and their treasured affection worked medical wonders. By the third day, Katie witnessed a radical transformation in Tristan's leg. It would be a month or more before the leg healed fully, but her poultices seemed to be warding off the return of serious infection, and her tinctures seemed to be strengthening his immune system. One pungent-smelling herb in particular seemed to work best, and Katie harvested some of its seeds, putting them in a leather pouch, which she dropped in her sweater pocket for safekeeping.

Free of fever, Tristan was up on his feet again, and his mind, clear at last, raced with plans. All of them included her. He could not bear the notion of giving her up. And Katie couldn't willingly leave the first man to whom she'd ever felt this close. She had no idea how long she would remain here, but she wanted it to last forever. She was even willing to risk leaving the cave—her apparent port of entry—to live her life with Tristan as fully as possible as long as they could. If Merlin, or Wodin, or some Halloween superstition had brought her here, these powerful forces could send her back to the future just as easily. She doubted the powers that be needed a cave or a mirror to activate her return journey.

Katie's main concern now was making sure that Tristan made it safely back to Camelot without succumbing to the Saxons. His sword arm was still weak, and he dared not risk a direct confrontation.

He didn't think there was any point waiting for the Saxons to give up the chase. They had attacked Tristan because he was wearing a cloak emblazoned with the sign of the pendragon—a dragon with wings. It had been a gift from King Arthur, and seeing Tristan wearing it, the Saxons had mistakenly assumed that he was a member of the royal family.

With few desirable options, Tristan and Katie decided to take a different route altogether. They would ride to nearby Rose Hill, one of King Arthur's secret getaways. There they could eat heartily, change into clean, dry clothes, and enjoy each other's company while Tristan's injuries mended. Then, when he was strong enough, they would try to outwit the Saxons together.

Katherine was eager to have a roof over her head again and enjoyed every minute of the ride to Rose Hill. Spring was in full bloom. At first it struck her as odd that autumn wasn't blustering over the land as it had been when she left Addison. But then she realized that over the course of more than a thousand years the earth's rotation had doubtless slowly changed the timing of the seasons.

The hilly terrain of sunken caves gave way to a lonely, mist-covered moor. Then their horse carried them with a rocking gait to a splendid meadow that dipped down and opened wide with a burst of green and patches of brilliantly colored flowers. There was a hill of roses, red and white, that sloped up to an expansive lodge, and rustic pathways along the way dotted with daffodils and lady slippers, lilacs and buttercups.

Butterflies flitted by leisurely, so close that Katie nearly caught one in her hand. And birds swooped down mere inches away from the high-stepping hooves of their mount, as if they had no fear of humans in this idyllic place. Katie breathed in the smell of sunshine and grass, the sweetness of flowers, and the comforting scent of leather that exuded from Tristan's tunic. She laid her head on his back, certain she had never been so content in all her life. Now she knew for certain that King Arthur's age was one of enchantment. If for no other reason than that the earth was still untouched by civilization, still pure and free and invigorating. And she wondered if it were possible that dragons really did exist here. Perhaps some prehistoric creatures roamed the earth, not quite extinct yet; a dinosaur, for example, that bards might call a dragon.

They rode up a narrow dirt road past the roses that climbed in pretty complexity up the hill to Arthur's lodge. It was a hodgepodge of building styles and materials.

"There is the servants' cottage," he said, pointing to a wattle-and-daub hut with a thatched roof.

Violets poured out of boxes planted in the shuttered windows, and smoke that smelled of roasting lamb billowed from a hole in the roof.

"How quaint," Katie said approvingly.

Then he pointed out a huge, rectangular hall made of wood, connected by a narrow wooden passageway.

"That's the old great hall. And next to it is the stone keep, which houses Arthur's private quarters."

The sun beat down on the buildings with cozy warmth.

"Are most castles made of wood or stone?" she asked.

"Most forts are wooden. But Arthur is fond of stone. He likes its permanence. And Lord Merlin advises Arthur's builders on how to erect them properly."

Katie recalled one of the legends about Merlin, that he raised the great monoliths at Stonehenge. Legends implied that he used magic, but perhaps instead he used premodern engineering principles.

"Well, would ye look at who's 'ere!" a voice cried out, and a plump woman burst out of the servants' house, wiping her hands on some sort of apron, her ruddy cheeks puffing up with a smile. "Oh, gads, 'tis Sir Tristan! Coom, Markum, give him welcome."

"Greetings, Winnefred!" Tristan called out with obvious affection. "I knew I could count on you being here."

He turned his head over his shoulder as he reined in. "Winnefred and Markum keep the lodge for Arthur. He comes here seldom, but it is always ready for him. And since it lays deep in Rose Valley, there is virtually no threat of attack here. There is naught but one man-at-arms to keep watch. Winnefred and Markum will take good care of us, but they will give us privacy, too."

He squeezed Katie's knee when he said the word *privacy,* and a frisson of pleasure sent a tremor through her body. His meaning was clear, and her thoughts were working along the same path. Ever since Tristan's health had improved, she'd been aware of his extraordinary masculinity and had longed to kiss him passionately. The deep and instant affection they'd felt for each other during his illness had turned into something altogether more sensual. When he wasn't aware of her scrutiny, she'd seen him staring at her with deep hunger shimmering in his eyes. She recognized the hunger because she felt it herself.

She'd been finding excuses to touch him—to fix his collar when it was askew, to brush a lock of hair out of his eyes when they were talking, to rub her hand against his when reaching for the same thing. It was almost as if she needed to touch him, like she needed air or water. Perhaps this was the place where they would give in to their desires.

Tristan reined in at the hut and helped Katie slide down to terra firma. Then he gingerly lifted his leg over the saddle and dismounted. Markum, an old man with brawny arms and kind eyes, took one look at Tristan's leg and winced. Then he nodded with confidence.

"Ye coom to the right place, Sir Tristan. We've no medicines, but we've Winnefred's food, and that'll half cure ye in itself."

Tristan clasped the man's forearm in warm greeting. "Winnefred's food has cured half the ailments in the king's army. It will be good enough for me."

Katie saw the look of affection winking in the beefy faces of the simple peasants. They looked up at the towering knight in awe, and she saw him suddenly from their perspective. No longer the wounded soldier, she saw Tristan for what he was: a brave, just, and powerful knight of King Arthur's court. One day he and his fellow men-at-arms would be the stuff of legends, but now he was very much a man. And he would be hers alone, at least for a few days.

She folded her arms, admiring the strength that exuded from his unusually blue eyes. They always held a smile, even when his wide, inviting lips were set firm. His long hair flowed away from his face, the gray at his temples mingled with the brown, exposing his rugged, wind-burned cheeks. She'd never seen a better-looking man nor one she wanted to make love with more.

She decided in that moment that she would give herself to him if only for one night. Sometimes love is that simple and not any less real for its brevity than love that lasts a lifetime. Love, she realized at last, was not the social functions and etiquette that had marked her relationship with Keith. It was the desire to touch another's soul, if only for a moment.

And for Tristan and Katie, whose future was uncertain, that would have to be enough.

Seven

After Tristan introduced the servants to Katie, and after they questioned her on her odd attire—pointing to her boyish pants and gasping in amazement when she demonstrated the zipper—Tristan invited her on a picnic to his favorite spot. Winnefred quickly packed a basket with meat pies and wine, butter, black bread, and fresh cheese. Tristan carried the basket while Katie followed with an arm full of blankets.

They walked down a grassy slope to a pond surrounded by so many apple trees they could scarcely see the water for all the bright pink blossoms. Their scent infused the air with luscious perfume, and Katie tossed back her head, inhaling it as the sun beat down on her cheeks. Her stomach rumbled, and she knew soon even that would be content.

"What a beautiful day!" she cried. "Oh, Tristan, I can't remember a time when I've felt so alive. For the last six months, my life has been so dreary."

"You have a purpose again," he said. "You were running from your destiny, and now you have embraced it. That is why your senses are coming alive."

"My destiny?" She quirked her brows. "I like the sound of that. But what exactly is my purpose?"

"To heal others. In ways they have never been healed before."

She thought about that while they walked on in silence. Her healing techniques would certainly be considered novel to people in the Dark Ages. But perhaps there was medical knowledge in Tristan's time that might be considered revolutionary in her world as well. If she brought back the seeds of Merlin's special herb to the twentieth century, who knows what diseases the harvested plants might cure. It was one of many new ideas that made her mind race with hope for the future. Perhaps Tristan was right. She could no longer deny her desire to make sick people healthy nor ignore the satisfaction she felt when it worked.

She grabbed his hand and they walked contentedly side by side over a bridge that led to a small island in the middle of the pond. From the center of the little island, Katie could see that the pond opened into a larger lake. The lake, Tristan informed her, was fed by a tributary that led to the ocean.

Katie tossed the blanket under the largest apple tree and sank down along its trunk with utter contentment. "I've never seen so many apple trees in one place. And they smell like the sweetest perfume."

"Yes, it is lovely, is it not?" He stood a moment, hands on his hips, admiring their surroundings. A fish jumped in the water with a splash, and he gazed down at the ripples left behind. "The only place I have seen more apple trees is at Avalon."

"Avalon?" She looked up at him a moment as the word triggered images of an enchanted isle where wise priestesses worshiped the goddess of old. She'd read every book on the Arthurian legends she could get her hands on. Katie started to remove the food from the basket. The bread was warm, heavy, and thick. No doubt delicious. "Tell me about Avalon. I think of it in the same mystical context as Atlantis or Shangri-La."

He looked at her as a half smile crawled slowly up one on his cheeks. "There you go again. Speaking blithely of places and things I've never heard of."

She laughed softly. "I'm sorry."

"Do not be. They call Avalon the Isle of Apples. That is where the Lady of the Lake lives. She's a sorceress."

"Nimue is her name, isn't it?" Katie said, the name popping up in her memory.

"Yes, she is Merlin's lover. Some say her powers are even greater than his. She certainly has the ability to heal. If I could have gotten to Avalon, I would not have needed your help."

"True," Katie said, pouring two cups of refreshing mint rose water. "I love thinking about medicine as magic and magic as medicine. Isn't Avalon a holy burial ground as well? That's where Arthur will be taken to be buried when he's slai—." She stopped abruptly. *When Arthur is slain by his nephew, Mordred,* she had almost said. She bit her tongue and her skin burned with remorse. She should know better than to talk about events affecting Tristan's future. That would interfere with the natural course of history. Hoping he hadn't realized what she was about to say, she offered him a cup.

"Here, my love," she said sweetly. "Drink up."

He didn't take it. He merely stared at her, as if he'd turned to stone.

"You know," he said at last. "You know what's going to happen in the future, don't you?"

She shook her head and looked down.

"Yes, you do. You know what will happen to Arthur and Camelot and the rest of it. You were about to say something about Arthur. Is he going to die?"

When she said nothing and refused to look him in the eye, he sat down, carefully extending his injured leg. He slipped the cup from her fingers and drank a little. When she looked at him again, she realized he wasn't angry, just curious and perhaps a little fearful of her knowledge. Merlin's prophecies were inspired guesses, whereas Katie's knowledge of the future was recorded fact.

"I do know what is going to happen, Tristan. But only in general terms. History books about this time period are very sketchy. Historians know that a real Arthur did exist, a military leader, but not the knight in shining armor as later stories anachronistically portrayed him. Plate armor wasn't invented until much later."

"Is he going to die?" Tristan said quietly, reaching out and squeezing her hand.

"Of course he's going to die!" she snapped. "We're all going to die someday."

"But when?"

She sighed and bit her lower lip. "If I told you that, it would affect your ability to fight for Arthur. It might lead you to take unnecessary risks and endanger yourself. I can't tell you about events if they will change because you have foreknowledge of them. All I can say is that Arthur will succeed in quelling the invading Saxons. He will succeed at keeping peace between his own warring Briton chieftains, and he will rule over many years of peace."

But when he dies, she silently added, *the Saxons will overpower your people. And one day they and the Anglos will overtake the Britons entirely, giving birth to a people the world one day would call the English.*

"How did you get to know Arthur so well?" she asked casually, trying to change the subject. She slathered a piece of bread with butter and cheese, handing it to him.

He exhaled a soundless laugh as memories came rushing back. "I caught the High King's notice during one of his early battles. Arthur's horse had fallen in a melee. He was surrounded by savage Saxons. I saw him from a distance and rode like hell to get to him.'' He took a bite of the bread and groaned with approval. ''Hmmm. Delicious.''

He swallowed and continued. ''Not long ago, I heard a bard singing a ballad about the events of that day. In the song I was portrayed as a soldier acting in a fit of divine battle madness, nearly flying over the Saxons that separated me from the king. But it was merely loyalty that drove me. I scooped him up on my horse and dismounted, fighting the enemy off singlehandedly until Arthur could get away.''

She flushed with pride over Tristan's bravery, understanding at last what his raw strength could mean to a king at the turning point of a battle. ''Was Arthur grateful?''

''To say the least,'' Tristan replied with an ironic grin. ''That night at camp, with my weary comrades gathered around crackling campfires, savoring our hard-won victory, I was called to the king's tent. I was more than a little excited. I entered and found him sitting in all his natural majesty in a high-backed chair, with Merlin standing behind him in the shadows.

''Arthur asked me if I realized what I had done.'' Tristan paused and leaned back on his straightened arms. His full, wide lips curled up at the corners. ''Naturally, I thought for a moment that I'd done something wrong.''

She chuckled. ''You are too humble.'' When Tristan merely shrugged noncommittally, she said, ''What did Arthur say then?''

''I remember every word. He said, 'You have saved a kingdom today.' Arthur spoke slowly, as if he were realizing it himself in that moment. 'All that my father Uther Pendragon fought for and all that my uncle Ambrosius fought for would have been lost today if not for you. You have fought bravely, Tristan of Ilchester.' ''

The words moved him even now, and he shut his eyes, rubbing away the moisture beneath his lids. Katie reached out and covered one of his hands with her own.

"You must be very proud, Tristan."

He wiped at the web of crow's feet that marked the tan skin at the corner of his eyes. "That's when Arthur gave me his father's cloak. He held it out to me—a heavy black cape with a pendragon emblazoned on the back. I'd seen Uther wear it in battle. It was, to me, the greatest symbol of royalty and pride.

"I tried to refuse the gift, but Arthur said I had earned it. He said his father's dream of a unified Britain would have died that day if not for me, and therefore Uther would want me to have it." He looked up and stroked her cheek with his knuckles. "It's good to share this with you."

"I'm awestruck, Tristan. And very curious. What happened to the cloak?"

He pointed in the direction of the stable. "It's in one of my saddlebags. I managed to tuck it away before the fever set in. I was wearing the cloak when those Saxons attacked a few days ago. They saw the sign of the pendragon and assumed I was related to Arthur. Their blows are badges of honor to me. All that I have ever wanted to do was fight for Arthur and free Britain from the invaders. Ever since I was seven."

She could tell by the grim lines that creased his forehead that something terrible had happened at that age. "Tell me about it."

"That's when my parents were brutally slain at the hands of Saxon warriors. Our village was burnt to the ground, and I went to live with my uncle in Ilchester. He was a warrior himself and scarcely knew how to rear a child. But he fed me. And he taught me to fight. He knew I would want to avenge my parents' death. And I succeeded in large measure the day I saved Arthur's life. Just as you've helped my cause, Katherine, by keeping me alive."

"I'd risk my life to save you if necessary," she said, surprised at how automatically and truthfully the words sprang from her lips.

"That's exactly what I said to Arthur that day. 'My lord,' I said, 'I would risk my life for you again and again. My life is yours.' Then Merlin spoke up in a wise croak from the shadows in the tent. 'No, Tristan of Ilchester,' the enchanter said, 'your life belongs to this kingdom. It is greater than all of us.'"

Katie shivered with awe. "I wish I had been there."

"I'll take you to Camelot to meet the king."

"I'd like that very much."

"And Merlin, when they return from Gaul. Merlin took an interest in me after that day. He's the one who told me you were coming."

She smiled and began to eat a delicious meat pie. "I wonder how he knew."

"He saw a vision. He told me a woman from the west would come to help me when I needed it the most. He said you'd have eyes as green as Britain and yellow hair like the invading Saxons, but you would come in peace from a country that did not yet exist. And your appearance in my life, he said, would affect the very fate of Britain itself. At least that's what I culled from what he uttered in his sonorous voice in one of his spine-chilling trances."

"What else did he say?"

"Oh, he said something about the eagle flying over the dragon and the buffalo standing side by side with the lion, though I did not know what a buffalo was. You probably do."

Her lips parted in a teasing grin. "As a matter of fact, I do."

"Tell me about it later," he said with a yawn. "This good food has made me sleepy. Right now, all I want to do is stretch out and doze awhile." He lay down and bent his arms, propping them under his head.

She leaned down and kissed his cheek. His eyes softened.

"What was that for?" he murmured, brushing a tendril of hair out of her eyes and tucking it behind her ear.

"I'm so proud of you, Tristan. You're a good man. Now, if you don't mind, I'm going to take a dip in the pond. I'll be naked. So keep your eyes closed."

"Must I?" he said with a wicked grin.

"I just want to get clean. Where I come from, I take baths every day, and sometimes twice a day. I'll be right back."

He nodded and shut his eyes and soon was fast asleep. Katie went to the pond's edge. The water was surprisingly warm for early spring. Just another part of the enchantment of this special place.

"Rose Hill," she murmured to herself as she peeled off her dirty clothing. She stepped in the water, plunging down in one fell swoop. She swam out toward the small canal that led to the larger lake, where waterfowl waded among reeds, their thin, elegant necks rising above the mist that hovered near the shoreline. She cut through the water, swinging arm over arm, feeling an incredible sense of exhilaration. She stopped in mid-stroke, however, when she felt a long, slithering creature brush along her legs.

"Oh!" Katie cried out, accidentally swallowing a gulp of water. She choked and whirled around, looking down but not seeing the enormous creature that must have bumped against her. "What on earth was that? A fish?"

She panted nervously as she tread water. Then, before her very eyes, not three feet away, a humped back rose above the silver surface as the fish, or snake, or monster—whatever it was—arched through the water.

"Tristan!" she shrieked at the top of her lungs. "Help me!"

But she knew he was too far away to hear her. With his injuries, he couldn't rescue her, even if he knew she was in danger. He could never swim this far. She began to swim frantically toward the short canal and back to the pond. If she'd been in the Olympics, she would've taken the gold.

"Tristan!" she cried out as she gasped for air when the

island was in sight. "Help me! There's a monster in here!"

When she reached a big rock that rose above the water, she scrambled onto it, naked and shaking with fear.

"What is it, my love?" Tristan called out, standing on the edge of the pond not fifteen feet away.

"Out there!" she cried, pointing toward the canal. "I-I saw something h-horrible."

"Well, all I can see is something very beautiful."

She turned her head back toward him, doing a slow burn. He was ogling her naked body, a devilish grin dimpling his handsome face.

"How *dare* you find me attractive when I was just nearly eaten by the Loch Ness monster! Look! There it is again. Oh, no!"

Katie shrieked as the creature slithered by the rock, arching out of the water as it passed.

"My God!" she gasped. "It has to be at least twenty feet long!"

"It is not a monster, my love," Tristan said calmly as he made his way to the rock, hopping toward her on a series of stones resting just beneath the surface. "It is a sea serpent. It must have wandered in from the ocean. Do not worry, though. They do not bite."

"No," she said sarcastically when he reached her, "it will just swallow me whole."

He laughed and scooped her naked, wet, and shivering body into his arms and carried her back over the stones to shore. When he lowered her to the ground, she gripped his tunic, looking up at him with excitement.

"Tristan, you called it a sea serpent. But do you realize what it really is? It's a prehistoric creature. They don't exist in my world. If I could get that back to my time period, I'd win the Nobel Prize for science!"

He threw back his head and laughed. "Lady Katherine, you do amuse me. First you are terrified of the creature, and now it is winning you prizes for your discoveries. You cannot quite decide whether you are a damsel in distress or a heroine from a bard's ballad, can you?''

A damsel in distress. That's what Lillian had called her. She missed Lil. She even missed her apartment.

"Katherine, you still do not know half your strength." His mirthful eyes grew sober as he put both hands on her shoulders and studied her with wisdom and love. "You have rediscovered your destiny in life. Now you have to recognize that you have the courage to follow it. You are strong, Katherine. Why do you not see that?''

He wrapped his arms around her, and she felt no awkwardness for her lack of clothing. She had nothing to hide from this man. She looked up at him.

"How do you know me so well?''

"I do not know how I know you, Katherine of Addison. But I do. I know that you have never truly been loved. And that you enjoy being held while listening to the sound of falling rain. And that you are infinitely kind. I saw that in your eyes the moment I met you, and my hunch was confirmed when you dressed my wounds at the cave. I think it hurt you as much as it hurt me. Promise me that whatever happens after this you *will* become a doctor. You are a natural healer.''

She nodded. "Yes, of course. I see now that I've been afraid to practice medicine for no reason. I was simply unwilling to accept my limitations. Oh, I love you, Tristan. I love you for who you are and for what you've done for me. You see me as I can be, not as I have been. And for that I will always love you.''

She reached up and pulled his head down until their lips met. His were warm and worked an instant magic. She coiled against him and felt her head grow light. She inhaled the musky scent of manhood and melted with sheer bliss. At last she was kissing the right man in the right place. Even in the right time.

Eight

She wrapped herself in a blanket, and they left the picnic basket under the tree, walking to Arthur's stone keep arm-in-arm. Tristan opened a side door that he knew Markum would leave unlocked for them. When he pushed open the thick oak door, they were greeted by a pillow of warm air.

Katie glanced around, looking for the welcome source of heat, and saw a brazier in the corner glowing red with burning peat. Tapestries hung in profusion, adorning dark stones with bright intensity. A large down bed was thick with warm and beautifully woven covers. Two chalices of the finest silver gleamed in the light of the torches that lined the wall. Katie had never seen a more cozy and inviting place. Apparently Winnefred and Markum knew exactly what Tristan and Katie had been planning, albeit secretly in their hearts.

"You must be cold. Climb in bed," he suggested and went to the table to pour two chalices of hot mulled wine. Then he sat down on the bed, where she lay propped up by pillows, the thick purple blankets tucked under her arms.

"Here's to your health," he said, raising his silver cup.

"Here's to the past," she returned with a contented smile, tapping the rim of her chalice to his.

"And to our future," he added with a significant nod.

She drank readily to that, though even thinking of the future made her queasy. How long would they be together? It was impossible to know. A sweet melancholy fell about them as the wine relaxed them. He took her free hand in both of his and traced her palm with his forefinger.

"I wish I were a fortune-teller," he said, a bittersweet mix of love and sadness deepening his voice. "Then I would know how long I have you. Katherine, I have been thinking. Do you know how long you will be here?"

He met her gaze, his brow furrowed, his eyes sharp and hungry for assurance. She swallowed a lump that formed in her throat.

"Perhaps forever," she said.

He sighed. "And perhaps not. Perhaps you were brought here to heal. Now that I am on the mend . . ."

She stared at the brazier that hissed and glowed red. "I don't know, Tristan. But I've been thinking about that as well. I've been here a few days, and my watch says it's now eight-thirty. That means that in my world I've only been gone an hour and a half. There are still three and half hours left of Halloween, or All Hallows' Eve as you'd call it. I wonder if, when the clock strikes midnight, I will be transported back."

"Why?" he asked simply, understanding little of the ar-bitrary units of time by which she measured her life.

She shrugged. "I don't know. But I can't help think my traveling here had something to do with Halloween."

"If that is the case, perhaps you will be here until this time next year, and we will have a year together."

She pursed her lips. "Perhaps. I would like that, Tristan." She looked down at her fingers entwined in her lap, adding in a whisper, "I'm not ready to leave you."

"Nor I you. I live in a special time, Katherine. I and my fellow men-at-arms sense that Destiny lives among us. We fight a great cause. Much of the year I live in the most enchanted place in the world—Camelot. You should see how magnificent it is, how vibrant. The best and brightest minds dwell there: the most valiant soldiers, the wisest bards, the most gracious and beautiful women, the best doctors, thinkers, and the holiest of men. We talk often of living in a world of peace, fairness, and justice. It is within our reach. I know it. But I would give it all up without a single regret if I could have you in exchange."

He drew her into his arms. They were strong and secure. He kissed her forehead, brushing his lips softly against her skin.

"How much time?" he murmured. "How long do we have?"

"I don't know," she replied, running her hands through his thick, long, brown and gray hair. "Let's just live as if there is no tomorrow."

"So be it."

He lay down beside her and drew back the covers, exposing her bare skin to the air. She shivered as the draft curled around her breasts. He kissed each one with exquisite passion and touched her gently in all the right places. She responded with a feverish intensity she didn't know she possessed, in turn igniting in him a passion that had been dormant too long. And by the time they made love, all thoughts of the world—his or hers—were vanquished.

For nearly a week, the world as they knew it existed solely in the confines of their cozy chamber. They felt, as new lovers often do, that they could sustain themselves for an eternity on love alone, emerging from bed only to take walks and pick flowers, to retrieve more food, and to chat over the fire with Winnefred and Markum. But whatever force that had brought them together was not content to let the lovers dwell forever in their idyll.

Two days after Tristan drank the last of the herbal tincture that Katie had concocted in Merlin's cave, and one day after the herbal ointment she'd made for his wounds ran out, Katie noticed a change in Tristan's leg. The deep gash that had begun to heal turned red again, then a sickly white. The pain returned, stealing his focus more and more by the hour. Before long, he was frowning whenever he walked. She knew he tried to hide the pain from her, but he couldn't mask his limp.

When Tristan's fever returned, Katie realized that her minor surgery and the herbs had abated his illness but had not cured it. She was confident that if she had more of the same plants, she could beat his illness in time. Unfortunately, Merlin's special plants weren't indigenous to Rose Hill.

Unchecked, the infection quickly spread throughout Tristan's system, and it became clear to Katie that nothing short of penicillin, a modern miracle, or even old-fashioned magic, would help him. If she didn't do something soon, Tristan would die.

Early the next morning, she went to the bed, sat down beside him, and stroked his hair away from his face. His cheeks were damp and feverish. She could see the life flowing out of him, and her heart silently screamed in agony.

"Tristan, I have to do something drastic to help you get better."

He managed to raise his eyelids to half mast and gazed at her with blurry focus. "I will be better soon," he said, licking his parched lips. "I promise."

Tears sprang to her eyes and she blinked them back. "No, my love, you will not get better. Not without a miracle. We have no more herbs. As you pointed out before, I am not God. I no longer even expect myself to be omnipotent. That was a foolish stage I had to get beyond. I freely admit that I need help to help you." She knelt by the bed so she could speak

close to his ear as she stroked his forehead. "I've been thinking, Tristan, that there is only one person who might help you
now."

He blinked, slowly absorbing her meaning, then frowned.
"Who?"

"The Lady of Avalon."

His cheek dimpled in a faint half smile. "What do you
know of her?"

"Only what you've told me. And what I've read. She prac-
tices the old arts of healing and sorcery. She knows secrets
that modern doctors spurn as illogical or evil. She can cure
you, Tristan, if we can just get you there."

"No. It is too far," he whispered, his strength failing.
"Never make it."

"I'll take you there on your horse. I'll strap you upright
behind me on the saddle, and I'll take the reins."

"You cannot ride."

"I beg your pardon," she said, gallows humor glinting in
her eyes. "I won first place in the horseback riding competition at Camp Wo-He-Lo Woods when I was twelve years
old."

He shook his head. "The Saxons will be waiting for us at
Willow Pass."

"I'm sure they've forgotten about you."

"No. Never. Pendragon . . ."

"Yes, I know you wore the Pendragon cloak. But we'll
keep it in the saddlebag. They'll never see it, and they won't
be expecting a lady on a horse. I'll fly past them before they
realize I'm not alone. Look, Tristan, I know it's risky, but I
have to try. I said I'd risk my life for you, and I meant it.
Now, the subject is closed. We're going to Avalon."

He was too weak to argue, and though she hated to act
unilaterally, she had to take command. She was strong enough
to bear the responsibility. She finally realized just how strong
she was. Love made her strong, and therefore there was no
choice. To Avalon they would go.

Nine

Winnefred and Markum did their best to prepare the young couple for the journey. Winnefred packed the saddlebags with meat and cheese and plenty of wine and water. Markum gave them two gray cloaks fastened with silver brooches to stave off the chill at night. And he gave Katie Tristan's sword. She wasn't sure she'd have the physical strength to wield it, but its presence made her feel safer. She discarded her borrowed gown and put back on her freshly cleaned pants, shirt, and sweaters, then said farewell to her loving hosts.

Katie and Tristan traveled the first day without incident, but on the second day, when they reached Willow Pass, two Saxon guards were waiting for them, just as Tristan had predicted. Expecting a possible encounter, Katie had rested their horse beforehand and then flew past the enemy campsite at full gallop. For two days she thought she'd outrun them, until she heard the sound of horse hooves behind them in the distance

Winded and exhausted, but also exhilarated by the chase, Katie managed to keep enough space between them to allow for a few hours' sleep at night. Following the crude map

Markum had sketched for her, they rode with the ground thundering beneath them, and Katie watched in wonder as the landscape changed.

The hilly terrain gave way to open moorlands dotted with purple and green heather. That desolate beauty was followed by scattered woods that thickened in density the farther they went. Wispy birch trees gave way to ancient and gnarled thickets of genuses she didn't recognize. Jagged stumps and twisted limbs sprouted from ground cover that became increasingly marshy. Peat grew thick, and reeds rose out of standing water. Bog mosses spewed a musty, overpoweringly fertile scent, making the air thick to breathe. Cottongrass and rushes rose in strawy bouquets. From gangly trees came the croaks of ravens, carrion crows, and the occasional call of a skylark.

Despite the danger coming from behind, Katie tugged on the reins, slowing their horse to a trot so she could absorb the mystical landscape. She was quite sure nothing like this primeval place existed in her world. She half expected a sorcerer to step in their path and wave them on with a magic staff. Perhaps even Merlin himself. Unfortunately, he was far away in Gaul.

She felt a coolness in the air that could come only from a large body of water, and soon the hanging trees gave way to a misty estuary. In the dark shadows that fell with burnt-red dusk, Katie saw the silhouette of a large body of land rising in the distance out of choppy, mist-shrouded water.

"Avalon!" she said excitedly and inhaled a whiff of apple blossoms on the wind. "It has to be the Isle of Apples! Tristan, we made it!"

Half unconscious, leaning heavily against her, he said nothing in reply.

She continued forward until she reached a lonely, craggy little dock that stretched like a crooked finger out from the water's edge into swirls of gray fog. She reined in at the edge of the dock.

"Hold tight, Tristan." She dismounted and tied up the reins. "I see a ferry. It will take us to the Lady of Avalon; I'm sure of it."

Barely conscious, clinging to the rope that bound him to the saddle, he nodded. She hurried out over creaking boards until she saw two figures tying a simple flat-bottomed boat to the dock.

"Hello! Can you help me? We need to travel to Avalon!"

Katie ran toward them but halted abruptly when one of the figures—a diminutive old woman clad in dark, tattered rags—turned and looked up at her.

"Eh, what is it, girl?" the old woman said.

Katie's blood turned cold as recognition burned through her like a flash of gunpowder.

"It's *you!*" She recognized the crooked nose with the wart, the missing teeth, the matted gray hair. "You're Clara. Crazy Clara. I saw you on the train. Don't you remember? On Halloween. You told me that he wasn't the one. Keith. You . . . you said I'd recognize my true love when I saw him. You were right. It's Tristan. He's on the horse. He needs help."

The old woman's moist, wrinkled lips curled slowly into a smile. She gave a raspy, cackling laugh. "Yes, missy, I remember. But he's not the one." She pointed to Tristan with a gnarled finger. "He's not the one."

Katie's breath stopped in her throat as confusion gripped her. "But . . . but he is, I know it! I love him. He taught me . . . he showed me who I am. Who I can be."

"But you are not that person yet," the old woman replied. "I told ye, watch for the sign of the dragon."

Katie ran her hands impatiently through her hair. "But he has the cloak. It's emblazoned with a Pendragon. It was worn by King Arthur's father, Uther Pendragon."

"But he's not wearing it," the woman fairly snarled, impatient herself. "Is he?"

"No, but—"

"Have you ever seen him wear it?"

Katie took a step back, flushing with anger. "You're not being fair. That's a technicality."

"It's not! Ask Lord Merlin."

"I don't know why I'm bothering to argue with you," Katie said, as much to herself as to Clara, trying to calm herself. "I love Tristan. And I'm going to save him. Look, I'm sorry. I don't mean to argue with you. Whether he's the one or not is immaterial. What's important is that he has to see the Lady of Avalon immediately!"

By now the second figure had joined them, a brawny old man who was obviously the ferryman. He put an arm protectively around the old woman.

"Ye listen to me wife," he said gruffly, narrowing his eyes suspiciously. "Ye cannot go to Avalon at this hour. We shut down for the night, we did."

"What happened to your . . . friend," the old woman said. "Was he wounded in battle?"

"Is there fighting nearby?" the old man said in an odd cadence.

"Not recently," Katie said. "But he was injured by Saxons. In fact, two of them are chasing us now."

The old couple exchanged wary glances.

"If we don't get on the ferry, they'll capture him and kill him. That is, if he doesn't die first from his illness. Please! We must hurry."

She'd said too much. The ferryman and his wife started backing away.

"We want no trouble here," he said, waving his hand. "Go away."

"You cannot bring the Saxons here," the old woman hissed angrily at Katie. "The Lady of the Lake has orders. She says the Saxons must never know of the Isle of Apples."

"They won't know about it if we hurry," Katie reasoned, desperation thinning her voice.

"No, go away!" the old man said, motioning to his wife to join him on the ferry. "We must away before the Saxons come, or they will know how to find the lady and her priestesses. Go away!"

The ferryman quickly untied the rope anchoring him to the dock, helped his wife on board, then shoved off into the lapping, dark water. Katie wanted to scream with frustration, but she knew it would do no good. She sank to her knees with a fierce groan. She had failed Tristan. She came to save him, and though she had helped, ultimately she had failed him.

"Help me!" she cried out, not knowing to whom she called. She would do anything to save Tristan's life. Anything. But what?

In the desperate silence that followed, while her own labored breath mingled with the sound of water lapping on the shore, she heard a new sound. Footsteps on the dock. She looked up sharply. Had the ferryman changed his mind?

No, the boat was receding in the mists. But she saw something else. Someone new. A third person. He stood at the end of the dock as if he'd materialized out of the mist. He began to walk toward her, and the moonlit gray fog gave birth to his powerful presence.

"Do not despair," he said in a voice as deep and ancient as the ocean. He stopped a foot away, towering over her.

She looked up in awe at his avalanche of long silver hair, his full gray beard, his bushy brows, and his warm but piercing brown eyes. He held a walking staff and wore a fantastic blue robe adorned with stars and moons that seemed to glow as if they were alive. Or was it an illusion?

"You're . . . you're a wizard," she sputtered, rising to her unsteady feet. When she finally got a good look at the infinity of his eyes, she broke out in a cold sweat. "Oh, good heavens! You're Merlin!"

His eyes winked with approval. "None other. Where is Tristan?"

"Up there. On the shore."

He put a heavy hand on her shoulder. "You have done well, girl. I knew I could count on you in my absence. Tristan of Ilchester will save this kingdom yet, thanks to you."

"But Tristan said you were in Gaul."

"I am. What you see is an illusion. That is why your work is not finished yet. Now, come and help me get him on the ferry. An illusion cannot carry a wounded soldier by himself."

"The ferry?" Katie glanced past him and saw the ferry returning to the dock. "Does the ferryman know you're here? I mean, if you're an illusion, how—?"

"Yes, they can see me. Just as you can. Now let us get to work."

With Merlin's help, Katie went to Tristan, unfastened him from the saddle, and pulled him down.

"What are you doing?" Tristan mumbled. Then he spotted the enchanter. "Merlin! I hoped you would come."

"He's going to save you," Katie said as she led Tristan to the dock, letting him lean his weight on her shoulder.

"No," Merlin said, "you are going to save him yourself, Katherine of Addison. You cannot fulfill your destiny until you finish this task."

By now they had reached the ferry, which was once again tied at the end of the dock.

"Lord Merlin, we cannot take him," the ferryman said, still clearly anxious, though obviously willing to do whatever Merlin the Enchanter ordered. "He will bring the Saxons to this shore and then to Avalon."

"I told her he wasn't the one," old Clara said irritably, pointing accusingly at Katie.

Merlin smiled patiently and turned to Katie with kindness in his eyes.

"She is right," he said, his deep voice gentle and commanding. "He is not the one."

Katie exhaled a sharp breath, as if she'd been stabbed in the back.

"I don't believe you," she said, growing angry at this triumvirate of nay-sayers. "I know what I feel for Tristan."

Pulling away from Merlin's gaze, she helped Tristan into the boat and onto a bench. She sat next to him and put her arm around his shoulder.

"I know what you are feeling," Merlin said, coming to the edge of the dock. "Your feelings are real. Yet even more important than the dictates of your heart is your purpose in life. Tristan of Ilchester has taught you that you must go back and be what you were meant to be. And you have enabled him to fulfill his destiny as well. He will save the king once again in the most important battle Britain will ever witness. Tristan will save this kingdom, you can be assured, because you saved his life."

The cold had begun to penetrate Katie's cape. In contrast, hot tears poured down her cheeks.

"Somehow," she said bitterly on a quivering breath, "your assurances give me little comfort."

"The Saxons are coming, Katherine," Merlin said, this time with stern authority. "You know what you have to do."

She *did* know. The realization washed over her as quickly as if Merlin had waved a magic wand. Perhaps he had. An invisible one. Merlin was right. Her destiny, and Tristan's, were far more important than their feelings. And unfortunately, they were destined to live in two different worlds.

"We are going to Avalon," Tristan said, raising his head and regarding her with bleary eyes, only half aware of the conversation going on around him. "Let us proceed, Katherine. Why are you waiting?"

She looked up at Merlin with sad resignation. Then she knelt before Tristan, taking his hands in hers with all the tenderness in her soul.

"Tristan, my darling," she said, "Merlin will take you to

Avalon. I must . . . must go away for a while. If I can come back, I will, I promise you.''

He looked up at Merlin, understanding slowly dawning. Then he pounded a fist on the bench. ''No!'' he said fiercely, his emotions paining him more than his leg ever could. ''You are leaving me forever. I know it. Do not do this, Katherine. We must stay together as long as we can.''

''Merlin says—''

''Do not listen to him! He is just an enchanter, not a man. He has no heart!''

''He does,'' she whispered, ''but he's not concerned about hearts right now. You will do great things, Tristan. And I have to let you do them.''

The sound of horse hooves filtered past them on a soft breeze.

''They are coming,'' the ferryman said, beginning to unfasten the moorings. ''Better hurry.''

She stood and unlatched the gray cape clasped at her throat. She put the silver brooch in her pocket and threw the cape over Tristan's legs.

''No, keep it,'' he argued, despair dripping in his voice. ''You will get cold. If I cannot protect you, at least it can keep you warm.''

She smiled down at him. ''I don't need protection. Remember? You taught me that. I can take care of myself.''

She started for the horse to retrieve the Pendragon cloak from the saddlebags, but she realized that Merlin already held it in his arms. He must have employed some sleight of hand. He stepped onto the boat and proffered it to her.

''Take good care of it,'' he said. ''One day this will be the only true evidence that Camelot ever existed.''

She nodded and hurled the heavy garment over her shoulders. Unfastening the gold dragon brooch pinned at the collar, she tried to clasp the cape at her neck. But she pricked a finger, and the brooch clattered to the floor, falling through the floor boards.

"Oh, no!"

"Do not worry," Merlin reassured her. "Nothing of importance is ever truly lost."

Nodding, she retrieved the silver brooch from her pocket and quickly fixed the Pendragon cloak at her neck.

Watching her, Tristan knew at last what she was planning to do, what Merlin had intended all along.

"I'm sorry, my love," she said, spreading the garment around her. "But I have to take your beloved cape with me."

"They will kill you when they see you wearing it," Tristan said simply.

"I'm a good rider. I'll outrun them."

"No!"

"I have to distract them, or the ferryman won't take you to Avalon. The Saxons will see this cloak and think it's you. I'll lead them far away from this shore."

"No!" Tristan shouted with unexpected force. He turned to Merlin with a savage scowl. "Why do you not do something? Why must she sacrifice herself?"

"I wouldn't deny her this for all the world," Merlin said calmly, as if he knew much more than either of them.

Katie sat next to Tristan, hooked her arm through his, and whispered in his ear. "Tristan, I came here to save you. Let me have that. Give me that gift. I told you I would risk my life for you. Let me do this for you, my love. Let me give for a change."

Tears gathered in his eyes as he recognized the bitter taste of his own defeat. Love did not make him master over her. She had to follow her own destiny.

"Damn Merlin!" he cursed, his voice cracking. "He said you would come, but he did not tell me you would leave so soon."

She glanced at her watch. As she might have guessed, it

was one minute and fifty-five seconds before midnight. What could she say in the short time left to them to make him understand? How much would five seconds in her world equal in his time?

"Tristan, I do this not only for you, but for the world where I come from. You have no idea what a fantastic legend Camelot is to my people! It's one of the last true legends in the cynical world in which I live. What would people in the future do without the dream of King Arthur and Merlin?"

Tristan listened quietly. Her logic seemed to penetrate his feverish mind and calm him. She wondered what else she could tell him without saying too much.

"You asked me once what I knew of the future," she continued. "Arthur will fight twelve great battles. And Tristan, you must be there for all of them. You must fight for your cause and your king. He needs you. With your help, history will never forget that in this time of great darkness, there was one shining bright gem of a kingdom known as Camelot."

She tenderly kissed his lips, so much being said in one silent gesture. Then she looked up at Merlin and could see from the sadness in his eyes that he, too, knew of the twelve great battles. And he knew the time and circumstances of Arthur's death. It was a heavy burden to bear, and admiration was added to the awe that she felt for the enchanter.

"Hurry up, lass," the old ferryman growled, nervously looking up at the shore. "They will be here soon."

She hugged Tristan one last time, then tore herself away, never looking back. She went on shore, mounted up, and spread the Pendragon cloak out behind her so the emblem would be clearly visible. Feeling the glory and agony of her sacrifice—and the love it represented—she galloped away, straight into the arms of the enemy.

The last thing she heard was the sound of Tristan's bellowing voice crying, "Katherine! Katherine! Katherine!"

Ten

She came to in front of the mirror and saw her image splinter as the glass shattered into a hundred separate pieces. The cold sound of cracking glass made her shiver. Then she started to shake in earnest. She looked around and saw wind billowing through sheer curtains. She heard the radiator knocking and hissing. The clock ticking. The wooden floor creaking.

She was home!

She glanced at the shadows, and seeing nothing but the familiar—the boring, dull familiar—she dropped her face in her hands and cried. Not only because she missed Tristan already, but because she was so grateful to him. She was a different woman, thanks to him. Her life would never be the same.

She wiped her eyes and fought a wave of vertigo as memories of the past waxed and waned in the light of her present reality. The last thing she remembered was rounding a corner in the woods and running straight into the Saxon warriors. Then all went blank.

Tristan. She hugged herself. Oh, how she would miss him! When she shut her eyes, she could still smell him, still feel the peculiar softness of his skin and the spectacular strength of the muscles beneath it. She could still see his handsome face: his high cheeks, his cleft chin, his dashing hair with the distinctive wings of gray.

"Oh, Tristan," she whispered, her heart wrenching with sorrow. "How will I go on without you?"

She slowly lowered her arms as she accepted the truth. She would never see him again. The mirror had cracked. She had no doubt that was Merlin's doing. He was quite emphatic that she had important things to accomplish in her world. There was no going back.

But back to where? Had she truly lived the last two weeks in King Arthur's time? Or had it been a dream? She looked down at her wristwatch, holding it up to the moonlight that filtered through the window. The electricity was *still* out! She squinted at the watch.

"It's midnight. On the button."

If it had been a dream, she had been asleep for four hours. If it had been real, she'd been back in time for about two weeks. How she would ever know the truth? Who could she even talk to about her adventure? They'd have her committed.

She sat up and heavy silk slid over her shoulders. The cape! It fell down over the back of her chair. So it had come back with her! As Merlin said, it was the only irrefutable evidence that Camelot existed. She felt for her pocket. The pouch of herb seeds was still there! Overjoyed, she stood and seized the cape, embracing it, hugging it as if it were Tristan himself.

"Oh, Tristan, you did exist. I didn't invent you. There really was a Camelot."

She hugged the cape a long time, then sighed with resignation and carefully folded it up, tucking it into the trunk her grandmother had given her as a hope chest. There it would stay with Granny's old-fashioned trousseau, a testimony to past love.

Still feeling empty and disoriented, she wandered into the living room and noticed a flashing and spinning red light reflected on the wall and heard radio broadcasts from a police car ricocheting off the buildings on her street. She was definitely back in modern times. She raised the open window farther and looked down at the street. Two police cars were parked close to the curb, and a plainclothes officer was coming out of British Isles Antiques.

"Lillian!" she said, her scalp prickling with foreboding. "Something has happened to Lillian."

Suddenly she remembered Woden's Curse and bolted for the door. She scrambled down the steps, out the main door, and reached the door to Lillian's shop just as a uniformed police officer was exiting.

"Excuse me," she said. "I—"

"You can't come in here, miss, there is a police investigation going on."

"What happened?"

"Vandalism. Somebody broke in here when the lights went out on this block. Did some major damage."

"Oh, no." Katie's heart sank. "Poor Lillian."

"You know her?"

"Yes. Yes, I'm a good friend. Is she all right?" She craned her neck to see over the officer's shoulder. Just then, the lights flickered on in the entire building. Someone inside the shop put his hands together in mock applause, shouting, "It's about time!"

"Where is Lillian?" Katie said. "Is she in there?"

His eyes narrowed suspiciously on her. "Now, who did you say you were?"

"Katie Montgomery. I'm a dear friend of Lillian's. I live upstairs. Maybe I can help you. Lillian said someone broke a windowpane earlier today."

"We rang your doorbell and didn't get an answer," the officer said, eyeing her suspiciously.

Katie forced a light smile. "I was . . . occupied."

"Go on." He waved her in. "You can talk to the investigator, Sergeant McGraw. Tell him what you know."

Katie walked in and glanced around but didn't see Lillian anywhere. Nor did she see any vandalism. When a detective in a brown suit came out of the mirror room smoking a cigarette, she introduced herself. He asked her a few questions about Lillian's habits and store hours. Katie grew increasingly concerned.

"Is Lillian here?" Katie said. "No one will tell me where she is."

"She's in the hospital." The officer took a last drag on his cigarette and threw it on the marble floor, twisting it out under his shoe.

Katie stifled a grimace of disapproval. "Is she ill? What happened?"

"After picking her son up at the airport, they stopped here so she could show him her latest antiques. When she saw the vandalism, she collapsed."

"How is she now?"

"She's spending the night at Glendon Memorial Hospital. Nothing serious. Her son is here, if you want more details. Will you be around tomorrow? I may have some follow-up questions."

Katie assured the detective she would be and gave him her phone number. When he went back out to the squad cars, Katie went to the mirror room. That's when she saw the extent of the damage. Dozens and dozens of mirrors, big and small, had been shattered. Silver glass littered the white tile floor.

"Oh, dear Lord," she softly exclaimed.

Katie was first struck by the monetary loss this represented for Lillian. Then she was saddened by the destruction of so much history. Each piece told a story of olden days gone by. And perhaps each mirror opened a door to the past likes hers had. Now that was all lost. And finally, Katie felt an erie chill. These mirrors had shattered just as her own had. If they had been broken for some time, perhaps they'd shattered when Katie first went back in time. Her own had broken only on her return. Again, perhaps that was Merlin's doing.

"Or perhaps it's simply Woden's Curse," she said to herself on a quivering breath.

"Woden's Curse?" an amused voice replied, then a man stepped out from behind the tallest mirror.

She took one look at him—at the blue eyes, and the distinctive shock of gray at the temples, and the cleft chin—and nearly fainted.

"Tristan! It's you!" Overcoming her shock, she ran the distance, dodging broken shards of glass on the floor and threw herself into his arms. "Oh, Tristan, I thought I'd never see you again."

He wrapped his arms around her and she felt comfortable for the first time since her return. She didn't know how or why he was here, but it didn't matter. The important thing was that they were holding each other.

Except that his embrace was tentative. She blinked her eyes open and focused on the Montblanc pen in his jacket pocket, then inhaled spicy aftershave. She frowned and started to withdraw from his arms. This wasn't Tristan's scent. He always smelled of leather and wood smoke.

Disappointed almost to the point of tears, she compressed her lips and drew up the last of her dignity. She slowly pulled away and looked up at the stranger smiling down at her with amusement wreathing his blue eyes. It wasn't Tristan at all. This man was too thin, though he had the same high cheeks and the same shoulder-length hair. In fact, the resemblance was uncanny.

"I'm sorry. I thought you were Tristan."

"I am. Tristan Bloodsworth. But my friends call me Stan for short."

She blinked at him, refocusing, then saw something new in his face: Lillian's intelligence, but with a masculine bent.

"*You're Stan?*" she said, feeling like the village idiot. "Stan Bloodsworth?"

He nodded. "Yes, I'm Lillian's son. I'm not who you thought I was." He gave her a wry grin. "But you can still hug me if you'd like."

She felt the heat of blood rushing to her cheeks and nervously tucked a strand of hair behind an ear. "I'm sorry. I thought you were . . . someone else."

"Someone named Tristan," he replied musingly, crossing his arms with elegant ease. "There are not too many people with that name."

She forced a smile. Talking with a stranger, even a handsome one related to her dearest friend, was almost more than she could handle after her incredible experience.

"Lillian never told me your name was Tristan."

His eyes lit with recognition. "You must be Katie!" He reached down and took her hand in his, shaking it warmly. "I've heard so much about you."

Her mind veered back to Rose Hill, and she forced herself to concentrate on the present. She gently pulled her hand away. "Where . . . where did you get such an unusual name?"

"One of my Briton forefathers was named Tristan of Ilchester."

The name was like a thunderbolt striking her heart. "You know about him?"

"He was one of King Arthur's great knights. He turned the tide in the battle of Mount Badon, a crucial victory for Arthur in his fight against the Saxons. I found that out not too long ago on the Internet from some recently translated bardic poems. You mentioned Woden's Curse a moment ago. That legend harkens back to the Dark Ages as well.

Tristan of Ilchester was said to have outrun the Saxons with the aid of a mysterious woman named Katherine. Outwitted, the angry Saxons called on Woden to curse his ancestors ever after. My distant relative was said to have possessed King Arthur's cloak.''

''Really?'' Katie swallowed hard. ''Whatever happened to it?''

''Lost to antiquity. Few artifacts have survived since that time.''

''I see.'' Katherine tried to make her expression one of passive curiosity. ''And what of the mysterious lady who helped Tristan of Ilchester? Her name was really Katherine?''

''Yes, though that's not exactly how it was spelled or pronounced in the olden days. At any rate, our hero apparently lost Katherine as well. But he never forgot her. He named a daughter after her, and there have been many Katherines since then in our family tree.''

She covered her face with her hands, willing herself not to weep in front of this stranger.

''Are you all right? Is it something I said?''

She took a deep breath and recovered her composure. ''I'm sorry.'' She lowered her hands. ''I'm just worried about Lillian.''

''She'll be fine. She was just overcome after seeing the damage here. She's been working too hard. They did a battery of tests at Glendon Memorial, and they all came out negative. They're just keeping her overnight for observation.''

''Good. Well, I'd better get back upstairs. It's late. This is still Halloween night, isn't it?''

He cocked his head and gave her a quizzical smile. ''Actually, it's early the next day. Are you sure you're well?''

She nodded. ''Tell Lil I'll stop by her house after work.''

''Join us there for tea, won't you?'' he said as she headed for the door, and she noticed for the first time his attractive, elegant British accent.

She paused, not at all sure she was ready to visit with anyone. Not at all sure she was prepared for a life without Tristan. But something in his expression—something intimately familiar—made her nod.

"Perhaps I will."

Eleven

Three months later, Katie sat at a bistro table at Chloe's Café, admiring the quaint storefronts that bordered Main Street in downtown Addison. She felt a little silly wearing her hospital whites in public, but Stan said he had to see her, and this was the only time she could sneak away from her hospital rotation. Her internship was as grueling—and thrilling—as she had imagined it would be.

Katie glanced anxiously at her watch. Stan was five minutes late. She realized she was excited to see him. She gazed across the busy lunchroom crowd just in time to see him make his entrance. His presence was so striking that those around him turned to stare. He towered over everyone in sight, and his handsome face was lined with kindness and intelligence.

His London Fog was splattered appropriately with rain. He shook out his umbrella near the hostess's desk and searched the crowd. Finding Katie with his dazzling blue eyes, his wide lips broke into an engaging smile. His shoulder-length hair was drawn back in a ponytail. Apparently, it was acceptable for the president of a British tea company to have long hair. He looked very chic. It suited him well, and Katie felt twinges of undeniable attraction. Attraction that had steadily grown in the three months they'd been dating.

Her grief over the loss of Tristan had been abating slowly since her return to Addison. In truth, she'd had little time to wallow in self-pity since she'd reentered medical school. And Stan's charming attention had distracted her as well. He'd been pursuing Katie with relentless, subtle persuasion from the moment they'd met. She had to admit that when he returned to London last month, she'd missed him a lot.

"Hello," he said when he reached the table. He kissed her cheek and sat down opposite her. "You look lovely today."

She flushed with pleasure at his compliment. "Thanks." Then she looked down and remembered what she was wearing. "Oh. You were joking."

"Not really," he said, and another grin dimpled his handsome face. "You'd look lovely in anything, Katie. I mean it."

She laughed. "Remind me never to go to England. If all British gentleman are sweet talkers like you, I won't have a chance."

"You're doing better, aren't you?" he said as he twisted the stem of his water glass, eyeing her penetratingly.

She frowned. "What do you mean?"

"I don't know what happened to you on Halloween, but whatever it was, you're finally recovering from it. There's a . . . joie de vivre . . . in you I didn't see before."

"How would you know? You didn't even know me before that night."

His face broke into a knowing grin. "I know things about you, Katie." His words were eerily familiar. "I know you've never truly been loved before."

Katie was sipping water and choked. She pressed her napkin to her mouth and coughed. Then she frowned at him in amazement. "How do you know that?"

He blinked, and a thoughtful look filled his blue eyes. "Lillian probably told me."

"She's a regular Merlin," Katie said, sure he wouldn't catch the irony. She hadn't told Stan about her time travel or the cape, though if she told anyone, she was sure Stan would be the one who wouldn't laugh in disbelief.

He signaled the waitress for service. They ordered quiche and salad, then he scooped Katie's hands in his. He traced her palm with a forefinger. "What are you going to do with the rest of your life?"

"Oh, I don't know. I thought I'd watch soap operas for a few years, then write a treatise on my belly button."

The waitress brought a pot of tea and two cups, then returned to the kitchen.

"You plan to have a private practice?" he inquired.

She studied him closely. He was definitely up to something. "Is this why you were so anxious to meet me today? To hear my life's agenda?"

"Yes, as a matter of fact."

"Well, when I'm done with school, I want to do some research in the area of holistic medicine. I have a few . . . herbal remedies . . . that will be a boon to mankind."

He raised his brows. "I'm intrigued. Where did you find these remedies?"

In her mind's eyes, she pictured Merlin's stash of herbs in the cave and the pouch of seeds she'd brought and she smiled. "I can't reveal my sources."

"But can you reveal your heart?"

Katie laughed, suddenly self-conscious. She withdrew her hands from his and poured two cups of tea, handing him one. "What do you mean?"

"You know what you want in life, Katie."

"Yes, you're right. I didn't always. But I do now."

"So now you can focus on . . . other matters. Like love." He cleared his throat and leaned closer. "I'm not one to beat around the bush, Katie. As you know, I'm expanding my tea company to America. I'll be basing my operations here in

Addison. It's not far from New York. It has a lot going for it: low rent, quaint landscapes, and one utterly enchanting medical student.''

She blushed. She hadn't realized how serious Stan's feelings for her had become.

''I won't back you into a corner, Katie.'' Remembering his raincoat, he shrugged it off his shoulders, letting it drop over the back of his chair. ''All I ask is that you think seriously about including me in your future.''

''Stan, I—'' she began to protest but stopped abruptly when she saw gold glinting from the lapel of his tweed sport coat. It was a dragon brooch, obviously an antique, and one she'd seen before. There could be no mistaking it. Her mouth went dry. Blood whooshed with a pounding pulse in her ears.

''Where . . . wh-where did you get that?''

He followed her shocked gaze to the brooch. ''This? I found it in one of the trunks my mother left at our family home in Cornwall.''

''It's a dragon,'' Katie said breathlessly.

''Yes, lovely, isn't it? So what do you say to my proposal? Will you at least think about me as you're planning your future? Try not to do your residency in Timbuktu, will you?''

She swallowed thickly and gazed at him with new clarity. ''Of course. I . . . I will try not to wander too far off, Stan.''

''Call me Tristan,'' he said, smiling with deep satisfaction. ''And I'll stop using your nickname. If I play my cards right, maybe I can add another Katherine to our family tree.''

They talked excitedly about the future, and when the food came, Katie gobbled down a few bites. She gave Stan—Tristan, that is—a quick kiss and dashed back toward the hospital. She'd just passed Colby's Fruit Stand when she saw an old woman picking through a bin of apples. Something about her looked familiar, and Katie did a double take. The old woman looked up and nodded her head as if she'd been expecting

Katie and wondered what had taken her so long.

"Hello, missy," she said, turning to her with a triumphant though nearly toothless smile.

"Clara?" Katie asked. "Is it you?"

"Yes, it's me. Crazy Clara." She nodded as she polished the apple on her soiled and tattered coat, her ever-present garbage bag of belongings at her side. "Didn't think I'd forget all about you, eh? I told you, didn't I? He'd be *wearing* the sign of the dragon. He's the one."

Katherine nodded. "Yes, I remember. Clara, did Merlin send you to me?"

The bag lady glowered at her. "Merlin? You sound as batty as half the women I sleep next to on the floor at Hope Mission." She wagged a finger at her. "Careful, missy, or they'll start calling you crazy, too."

She winked at Katherine and bit into her apple. Then she turned and walked away, cackling with satisfaction.

Suddenly, Tristan appeared in the distance, pulling on his raincoat as he jogged toward Katie. He brushed past Crazy Clara in his haste.

"Katherine! Wait up!"

He was breathless by the time he reached her. "I forgot something." He reached out and gripped her arms, pulling her close with surprising strength. Then he kissed her with equally surprising passion. But what stunned Katie most was her reaction. She melted in his arms. When he ended the kiss, it was a long while before she opened her eyes. Then she blinked up at him with mischief.

"Tristan. May I ask you something? Do you believe in superstitions? Wives' tales? That sort of thing?"

Grinning, he nodded. "Yes. Why do you ask?"

"Oh, no particular reason." Then she wrapped her arms around her man in the mirror and kissed him again.

TANGLED DREAMS

LORI FOSTER

One

Even though it was an incredibly busy night at the bar, even though he could barely hear the newest order over the din of loud conversation, music, and laughter, he heard her. Her every thought. Chase watched her, saw that her mouth wasn't moving, that she wasn't actually talking, but he could still listen to her.

She was on the other side of the bar, standing by a group of Halloween decorations that his sister-in-law had designed out of a bunch of pumpkins he and his brothers had carved. The haystack and jack-o'-lanterns were festive and provided an amusing backdrop to the serious expression on Allison Barrow's face. He'd known her several months now, ever since his brother had married her best friend and boss, but he'd never before noticed how cute her round, wire-framed glasses looked on her small nose or the fact that she had a tendency to straighten them needlessly.

He noticed now. But why?

His youngest brother, Mack, bumped into him. "Hey, Chase, orders are piling up here. You want to stop daydreaming and help me out?"

Chase gave Mack a distracted glance. "Come here a minute, will you?"

Mack paused. "What?"

"Over here. Come on. Now stop right there." Chase positioned him exactly where he'd been standing. Mack was in his last year of college, still studious and alert. Surely he'd pick up on something. "Now, look over there at Allison. See her, right past the redhead with the skinny guy in a suit? By that Halloween display?"

"Yeah, so?"

"What's she saying?"

Mack turned to stare at Chase in disbelief. "What's she saying? How the hell should I know? I can barely hear you, and you're only two inches away from me."

Frustrated, unable to really explain, Chase said, "Well, look at her, dammit, and try."

With a sound of disgust, Mack again stared toward Allison. Chase saw his gaze warm a little, then go over her from head to toe, and for some reason, that annoyed him. Now that he'd really noticed Allison, he didn't particularly want Mack doing the same. He'd always thought Allison was cute, in an understated, sort of just-there way, but suddenly she looked very sexy to him. She was twenty-five, on the short side, dark blue eyes, medium blonde hair. Nothing special. Certainly not the type of woman to appeal to his baser side. But tonight he couldn't pull his attention away from her. He suddenly heard her every thought when he'd sure as hell never been a mind reader before. And he only heard Allison, no one else. There was something going on between them, and it didn't make any sense.

"Well?" Chase prompted.

"She looks different, doesn't she?"

"It's the clothes," Chase explained, having noted the difference himself. It had taken him several minutes to finally pinpoint what made her look so unusual tonight, so . . . sensual. "She's wearing some sort of old-fashioned, vintage dress."

In truth, she looked like a woman straight out of film noir. The dress was a deep purple gray, and even from a distance, Chase could see that the color did things for her eyes. Or were her eyes just brighter tonight, more alert?

There was subtle black beading on the top of the dress that caught the bar lights and drew his attention repeatedly to her less-than-outstanding bustline. At least, he'd never thought it outstanding before. But now . . . Now he was imagining her naked and almost going crazy because of it.

The waistline was tight, showing off her trim build, and when she turned, Chase not only saw that she had on seamed stockings but also that the damn dress had a flat bustle of sorts, a little layering of soft material that draped real nice over her pert behind, a behind that would feel just right against his pelvis if he took her from the back . . .

"It looks . . . I dunno, kind of sexy on her, doesn't it?"

"Mack." Pulled from his erotic thoughts, Chase said it as a warning, surprising himself and his brother. His tone had smacked of possessiveness, and he didn't like it, but he also didn't like another man, not even his brother, thinking Allison was sexy. He wasn't quite used to himself thinking it yet. "Pay attention."

"To what? From what I can tell, she's not saying anything. She's just standing there all by herself, looking sweet. In fact, she looks a little lost."

Chase rubbed his face. "So you don't hear anything?"

With a strange look, Mack asked, "What exactly am I supposed to be hearing?"

Damn. There was no way Chase could repeat the thoughts he'd picked up on so clearly. They were fairly . . . intimate. Explicit thoughts. Sexual thoughts. *About him.* He almost groaned. "Never mind. Forget I said anything."

Mack frowned at him. "Hey, you okay?"

"Yeah, fine. Go on before we get mobbed by disgruntled customers. You take that end of the bar, and I'll handle this end."

With one last curious look at his brother, Mack sauntered off. The bar, owned by the brothers, was especially packed tonight. It had gone from being a popular watering hole to a regular hangout. People not only drank there, they danced and played billiards and pinball. Cole, the oldest brother and recently married, was thinking of expanding into the empty building next door. He'd discussed his plans with Chase just the other day, and Chase was all for it, especially if it meant they'd hire in some help. The bar was plenty prosperous enough now to support several additional employees, and with Zane, the third brother, getting his own computer business off the ground, and Mack finishing up college, it was certain the two younger brothers would likely work less and less at the bar.

Cole had originally bought it to support the family after their parents had died. He'd worked damned hard, making ends meet and taking care of three much younger brothers. Chase, as the second oldest at twenty-seven, was still nine years younger than Cole, with Zane twenty-four and Mack just turned twenty-two. Chase had always tried to help out as much as possible, and he and Cole were friends, as well as being as close as brothers could be, but none of them had expected the bar to eventually be so popular. It had given them a great start in life and had guaranteed employment for the younger brothers, but it had served its purpose and it was time to think of the future.

Their clientele was as much female as otherwise, being that until Cole's recent marriage, they'd all been bachelors—according to the local papers, the most popular bachelors Thomasville, Kentucky, had to offer. A lot of women lamented Cole's altered state, which sent an overflow of attention to the remaining brothers. Chase smiled. He wasn't all that interested, being something of a recluse and extremely particular in his sexual appetites, but Zane and Mack sure appreciated all the female adoration.

The six to eight o'clock rush was finally starting to wind down when Chase was hit with another of Allison's vivid internal dialogues. He'd been fending off the stray thoughts, doing his best to ignore them, but there was no way to keep this one out. A tray in his hands, a dishrag over his shoulder, he paused on his way to the sink, like someone had frozen him in mid-step.

Such nice shoulders. So sexy. Probably hard and smooth to the touch. And hot. They'd move when he thrust, the muscles shifting . . .

And then a visual image joined the words, an erotic picture of him making love to Allison. It was carnal, sensual, and showed him exactly what she'd look like naked, laid out beneath him, straining against him while he drove into her. Her small breasts were flushed, her pale pink nipples were puckered tight. Her eyes were closed, her blonde hair fanned out on a pillow, her hands desperately clutching his shoulders . . .

The tray almost slipped out of his hands, and he barely managed to catch it. He shook his head, trying to clear it, totally overwhelmed by a wave of raging lust and heated need. He turned to stare at her.

She was looking at him, and as he stared, gaze intent, her face turned pink and she ducked her head. Like a sleepwalker, Chase plunked the tray on the bar, threw the dishrag to the side, and started toward her.

She looked up at him, her eyes now rounding with alarm, and she took a hasty step back, but the haystack and pumpkins were there, crowded into the corner, making it impossible for her to flee. Which was just as well, because if she'd run, he'd have simply chased her down. All he could think of was getting his hands on her.

Chase stalked her, keeping her in sight, stepping around

those people loitering or dancing in the middle of the floor, dodging tables and ignoring greetings. He didn't like being played with, and while he didn't know how she did it, he knew Allison was in some way responsible.

He stopped right in front of her and she looked up at him, one hand pressed wide over her heart as if to keep it contained in her chest. He started to question her, but then he noticed her lips, soft, pink, parted slightly, and he wanted so badly to kiss her he couldn't think straight. He could almost taste her on his tongue, hot and wet and woman sweet. His hands shook—hell, his whole body shook.

Like a wild animal scenting a female in heat, it took all his concentration to control his basic urges. He'd *never* felt this way before, not even with the most accommodating women, and they were rare indeed. His desires were usually specific, a little risqué to the average woman, something that needed to be catered to in order to achieve mind-blowing pleasure. He simply didn't get overwhelmed with lust at the mere sight of a woman.

Anger washed over him, making him tremble. He didn't want to notice her, dammit. She'd never affected him this way before, so why now? How did she do it? He stared down at her, at that tempting mouth, and every muscle in his body tensed. He cursed softly.

Oh God. Maybe I should have chosen Zane. He'd have been willing at least, and so much easier. He wouldn't question what was happening . . .

"Like hell!" Chase took her shoulders and shook her slightly. Through clenched teeth, he growled, "You're right, Zane wouldn't hesitate; he'd probably already have you in the back room with your little bustle in the air. But I'm not Zane, and I didn't start this, you did."

She stared at him, her shock apparent, her face draining of color.

Jealousy made him a little rougher, a little less discreet than he'd normally be. He took care to keep his private life private. Not that he was a monk, but he sure as hell wasn't the outgoing, obvious ladies' man that his younger brother Zane was. His hands tightened on her narrow shoulders and he leaned low to say, "You can just get thoughts of Zane right out of your head."

She blinked up at him, the pulse in her throat going wild. "What . . . what are you talking about?"

They were so close, her glasses fogged just a little, then slipped down the bridge of her nose. Chase could see small flecks of gold in her deep blue eyes, like little explosions of heat. His jaw worked for a moment, then he said with just a touch more calm, "How dare you even consider my brother?"

She gasped, putting both her palms on his chest. The touch burned him, making the lust that much worse. He wanted to howl. He had never in his adult life had this happen, had lust rage over him so suddenly, so uncontrollably. Hell, of the four brothers, he was the quietest, the most discriminating in outward appearances. And control, especially with a woman, was something he insisted on.

She glanced around, her movements nervous, then whispered in a rush, "Chase, what in the world is wrong with you?" Her face was flushed, her eyes round, and she looked embarrassed and alarmed and very worried.

Chase, too, glanced around. Several people were looking at him, including his damned brothers. *They must have radar,* he thought, wondering how all three of them had known he was going to make a fool of himself. But the fact that he had, that it was over a woman, was rare enough that he knew they wouldn't ignore it or let him forget it. He simply didn't cause scenes, ever, but especially not over women.

Turning back to Allison, striving for a pleasant look rather than that of a crazy man, he said, "I'd like to talk to you. In private." The words slipped out through his teeth and the parody of a smile he'd forced to his mouth.

She rolled her lips in and bit them, her gaze still wary, then nodded. But she looked far from willing. She looked nervous as hell. He could *feel* her nervousness, damn her, just like he'd felt everything else.

Holding her arm in case she changed her mind, Chase led her past the bar toward the back office. Mack stood behind the bar, shaking his head in wonder. Cole, standing in his path, frowned in concern, and Zane, surrounded by a group of women, grinned like the village idiot. Ignoring the two younger brothers, Chase stopped in front of Cole and said, "I need a few minutes of privacy."

Looking between him and Allison, Cole narrowed his eyes.

There was no way Chase could explain, so he said simply and firmly, "I'll be back out as soon as I can," and his tone alone forestalled any arguments.

Cole looked hesitant, then finally he nodded. "Take your time. We can handle things now."

"Thanks." Chase turned away, and Allison stumbled along beside him. He realized it looked like he was dragging her along, but that was only because she was holding back a bit. Chase glanced down at her. "You're causing a scene."

"Me?" They were now out of sight of the main room of the bar, and she again held back as Chase opened the office door. "You're the one doing the caveman routine. What in the world is the matter with you?"

He snorted. "Like you don't know." Hell, she'd been thinking about him all night, taunting him with those personal, private, *sexual* thoughts of hers. He didn't know how he knew it, but he did, and his conviction was so strong he didn't doubt it for a moment. He gently propelled her into the office and shut the door.

The lock turned with a quiet click.

Only one light was on, a small lamp sitting on the desk. Chase watched as Allison backed up a few steps, then stopped and braced herself. For what?

"Allison . . ."

You can do this, you can do this, you can . . .

"Do *what?*" Chase barked, advancing on her, again losing his temper. Startled, she jumped back and her knees hit the soft, slightly worn sofa that Cole had installed years ago when long nights sometimes made it necessary to nap at the bar. Allison lost her balance and she tumbled gracefully onto the sofa, the soft, flared skirt of that killer dress fanning around her. Her spine pressed hard to the back of the sofa in alarm. She started to jump up again, but Chase stepped so close she couldn't, not without plastering herself against him.

And judging by her expression, she didn't want to do that.

She eyed him, then whispered, "I don't know what you're talking about."

He leaned down, one hand on the back of the sofa next to her head, the other on the arm next to her side, pinning her in. "You want me. You've been thinking about me all night, distracting me, invading my head. Now you're trying to give yourself a pep talk and—"

Her eyes flared wide like saucers, and she fumbled with her glasses. Her mouth moved, but no words came out. Finally, she sputtered, "How on earth do you know that?"

He frowned, tilting his head to study her carefully. Her old-fashioned dress was a major turn-on for him, and he fully appreciated the feminine, sultry picture she presented. It affected him somehow, but he couldn't say exactly why.

"Chase?"

She sounded honestly surprised, and then he felt her shock roll over him and knew she'd had no idea he'd been listening in on her ruminations. She hadn't silently talked to him on purpose, he'd just suddenly been able to read her. *Why?*

Chase touched her cheek, feeling the heat of her blush. She was mortified to discover he knew her thoughts. Some of his anger evaporated, and he wanted to reassure her somehow, but first they had to figure out what was going on.

Standing up straight again, he said, "Don't move."

She shook her head, mute. Her thoughts were such a jumble he almost smiled. Poor little thing. She was as confounded as he. And now that he knew she wasn't controlling the situation, wasn't controlling him, he could almost appreciate the novelty of it.

He touched the tip of her nose, then a loose blonde curl by her temple. He liked touching her, he thought, then immediately withdrew. He didn't want to like touching her. "This is going to take some time to sort out. I'm going to go get us a couple of drinks, then we'll talk, okay?"

Her chest rose and fell rapidly, making the beaded bodice glitter. She looked away. "Okay."

"Allison?"

Her gaze came back to him reluctantly.

"It's all right." He searched her face, noticing how pretty her eyes looked, how they weren't just a dark blue, but a multitude of blue shades, complex and original. "That you want me, I mean."

Her lashes lowered, her hands fisted in her lap, and she whispered, "Oh God."

Smiling now, feeling like he was finally getting the upper hand, Chase walked out. Damn, he didn't know what was going on, but one thing was certain: Allison hadn't denied wanting him. She hadn't denied anything. She'd been too upset and embarrassed and confused to do more than stare up a him, letting him absorb her thoughts, letting him experience her desire.

And her desire sparked his own.

He was so hot, he thought he could breathe steam. His muscles were tensed, his abdomen tight. He felt like he'd been indulging in an hour of specialized foreplay, and in a way, he supposed he had, listening in on Allison's thoughts, seeing her small fantasies. They'd been almost real, and had affected him like a touch.

This whole thing went beyond the realm of reality. If someone had tried to tell him any of this was possible, he'd have laughed. Mind reading? Ha. He hadn't believed such a thing existed, but now he knew it did.

Even stranger than that was Allison, suddenly looking so appealing, suddenly wanting *him*. He'd always been polite to her but distant, because he'd instinctively felt she wouldn't meet his needs. She was mostly quiet, a little perky but in a cute, friendly way, not overtly sexual. A small woman with sweet features, not a single risqué or daring thing about her. She didn't in any way look like a woman who would indulge his sexual demands. So he'd been merely polite and she'd always been the same.

Now he knew her quiet facade hid some heated urges, and though they weren't on a par with his, they intrigued the hell out of him.

Hurrying, he went behind the bar and grabbed two colas. Cole tried to talk to him, but he put him off. Hell, there was no way to explain the unexplainable. Cole would think he'd gone off the deep end.

Mack and Zane started whispering, their heads together, but he ignored them, too, not even bothering to give them a second glance.

Even this far away from Allison, he still knew what she was thinking, and he wanted to get back to her, to reassure her. She was afraid of what he'd think, racking her brain for an explanation he'd accept. Her uncertainty was understandable, even endearing, given the bizarre situation.

For whatever reason, she suddenly wanted him, and he didn't really think he should turn her down. Hell no. Whatever was frightening her—and she was frightened—he'd take care of it.

Cole walked up to him again. "Chase . . ."

"It's under control, Cole. Don't worry."

Cole searched his face, not looking the least bit convinced. "But . . . *Allison?*"

Chase grinned. "Yeah, I know. Pretty surprising, huh? Maybe there's some black magic at work, considering it's almost Halloween, or there's a full moon out tonight or something. Who knows?"

Cole didn't respond to the joke. "Do you know what you're doing, Chase?"

Considering that a fair question since he wasn't behaving at all like himself, Chase shrugged. "I'm working it out. That's all I can tell you for now."

Cole still looked concerned, but he let it go, saying only, "Just remember she's my wife's friend and assistant. I don't want to end up in the doghouse because of you."

Chase laughed. As he headed back to the office, colas and napkins in his hands, he dodged under a black paper cat and an orange paper jack-o'-lantern hanging from the ceiling. Maybe Halloween really did have something to do with this sudden power of his to read Allison, to see things in her he'd never seen before.

If so, he intended to enjoy it while it lasted.

But first, he wanted some answers.

Two

Allison paced the office as she waited for Chase to return. She'd never been in here before, and beyond her nervousness was a curiosity that kept her looking around. Cole mostly used the office, since he was the bookkeeper of the bar. Chase generally contented himself with being a bartender—and an unusual one at that. He wasn't chatty, was more of a listener than not. He had the incredible knack for keeping disagreements at a minimum, negating the need for a bouncer. The bar was a lively place, but it was friendly, and totally acceptable to a family man or woman.

The office was large with a massive desk at one end and a plush sofa against the adjacent wall. A few chairs were scattered about with a filing cabinet or two. Photos of the brothers at various ages hung on the wall, and with her heart pounding, Allison went to peer at an aged photo of Chase. He was younger, but even then she could see the hidden fire in him, the repressed energy that everyone else seemed to miss, accepting him as the *quiet brother.* She shook her head. He was still incredibly gorgeous and her stomach knotted. It suddenly seemed like much too much.

"Darn it, Rose, I knew this was a bad idea. He's actually angry that I want him. Why wasn't Jack good enough? He couldn't read my mind, and we both know he was more than willing, even if he didn't exactly make my pulse race the way Chase does. He had no idea what you were planning. It would have been so much—"

The door slammed and she turned to see Chase, drinks in his hands and a frown on his face. "First my brother Zane, and now some bozo named Jack. How many men are you daydreaming about?"

He was angry again—

"Damn right I'm angry!"

Her own temper sparked, obliterating some of her nervousness. "Stop doing that! Stop reading my mind."

He stared at her, and very slowly his frown smoothed out. He looked disgruntled as he stepped into the office and set the drinks on the desk. "I can't help it. It's like you're screaming into my head."

"But why?" Her hands twisted together in nervousness. "I don't understand."

"Hell if I know. You came in tonight and just like that, I heard you thinking about me."

If her face got any hotter, her ears were going to catch on fire. Mustering her courage, determined to see this through—a thought he obviously read, judging by his smile—she admitted, "I've done that before."

"Thought about me?"

She swallowed hard and nodded. "Yes."

Eyes narrowed sensually, he stepped closer. His voice was low and heated when he asked, "Sexual thoughts?"

Her stomach did quick little flips of excitement. "Yes."

"I never guessed."

"I know. You've never even noticed me." That was painfully true, and there'd been many a night when she'd gone home feeling heartsick because she was all but invisible to him.

Chase reached out and touched her cheek again. "I'm sorry."

Darn it, she had to censor her thoughts a little better or she'd never be able to get through this.

Chase grinned. "Don't bother on my account. I kind of like reading your mind."

With the most ferocious frown she could muster, she said, "Well, I don't like it!"

He looked very annoyed again. "Because you're also thinking about Zane and this Jack person?"

"No!" She shook her head, flustered to the core. Seeing no hope for it, she admitted quietly, "I don't want Zane or Jack. Not like . . ."

His gaze softened. "Like you want me?"

"Yes. But none of it matters. I don't need to be a mind reader to know you couldn't care less about me. I'm sorry if my thoughts are suddenly intruding in your head, but I don't really know what I can do about it."

His frown was back, only now it looked more confused than angry. "You want me, but you don't want to do anything about it?"

Allison turned away. This was the tricky part—

Chase swung her back around and up close to his chest. His hands held her firmly, not hurting, but making certain she couldn't move away. Allison thought he'd shake her again, and she braced herself, but no sooner did she think it than he narrowed his eyes and sighed. "Dammit, I would never hurt you, okay?" When she didn't answer right away, he added, "I promise. Trust me."

Heart tripping at his deep, compelling tone, she said, "Okay."

"Good." There was a wealth of satisfaction in his heated gaze, but also determination. He tugged her the tiniest bit closer, until she gasped. "Now let's get something straight. I don't want you to try planning and plotting against me. It's only tricky if you're not honest with me."

Being so near to him was muddling her brain, making logical explanations difficult. "I . . . I can't be honest with you."

"Why not?"

"You won't believe me, and you'll think I'm nuts, and you won't want anything to do with me, but I need you to . . ." She closed her mouth, appalled by how much she'd just blurted out.

His gaze moved from a fascinated study of her eyes, to her mouth, then down to her breasts. His fingers on her arms turned caressing, persuasive. In a soft, gentle tone, he said, "This whole situation is nuts, so I doubt you can add much lunacy to it. And to be truthful, I'm finding I want a lot to do with you. Maybe it's just a masculine gut reaction to knowing how much you want me, but I've had a hard-on since you first started thinking about me. And it's you I've got pictured in my brain, not any other woman."

Allison groaned. His words were like an aphrodisiac, making her blood race, her toes curl. Rose couldn't have planned this any better if she'd tried. But it was all wrong. Even if he was now willing to do what she needed him to do, it wasn't because—

Chase leaned down and pressed his mouth to her temple. "Tell me what you need me to do, honey."

Honey. He'd never called her that before. She liked it.

"I'm glad."

Her head dropped forward to bounce against his chest and she groaned again, this time thoroughly flustered at her wayward thoughts.

Chase chuckled, nuzzling against her crown. "I'm sorry. Would you rather I didn't answer your thoughts?"

She shook her head. This situation was so bizarre, it bordered on comical. But then, everything that had happened to her since moving into the house was beyond belief. "No. It's just . . . disconcerting."

His hands stroked up and down her back, and her eyes closed as she basked in the heat of his touch. He kissed her brow and said, "To me, too, you know. My brothers are probably out there huddled together, coming up with every wrong conclusion there is. It's for certain they're not anywhere close to the truth."

Alarmed, she pushed back to look up at him. "You're not going to tell them, are you?" It was bad enough that Chase had been drawn in, but she didn't want or need anyone else to find out all her secrets.

Chase cupped her cheek, his touch so tender she could barely find her breath. "I don't know. I'm not even sure yet what's going on. But if it'll make you feel better, for now I won't say anything."

Her eyes closed in relief. "Thank you."

"What secrets do you have?"

Darn. She hadn't meant to let that slip. Then realizing she might as well have spoken out loud, she said, "Just give me a little time, okay?"

"Time for what?"

"Time to figure out how to tell you, how to get used to this, how to prepare myself."

He didn't look like he wanted to agree. In fact, he looked very disagreeable, but he finally nodded. "Answer a few questions for me, then."

"If I can."

"Who's Jack?"

That was easy enough, though not a very desirable topic. "He's a man I've been dating. He wants to get serious, but I don't."

He looked far from pleased by her explanation. "Why?"

"He's not . . . right for me."

"In what way?"

Chase made it very difficult to talk when he kept touching her, his big hands smoothing over her shoulders, her back. And he stared at her mouth, making her self-conscious.

And he damn well knew it.

He shook his head. His voice was deep and affected, husky with desire. "I'm sorry. It's just that I can't stop thinking about kissing you—and a lot of others things. Things that'd likely have you hightailing your pretty little behind out of here as fast as you can."

Ignoring most of what he said only because it didn't make sense to her, she asked, "You . . . you really want to kiss me?"

"Oh yeah." His voice dropped even more and he stared at her lips. "But I can tell you don't really want me to. Yet."

Allison tried to step away, but he wouldn't let her go, so instead she covered her face. "This is so difficult."

She found herself hauled up against Chase's chest, his arms wrapped tight around her, comforting her. "I don't mean to make it—whatever *it* is—harder for you, honey. But I can feel your confusion. You want me, but you don't want to want me. Have I got that right?"

She sighed. He smelled so good, and it felt so good to be this close to him. More than anything she wanted to be with him, in every way imaginable.

He drew in a deep breath. *"Every* way?"

She stared at him, speechless. That had sounded too ominous by half. Still, she would have agreed, but there were stipulations that she couldn't ignore.

His eyes narrowed. "What stipulations?"

Darn it, she had no privacy at all! It took all her control to hold back her fist. She wanted really badly to punch him.

Chase held her tighter. "None of that."

This time she didn't even question his right to know her thoughts. Thoroughly disgruntled, accepting there was no way she could sort out her thoughts in her own head, she groaned and pushed back to glare at him. "Do you think I should be happy to want a man who doesn't want me?"

"But I just told you—"

"Right. That you . . . have an erection." Her face burned, but she didn't look away from him. "I know. But that's not because of *me*. Chase, you don't even know me, and you've never wanted to know me."

He was quiet, watching her closely.

"I think in the eight months that Sophie and your brother have been married, you've said about a dozen sentences to me, all of them mundane cordial niceties. How're you doing? Nice weather we're having. That sort of thing. Now, just because you know I've fantasized about you a little—"

"A lot."

"Okay a lot—"

One corner of his firm mouth kicked up. "Tell me some of the fantasies."

His voice was low, commanding, making her insides tingle. She frowned severely. "No. Besides, you'll probably know them soon enough as it is."

His brows lifted. "You've got plans, do you?"

She opened her mouth, then saw his taunting smirk and wanted to slug him again. "No! I meant that you'd probably just read my mind and know them, though I swear I'm going to do my best *not* to think about you at all."

"Party pooper."

"It's not funny, Chase."

He grinned and kissed the end of her nose. "From my perspective it is. There's not a man alive who wouldn't pay good money to be where I am right now. It's not often a fellow can actually understand a woman or know her thoughts."

She snorted. "Like you can even begin to understand."

He ignored that. "And I really am curious about these fantasies, but I'll wait, if you insist. Now, about that other nonsense you rattled off."

Her wariness returned. "What nonsense?"

"Me not wanting you. Okay, so I'll admit I'd never really paid much attention to you before. I never pay much attention to any woman, at least not for long, but especially not a woman who's a friend and assistant to my sister-in-law. I have no intention of getting involved long-term with anyone, and your relationship with Sophie puts you just a little bit too close to home for comfort. You're not the type of woman for a one night stand, and one night stands are about the only speed I go these days, so I ignored you. It really didn't have anything to do with you."

She stared at him, disbelieving such words had actually come from his mouth. "My goodness. All that? So your disregard for me was actually something of a compliment, because I'm above such casual notice?"

"Don't be snide."

"Snide? I don't believe a thing you said. Since I've known you, I've seen you with three women, and if they were any indication of the type of female you gravitate toward, then I have no problem at all understanding why you've always ignored me, and it didn't have a lot to do with my friendship with Sophie."

He'd stiffened at her first mention of the women. "Meaning?"

"Meaning the women you go for are always beautiful and. . . . and well, stacked." She winced at her own word choice, but it was absolutely true. While she was full through the hips, lacking in the upper works, and of a very ordinary appearance overall, Chase had shown a preference for tall, slim, busty women—none of which could be applied to her.

He chastised her with a shake of his head. "Women are so damn weird."

"Weird!"

"And so hung up on their bodies. Allison, there's absolutely nothing wrong with how you're built."

Her mouth twisted. She obviously didn't have a single sacred thought.

"No, absolutely not, especially when you're thinking all kinds of ignorant things."

"Ignorant things? Chase, I have mirrors in my house, and I know what I look like."

"You look fine, better than fine, and it wasn't the look of those women that drew me."

"Then what?"

He hesitated, studied her closely, then smiled. "Not yet, honey. But maybe, given half a chance, I'll explain it to you someday."

The deliberate secrecy annoyed her. "See? You're obviously just not interested."

His own temper sparked at her stubbornness. "Then explain why I still have a damned erection!"

He no sooner shouted that than a tentative tap sounded at the door. They both turned, appalled. Chase recovered first, saying in a bark, "What is it?"

There was barely repressed laughter in Mack's voice when he called out, "Uh, there's a guy here looking for Allison."

"Uh-oh." She cleared her throat as Chase turned slowly to glare at her, then she answered Mack nervously, saying, "I'll, uh, be right out."

Chase looked like a thundercloud. "Who the hell is looking for you?"

"Jack?" She posed her answer as a question, not sure how he'd react.

Working his jaw, Chase stood silent for a moment, then finally said, "You'll tell him to leave."

"No, I will not! Chase, we agreed to meet here tonight before I knew any of this would happen. I need to talk to him, to tell him—"

"That you want me."

"No! I'm not going to tell him that."

"Then I will."

He turned toward the door, and Allison launched herself at him, wrapping her arms tight around his waist and digging in her heels. "Wait! You don't understand!"

Chase easily pulled her around in front of him, then pinned her to the door with his hands on her shoulders, his hips pressed to her belly. Her heart skipped two beats, then went into frantic overdrive. His breath fanned her cheek and his gaze was hot. With his lips almost touching hers, he said, "I don't want you to see anyone but me."

His scent enveloped her, his nearness made heat bloom inside her. She'd wanted this for so long, but not this way, not when he'd more or less been coerced.

"No one is coercing me, Allison. I want you, plain and simple."

"There's absolutely nothing simple about this and you know it." Still, did she have any choice? Rose was counting on her, and so was Burke. She licked her lips and could almost taste him. "There's a lot I have to explain to you yet."

His hips pressed closer, letting her feel the long, hard length of his erection, making her gasp. "Like who the hell Rose and Burke are?"

Her glasses were crooked and she straightened them, staring at his throat rather than meeting his eyes. "Yes. And . . . and why I think you should come to my house and. . . . and make love to me."

She peeked up at him. The heat of his gaze burned her up from the inside out. And then he kissed her, his mouth voracious, his tongue stroking. She clutched at him, overwhelmed and turned on and unable to rationalize what was happening. Unexpectedly, he caught her hands and pinned them over her head, then groaned deeply.

When he pulled away just the tiniest bit, he said roughly, "Get rid of the other man, Allison."

She practically hung there in his grasp, on her tiptoes, her arms stretched out, his pelvis pressed to her, keeping her still. "I . . . I will," she managed to stammer around her excitement. "But I have to do it right."

"Tell him to get lost."

"That would be cruel." She said it as a gentle reprimand, then quickly added, "He's a nice man, Chase. And he's serious about me. He asked me to marry him, so I can't just dump him like that."

Chase stared at her for a long moment, and she could see he fought an internal battle. Finally his eyes squeezed shut, and he whispered, "I've never been jealous before. I don't like it."

"You have no reason to be."

He kissed her again, softer this time, consuming, with so much tenderness it felt like her heart was swelling in her chest, nearly choking her.

"Don't let him touch you. Promise me."

"No." His kiss and his words left her nearly panting. "No, I won't."

With a sigh, he carefully, slowly released her wrists and stepped away from her. "Let's go before Mack starts telling everyone that I have a hard-on and I'm shouting about it."

Horrified by such a possibility, she asked, "He wouldn't, would he?"

"Hell yes, he would, if he thought it'd embarrass me. That is, he'd tell Zane and Cole. And they're the two I'd most prefer didn't know."

But when they stepped back into the bar, all three brothers stood there, grinning like magpies, and Allison knew Mack had already blabbed. Luckily, it was only Chase they seemed intent on teasing. But then Jack spoke up from behind them, drawing everyone's attention.

"Allison? What the hell's going on?"

She looked at Jack, silently begging for him not to start anything, but it was Chase who answered those thoughts, saying forcefully, "Forget it, honey," as he stepped forward. All three of his brothers crowded behind him.

Jack stiffened his spine. He was every bit as tall as Chase, topping six feet, but was Chase's exact opposite in every other way. While Chase was dark with golden brown eyes, Jack was blond with bright green eyes. They looked like two wolf-hounds ready to bite each other. Allison was mortified.

"Cole, do something!"

He blinked at her, then turned to his brother. "Knock it off, Chase."

Both Chase and Jack ignored him. Cole shrugged at her, as if saying, *I tried*. But then he suggested, "At least make it private, Chase. You're embarrassing her."

Chase nodded agreement to that and turned to go back in the office. Jack followed him against Allison's protests.

Exasperated, Allison hurried in on Jack's heels, and shut the door behind her. "This is not necessary."

Chase said, "I think he disagrees."

In his most provoking tone, Jack said, "You're right, I do."

Trying desperately to salvage the moment, Allison said, "Jack, it's not even what you think."

Chase snorted. "Unless he's an idiot, it's exactly what he thinks."

Allison whirled to face him. "You promised, damn it!" Chase didn't even look at her, his attention fixed on Jack.

But he did say, "I promised to give you time to talk to him. But I didn't say anything about letting him yell at you."

"Allison?"

Jack sounded out of patience, and she turned to him again, saying in a whisper, "It was Rose's idea. I swear. I'll explain later . . ."

"Rose?" Suddenly Jack's expression relaxed and he even chuckled as he glanced at Chase with an amused look. "So you're letting Rose call the shots again, huh?" He shook his head, laughing at her.

Chase took an aggressive step forward. "Allison, maybe it's time you told me who the hell Rose is."

With a lift of his brows, Jack said, "I can explain, though I doubt you'll believe it any more than I do."

He was still amused, and seeing no hope for it, Allison decided she had nothing to lose. She frowned at both men. "Jack, you can forget our date tonight. In fact, you can forget any dates!"

Jack glared. Anger crowded his features, then a near panic. "Damn it, Allison . . ."

She crossed her arms over her chest.

Jack glanced at Chase, then narrowed his gaze on her face again. "I'll call you later when you've had a chance to calm down." And in a huff, he stormed out, slamming the door behind him.

Chase shook his head. Now that Jack was gone, he looked relaxed and under control again. His gaze lit on Allison, and he teased, "I thought you claimed he was a nice guy."

"And you!" She was practically fuming, she was so mad. Nothing had gone as expected, and she'd had more surprises tonight than one woman could bear. "I've decided you're not worth the trouble, no matter what Rose thinks!"

She turned to the door, ready to make a grand exodus, but Chase's hand flattened on it before she could get it open. Speaking close to her ear, he growled, "I don't get off till late tonight, so it'll have to be tomorrow morning. But we'll get together at ten to talk. Which is damned early for me, so I hope you appreciate the concession to my sleep."

"I won't—"

"We have a lot to discuss, and I think I'm showing a great deal of patience, all things considered."

She wanted to tell him to go to hell. She wanted to go hide somewhere, considering how horrible the evening had turned.

"But you won't, will you, honey?"

She turned the doorknob and he let the door open. As she

stepped out, thoroughly defeated, she growled, "I suppose not. Good night, Chase."

"Ten o'clock, Allison. Don't make me wait."

Arrogant, obnoxious, controlling jerk . . .

She heard him laugh, and she groaned. Fleeing seemed her only option, and she did so quickly. But as she left the bar, she felt all four brothers watching her, and she knew, from here on out, nothing would be the same.

Three

Chase was distracted as he finished closing down the bar. It was almost two in the morning, and he and Zane were alone. Mack had taken off hours ago to catch some sleep before his morning classes, and Cole always left early these days, now that he had a wife waiting at home for him. Chase grinned, thinking about Sophie. She was awfully sweet, and the way she'd played Cole just before they were married was something he'd never forget, the stuff fantasies were made of. Cole hadn't stood a chance, and Chase considered him damn lucky to have her.

But thinking of Sophie and Cole reminded him of something that had been niggling at the back of his mind ever since Allison had stormed out of the bar, her thoughts confused and her frustration level high. Hell, his frustration was through the roof. He was still mildly aroused, even though she was gone. He couldn't get her out of his mind, and though he couldn't read her so clearly now that she wasn't close, he still got the occasional glimpse of her thoughts and it kept his desire on a keen edge.

Small talk with customers had been almost impossible tonight.

Zane came out of the back room, whistling. Out of all the brothers, he was the rowdiest. Zane seemed to have a little wildness in him that no one would ever be able to erase. Cole had never really tried, preferring just to temper that energy whenever possible. It had never bothered Chase before, but now, he kept thinking of how Allison had briefly considered Zane, and it bothered him a lot.

Zane looked up and caught Chase staring. The whistling stopped. "What'd I do?"

"Nothing. At least, I hope not."

Reaching for his coat off a hook in the hallway, snagging Chase's also, Zane started forward. "What does that mean?"

"I want to ask you something, Zane, and I want a straight answer, okay?"

Zane tossed Chase his coat, then propped his hands on his hips. "At twenty-four, don't you think I'm a little old for a lecture?"

"I wasn't going to lecture you."

"Oh." He grinned. "Well, good. Because I wasn't going to listen."

Chase perched on a bar stool and stared at his brother. "You remember back when Cole and Sophie first hooked up?"

"How could I forget?" Zane lifted himself onto the edge of the bar. "Hell, Cole was so damned amusing, I worked extra hours, neglecting my own business, just to get to watch him fumble around."

Chase grinned, too. "He did have a hard time of it, didn't he?"

"Aw, well, Sophie made it worth his while."

"You knew Allison back then, didn't you? I mean, even before Sophie and Cole hooked up." He'd sort of blurted that out, but he was getting edgier by the minute, prompted by some unknown discontent, like something was wrong, but he didn't know what.

Zane shrugged. "I know just about every woman in town, Allison included, but probably not the way you're thinking, judging by your frown." He grinned. "I asked her out, but she turned me down flat."

That surprised Chase. "She did?"

"Yeah, several times, in fact."

So Zane had asked her out more than once? He didn't like that. "You never said anything."

"Like you expected me to brag that I was turned out cold? Get real. Besides, from the way the two of you carried on today, I have to wonder if she wasn't hung up on you way back then. You can be damn blind when it comes to women, Chase."

"What's that supposed to mean?"

"It means a lot of women try to get your attention, but you don't take the bait."

Because they were nice, conservative women who most likely wouldn't meet his appetites. He shook his head. "I date."

"Yeah, about five times a year." He snorted. "That's barely enough to keep a man alive. I figure every so often your libido takes over, and you cave. Other than that, you're a man of ice."

"Maybe I just don't like to spread myself so thin."

Zane chuckled. "You were sure spreading it around today. The way you corralled Allison into the back room reminded me of a stallion herding a mare. Not at all subtle."

Chase made a disgusted face and muttered, "Yeah, well, I don't know what got into me today." But even as he resolved to regain his iron control, his uneasiness grew, prompting him to leave. He stood up and pushed in the bar stool.

Zane slid off the bar and buttoned up his coat, preparing to follow Chase out. "If I'm not mistaken," Zane said, "I think it's called lust. And about time, I'd say.''

Suddenly, Chase had to see Allison. The urge to go to her was overwhelming, as bad as the turbulent lust had been. He had to fight to keep from rushing out, making a fool of himself again. Only the fact that he didn't have her exact address held him back. He glanced at his brother and wanted to wince. Zane was giving him a rather knowing look.

''I don't suppose you know—''

Zane chuckled. ''She lives on State Street, not too far from here. It's a big old cream-colored clapboard farmhouse, and you can't miss it because the roof sticks up way higher than any of the others.''

Narrowing his eyes, Chase asked, ''How do you know?''

''Well, I haven't been there wooing her, if that's what you're worried about. Besides, like I already told you, she wasn't interested in me. From what I understand, she inherited the house from an old spinster aunt. I helped out about a month ago when Cole and Sophie moved her in there.''

''Thanks.'' Chase headed out the door, driven by some vague urgency he couldn't suppress. He tossed a quick look at Zane. ''Lock up, will you?''

Zane blinked in astonishment. ''You're not going over there now, are you?''

Chase didn't answer him. He didn't have time. Before he was completely through the door, he was flat-out running. He had to get to Allison. Why, he didn't know, but the panic was real, making his heart race and his jaw lock. Within minutes he was in his car, driving too fast, and just as he turned the corner on State Street, he was able to clearly hear her again, her every thought, her every word. And what he heard caused him an unreasonable amount of anger.

It's not that I mind you being here, really. It just makes me a little nervous because it's not something I'm used to. Especially when I'm trying to bathe. Couldn't you go away for just a little while until I finish up?

Someone was with her while she was trying to take a bath? And he refused to leave?

Allison's nervousness was real, flooding his senses. In fact, her nervousness bordered on fear, and Chase was suddenly so enraged, a red haze crowded his vision. He parked his car in the driveway with a screech, thankful that she didn't have any near neighbors on the older, quiet street. He jumped out of his car, stormed up the paved entry walk to the immense wooden front porch decorated with a huge jack-o'-lantern and some cornstalks, but as he started to pound on the door, he noticed a narrow window to the side of the front room was opened just a crack. In late October, the evening air was cool enough that all the windows should have been shut, especially considering she was a woman alone, on a dead end street, and it was nearing three in the morning. His instincts kicked in.

Chase crept to the window and slid through it silently. Once inside, he closed and latched it, then looked around. He seemed to be in a parlor of sorts with carved, embroidered furniture, plenty of crocheted doilies, and lamps with fabric shades. Even though the room was dim, enough light came from the hall chandelier to let him clearly see the flocked, flowery wallpaper. He felt like he'd stepped back in time.

The house was dated enough to boggle his senses.

He explored cautiously, leaving the parlor and sneaking a peek into the adjacent rooms, one a library lined with dark, heavy wooden shelves, the other a more modern family room with a TV and overstuffed couch. The rooms were long and narrow with arched doorways and heavy drapes, and they opened to a central hall. At the end of the hall he could see a spacious country kitchen, and next to it, a small bath with black and pink ceramic tile on the floor and walls. Right inside the front door, to the left, was an incredible winding, ornate wooden staircase that led to the second floor.

Hearing a creak from above, Chase looked up. From the

sounds of it, Allison was up there talking quietly with someone.

Jealousy, hot and dark, raced over his nerve endings, along with the need to protect. He could still feel her unease, and when he found out who was responsible, they'd be sorry. He crept upstairs. Each damn step seemed to groan beneath his weight, the typical speakings of an old house. The urgency suddenly quieted, replaced by annoyance—not his annoyance, so maybe it was hers?

The stairway ended with another hall. At one end was a large, narrow, diamond-paned window showing the dark night beyond, with two bedrooms, one on either side of the hall, in between. At the other end was a master bedroom and a larger bathroom, and that's where Chase headed. He could hear Allison clearly now, and his brows drew tight. Who the hell was she talking to? He paused outside the bathroom door and listened.

"Really, the idea is ludicrous. I can't sleep with Chase when he doesn't truly want me. And before you say it, you know it's just that darn trick you played on me, letting him read my mind, that has him reacting right now." She groaned. "When I think of all the stuff I imagined, it's *so* embarrassing. If it wasn't for that, he'd still think I was invisible.

"Oh, no. That dress had nothing to do with it, though I admit I liked wearing it. It made me feel sexy, whether it actually worked or not." She laughed slightly. "The underthings were great. I loved them."

Chase peeked around the open door, his eyes narrowed. But there was no one in the room. Just Allison. Naked. In a tub of bubbles.

Her blonde hair was pinned on top of her head, little ringlets falling free, and her bare arms rested along the sides of the free-standing, claw-footed white porcelain tub. Her eyes were closed and her soft mouth smiled.

She sighed deeply, and one small pink nipple appeared

above the froth of bubbles. Chase stared, mesmerized, unable to speak, barely able to breathe.

"I appreciate your efforts, guys, I really do. But I'm not at all sure I can go through with it, so let's just forget about Chase, okay?"

Chase stepped completely into the bathroom, his body pulsing with need. "Let's don't."

With a loud squeal and a lot of thrashing and splashing, Allison turned to see him. She knelt in the tub, her hands crossed over her chest, her eyes wide. She didn't have her glasses on and she stared at him hard.

Automatically, he said, "It's me, Chase."

"I know who it is! What in the world are you doing in here! This is my bathroom. How did you get in?"

He opened his mouth, but she interrupted him, shouting, "Never mind that! Just get out!"

He frowned. "Who were you talking to, Allison?"

She groaned. "Oh God, I don't believe this. I don't believe this, it isn't happening. . . ."

"Are you going to get hysterical on me?"

"Yes!"

She glared up at him, her big blue eyes rounded owlishly as she tried to see him without her glasses. She was still crouched in the tub, the bubbles reaching her hips, and her hands somewhat inadequate to completely cover her breasts. She was small, but the soft, white, rounded flesh showing from around her crossed arms was very distracting. And here she'd thought herself lacking . . .

Chase cleared his throat. "I'll step out in the hall, but make it quick. You have some explaining to do."

He walked out and dropped back against the wall, his eyes closed, his stomach muscles pulled tight. He'd left the bathroom door open and heard her growl, "Don't you dare peek!"

He just shook his head. "Hurry up, will you? My patience is pretty thin right now."

There was a flurry of splashing and mumbled cursing, then Allison, leaving a trail of water, padded barefoot out of the bathroom, an ancient embroidered chenille robe wrapped tightly around her, her glasses once again in place. Bubbles clung to the end of a ringlet over her right ear, and her throat and upper chest were still wet. The robe covered her, but the neckline dipped low enough that he could just make out the edging of white lawn underwear. Again, something vintage? When she stomped over to face him, the robe parted over her legs and he saw old-fashioned drawers that just reached her knees. His heart rate accelerated, but she quickly pulled the robe closed again.

She greeted him with a pointed finger poked into his chest. "How dare you barge in here, intruding on my privacy!"

Chase grabbed her hand, pulled her close, and gave in to the need to kiss her. She was still warm and damp, and she smelled like flowers. He held her head between his hands, urging her to her tiptoes, then kissed her long and soft and deep, eating at her mouth, capturing her tongue and drawing it into his own mouth. She groaned softly, and the hallway lights blinked happily around them.

"What the hell?" Chase looked up, but there was no one there. "What happened to the lights?"

Her hands remained fisted in his shirt, her expression dazed, her lips still parted. Around panting breaths, she said, "Hmmm?"

"The lights blinked, almost like a strobe."

"Oh." Very slowly, she pushed herself away from him, then straightened her glasses. She looked around with a frown. "It's an old house. The wiring is sometimes . . . temperamental."

Chase stared at her, saw her trying to gather herself, and shook his head. "Damn, honey, you look sexy as hell." He lifted an edge of the robe. "What have you got on under there?"

Her eyes widened and she clutched the robe. "Chase, stop it."

He stepped toward her, and she backed up. "Who were you talking to, Allison?"

"Myself?"

He shook his head. "I'm not believing it. Try again."

"You can see there's no one here."

"The window downstairs is open."

"It is?"

"Yes." He couldn't quite keep his gaze on her face, not after seeing her practically naked—and liking very much what he saw. He was so hard he hurt, and his imagination was going wild, thinking of all the things he'd like to do to her. "Don't you think that's a little risky, being you're here alone?"

"I didn't open the window, Chase."

His brows pulled down again, because she sounded totally unconcerned as she said that. Then she added, "What are you doing here, anyway? It's kind of late for a social call, isn't it?"

Why was he here? Damn, how could he tell her he'd been worried? That he'd felt something was wrong? He started to say just that when suddenly the lights flickered again, almost going crazy, and seconds later there was a crash downstairs. Chase grabbed Allison's arm, shoved her into the bathroom, and shouted, "Lock the door," before rushing down the stairs. His instincts were screaming an alarm, and he didn't wait to see if Allison would do as she was told. He just took it for granted that she would.

Bounding down the steps two at a time, an awkward task given the lights danced wildly, he reached the bottom in just a few seconds. He heard another noise, like a distant thump, and followed the sound into the parlor where he'd entered. As he bolted into the room, he saw that the wind had picked up a heavy curtain hanging over the window he'd climbed through minutes before.

He distinctly recalled closing and locking that window. Someone had just left the house.

He moved silently across the room, his gaze searching everywhere, checking out every corner. But the fact that the window was open when he got here, and then opened again, led him to believe someone had been in the house and had now left. Otherwise, how did the window get open, when it locked from the inside and he himself had just locked it?

He turned to go back to check on Allison and ran right into her. She would have landed on her sweet behind if he hadn't caught her upper arms and steadied her.

"Dammit! I thought I told you to stay upstairs." He wasn't at all pleased that she'd disregarded his orders.

She glared right back at him. "This is my house. And besides, I knew nothing was wrong. A house this old makes all kind of noises. There was no reason to be alarmed."

He wanted to shake her. This propensity he had for losing his temper and rattling her teeth was disturbing in the extreme. He'd never really lost his temper with a woman in his life, and he'd sure as hell never taken to shaking them. In fact, he took extra pleasure in maintaining icy control, in holding the reins of command gently. It was a big turn-on for him.

But Allison made him forget all that.

He leaned down close until their noses almost touched and said in a low growl, "Someone was just in your house."

She scoffed.

"Dammit, Allison, how much proof do you need? When I got here, the window was open, which was how I got in, by the way. But then I closed and locked it. Only now it's wide open again and a table's knocked over and there's a broken dish on the floor. So unless you're going to tell me this house is inhabited by ghosts, you'll have to admit—"

"It is."

Her blurted statement and small wince had him verbally backing up. "It is, what?"

She drew a long breath and he felt her shoring up her courage, preparing herself, then she whispered, "It is inhabited by ghosts."

He had the horrifying suspicion she was serious. "Come again?"

With another deep breath, she looked up at him, then said, "The house comes with two ghosts. If you'd like, I could introduce you to Rose and Burke."

Four

Allison waited anxiously while Chase did no more than stare down at her. He looked skeptical and a little concerned. Finally he said, ''Are you all right?''

''Chase.'' She took his hand and led him to a couch, forced him to sit, then turned on a few lamps. He was right. There was a knocked-over table and a broken dish. She frowned and said to the room at large, ''Very funny, Rose. If you wanted to scare him off, you're succeeding.''

''Uh, Allison—''

She waved him to silence, propped her hands on her hips over the soft robe, and looked around. ''Well, Rose? You got him here, so the least you can do is come out and show yourself. What? No more blinking lights? No more parlor tricks?''

Nothing. She frowned again, then glanced worriedly at Chase. He watched her like she'd grown an extra head. She raked a hand through her disheveled bangs, somewhat embarrassed. Darned aggravating ghosts.

''Uh, listen honey.'' Chase spoke very gently, very softly. He patted the couch cushion beside him. ''Why don't you sit down here for a minute and I'll go see if I can get us something to drink.''

When she shook her head at him, he left the couch to stand beside her, trying to urge her to the seat he'd just vacated.

She made a sound of disgust. ''It must have been Burke. Rose is pretty nice most of the time, though she's sometimes a little crotchety. But Burke''—and here she raised her voice to make certain he'd hear—''can be a real pain!''

A cold draft filled the room, making her shiver. Chase looked around, then chafed her arms roughly to warm her. ''Do you have another window open?''

''No, that's just Burke. He hates it when I insult him.''

He eyed her dubiously. ''On second thought, I don't want to leave you alone. Why don't we go into the kitchen together?''

Allison laughed. ''Chase, you can read my mind. Can't you tell I'm not making it up?''

She might have been made of fine china, the way he now handled her. ''I can tell you think you're actually talking to ghosts.'' He put a rather brotherly arm around her and urged her into the hallway. ''But don't worry about that right now. Let's just go to the kitchen, and while you get something to drink, I'll check the other windows. There's definitely one open. Your hair is blowing around.''

She lifted one hand and shoved a loose curl behind her ear. Her gaze searched every corner of the hallway and all the rooms as she passed, but Rose and Burke were hiding for some damn reason.

''Shhh. It's okay. Here, just sit a minute while I go check the windows and doors.''

Allison sighed. ''I'm not going to break, Chase.''

''I know that.'' Then he very carefully smoothed her hair in a way that reminded her of a puppy being petted. ''I'll be right back, honey.'' He jogged out of the room.

Allison looked around her empty kitchen and wanted to scream. She said aloud, "Well, I hope you're happy now. He thinks I'm loony. And I seriously doubt discrediting my mental faculties is going to inspire him to lust."

A warm breeze blew over her, taking away the chill. "Thanks. I hate being cold." Then she covered her face. "Guys, this is never going to work. I know you thought it would, but—"

Chase walked back in, a severe frown on his face. She knew he wanted to say something about her conversation with ghosts that he didn't believe in, but he refrained. "Everything on this floor is closed up and locked. I didn't check upstairs yet, but the breeze seems to be gone."

She eyed him carefully. "Of course it is."

"Actually, for such an old house, the locks are pretty secure. Were they changed recently?"

A safe enough topic, she decided. "My aunt, who I inherited the house from, had never married. She lived alone here, and it made her nervous. I think she updated the locks every two years, and she had them all checked regularly." Allison added with a grin, "Living with ghosts made her really nervous. She didn't accept it nearly as well as I have."

Pulling a chair up close so that their knees almost touched, Chase seated himself. He took her hands and stared her in the eye. "Forget your ghosts for a second, okay? You have a real problem."

"What?"

"Honey, I opened the front door and right off the edge of your porch, there's footprints in the dirt. Big prints. Not yours." He glanced down at her small bare feet, then with another frown, added, "Someone went out the window in a hurry, then leaped off the porch. Not a damn ghost, a flesh-and-blood man. Someone was here in the house with you."

Every small hair on her neck stood at attention while she stared frozen, straight into Chase Winston's dark, serious gaze.

So that was why she'd been feeling so nervous and why Burke and Rose had invaded her bath.

Chase made an impatient sound. "Allison, I don't understand—"

She waved him to silence, finally ungluing her tongue from the roof of her mouth. "Don't you see? Usually they respect my privacy. They're around, but they don't intrude—at least, not much—and certainly not when I'm changing clothes or bathing. But tonight they kept hanging around the bathroom, and even though they're just ghosts, it really did make me nervous. I mean, I was *naked.*"

Chase blinked slowly. "Yeah, I noticed."

She ignored that and continued to reason things out. "At least, I thought that was why I was nervous. But now I think it must have been the intruder. Rose wanted me to be nervous, to understand . . . Oh God." The enormity of it hit her. "Someone was in my house!"

Chase bit the side of his mouth, and she could feel him thinking, sorting out what he'd say, how to address what he considered sheer fancy on her part. Finally, he lifted a hand to her cheek and tried a small smile. "Honey, you're telling me there's ghosts in your house, but that doesn't bother you. It's only the idea of a real man—"

"Oh, for pity's sake, Chase. You're a real man, and I'm not afraid of you. But then you don't sneak in through windows!"

His thumb brushed over her temple, distracting her. "Actually, I did."

She struggled to get her mind back on track and away from that big, warm thumb. "You know what I mean. You came because you were worried about me. Hey! That's it. Just like Rose transferred my thoughts to you at the bar, she must have let you know about the intruder. Can you just imagine what might have happened if you hadn't shown up?" She shuddered in very real fear. "I guess I owe Rose my thanks."

Chase appeared to be considering everything she'd said. "Okay, let's deal with that first. Why did you leave the window unlocked?"

Allison huffed. "I'm not an idiot, Chase."

"But . . ."

"I didn't leave the window open," she insisted. "And before you even think it, Rose or Burke would never do such a thing."

Chase lifted his gaze to the ceiling. "I wasn't going to suggest they might."

"Oh, that's right. You don't believe in them."

"What I believe is that someone broke in here, and they got in through the window. It didn't look to me like they'd broken in, rather they just opened the window because it wasn't locked."

"But they're always locked."

"This one wasn't."

She pondered that. How could such a thing have happened? The lights flickered again and both she and Chase looked up at the old Tiffany-style chandelier hanging over the kitchen table. Allison pursed her mouth. "See there? I think Rose or Burke have an idea, but because they're fickle and determined on their own course, they won't just come right out and tell me about it."

"They, ah, talk to you, do they?"

"I don't know if I'd call it talking. I mean, I hear them, but I don't know that they're actually saying anything. You understand?"

His expression was ironic. "Certainly. What's not to understand?"

She narrowed her eyes at him. "You claim to hear me when I'm not talking to you."

"But you're not a ghost."

"So?"

He opened his mouth, then closed it.

Satisfied that he'd listen, Allison stood to pace. "The thing is, they didn't come right out and tell me, but they did do the next best thing, which was to send you here." Then she glanced at him again, and the look on his face didn't encourage her. "I'm sorry you're out so late tonight. You must be exhausted after working all day."

Chase looked like he either wanted to strangle her or lay her out on the table and do wickedly sexy things to her. She gulped, knowing which she'd prefer.

"I know which I'd prefer, too," he said pointedly, staring at the way her robe gaped at her throat, "but I think we need to get a few things straightened out here first."

"Like my sanity?"

"I'm not suggesting you're insane—"

She began pacing again. "I'm not confused or making it up or imagining it, either. You saw the lights. Well, they do that to show they're agitated or excited. Which proves Rose and Burke are real. Or, that is, they're as real as ghosts can be."

"Because of some flickering lights? Honey, I hate to tell you, but this old house probably has lots of glitches in it. It's ancient enough to be falling apart. Damn, just look at the kitchen."

There was a touch of criticism in his tone as he looked around at the kitchen she loved so much. She saw his gaze linger on the old-fashioned free-standing sink with the hand pump at one end. Protectiveness for her house rose like a tide within her. "I happen to love my house."

He shook his head. "It looks to me like it needs some major fixing up."

No sooner did the words leave his mouth than a large plastic bowl filled with fruit toppled off the top of the rounded refrigerator to pummel his head. Chase jumped up, cursing and looking around, his body tensed. A plump orange rolled across the floor, stopping when it hit Allison's bare foot. She bent to pick it up. Several apples, a banana, and a few grapes were littered around him. Chase's look of insult was replaced by disbelief. "How the hell did that happen?"

"Burke?" When Chase scowled at her, she shrugged. "He loves this house. He bought it for Rose after they married, sort of a little love nest, though in this day and age the house would be considered huge. But anyway, Burke doesn't take kindly to someone insulting it, so if I were you, I'd be careful what I said."

"Dammit, Allison, that's ridiculous. Besides, I wasn't insulting the house, only commenting on the obvious."

"I guess Burke didn't like your comments."

He shook his head. "The floor slants, that's all. Even the walls are crooked. The bowl was bound to topple sooner or later. It was just coincidence that it happened to fall on me just then."

"If you say so."

He crossed his arms over his chest and leaned back against the refrigerator. It was such an old, squat appliance, his head was above the top now that he was standing. "I'd just gotten off work when I had the feeling you were upset about something. What are you doing up this late, honey?"

She fidgeted, wondering how much to tell him, but one look at his face and she knew he'd just read her mind if she attempted to hold anything back. Still, it was so embarrassing . . .

"Out with it, babe. All this hedging will just make it worse."

She bit her lip, knowing he was right but resenting him all the same. She should have had at least until tomorrow to get her thoughts together. "I couldn't sleep. I kept . . . kept thinking about you and that you'd kissed me and how wonderful it was." His gaze darkened, and his look became almost tactile. She shivered again, this time in reaction. Then she added softly, "And I kept thinking that it was all wrong."

His shoulders tensed while he looked her over from head to foot. "What's wrong about it?"

He sounded gentle again, but determined. Allison cleared her throat. "You don't really want me, Chase. I think Rose has done something to you to make you think you do. It's kind of a long story—"

"Do you have to be at work early tomorrow?"

"No. Not until noon. Sophie's opening it up tomorrow."

"So, we have plenty of time for you to explain this long story to me then, right?"

Unfortunately, she couldn't think of any reason to refuse him.

He smiled. "First, I think we need to call the police about the break-in."

"No!" Even as she said it, the lights flickered crazily.

Chase's expression hardened as he glared at the lights. "Allison, a man was in your house. If I hadn't shown up when I did, you might have been hurt—"

"It was probably just a prankster, you know, a kid messing around because of Halloween."

"It isn't Halloween yet."

"But you know that sort of thing always starts early. And now he's gone, and I'll be sure to double-check the windows every night from now on, so there's really no reason to worry. And no reason to bother the police."

Chase wasn't an easy man to fool. He leaned over and trapped Allison against the butcher block counter. "What's going on, Allison? Why the aversion to the police?"

With him this close, she could see how thick his eyelashes were, could smell him . . .

"Dammit, forget my eyelashes! I'm not trying to seduce you. At least, not yet. I want to know why you won't call the police."

She looked at his incredibly sexy mouth, saw it quirk slightly, then blurted, "Rose and Burke hate having people rummage through the place. It makes them nervous.''

His eyebrows shot up incredulously. ''Nervous ghosts?''

''Well . . . yeah.''

Straightening again, he rubbed the back of his neck. But Allison's gaze dipped over his body—so gorgeous—and her attention got stuck on the fact that he was hard again. His jeans fit him snugly and the soft, faded material hugged that part of his body, making heat explode inside her, her stomach twist in need.

He groaned. ''You're making me crazy, babe.''

''I . . . I think you need to see something.'' She gulped. ''Before we go any farther, I mean.''

He leveled a look on her, hot and expectant.

''It's . . . it's upstairs. In my bedroom.''

He smiled.

Shifting nervously, Allison said, ''I'll just go up and get dressed, and then I'll show you—''

Chase took her arms and half lifted her off her feet. He shook his head. ''I like you just the way you are,'' he whispered, then kissed her gently, showing a lot of restraint. ''You look sexy as hell with your hair pinned up, that soft robe giving me sneak peeks every now and again of that sexy cotton underwear, and your glasses perched on your nose that way.''

She clutched the robe shut to rid the possibility of any further sneak peeks, then asked with a squeak, ''You like the corset cover and drawers?''

''What I've seen of them, yes. Do you intend to model for me?''

Her brain went blank at the idea of dropping her robe for him. He grinned, and she quickly asked, ''You think my glasses are sexy, too?''

Pulling her up flush against him, he said, ''I think everything about you is sexy, and your damned ghosts don't have a thing to do with it.''

"But . . . my glasses?"

He smiled again. "Let's go upstairs, honey. I think I've waited long enough."

Eyes wide, she said, "But I have to show you something before you start getting . . . um . . . amorous."

One large hand stroked her waist. "I'm already amorous."

"Chase . . ."

"You can show me what you think is so important, but it won't make any difference."

Allison turned to nervously lead the way to her bedroom. Under her breath she muttered, "Wanna bet?"

But Chase heard her, and he rewarded her sarcasm with a small smack on the bottom, then left his hand there, caressing. It took all her resolution to climb the stairs. And once they were in her bedroom, she avoided looking at him, knowing if she did, she'd jump his bones and they'd never get around to the important stuff.

Hurrying to her nightstand, she opened the top drawer and pulled out an old, red leather-bound journal. She thrust it toward Chase. "I haven't shown this to anyone else. But I think you should read at least part of it before we do anything."

He stared at the book, stared at her, and then stared at the huge, four-poster mahogany bed, and he sighed. Taking the book, he said, "I sure don't have any complaints on your bed, honey. It looks plenty big enough, and the four posters are giving me some interesting ideas." He looked at her, searched her face, then asked, "How about you?"

She gulped. "How about me, what?"

Nodding toward the bed, he asked, "Any interesting ideas?"

She could just tell he was reading her mind, and what was in it was too explicit for words. Ideas? Heck yes, she had ideas, and all of them had him naked for her pleasure.

Chase grinned, then sat on the edge of the mattress. "Not

exactly the images I'm having, but we'll work on it.'' He held up the book. ''Just as soon as I finish this.''

He settled himself comfortably with a pillow behind his head, at his leisure. With one last glance at Allison, standing there with her mouth open, he murmured, ''You're just damn lucky that I'm a fast reader.''

And there was a promise to those words that had her catching her breath and shivering from the inside out. ''I think I'll go get us those drinks we kept talking about.''

''And something to eat? I'm starved.''

''I'll see what I can dredge up.'' She fled the room, unable to look at him as he read the damning words in the journal that told what his purpose tonight would be.

Five

Allison made four peanut butter and jelly sandwiches and poured two large glasses of milk. Rose and Burke were mysteriously absent, and she had the feeling they were watching Chase read. She felt so bad for them, she sincerely hoped Chase would be able to accommodate what needed to be done.

She'd been downstairs over twenty minutes and decided putting it off any longer was just plain cowardly. Still, she dragged her feet as she went up the steps. Sure enough, when she entered the bedroom, she saw both Burke and Rose hovering over Chase, who still had his nose buried in the journal. Now, however, he'd taken off his boots and had his sock-covered feet crossed at the ankle, with one long arm behind his head. He was so tall, his stretched-out form went from the head of the bed to the very end, when she often felt lost in the incredible size of it.

When she stopped in the doorway, his gaze lifted to her, but otherwise he didn't move. His expression was speculative and lazy.

She cleared her throat, ignoring Rose and Burke. "I, ah,

made you some peanut butter and jelly sandwiches. I hope that's okay?''

He laid the open book on the mattress, spine out, and rolled to his side, propping his head on a fist. He still didn't say anything.

''Um, interesting reading?''

''Very.''

''How far did you get?''

''Far enough to know now what it is you want me to do.''

''Oh.'' Her face heated and she inched closer to hand him the tray of sandwiches.

Chase set it in the middle of the bed, then patted the other side, indicating she should sit down with him. Very tentatively, she slid onto the mattress. She smoothed the robe over her outstretched legs, kept her back straight, and settled her hands in her lap. Just to give herself something to do, she picked up half a sandwich and took a small bite while staring at her bare feet.

Chase, knowing exactly how nervous she was, waited until she had her mouth full to say, ''I'm supposed to be your *grand passion,* right?''

And Allison promptly choked.

Chase made no move to assist her, instead picking up his own half of a sandwich and eating it in two bites while watching her struggle for a breath.

Allison wheezed and snuffled and when she could finally talk without rasping, she asked carefully, ''Did you get to the part about the jewels?''

''Um-hmm. Burke gave Rose jewels as a sign of his love, but when he died with the measles, and she, too, got sick from never leaving his bedside, nursing him until his death, she hid them in the house so none of her damned relatives could steal them. They were, in Rose's words, a symbol of *grand passion,* and neither she nor Burke wanted them getting into the wrong hands.''

Allison toyed nervously with a curl that had escaped her hairpins to hang to her shoulder. "That's right. And in fact, Rose did die of the same thing, only she went a little faster than Burke did because she was already so weak from taking care of him." She glanced at him. "Isn't that sad?"

Chase shrugged. "I suppose a wife who loved a husband would do exactly that. Or vice versa."

His answer obviously pleased the ghosts, considering how the lights twinkled happily and a warm glow seemed to fill the room. This time, Chase didn't even seem to notice the lights. All his attention was on Allison.

She cleared her throat. "They're not really a symbol of everlasting love or anything like that." She peeked at him through her lashes. "But Rose and Burke at least want the female relative who inherits the jewels to be . . . um . . . *passionate*. So far, there's been no one they feel fits the bill, so they've kept the jewels hidden, and they've been stuck here, not wanting to leave until the legacy of the jewels has been passed on."

"So it's an actual legacy of passion?"

Allison wasn't sure if he was teasing or not or if he believed any of it or not. His expression gave nothing away. "When they both died, they left the house to one of Burke's sisters, Maryann. But Maryann's young husband had already died, and she never remarried. Her only daughter, Cybil, inherited next, but she never even seemed interested in the idea of marriage. Rose didn't consider either of them women of . . . um . . . *fire*. Like herself. The women didn't believe in the ghosts and weren't that interested in men. It's Rose's worry about the jewels getting into the wrong hands that's keeping them both grounded on this plane instead of finding peace."

Chase ate another sandwich and drank half his milk, still looking at her in that watchful, curious way, as if waiting to pounce on her. "Rose didn't have any other relatives that suited her?"

Allison shook her head, and two more curls tumbled free. She tried to stick them back up, but somewhere along the way, she'd lost a pin or two. Chase's gaze skimmed her hair, lazy and hot, then came back to her face.

"I, ah . . . no, Rose's relatives all thought she'd married beneath herself, and most of them disowned her. That's why the jewels were so important. Burke had to work really hard to afford something for her that he thought her family would find adequate. But Rose never wanted anything material from him. Still, he bought her this house and the jewels and—"

"And they had a very passionate marriage."

Allison ducked her head. "Yes." Then in a smaller voice, she added, "That was all Rose ever expected from him. But he was an entrepreneur, and it wasn't long before they were actually doing pretty well. Rose had always believed in him, so she wasn't surprised. And it didn't make her love him more. And by then her family all wanted her back, but she was devoted solely to Burke and didn't want to associate with a family that hadn't accepted him based on the wonderful man he was rather than his material worth."

The last sandwich was gone, wolfed down by Chase. She'd only eaten a half. Chase finished his milk, then set the whole tray aside on the nightstand. He reached for Allison, and she stiffened, both in excitement and wary nervousness. She squeezed her eyes shut.

Chase paused, his hand now gently rubbing her arm. "I take it you're willing to fulfill the role of the passionate heir?"

Not quite meeting his gaze, she said, "Rose thinks I would suffice, though truth is, I've never considered myself a particularly passionate woman."

"No?" His fingers trailed up and down her arm, then across her throat.

Allison swallowed audibly. "You'd probably find out soon enough, considering things are progressing right along here, but I'm actually still a . . . a virgin."

Chase froze, then with a growl he dropped back on the bed and covered his eyes with a forearm. "I don't damn well believe this."

Allison peered over at him. He seemed to be in pain, his body taut, his mouth a firm line, his jaw locked. "Chase, are you all right?"

His laugh wasn't at all humorous. "A damned virgin," he muttered.

"Well, I'd hardly consider myself damned. I just never met anyone . . . um, except you . . . that I wanted to get all that involved with. Sexually I mean. And being as you weren't interested . . ."

"This is incredible. A *virgin.*"

"You don't need to drive it into the ground."

Just that quick, Chase was over her, causing her to yelp in surprise before her breath was completely stolen away by the look in his eyes and the pressure of his wide chest over hers. He caught her hands in one of his and raised them over her head, effectively pinning her in place so she could do no more than blink. Through clenched teeth, he muttered, "Do you have any idea what I wanted to do to you?"

She opened her mouth but could only squeak.

Chase gently smoothed her hair away from her face, the careful touch in direct contrast to how he held her and the roughness of his tone. "You know so little about me, sweetheart."

Suddenly the lights turned dazzling bright, making them both squint against the glare. Allison turned her head to look in the corner at Rose—and her mouth fell open in shock. "Oh my God."

Chase shielded his eyes with a hand and barked, "What?"

She turned back to him, so surprised even the light couldn't bother her. "Is it true?"

"Is what true, damn it?"

"What Rose just said."

"I didn't hear her say a damn thing. Are you telling me the ghosts are here with us now?"

He couldn't see them. Allison registered that fact and wondered how she'd ever convince him. Then just as quickly she realized that if what Rose claimed about him was true, he probably wouldn't need much convincing.

Chase pressed his chest closer, effectively pulling her from her thoughts. With a near sneer, he asked, "And what exactly is it that Rose has said about me?"

She almost couldn't utter the words. It took two swallows, and a great deal of effort to whisper, "She says you're . . . you're kinky."

"Kinky!"

Allison nodded. "She says you like to . . . to dominate in bed." Chase's expression was almost comical in his disbelief. "She says that's why you're so choosy about who you sleep with, why you ignored me, because you didn't think I'd get into sex games with you or that I wouldn't indulge your preferences for a little bondage and—"

Chase laid a hand over her mouth, halting the flow of words. He whispered, as if he didn't want anyone else to hear, "There really are ghosts?"

Allison nodded.

The look of disbelief left his face to be replaced by outrage. He glared and thrust himself away from her, rolling off the bed and onto his feet in one quick, fluid movement. He searched the room, but the lights were dim again and Rose and Burke were hiding. Chase turned his accusing gaze on Allison, who hadn't moved a single muscle. She was still too fascinated by the idea of being at Chase's sexual mercy. She didn't know exactly what he'd do or how much mercy he'd have, but she was more than a little anxious to find out.

"Oh no you don't! Don't start trying to distract me again with sex." He pointed a finger at her. "You expected me to make love to you tonight, and you knew all along they'd be watching? You set me up as entertainment for them? Rose and Burke can't just be normal ghosts, oh no, they have to be damned voyeur ghosts!''

A pillow shot off the bed to hit Chase square in the face. He slapped it aside, but another took its place. Chase cursed and said, ''Oh great. Now I've pissed off a ghost! It doesn't get much better than this, does it, Allison!''

Still lying there, feeling a lot more confident about the situation now, Allison grinned and said, ''Then you believe in them?''

Running an agitated hand through his hair, Chase said, ''Why not? It makes as much sense as anything else.''

She looked ready to giggle. Chase realized he was behaving in an absurd way. There was Allison, spread out on a bed, looking so damned ripe and ready it made his teeth ache. And he was provoking ghosts.

It also dawned on him that she didn't seem overly repelled by the idea of him dominating her. In fact, if he was reading her right—and he knew he was—she was intrigued. *Well, how about that.*

Another pillow hit him.

''I think Rose wants you to apologize. She said she kept her eyes closed whenever Burke made love to her, so she sure as certain doesn't have any urge to watch you.''

A reluctant smile curved his mouth. The uniqueness of the situation was finally starting to sink in. ''She said that, did she?''

''Yes.'' Allison hesitated, then added, ''But Burke says it isn't true, that she used to devour him with her eyes when they made love. He says Rose has the most beautiful, expressive eyes in the whole world.''

Despite himself, Chase was touched by the sentimental words. *Ghosts.* And not just any ghosts, but passionate ghosts who joked and teased and loved. Who would have believed it? Allison had to be telling the truth because how else could she have known? And the damned pillows had literally flown off the bed without her help. She'd done no more than lay there, watching him. Waiting.

In a way, he was grateful, because Rose and Burke had given him Allison. Without their interference, he never would have seen the depths of her, and seeing her now, so anxious to take part in everything he wanted to do with her, he couldn't imagine not being with her.

He stepped over closer to the bed. "Tell me something, honey. Did you think to try this with Jack?"

She wrinkled her nose but apparently felt there was no point in lying. "I needed to do something passionate so Burke and Rose could move on. They don't mind being here, but they're not settled. Only they didn't want me with Jack—and I have to admit I'm glad. He's a nice guy, despite how he acted at your bar, and he's been very considerate, very helpful to me. But I couldn't quite get into the idea of . . . of . . ."

Chase felt his heart swell at her pink cheeks and stammering tone. Very gently, he said, "You couldn't imagine being passionate with him?"

She nodded, then added in a whisper, "I tried to think about him that way, but it always ended up being you in my fantasies. And somehow Rose just sort of knew that. She insisted I should go after you, even though I told her it was useless. She even selected the stuff I'd wear—"

"Ah, that killer dress from yesterday?"

She nodded. "Rose found it in the attic."

"Was it hers?"

"No. She told me she really likes this modern, shorter style though." Allison smiled. "To Rose, it seems really risqué."

He lifted a brow and looked her over slowly. "To me, too."

"Really?" She gulped, then forged on. "Rose even picked out the stuff I'm wearing now, but at the time, I didn't know you'd ever see me in it."

He knelt on the bed beside her and without a word, un-knotted the fabric belt to her robe to pull it open. He stared down at the soft-as-silk cotton chemise and drawers. There was a flawless rose crocheted on the neckline of the chemise right above a row of tiny shell buttons, and more roses on the front of each leg. The drawers closed up in front with a wide, intriguing flap—big enough for a man's hand. Chase breathed hard. "You can tell Rose I heartily approve."

Allison smiled. "You just told her yourself."

He stared down at her soft breasts, her small nipples hard and straining against the cotton material. He felt his nostrils flare, felt a twisting in his guts. Without lifting his gaze, he said, "Beat it, guys. Allison and I have some business to attend to."

The lights dimmed so that only a soft glow touched the bed, then a slight warm breeze passed over him and he knew Burke and Rose had given them privacy. He wasted no more time. Straddling her hips, he stared down at her body, at the way her chest rose and fell with her deep breaths. He unbuttoned his shirt and shrugged it off.

Allison groaned at the sight of his bare chest and started to reach for him. He smiled and caught her hands.

"No, I have a certain way I like to do things, sweetheart. And seeing as we'll be doing this a lot—"

"We will?"

"Oh yeah. Definitely. So we might as well start out right." He pulled her into a sitting position and removed her glasses, tossing them aside, then stripped the robe off her shoulders. Holding her wide gaze, he pulled the soft, chenille belt out of the belt loops.

He could feel her trembling, both alarmed and excited. "Don't ever be afraid of me, Allison," he ordered quietly. She licked her lips, eyeing that soft belt, then nodded.

"Good girl." Her acceptance pleased and provoked him. "Now, lie back down."

She was practically panting, her eyes unblinking, her lips parted. Chase couldn't help but smile at her. "Put your arms over your head, as far as you can. Try to reach the top of the bed."

She gulped, but she slowly did as he ordered. Blood rushed through his veins at her compliance. And better still, he could feel her excitement, almost as great as his own. It was like she was his exact match, a perfect soul mate, and his body and mind recognized that fact, making all the feelings more acute, more important.

Taking his time, making the anticipation build, he held her wrists together and looped the belt around them, then tied it to one of the sturdy posts at the top of the bed. When he was confident that the knot would hold, he trailed his fingers down her bare arms to her armpits, then over her collar bone. She shivered slightly, twisting, and he whispered, "No, don't move."

She stilled instantly.

He eyed her taut form. "Are you uncomfortable?"

"No."

That was the tiniest voice he'd ever heard from her, and he recognized the aroused tone. He touched the rose on her bodice. "I'm going to look at your naked breasts now, Allison."

She started to close her eyes, but again, he reprimanded her. "I want you to watch me," he instructed gently.

Her teeth sank into her bottom lip, but she kept her gaze on his face. The tiny buttons slid easily out of the silk loops, and little by little, he bared her. Her breasts were small, some of the fullness removed by her stretched—out position. He felt her touch of embarrassment but refused to allow it to interfere with her enjoyment.

Closing his fingers around one taut nipple, he said, "You're more beautiful than any woman I've ever seen."

She started to speak, and he pinched lightly, tugging. Her words evaporated into a gasp.

"You like that?"

"*Yes.*"

He lifted his other hand, plying both breasts. Her back arched, ignoring his order to remain still, but he let the small disobedience pass. She looked sexy as hell writhing under his hands, and he enjoyed watching her, enjoyed feeling her waves of carnal pleasure pass through him.

Without a single word of warning, he leaned down and replaced one hand with his mouth. She cried out at the sweet, soft tugging and the stroke of his tongue.

"Shhh." He blew softly on her now wet nipple.

"Chase, I can't stand it."

"Yes you can."

He felt her frustration explode, felt her body tensing even more. She was drawn so tight, her entire body jerked when he lightly nipped her with his teeth. He tightened his thighs around her hips, holding her still, forcing her to his will.

He switched to her other breast, treating it to the same sensual torture. Around her nipple, he whispered, "I learned early on how much I love controlling a woman this way, being in charge of her pleasure, mastering her with sex. But I love controlling you even more."

She groaned and tried to lift her legs but couldn't. He smiled. "None of that now. I told you to be still."

"Chase . . ."

"It's all right. Let's see what we can do about these bottoms."

Sitting up, he positioned himself so that her upper thighs, clamped tightly shut, were accessible to his hands. Through the soft cotton, he stroked one finger over the center seam of the drawers.

Allison's head twisted from side to side and she tugged on the bindings of her wrists. It was an instinctive reaction, he knew, to try to free herself even though she didn't really want to be free. He could feel everything she felt, and it doubled his pleasure knowing his own unique form of foreplay drove her crazy with need. She was already wet, the drawers damp where his finger continued to stroke. He was careful to barely touch her, to avoid letting her get too close to the edge.

Her belly hollowed out and her breasts thrust upward as she tried to strain closer to his taunting finger. He watched her face as he asked, "What do you want, Allison?"

"I don't know," she answered on a wail.

"Yes, you do. Don't lie to me."

She squeezed her eyes shut and he lifted his hand. "I told you not to do that."

Gulping air, she forced her eyes open again. "I want you to touch me."

"Like this?" His finger slid down, dipped, came away.

A great shudder passed over. "No. Under . . . under the drawers."

His body rocked with his heartbeat. He slid his hand inside the seam, barely touching her. "Like this?"

She tried to thrust against him, but he pulled away again. "Oh, please."

"Tell me, honey."

"I want . . . I want your fingers inside me."

Her face was bright red, both with frenzied need and embarrassment. Chase was so pleased with her, he leaned down and kissed her mouth hungrily, thrusting his tongue deep, his control almost shattered by her innocently whispered words. When he pulled back again, she stared at him expectantly, her breath held. He opened the seam of the drawers, laying the material wide.

Her feminine curls were dark blonde, damp, and he wanted to taste her very badly. He locked his jaw against the temptation and insinuated one long finger between her folds, feeling her wetness, the warmth of her. His penetration was eased by her excitement, but the tightness of her nearly did him in.

Allison let out a low, keening cry as he forced his finger deeper. "Is this what you wanted, baby?"

She didn't answer, her hips working against him, almost lifting his weight from the bed. He pulled back, watching her face closely, then thrust again, hard and deep.

She screamed with pleasure. *His name.*

Cursing viciously, Chase levered himself to the side. He pushed her legs wide, then held them there when she instinctively tried to close them again. The material of the drawers was in his way and he ripped it open wider, wanting to see all of her, vulnerable, open and ready for him.

Allison was stunned. He could feel her sudden confusion and anticipation. He slipped his finger into her again, then added another. Her hips bucked, and that was all the provocation he needed. Bending down, he took her in his mouth, his tongue hot and rough and insistent. He found her small clitoris and sucked gently.

Allison climaxed with a shock of incredible pleasure that shook her whole body, and he felt it all, felt her trembling, her emotional turmoil, her greed. He cupped her hips, lifting her tighter against his mouth, refusing to let her orgasm fade despite her cries and weak struggles. When finally she stilled, going boneless beneath him, he climbed off the bed and furiously stripped off his jeans and shorts.

"Allison?"

Her eyes barely opened—until she saw he was naked. Then her big blue eyes flared wide, looking him over in great detail. "Are your arms okay, sweetheart?"

She squinted at him, trying to see him more clearly, and he smiled. "I want to touch you, Chase."

"That's not what I asked."

Her legs shifted restlessly, then she nodded. "I'm not in any discomfort, if that's what you mean."

"Good. And don't worry. You'll get your turn. But for now—" His gaze burned over her again. Her legs were still open, her damp curls framed by lacy cotton. "—For now, I like you just the way you are."

He slid a condom on and moved over her. After gently lowering himself onto her, he held her face and said against her mouth, "I like making love to you like this, Allison. Will you mind if we do this often?"

She blinked at him, then mutely shook her head.

"Good. I think I'd enjoy keeping you tied to my bed forever."

"Chase . . ."

He could feel the questions she wanted to ask, questions about the future. But he couldn't even explain to himself what he felt, the rightness of being with her, the intensified pleasure of his naked body touching hers. She felt like his soul mate, like just being with her would be enough to make him whole. He realized how alive he'd felt since last night, when he'd first started sparring with her, wanting her, trying to understand her and get to know her better. He felt unbearably possessive, and he knew the feeling wouldn't go away anytime soon. Probably never.

He kissed her to stop any further questions and calm his own tumultuous thoughts, then reached down and carefully opened her to his first thrust. The bed rocked gently and she moaned into his mouth.

"So tight, honey. So damn wet. God, you feel good."

Her body resisted him at first, then, as if being welcomed home, she accepted him, his size and length, letting him in until he filled her completely. She gasped, arching her neck back, her tied hands curling into fists. Her muscles clenched and unclenched in small spasms, her entire body trembling. It was incredible and mind-blowing, and he couldn't pace himself, couldn't hold back to tease further.

He met her eager gaze as he balanced himself on his elbows and tried to control the depth of his steady thrusts. His jaw locked with the effort, his shoulders straining.

The damned bed, apparently on uneven legs, rocked back and forth with his every movement. He slid his hands over her breasts, felt her nipples tight against his palms, felt her hips lifting, seeking, her muscles squeezing around his erection as he thrust harder and faster, and he was gone, closing his eyes against the too intense pleasure of it.

Nothing in this life had ever felt so right.

He knew then that he couldn't ever lose her.

Six

Long minutes later, Chase became aware of Allison shifting beneath him. Good lord, had he fallen asleep? Appalled, he lifted himself to stare down at her. Her face looked so precious to him, glowing, flushed, happy, and also a little timid. He smiled and kissed her gently, then smoothed her mussed hair, now more unpinned than not. "Are you all right?"

She ducked her head shyly and attempted a restrained stretch. "I'm wonderful."

He looked up at her wrists, then reached to untie her. Lowering her arms carefully, he began to rub them, easing any tenderness she might feel. "I've never made love to a virgin before." He grinned at her. "It was a uniquely satisfying experience."

She gave him a quick glance. "I've never been tied up before. I doubt I would have enjoyed it with anyone else but you."

"And with me?"

"It was . . . incredible. You're incredible."

Chase rolled to his back and pulled her on top. She wasted no time in doing some of the exploring she'd missed out on due to her restraints. Her hands coasted over his chest and she sighed in wonder. "You are one devastatingly beautiful man, Chase Winston."

Satisfaction settled into his bones. Life didn't get any better than having a naked Allison sprawled over him, his body replete from loving her, his mind at peace with the knowledge that she was his.

When she bent to press her soft lips to his chest, he laughed and resettled her against him. "Behave, woman. It's almost four in the morning. Don't you think we need some sleep?"

She made a pouting face at him. "I thought you said I'd have my turn."

"You will. Tomorrow."

She looked his length over greedily. "Will I get to tie you up?"

"Hell no." The frown she gave him now was mutinous, and he kissed her thoroughly in between chuckles. "The effect isn't at all the same, I promise. Besides, there are a few things I still want to do to you."

"Chase . . ." Her eyes were suddenly glowing warmly again.

He touched her cheek. "You're an intelligent, independent, sexy woman, Allison Barrows. I wouldn't have you any other way. Except," he added when she looked flustered at his praise, "in the bedroom. In here, I'm in charge. And I already know how much you like it, sweetheart, so don't bother protesting."

Allison picked up a pillow to smack him with it. The bed teetered. Chase caught the pillow, then frowned. "Has this damn bed always been uneven?"

Still looking disgruntled that he could so easily know her thoughts, she muttered, "Not that I've noticed. But then you probably weigh a hundred pounds more than me. I don't think I could make this bed move if I tried."

Chase sat up and rocked experimentally, then felt the enormous bed wobble again. With a dark suspicion, he climbed off the mattress and looked down at the thick posts supporting the massive bed. Placing one hand on the edge of the mattress, he pushed. The bottom left leg of the bed lifted and fell because it was almost a quarter inch short. Chase noticed a small corner of cloth poking out. He bent down, but it was stuck inside the bottom of the leg. "Allison, come here a minute."

"What is it?" She peered over the side of the bed, squinting in an effort to see clearly without her glasses. Her gaze was on his naked body, not the bed.

Chase shook his head in amusement, then tugged on his jeans so her attention wouldn't be divided. "See if you can pull that piece of material out when I lift the edge of the bed."

Chase was momentarily diverted from his quest when Allison scrambled off the mattress, breasts bare, drawers gaping open and hanging low on her lush hips. He felt a fresh wave of heat and almost forgot his purpose, especially when she went on all fours in front of him, then looked up. "Well?"

Damn. The erotic images that crept into his mind were probably still illegal in some states. It took all Chase's resolution to reach down and heft the edge of the heavy bed. He barely managed to lift it two inches, but Allison quickly tugged out the thin piece of white lawn. It had something written on it.

"What did you do with my glasses?"

Chase reached for the small square of material, but she held it out of reach. "I got it. I want to look first."

"Allison . . ."

She narrowed her eyes at him, still sitting on the floor. "You can control the sex, Chase, but that's all."

With a slow, satisfied grin, he picked up her glasses, then sat on the floor beside her, his back to the bed. "That's all I want to control, babe, so I guess we're in agreement." He slipped the glasses on her nose while she watched him warily.

"Somehow I'm not sure I won that one."

He leaned closer, eyeing a pert breast. "Later, when I'm showing you a position I'm particularly fond of, you'll be more certain."

She reluctantly pulled her gaze away from him and stared at the scrap of material. "Oh my God! Do you realize what this is?"

"Since you won't let me look, no."

"It's the directions to where the jewels are hidden!"

Despite himself, Chase felt the rise of enthusiasm. "A map?"

"Not really. I mean, it just directs us to a certain spot in the basement. And judging by how complicated this is, without the note, we'd never find the jewels."

The laughter erupted, so hearty he almost fell over. Allison smacked his shoulder. "What?"

"Don't you see?" He wiped tears from his eyes and chuckled some more. "The note is hidden in a leg of the bed, and the only way anyone would know about it is—"

Her eyes widened. "If they indulged in some pretty passionate activity in that bed! Otherwise, the bed is so heavy, it would never rock, and no one would ever notice the hidden note."

"Exactly. You have to admit, Rose was pretty damned clever."

Allison jumped to her feet. "Come on."

"Whoa." Chase held her hand and pulled her back to stand between his wide-spread legs. "Don't you think you should put something on first?"

"Why?"

"Because if you don't," he said succinctly, leaning forward to kiss her belly, "I won't be responsible for the fact that we never make it to the basement."

"We won't?"

He stared at one taunting nipple. "No, we won't."

Allison grinned. "You make me feel very sexy, Chase."

"That's because you are very sexy. Incredibly sexy."

"And here I'd always heard virgins weren't supposed to enjoy their first time."

Chase cupped both her breasts, his interest in cold jewels fading quickly. "You're not the average virgin, honey."

She flashed him a coy smile and stepped away toward her closet. "Or maybe you just have a rather unique way about you that . . . stimulates my sexier side." She wiggled out of her drawers and pulled a dress off the rod. She slipped it on over her head. Chase stared.

It was another old-fashioned dress, fitted across the top, calf-length. It had no collar, just sort of scooped down in a narrow *V* over her naked breasts. There were about a zillion little tiny covered buttons down the front that fit into narrow, covered loops. Chase watched her start buttoning and knew it would take an excruciatingly long time to get her back out of that dress. To him, it looked like an opportunity for endless foreplay.

He already looked forward to the effort.

She pulled out chunky heeled shoes, then said with a wink, "These are my Brighton Beach hooker shoes."

Chase narrowed his gaze. "You're naked underneath."

"I know." And just that easily, she sauntered out of the room. "Come on, Chase. I'll show you the way to the basement."

Chase grinned as he followed her, watching the tantalizing sway of her behind in the full skirt.

Allison had the foresight to grab a flashlight from the kitchen. Once in the basement, they had a hard time maneuvering across the packed-dirt floor. The one bare bulb hanging at the bottom of the stairs wasn't adequate to light their way. The basement was musty, the walls damp. They followed the directions carefully, counting off steps, making abrupt turns, steering around the odd pipe. They came to a stop in the far corner where the rough edge of a protruding, homemade laundry chute was just visible from the ceiling beams. Chase stared down at a rusted tub beneath it.

Fascinated, Allison paced around him. "That's the old laundry chute, from when Rose used to have to do the wash with a wringer-type washer. Burke built it for her. When they first got this house, they couldn't afford a maid of any kind, so he tried to make it as organized for her as he could. The chute starts under the sink in the hall bathroom, but a former heir had it boarded up when a modern laundry room was built off the kitchen."

"We need something to climb on," Chase said, moving to stand just beneath the chute. He aimed the flashlight at the square of linen in Allison's hand. "It says the jewels are directly up from here."

The flashlight beam bounced over the long, deep chute, then inside it. About two feet up, taped flat against the inside, was a narrow box. "Well, I'll be damned," Chase whispered slowly.

"Is it the jewels?"

"I think so."

Chase felt Allison's excitement roll over him, and then a thought occurred to him. "Where are Burke and Rose? There hasn't been a single light flicker or breeze or anything. Not since . . ."

Allison froze. "Not since you asked them for some privacy."

Chase gently touched her cheek. "Maybe they realized things would work out."

Allison bit her lip, her eyes huge behind her glasses; then she whispered, "Will they?"

They both jumped when a third voice intruded, amused and condescending. "Don't tell me you actually believe in that ghost nonsense."

Allison whirled around. "Jack?"

Chase stepped forward, forcing her behind his back. Jack

stood at the bottom of the steps beneath the feeble bulb. In his hand was a gun. Very calmly, Chase asked, "Visiting again?"

Jack merely smiled. "Yes. That was me you found in the house tonight. I thought Allison would be in bed, and God knows, I never figured on you visiting that late. But not only did you visit, you stayed." His expression hardened and he glared at Allison, who stood on tiptoe to peek over Chase's shoulder. "After you sent me off without the slightest regret, I never suspected it was so you could have another man over. Somehow I had the impression you were a nice girl."

Allison gasped, but it wasn't the insult that shocked her. "How did you get in? I locked the front door behind you myself!"

"Ah, but first we went to the parlor and talked, and while you were busy explaining to me why we couldn't see each other anymore, I unlocked the window. You thought I was staring despondently, when I was actually planning." He smirked. "Your door is now a little damaged by the way."

"But why?"

"For the jewels, of course. You told me they were here somewhere, I want them. They must be worth a fortune."

Chase said nothing. He was busy watching the bulb over Jack's head dim slightly, then turn bright again. A small smile touched his mouth. "You want the jewels, you bastard? Fine, they're up there."

He pointed at the chute, but Jack just shook his head. "I think you can fetch them down for me. And Allison can come over here by me to wait."

"No."

Jack raised the gun. "I'm not asking, bartender. I'm telling you."

Before Chase could stop her, she darted around him toward Jack. He saw her glance up at the light. He hoped like hell they weren't both nuts, trusting in ghosts that might not even be around anymore.

Once Allison was pinned to his side, Jack said, "Well hurry it up. Get the damned jewels."

Not willing to waste a single moment with Allison so close to the other man, Chase turned over the heavy, rusted-out laundry tub and climbed on top of it. His fingertips could just barely reach the package. He used the edge of the flashlight to work it loose, and finally, after several minutes, it fell down into his grasp.

"Give it to me."

Jack held out one hand, and Chase started toward him, but the gun lifted. "No, toss it to Allison." He shoved Allison forward, and she stumbled, then righted herself. Staring at Chase, she held out her arms. He carefully tossed the heavy package and she caught it in both hands.

Jack grinned and snatched it away from her. "Excellent. You know, I'm thrilled to finally have these, but I swear, Allison, I would have enjoyed having you, too."

She shuddered in revulsion, then sneered at him. "I didn't want you, though, and that's all that matters."

He laughed. "Because your damned ghost said it had to be *passionate?*" He gave Chase a man-to-man look. "Can you believe that nonsense? When she first explained it to me, I went along. I mean, what the hell, she's pathetically naive, and I figured it'd be fun."

Chase turned his molten-hot gaze on Allison. "You actually planned to sleep with this bastard? You went so far as to explain to him why?"

Allison's face turned bright red. "I didn't think you would be . . ."

"Obviously. Hell, Allison, even Zane would be preferable to him."

She lowered her head, chagrined.

Chase inched closer. He didn't know quite what Jack had

planned, but he didn't doubt for a minute that it wouldn't be pleasant.

Before he could take two steps, Jack snarled at him. "That's enough. Both of you, over in the corner."

Allison stared up at him. "What are you going to do?"

"I'm going to lock you both down here until I can get away, that's all."

But Chase knew he was lying. His brow furrowed as he realized exactly what Jack would do. Had Rose let him read another mind? "You're going to set the house on fire."

Jack looked abashed at first, then wary. "How did you know?"

"Rose told me."

Jack began backing carefully up the steps, keeping the gun on Chase the whole time. He tried for a sneer but wasn't overly successful. "I don't believe in ghosts."

The lightbulb flickered, almost going out, then blazing so brightly, Jack had to lift one hand to shield his eyes.

Chase smiled. "Neither did I, until I met two of them."

"It a trick! How the hell are you doing it?"

"I'm not. Rose and Burke are. And if you're smart, you'll put the gun away and give Allison back her jewels."

"Ha!" He had almost reached the top step. "So she can sell them?"

Allison gasped. "I would never do that!"

Jack stopped on the top step. A cold wind blew down the stairs with an eerie whistle. Jack's breath frosted as he shouted, "Stop it!" He lifted the gun. "I don't know how you're doing it, but—"

Suddenly he was pushed forward and his gun hand went up in the air, then resounded with a loud crack as Jack instinctively pulled the trigger. Allison covered her ears, while Chase covered her with his body. Jack lost his balance and tumbled head over heels down the hard stairs, squealing the whole way.

He landed in a heap, the gun skidding a good three feet from him. Chase jumped up and grabbed it, then leaned over Jack. The man was unconscious but alive. Judging by the twist of his right leg, it was broken. He turned to Allison and held out his arms.

With a small gasp, she ran to him, and it felt so good to hold her, to know she was again safe, he knew for certain he'd never let her go.

Suddenly there was a flurry of footsteps from above. *"Chase!"*

Chase lifted his brows. "Cole? What the hell are you doing here?"

Not only Cole filled the open doorway at the top of the narrow stairs. Zane and Mack, both wide-eyed, joined him. "What the hell happened? We walked in, and here's this maniac, holding a gun and shouting."

"It's just Allison's old boyfriend," Chase explained, and though he was still holding her close with one arm, she managed to punch him in the side. He grinned and pulled her closer, then started up the stairs.

Zane peered down at him. "We were rushing over to help, but then . . ." He looked at Cole. "Did you, uh, push him down the stairs?"

Cole stiffened. "Me? I thought you did it somehow."

"Well, no." They both turned to Mack.

"Don't look at me!"

Chase chuckled as he joined his brothers upstairs. "It's a long story."

"Then you better make it quick. I, uh, called the police."

"Why the hell did you do that?"

Cole shook his head, then looked away. "Damned if I know. I was sleeping with my wife— which is usually enough distraction to block out the rest of world—and suddenly I just . . . knew you were in trouble." He shrugged. "It was the strangest damn thing. I called the cops, then Zane and Mack, and we all met outside.''

The kitchen where they had all clustered suddenly glowed with warmth. The brothers looked around. Mack turned to Zane. "I think I'm ready to get the hell out of here."

Zane nodded. "I'm with you." They both turned to go. "If you need us for anything later on, just give a holler."

Mack snickered as they walked out. "First Cole, and now Chase. I can't wait to see what the hell you get into."

"Ha! I hope you're not holding your breath, because you'll be the next entertainment, not me."

"I'm still in school!"

"And I'm having way too much fun to start acting crazy over one particular woman."

Their voices faded as they went through the house to the front door. Cole, Chase, and Allison stared after them.

After shaking his head, Chase raised a brow at Cole. "What about you? You going to stick around?"

Cole sighed. "Well, I did leave a rather warm, willing female in my bed." Then he laughed. "But I suppose Sophie will wait. Hell, I'm anxious to see how you rationalize this to the cops."

It was several hours before the police left, content with the explanation that Jack was simply an insane intruder, the story neatly shored up by his loud claims of ghosts.

Allison and Chase were alone, back in the massive bed. It had taken Chase quite some time to get the dress off her, but the end result had been spectacular. Allison curled up at his side, then sighed.

Chase smoothed her hair. "What are you thinking, sweetheart?"

She froze, turning quickly to look up at him. "Don't you know?"

The expression on his face was comical. "Uh, no."

Her heart pounding madly, she asked, "You can't read my mind anymore?"

Chase frowned, then shook his head. "I don't have a single clue."

"Oh God, Does that mean Rose and Burke are really gone? Have they moved on?"

Chase touched the modest emerald and diamond necklace around Allison's throat. The jewels weren't ostentatious or enormously valuable, except maybe to a collector. But they were beautiful, and she'd cried as Chase hooked the latch at the back of the necklace and helped her to slip the pierced earrings in. The ring was a little big for her fingers, so it was now on Chase's pinkie.

He kissed her cheek. "The jewels are where they belong, sweetheart. It's only right that they find peace now."

"I'll miss them."

"But you still have me."

His small jest didn't make her feel much better. Would she have Chase? A thought occurred to her, and she asked, "Could you read my mind while we were, you know. Making love?"

Her face felt bright red, thinking of the way Chase had lingered over removing the dress, how he'd positioned her on the edge of the bed, how she'd eventually pleaded with him to take her.

He pulled her up over his chest and framed her face with his hands. "Come to think of it, no. But I didn't need to read your mind when your little moans told me everything I needed to know."

She swallowed hard. "Chase? Do you really like my old-fashioned dresses? I mean, there's trunks full of them, left over from one of the spinsters, and I like wearing them and—"

He placed a hand over her mouth. "Hell yes, I like them. They're the type that inspire fantasies, sweetheart. At least, they do when you're wearing them."

She pulled his hand away and asked, "Do you like my

house? Because I don't ever want to leave here. I know it needs some work, but—''

Again, he covered her mouth, this time grinning. ''I like your house. A lot. I think it'd be fun to do some repairs, without changing the looks of things.''

With her words muffled against his palm, she asked boldly, ''Do you like me?''

Very slowly he shook his head. ''No. I don't *like* you.'' Her heart nearly punched out of her chest, and it was all she could do not to wail. The disappointment seemed like a live thing inside her. Then he lowered his hand and kissed her and he whispered, ''I love you. All of you.''

''You love me?''

''I've never known a woman like you, Allison. How the hell could I not fall in love with you? You casually converse with ghosts, defending them, fighting for them. Befriending them. You burn me up in bed, taking everything I have and giving it back tenfold. But you make the rest of the world think you're such a good little girl. You even turned down Zane, and that makes you unique as hell.'' He grinned, tangling his fingers in her hair. ''You're smart and independent and brave, and best of all, you love me, too.''

With tears threatening, she whispered, ''Did you read my mind to know all that?''

He very slowly shook his head. ''No. It's right there, in your pretty blue eyes for me to see. You do love me, don't you, sweetheart?''

''Yes. I have, almost from the first time I saw you.''

''Will you continue to indulge me in the bedroom?''

She bobbed her head. ''Oh yes.''

This time he laughed out loud. ''You sounded awfully eager when you said that.''

She pressed her forehead to his rock-hard shoulder. ''I'm so glad Rose tangled up my dreams and sent them to you.''

"I'm so glad you had the good sense to dream about me in the first place."

They both grinned, and then Chase rolled her beneath him. They neither one noticed, but there was one last, happy flicker of a light—and then it was gone.

PANDORA'S BOTTLE

EILEEN WILKS

One

In a world where magic is real but distrusted, those touched by the Gift have long been persecuted. Many of the Gifted who survived the purges fell victim to the less violent but still destructive tide of social disapproval that began with the Victorian Age, and they turned their backs on their heritage. Now, as another century draws to a close, the wild forces are waking from their century-long sleep.

Dora was barefoot, flustered, and running late. Not her usual self at all. But even the most practical of women could be excused for being excited under the circumstances, she told herself as she knelt on the floor next to her bed. It wasn't every day she left for a passionate interlude with the man she loved.

Their very *first* passionate interlude. At last.

John had asked her to go away with him, to stay for a few days at the old house that had been in his family for generations. He'd said he had something important to tell her, and something important to ask her.

Tingles danced happily over her skin. She knew what that meant. Tonight—or maybe this afternoon—John would propose.

But it wasn't tonight yet. It was morning, and she still didn't have her cat.

Dora dragged her attention back to the present, lifting the eyelet bed skirt to peer beneath her bed. "Come on, Mitzi," she said to the pair of bright green eyes glaring at her from just out of arm's reach. For a second, those glowing eyes conjured wispy traces of the dream she'd had last night: the long, involved, heated dream she'd had more than once lately. The one she never quite remembered upon waking, though it left her body aching and her mind unsettled.

Dora shook her head impatiently. "Mitzi, I'm late. I know you aren't fond of the carrier, but—"

The doorbell rang. She stood and smoothed an imaginary crease from her navy wool slacks, glancing at the clock on her bedside table, which claimed that ten o'clock was still seven minutes away.

Was John early? Seven minutes wouldn't mean much with another man, but John was as dependable as an atomic clock. Maybe he was as eager for this trip as she. That thought sent another tingle of anticipation skittering over Dora as she headed for the living room, but common sense reasserted itself by the time she reached for the doorknob. Given the alternatives—that John was early, or that her clock was slow—it was more likely that her clock was slow.

She stifled a sigh as she opened the door.

"Ready?" John asked.

The sight of him standing at her door gave her a familiar rush of pleasure. He dressed like the conservative, successful stockbroker he was, but the Arabic side of his heritage lent him an intriguing air of mystery that drew Dora in spite of herself. Certainly he did nothing to cultivate such an impression. But his skin was the dusky gold of the desert sand at sunset, and his short hair was as black as the depths of Aladdin's cave. His eyes were black, too, and deeply set beneath eyebrows with a faintly exotic slant.

Appearances were often deceiving, she thought with a fond smile. Beneath that mysterious exterior lurked a perfectly ordinary man. Just her type. "I'm not quite ready," she admitted, stepping aside so he could come in.

Those winged eyebrows lifted in surprise as he bent and brushed a kiss across her lips. "Anything wrong?"

The way she felt after receiving that too-brief kiss was familiar, too. Warm, stirred and . . . something else. Some feeling she'd never quite pinned down. That she couldn't identify the feeling bothered her. Dora was an information specialist. She had nothing against emotions; she simply preferred them to behave reasonably or at least come with a proper label. "My mother called while I was packing."

"Ah." He nodded. "Did you reassure her about our trip?"

"I did my best, but you know Mom. She enjoys worrying." Of course, John didn't know exactly what was worrying Sandra Kitlock about this trip, and Dora didn't plan to tell him. "She's still afraid you might be the kind of man you look like, instead of the kind of man I keep telling her you are."

"Boring, you mean?"

Was it just her imagination or did his smile not quite reach his eyes? "Dependable. We're so much alike, aren't we?" They had both been cursed with unusual looks that all too often led people to expect all the wrong things from them: things like adventure and impulse and excitement.

"I think we are alike," he said very seriously. "I really do."

That seemed an overly solemn response, even for John. "Of course we are. Would you like a cup of coffee before we leave? I haven't unplugged the pot yet." Coffee—hot, dark, ridiculously strong—was one of his few vices.

He followed her to the kitchen. "I'll help myself while you finish packing."

She took the hint that he'd like to get back on schedule and changed direction, going to the refrigerator. "I'm all packed, but Mitzi saw me getting the suitcase out. She darted under the bed and won't come out."

"I doubt that your cat understands the significance of a suitcase."

"Of course she does. She's furry, not stupid." Dora took out a package of lunch meat. "But she won't be able to resist this. Turkey is her favorite."

"I remember," he said dryly, and took a sip of coffee. "It was worth sacrificing my sandwich to make friends with her, though. You're very fond of your cat."

"All of us dedicated spinsters have cats," she said cheerfully as she started for her bedroom. "It's expected." Dora had never thought she would marry. Partly that was due to her appearance; the kind of men who were drawn to the underfed-pixie look didn't interest her. Partly it was due to her independent nature. She'd never felt a driving need to be part of a couple.

He followed her to the living room, where he paused by her stereo. "It's time for the news. Mind if I turn on your radio while you bribe your cat?"

"Go ahead." She knew John wasn't comfortable without frequent updates on market conditions. She knelt beside the bed and tucked the bed skirt up out of the way, dangling the slice of lunch meat enticingly.

For a few minutes Mitzi watched the meat, Dora watched Mitzi, and John listened to the news. Dora could hear the murmur of the newscaster faintly until John clicked off the radio and came to stand in her doorway. "We need to get going. Boynton is only a few miles from the house, and the marchers are supposed to reach there around noon. I don't want to run into them."

"What marchers?" Dora jiggled the lunch meat.

"You must have heard of them. The Supernatural Alliance is staging a big Halloween march on Washington."

"Oh, *them.*" She made a face. "They're demanding their civil rights or something like that, aren't they? I guess I haven't been paying attention. It all seems so—well, so tacky. All those people publicly admitting to their peculiarities."

"Peculiarities?" His eyebrows lifted. "That's one way to put it. Anyway, a couple of hate groups are threatening to stop the marchers any way they can. It could get ugly, and I don't want you nearby if it does."

Mitzi darted out, snatched the turkey—and Dora snatched the cat. "Got you," she said smugly. The cat glared, lunch meat dangling from her mouth, as Dora stood.

John frowned. "Be careful. That animal looks ready to draw blood."

"Mitzi would never hurt me. She's just mad because I won this round." Dora proved her point by stuffing the reluctant cat into her carrier.

"You know, Dora, I thought you would be a bit more tolerant of people like those marchers who are . . . differently endowed."

She glanced at him, surprised, as she latched the carrier. "You sound so politically correct."

"Call it whatever you like. Almost everyone has someone touched by the Gift in their family tree."

"I suppose that's true, but most of us don't go around bragging about it." Dora didn't like the direction the conversation was taking. It reminded her that she'd kept one small secret from the man she hoped to marry. "All this talk of being Gifted—well, it really isn't the sort of thing decent people discuss, is it? Much less draw attention to, the way these marchers are doing."

He didn't speak, his expression so strange and grim that he didn't look quite like the man she knew.

"John?" Troubled, she moved over to him. "You're in a funny mood this morning. Is something wrong?"

He sighed and once again looked normal. Grumpy, but normal. "Nothing. Can we go now?"

She frowned. "You know, I get the impression you aren't looking forward to our trip as much as I am."

"I'm looking forward to part of it very much," he growled, and pulled her to him. His mouth came down on hers.

His sudden ardor startled her. John was always careful about kisses. Neither of them were impulsive people, so they'd agreed to take things slowly. John took that decision seriously—maybe more seriously than Dora wanted him to. They'd dated for four months now, and he'd maintained a steely control over his passions the whole time.

Assuming he really did feel passionate about her.

But that was the reason for this trip, wasn't it? It was time to take their relationship to another level. Dora wrapped her arms around John's shoulders and savored the feel of his body, so solid and strong, against hers. The tingles came back, chasing each other over her skin as he deepened the kiss, his mouth making wonderful promises about what lay in store for them both. Oh, he did stir her. Yet she felt something else, too: some vague frustration, something . . . missing.

Her eyes came open in the middle of the kiss. Something missing?

She squirmed. If he'd just touch her somewhere more intimate than her back and shoulders, put those big, warm hands of his on her . . .

He pulled his head back. "Dora . . ." He sounded hoarse. His hands stayed at her waist, but they gripped her tightly. Urgently. "I have to ask you something."

"Yes?" Maybe he didn't want to wait until they reached his home to take their relationship to the next level. She didn't mind. In fact, she'd be glad. Would he urge her over to the bed? She wondered. Slip the buttons on her lacy white shirt from their buttonholes one at a time while he asked her if she minded if they started their trip later . . . much later?

"Dora, where did you get your name?"

"What?" She blinked.

"Your full name. Pandora Elsbeth Kitlock. It's . . . unusual."

Disappointment crashed through her. She struggled to stay calm. Reasonable. "Get stuffed." She pushed him away, turned, and grabbed the cat carrier, which elicited a protest from Mitzi. "Let's go. If you still want to. If you're at all interested in—in—"

"I'm interested," he growled. "But there's something I— oh, hell." He ran a hand over the top of his head, barely messing up his neat hair. "I'm making a mess of this. Never mind. I know I've confused you. I'll explain everything— everything I can, anyway—when we get to Century's End."

"Talk about odd names," she muttered, starting for the door. "Century's End is beyond unusual, if you ask me. Lots of homes were built at the end of the last century, but their owners didn't feel compelled to name them to reflect the fact."

"Dora." He hadn't moved.

"What?" She paused in the bedroom doorway. She knew she sounded sulky. She didn't care.

"Don't you think you're forgetting something?"

"My suitcase, you mean? For some reason I thought you might get that for me, since I've got Mitzi's carrier, but if you don't think you can manage—"

"No. Your shoes." A smile tugged at one corner of his mouth.

She looked down. "Oh." Good grief. She'd forgotten she was barefoot.

He walked over to her and rested his hands on her shoulders, smiling tenderly. "I am extremely flattered that you forgot them, you know. It does wonders for my ego to think I can have such an effect on you."

Her ego, on the other hand, was flapping around her ankles in tatters. She sighed and set down the cat carrier. "What kind of effect do I have on you?"

"You know the answer to that." He touched his fingertips to her cheek in the lightest of caresses. "I love you."

That brought a smile back to her heart, softening her disappointment. She stood on tiptoe to give him a kiss on the cheek. "I love you, too."

"Do you?" That cloaked, mysterious quality was back, making his eyes darker than ever, impossible to read. "Are you sure?"

Dora realized that he, too, needed reassurance. Maybe he was suffering from some sort of male performance anxiety. After all, they'd both been waiting for this a long time. It would be only natural for him to worry that he might not live up to her expectations. She gave him a gentle smile. "I wouldn't be going away with you if I weren't sure."

"Good. Maybe everything will work out, then." He dropped his hands, looking unexpectedly fierce. "I'll make damned sure it works out."

Poor John. He *was* anxious. She would have to be more patient. "Hey, I'm part of this relationship, too. The way things, uh, work out between us is up to me as much as it is you."

"True." But the twist to his mouth looked more like irony than relief. "Well, let's get going. I'm going to have to bend a few speed limits to get us there before those marchers reach Boynton."

She liked the idea that her rule-abiding John was willing to bend a law or two in order to reach their rendezvous as quickly as possible. She just wished his haste came from an urgent need to get her into his bed instead of such a sound, practical reason. Stifling a sigh, she went to get her shoes.

Two

He hadn't made a complete muddle of things, John assured himself as he turned into the long, winding drive that led to Century's End. Dora had been mad at him earlier, and he didn't blame her. Sexual frustration could put anyone on edge, even a levelheaded woman like Dora. God knew he'd lived in a constant state of arousal and frustration himself the past four months, and it hadn't done his temper any good.

The closer he came to Century's End, the more nervous he felt. So much was riding on this. He badly wanted to do everything right. He'd even called his mother to ask her advice. Now, John loved his sweet, down-to-earth mother dearly, but normally she would be the last person he would consult about his love life.

But no one else knew what he was up against.

She hadn't made him feel any better. "Give her romance," his mother had told him. "I don't care how practical a woman is, she wants to be swept off her feet at least once in her life."

"I don't know how to sweep a woman off her feet," he'd protested.

"I know, dear," she'd said with a sigh. "But your rival does."

He'd rented a bunch of old movies and watched them, trying to figure out what, exactly, women considered romantic. Very little of it made sense to him. He couldn't picture himself abducting a woman. He didn't dare stage any big seduction, not when the consequences were so uncertain. His father had warned him about that before he died: "Don't take her to bed," he had said. "When you find the one woman, the right woman, you'll want her like you've never wanted a woman before. But wait until she's made her choice. That's the way it has to be in our family. The choosing comes first."

Besides, it would have been unfair to Dora to pressure her into bed before she knew the truth. John had tried to come up with other, less perilous romantic deeds, but he didn't know how to ride a horse, much less how to swing Dora up on the saddle in front of him for a passionate kiss. It sounded uncomfortable. Most of the things that were labeled romantic sounded uncomfortable, impractical, or downright dangerous. Sometimes all three.

He'd settled for sending her flowers frequently, but he suspected that flowers, however pretty, didn't qualify as sweeping a woman off her feet.

As they passed the edge of Boynton, he speeded up. The turnoff to Century's End wasn't far now. John hadn't made the trip to his old family home since his mother moved to Florida last year, and he had decidedly mixed feelings about the place.

Memories hid in every curve of the winding road, adding their subtle shading to the brilliant autumnal dress of the trees that formed the small woods near Century's End. Most of the memories connected to this place were pleasant. It was the other ones that disturbed him. Dream memories. All too often lately he had dreamed . . . of seductions, fast horses, and the quick, flashing weight of a saber in his hand. And sometimes . . .

He glanced at Dora, uneasy. Sometimes he dreamed of magic. Magic sliding like wine through his system, prickling his skin from the inside out. *Not surprising*, he told himself. Not the dreams nor their seductive allure. It was very close to Halloween.

Dora was looking straight ahead, which made him smile. Dora was a very straightforward woman. It was one of the things he loved about her, though it meant she might not understand why he'd kept such a large secret from her.

Not that he'd had any choice.

She looked so pretty to him, so *right*. She had the short, rampant curls of a 1920s flapper and the cupid's-bow mouth of a Victorian heroine. He stole another glance or two away from his driving so he could admire the fluid curve of her cheek, the cool, lucid glow of her big gray eyes. She made him think of things like fairy dust and moonglow.

Of course, he would never tell her that. She'd mentioned more than once how tired she was of being compared to a sprite. But she did resemble one.

Perhaps she sensed his attention. She glanced over at him, a tentative smile on her pretty mouth. "We didn't see any sign of those marchers you were worried about."

"No, we made pretty good time. Maybe they were slower than they'd expected to be. I suppose it wouldn't be easy to get a bunch of witches, conjurers, brownies, and sprites to follow a schedule."

"I guess not. Do you think they do have some of the Folk in their march?"

She sounded wistful. He glanced at her, surprised. "Well, none of the sidhe, of course. There hasn't been a confirmed sighting of any of the greater fairy folk on the East Coast for over fifty years, but there's a brownie reservation nearby, and where you have brownies, you're sure to find sprites. I understand a few of the less common nature elementals have settled there, too. The Alliance might well have attracted some of them to their cause.''

''I've always wanted to see a brownie.''

''Not a sprite?''

''I already know what they look like,'' she said wryly.

He smiled. ''Didn't you ever visit a preserve or a reservation when you were little?''

''Mama didn't encourage an interest in supernatural creatures. She isn't prejudiced,'' she added quickly. ''She just thinks we weren't intended to mix.''

''How do you feel about—mixing?'' he asked, careful to sound only mildly interested. They were rounding the last curve in the tree-lined drive. Any second now, they would see Century's End.

She shifted uncomfortably. ''Well, I don't—oh, my God!''

Her exclamation didn't alarm him. The house often drew that kind of reaction. ''It is a little different,'' he said as they pulled up to the front.

''Different?'' She turned a disbelieving face on him. ''It looks like the *Arabian Nights* mated with *Gone With the Wind* and gave birth to—to—''

''My home,'' he finished dryly when she didn't seem able to complete the thought. He turned off the ignition. ''Welcome to Century's End.''

She opened the car door and got out, staring. ''I thought you came from a middle-class background, like me. When you asked me to stay at your family's place on the coast, I was picturing a nice cottage. This . . .'' She turned toward him, gesturing vaguely at the jumble of turrets and domes and antebellum columns behind her. ''I could call this place a lot of things. A cottage isn't one of them. I think I'm intimidated.''

He got out, too. ''My father was an accountant. You can't get much more middle class than that. This . . . inheritance of mine comes from my great-grandfather. Old Hassan was rich, but most of the money's long gone. He set up a trust for the house, however, so that it would be well cared for, no matter what happened to the rest of his fortune." He couldn't keep the bitterness from his voice when he added, "Hassan Ibn Reyen Ben Jamur was very big on passing things down through the generations."

"Hassan Ibn what?"

"His son Anglicized the name to Raven." He popped the trunk and got their suitcases out. Dora's reaction to the visible part of his heritage was not encouraging.

"Oh." There was a loud meow from the backseat. "Goodness, I'm forgetting about Mitzi. Are there servants?" she asked, opening the door and reaching for the carrier.

"A housekeeper. Mrs. Millrow. There's a service that takes care of the grounds."

She sighed. "A housekeeper."

"You don't like the idea of servants?"

"I just thought we'd have more privacy than this." There was a delicate flush high on her cheekbones.

She was thinking about bedrooms, he realized suddenly. About where they would sleep, and the fact that the housekeeper would know where they were sleeping. And it embarrassed her. A woman who was being swept off her feet wouldn't notice any embarrassment, though, would she? Coming to a quick decision, John set the suitcases down and picked Dora up instead. Like that Rhett Butler fellow had done.

Dora and her cat both squawked in surprise. Dora threw her free arm around his neck. The cat growled.

An unromantic man like himself might have trouble sweeping a woman off her feet emotionally, he thought as he started up the steps. But maybe doing it literally was the next best thing.

"What in the world are you doing?" she cried, the cat carrier dangling from one hand while the other one clutched his neck tightly, her nails digging into his skin. He winced.

Dora didn't sound swept off her feet. Maybe his attempt at

romance wasn't having the right effect on her, but it was having a definite effect on him. She felt damned good in his arms. He did wish she would quit wiggling so much, though. The romantic aspect of the act would be spoiled if he dropped her.

"John—John, put me down. I don't know what your housekeeper is going to think!"

"Best to get the embarrassment over with all at once." He reached the door and realized he hadn't the foggiest idea how to get inside. Maybe he could have supported her with only one arm long enough to get the door open if she hadn't had the cat carrier, but that awkward burden kept her from leaning into him enough for him to get her balanced right. He considered the problem a moment. "I think you'll have to knock," he said at last.

Her eyes, wide with disbelief, stared into his from a very few inches away. The slow ache of hunger, never far from him these days, began to pulse through his body. If he lowered his head the tiniest bit, he could take that pretty mouth with his and—

The lips he was studying turned up at the corners. She giggled. "You've gone crazy. Stark, staring bonkers. How am I going to knock when I've got Mitzi's carrier?"

He was ready to consign her cat to the devil and opened his mouth to tell her so. Fortunately, the door opened just then without his intervention, and a sixtyish, six-foot-two amazon in a crisply starched apron stood framed in the doorway.

"Master John," Mrs. Millrow said in scandalized tones. "You put that young lady down right now. I never would have thought—that is—it *is* you, isn't it, Master John?"

He sighed. That Rhett fellow hadn't had to contend with a housekeeper who'd known him since he was a grubby brat. "It's me," he said, obediently easing Dora onto her feet. Dora looked confused, no doubt wondering who else his housekeeper thought he might be. Well, he couldn't explain that.

"Mrs. Millrow, I'd like you to meet my fiancée, Pandora Kitlock. Dora, this is the woman who helped my mother keep me on the straight and narrow when I was younger."

Mrs. Millrow took charge. "You come along with me, dear. I've got your room all ready. You'll like it. It has a nice view of the woods, and we're having excellent color in the leaves this year." She nodded in satisfaction as if she'd personally selected the leaves' autumn palette. "Master John can bring the suitcases in, and you can freshen up while I unpack. I've got a nice luncheon all ready for you—cold cuts and some of that Havarti cheese Master John likes so much, and some lovely grapes from the Greenleys down the road. I don't bake, but my cousin Ada does, so you'll have some nice, fresh bread with your luncheon."

The tide of Mrs. Millrow's loquacity carried Dora to the foot of the stairs before she managed to reply. "That sounds very, uh, nice, but I—"

"Of course, Master John insisted I set luncheon out in the library, of all places. Not that the library doesn't have a lovely view, but what's wrong with the dining room, I ask? But he wants to eat in the library, so I'll bring you along there as soon as you're unpacked. What's your kitty's name? He doesn't sound very happy in that carrier, does he? Master John told me you were bringing a cat, so I have a box all fixed up for him in the adjoining bath."

"My cat is a she, not a he, and her name is Mitzi," Dora said, speaking quickly to get as much in as possible. "John, are you coming?" She cast a beseeching glance back at him.

"I'll get the suitcases and be along shortly," he said with a reassuring smile and escaped out the front door.

In the library of Century's End, John paced.

He hadn't chosen this room for their lunch because he was fond of it. He wasn't, though the collision between East and

West had produced more harmonious results here than in some parts of the house. The hundreds of books showcased by the mellow wood of shelves and paneling looked quite Western but didn't clash with the Eastern elements. The ornately inlaid two-foot-high elephant looked whimsical rather than jarring between the overstuffed reading chairs by the window, and the embroidered cushions that took the place of chairs beside the low library table added a casual note.

There was also an old wooden box sitting on a pedestal near the window. A very old box. An intricately carved box slightly larger than a shoe box, and about the same shape that such a prosaic object would be if stood on end. A box that John paused to glare at.

The tug was stronger here. He'd lived with that annoying sensation most of his life, but usually it was faint enough that he could ignore it. Now, when he stood so close to the bottle inside that box, the tug felt rather like standing near a humming power line.

When he'd taken Dora's suitcases to her room and told her he'd wait for her in the library, Mrs. Millrow had still been there, trapping Dora with her endless flow of talk. John had been glad to get away without explanations. He'd thought it might help to have a few minutes alone to go over what he had to say to her.

Now he just wanted to get it over with. He fingered the box in his pocket—a small, black box with a ring inside. A ring he devoutly hoped Dora would let him put on her finger today.

But first, he had to tell her the truth about himself.

John told himself for the hundredth time that Dora was a reasonable woman. Once she understood his situation, she wouldn't blame him for what was out of his control. But now that the moment was nearly upon him, he couldn't sit down, couldn't quiet his mind. Dora said she loved him, but would a reasonable woman—even one who was in love—commit herself to a man with his heritage?

That was only half his worry. The other half . . . He scowled at the box on the pedestal. Dora loved him. She was *his,* and he wouldn't let anyone take her away from him. No matter what.

No matter *who.*

In a long hallway on the second floor, Dora stopped by a window overlooking a rose garden. A few spent blooms clung to the thorny stalks like ghosts of summer past. Dora sighed. The rose garden, according to some of the information lodged in Mrs. Millrow's endless flow of words, was on the south end of the house, and Dora needed to find the main entry hall, which faced north. She turned to go back the way she'd come.

This house was certainly confusing. Dora had left Mitzi in her bedroom ten minutes ago, along with Mrs. Millrow, who had begun unpacking Dora's things. The cat and the house-keeper had both protested—Mitzi, at the door she'd closed between them, and Mrs. Millrow at Dora's decision to find the library on her own. But Dora hadn't wanted her cat getting lost in this ridiculous sprawl of rooms and halls and stairs, and she hadn't wanted company. She'd felt the need for a few minutes to herself. The only way to get those minutes was to let Mrs. Millrow continue with her self-appointed task, while Dora found her own way to the place where both lunch and John awaited her.

John. Dora smiled mistily. It was typical of his considera-tion that he'd arranged for them to have separate bedrooms so she wouldn't feel pressured into anything. And yet . . . She sighed. She was ready to take the next step in their relation-ship, and it was contrary of her, but she wished he hadn't been quite so considerate this time. It would have been nice to think he wanted her badly enough to toss his scruples to the wind just this once.

But he *did* want her, she reminded herself. That was the reason for this trip.

Was he going to ask her to marry him before lunch, or after?

This was the craziest house, Dora thought as she made her way back to where she'd taken a wrong turn. It seemed designed around a madman's whim, untrammeled by logic. Rooms opened onto other rooms; stairs climbed to turrets or stopped at small, nameless chambers; halls turned or led to other halls that took one off in entirely the wrong direction. But Dora was not easily separated from logic, and eventually she found her way back to the grand staircase. From there she followed Mrs. Millrow's directions until she stood in front of a large, wooden door that ought to belong to the library.

She paused and rested a hand on her stomach. Goodness. Until that moment, she would have said she had no doubts at all about John, yet some tense feeling coiled tighter and tighter in her middle, making her half-sick with nerves.

How silly of her to get bridal jitters before John had asked her to marry him. She dismissed the reaction as unimportant and reached for the doorknob.

In a quiet place bounded by shadows curving over each other in layers of darkness that resembled walls, a man waited. He lounged on cushions embroidered far more beautifully than those in the library where John paced; the glitter of gold thread in those cushions caught light from the many small flames that burned in candles and sconces set here and there in his place. His hair was blacker than the shadows that hemmed him in. His eyes gleamed more brightly than the gold thread embellishing the cushions; green eyes, a green as bright and new and merciless as spring, set in a face that the two people who were about to come together in the library would have recognized instantly.

John's face. Except for those green, green eyes, his features were identical to the ones John saw every day in the mirror. But this man—who wasn't precisely a man, just as the place he waited wasn't precisely a place—couldn't see himself in a mirror. He cast no shadow in the daylight, nor would any surface reflect his image back to him. Not now. Not for the last hundred years.

He was hungry, very hungry, to own both of those things again. Along with all the other marvels of the flesh.

Jack waited patiently for the two people who could set him free to come together. Patience was a trait he'd acquired reluctantly, and he considered it as dull and irritating as most of the virtues. But for the last hundred years he'd had little opportunity to do anything but wait patiently . . . and dream.

In his dreams, he wasn't held captive by the shadows that defined this place. In his dreams, he wasn't alone.

He smiled as Dora opened the door to the library. He saw her in the way one sees in dreams; he felt her in his gut, in the wild stirring of his blood. Oh, she was the best yet: stronger, richer in ways she didn't comprehend, more complete than any of the other brides had been. She was the one. He knew it.

Of course, his alter ego was as drawn to her as he was. That was the way it worked. This was going to be quite a contest, he thought, and he laughed suddenly with the joy of competition, the anticipation of seduction and sex, the intoxication of the moment. His laugh was free and merry and owed little to a century's imprisonment.

Pandora was *his*. She didn't know it yet, and she was going to fight him, but that would only make her eventual surrender sweeter. And his rival's defeat all the more satisfying.

Three

Yes, Dora assured herself as she opened the door, this was definitely the library. The walls lined with books made that obvious. So did the presence of the tall man standing by the opposite wall, his lean shape backlit by the sunlight that poured in through the floor-to-ceiling windows.

He looked so good to her. It worried her sometimes, the degree of pleasure she took in just looking at John. Lust was hardly a sturdy foundation on which to build a relationship, after all. Especially since she suspected that part of her physical fascination with him came from the fact that he looked like everything she didn't trust—things like impulse and mystery and dark, wild pleasures. That was what worried her mother.

But she wasn't her mother, Dora reminded herself, and John's appearance was one reason he was so perfect for her. With John, she could safely indulge the part of herself that was secretly drawn to the forbidden. Because he wasn't really like that, no more than she was.

She cleared her throat and closed the door behind her. Her

stomach was tight with anticipation. "You have a lovely house. Weird, but lovely."

"Thank you." He was painfully polite. "Mrs. Millrow has set lunch out on what passes for a reading table in here. I'm afraid we can't sit in proper chairs, but if you don't mind sitting on a pillow—?"

"It looks lovely." Poor John—he looked so tense. Almost grim. Surely, she thought, he wouldn't be this worried unless he were planning to propose. She smiled encouragingly. "Shall we eat first, or talk? You, ah, did say there was something you wanted to ask me."

He nodded slowly. "First there's something I have to tell you." He turned, going to the low table, where he poured wine from a dark bottle into a heavy, cut-glass goblet. "Maybe you should have a glass of wine first."

She took the glass and looked at the wine dubiously. It was a red wine, heady and fragrant, a shade or two darker than blood. Anticipation was joined by a vague apprehension, making an unhappy muddle in her stomach. "You're making me nervous, John."

"I'm sorry. I . . . Dora, I haven't been entirely honest with you."

Not honest? Hope plummeted, lodging miserably in the confusion in her middle. Her fingers tightened on the heavy glass in her hand. Flatly, she said the worst thing she could think of. "You're married."

Both dark eyebrows flew up. "Married? No—no, it's nothing like that."

"Then what is it?"

"It's . . . hell," he muttered, pacing over to a waist-high pedestal in the corner. "This is even harder than I thought it would be. Dora, I love you. I want . . . I'm hoping . . . I intend to ask you to marry me. But you have to know something about my family first."

Relief washed through her, a giddy tide that lifted her up and left her smiling. "I can't imagine any family secret terrible enough to deserve such a dramatic buildup."

"Can't you?" He stood with his legs apart, as if braced against her reaction. "Try this one. I'm mortal. But my great-grandfather wasn't."

Not mortal? Shock froze her for a moment, but common sense reasserted itself. John was undoubtedly making too much of what was no more than a minor embarrassment, and that was partly her fault. He'd hinted at this, hadn't he? He'd talked about how most people had a Gifted relative somewhere in their family tree, and she'd given him that little lecture on how indecent it was to discuss such things. "What was he? A witch? A conjurer?"

He gave her an impatient glance. "Dora, even you must know that witches and others who are Gifted are entirely mortal. Listen to me: My great-grandfather was not mortal. Not until he married, at least. He was a djinn."

"A *what?*" She couldn't have heard what she thought she'd heard.

"A djinn. Most people here in the West say genie, but the correct pronunciation is djinn."

"I've never heard of someone with a—a *djinn* for a relative." Dora looked at the glass in her hand and considered drinking. No, she decided. She'd better keep a clear head. "I can see why you hesitated to tell me, but—you did say that *you're* mortal, didn't you?"

He nodded grimly. "I plan to stay that way, too."

That was an odd thing to say. Very odd. Foreboding settled in her stomach along with the other knotted feelings. Without thinking, she lifted the goblet and took a deep swallow. Then another. The wine was as sweet as summer, cool in her mouth yet warming as it reached her unsettled middle. "I have the feeling there's more."

"You're right." He didn't look happy about it. "Immortals

can't simply become mortal on a whim. When my great-grandfather chose to give up his powers in order to marry my great-grandmother, there were . . . conditions. A bargain was struck."

"A bargain?" Dora was reminded uneasily of several old fairy tales. Bargains between a mortal and a supernatural being or creature tended to work out poorly for the mortal. "Um—you're not going to tell me there's something in this bargain about your firstborn son, are you?"

"Not exactly."

"Not exactly?" She jerked, making the wine slosh in her glass. *"Not exactly?* John, there is no way on heaven or earth that I'd make any kind of bargain with the supernatural concerning any of my children!"

"Calm down," he said soothingly. "It's not that type of bargain. I just meant that when I have a son, he'll be bound by the same conditions that I am bound by." He started toward her.

Conditions. Bargains. *Magic.* Dora wasn't used to the sharp, sour taste of panic or the shrill sound of her own voice. She set the glass down with a sharp *chink* on the nearest surface, a freestanding bookcase. "What conditions?"

"It's not that bad." He stopped in front of her, looking so worried, so much like the man she'd fallen in love with, that guilt was added to all the other emotions. "I'm doing a lousy job of breaking this to you. Let me explain." He rested his hands on her shoulders.

The warmth of his hands helped smooth her feelings into an unsteady sort of calm, leaving a cold lump of dismay behind. She bit her lip and nodded at him to continue.

"Everything that made Hassan a djinn had to be stripped from him. But it couldn't just be destroyed. You can't destroy immortal qualities. So it—the magical part of him—was put away. Locked up. In there." He nodded at the tall box that sat on the pedestal in the corner. "There's a bottle inside that box."

A chill of superstitious horror sprinted up her spine. "A genie's bottle? Right here? In the room with us?"

"It can't get out. Not unless—well, I could release it. Or you could."

"Me?"

"That's one of the conditions. With every new generation, the choice between magic and mundane must be made again. The firstborn son makes his decision at, ah, puberty, but so must his—my—intended bride. Between now and midnight on All Hallow's Eve, you must choose between me and what's in that bottle." He tried a smile. "You might say that my family has bottled up all our worst impulses."

Dora swallowed. She didn't like this, not any of it, but at least he'd presented her with an easy decision. "Okay. I choose you."

"It doesn't work that way."

"Great." Dora pulled away from John. "I suppose there's some sort of mystical ceremony I'm supposed to go through? Some incantation I have to recite? John, I don't like magic! I don't like any of this!"

"I can't tell you what you're supposed to do, because it's never the same. The form the choosing takes is different for each Raven bride, but there's no ceremony or ritual involved."

"So what form did it take for your mother? Or your grandmother?"

"I can't tell you that."

She paced over to the window and turned to face him. The sight of him still made her heart give a little leap, though his beautiful face looked remote to her in that moment, set and unyielding. "Is that supposed to reassure me? I don't know the rules of this—this *bargain* your ancestor made, but I think you owe me more of an explanation than that."

"I didn't say I won't tell you. I *can't.*"

More magic. "How do I know what's true, then? If there are things you can't tell me, things you are magically bound from revealing, how do I know what's true?" A thought struck her. "Anyway, does all of mysterious choosing even apply? You haven't asked me to marry you. And I haven't said that I would."

He didn't move. "Even if you don't want to marry me, you'll still have to go through the choosing now."

John's quiet voice, his calm, reasonable manner—qualities she normally cherished in him—only made her feel frantic now. Trapped. "But that's not fair! Why? Why would I have to go through this unless I decide to marry you?"

"Because you're the only woman I'll ever love."

He spoke so sadly. So certainly. It broke through her building hysteria as nothing else could have done. She gave a little cry and went to him, and his arms opened for her, then closed tightly around her. "I'm sorry," she said, rubbing her face against the crisp cotton of his shirt and holding him just as tightly. "I'm sorry. I'm acting like such a fool. I do love you, John. I'm just so confused."

"This isn't fair to you. God knows I realized that, right from the start." He rubbed his cheek along the top of her head. "But I couldn't keep any of this from happening. The choosing is triggered by my feelings, not yours. By the choice my heart made for me." He ran his fingers over the nape of her neck, making her shiver, then cupped her face in his hands, gently urging her to look at him. "But there's no danger to you. I promise you that. I would never, ever put you in danger, Dora."

She was going to have to tell him. He wouldn't understand why she'd reacted so strongly unless she did, and Dora realized that she owed him that explanation. Still, she felt a deep reluctance. It was hard to find the right words. "Magic scares me. Anything connected with it scares me."

"I wish I knew how to make this easier on you. I knew

you didn't approve of magic, and I was glad of that, but I didn't realize how deep your feelings about it were.''

''There's something I should tell you, too. When I was twelve—*yipes!*'' She jumped as something rubbed against her ankles—something warm and furry. ''Good grief, Mitzi, you startled me!''

''Your cat?'' John sounded more startled than she was. In fact, he sounded almost horrified. He moved away suddenly. ''Dora, how did your cat get in here?''

''I don't know.'' Since John wasn't holding her anymore, she bent to pick Mitzi up. ''Cats are like that, John. It's no big deal. They're forever getting into places you could have sworn they couldn't.''

He was staring at the purring animal in her arms as if Mitzi were the embodiment of his worst nightmare. ''But the door is closed. It's been closed the entire time. How could she have gotten in?''

John wasn't a cat person, so he wasn't familiar with their habits, but his reaction seemed rather extreme to her. ''Cats are like that,'' she repeated patiently. ''They hate closed doors, so they figure out ways to get through them. I left Mitzi in my room, but she probably escaped when Mrs. Millrow left, then wandered down here while I was trying to find the library.'' She rubbed Mitzi affectionately under the chin. ''She's a clever cat. She must have come in when I did. We just didn't notice her.''

John ran his hand over his short, shiny hair. It fell back into place perfectly. ''I don't think I could have missed seeing her. I don't . . . Dora, wait here.'' He started for the door.

''Where are you going?''

''I'm going to ask Mrs. Millrow if she let your cat out.''

''Good grief, what does it matter? We've got a lot more important things to discuss than how my cat got out of my room!''

''It matters.'' He opened the door but paused before going

through it. "It matters one hell of a lot. I think you brought her here. You *called* her."

"Of course I brought her here. In her carrier. You're not making a great deal of sense, John."

"No, I mean here, to this room. I wondered, given your attachment to that damned cat—but lots of people like cats. Then there was your name. You may not be aware of this, but names are important in how the Gift is passed down. But you seemed so set against magic. I just didn't think it was possible."

"Didn't think *what* was possible?" Dora's growing dismay communicated itself to her pet, who started squirming. Distracted, Dora set her down.

John sighed and turned fully toward her. "If you are touched by the Gift, even slightly, it changes everything." He passed his hand over the top of his head again. This time his hair didn't fall back into place quite so perfectly. "*Everything*. Dora, I asked this once before, but you didn't answer. Where did you get your name?"

"M-my great-aunt. My father's aunt, actually. She was his favorite relative, and he named me for her. But he didn't know she was a—a practicing witch. No one knew, not for years and years, until she was quite old. She was watching a parade one day and absentmindedly levitated. She was trying to see over people's heads, you see, and forgot herself."

He looked sick. "You were named for a witch."

"Yes, but I've stayed away from all that! Ever since the unfortunate incident when I was twelve—"

"Unfortunate incident?" In three quick strides he was standing in front of her. "What happened when you were twelve?"

"It doesn't have anything to do with my cat, John. I didn't summon Mitzi, for heaven's sake."

"Just tell me, Dora." He put his hands on her shoulders. "It's important."

She flushed. "But it's so embarrassing. I was just experimenting, the way girls do sometimes. I didn't think it would really work—and it didn't, not the way I meant it to. Not that that excuses me," she said hastily. "I knew better, but I was only twelve, after all."

"What happened?"

"It was at the big pep rally. I'd wanted to be a cheerleader so badly, but Sunny Fiddleman tripped me when I tried out. She did it on purpose, John!" Remembered indignation flooded her. "She did other things, too, to make me look dumb, but everyone thought Sunny was so sweet, so perfect. No one believed me. Mrs. Jones—the cheerleading coach— even lectured me on how I shouldn't blame others for my own mistakes. So Sunny got the cheerleader spot, and she told everyone I was a liar and a sneak and no one would talk to me, and I—well, I decided to teach her a lesson."

"Keep going," he said grimly.

"I wanted to make her trip in front of everyone, like she'd done to me. Only I was up in the bleachers so I couldn't do it in person, so . . . there's this silly little spell I made up when I was little. It sort of undoes things. Like shoelaces. That's all I meant to happen, but somehow it made *everything* come undone—Sunny's shoelaces, and the braid in her hair, and— and the seams on her clothes."

Dora paused, searching his face to see how he was taking this. *Not well,* she thought. His lips were thin when he spoke. "You used a spell that made her clothes fall off."

She nodded miserably. "They found out, of course. One of the teachers was a Sensitive, and my friend Belle heard me whisper the spell." Belle had been her best friend at the time, but she'd turned Dora in and had never spoken to her again. "It was awful. I was suspended, of course, but that wasn't all. Our house was egged. The neighbors wouldn't speak to us, and my father had problems at his job. He ended up taking a transfer so we could start over elsewhere."

His hands fell away from her shoulders. He spoke flatly, like a judge pronouncing sentence. "Dora, you're a witch."

Stung, she snapped, "No, I'm not! You can't be a witch unless you practice the Craft, and I don't! I learned my lesson!"

"All right, then, you're Gifted but not a witch. Good God, Dora, why didn't you tell me?"

"Because it was the most humiliating time in my life, and it happened so long ago—and you don't have any business looking at me like that, not when you're descended from a djinn yourself!"

He started to pace, muttering as he moved. "Maybe it will be okay. The trauma made you repress the Gift. Maybe that will shield you. Unless it works the other way around, and ignorance leaves you more open . . ."

"Open to what? John, you're scaring me."

He stopped, looked at her without speaking for a second, then came to her and grabbed her hand. "Come here." He tugged her over to the corner where the box waited on its pedestal. "What do you feel?"

"Angry. Embarrassed. Scared. What am I *supposed* to feel?"

"You don't feel anything about this?" He gestured at the box that held the bottle. "No tug, or anything like that?"

She shook her head.

"Thank God." His breath came out in a long sigh. "I know I'm confusing you. It's just—" He broke off and looked at her, his eyes bleak. "My father and grandfather warned me never to become involved with a Gifted woman. I'm not sure why, not exactly, but your Gift will change the way the choosing happens. Especially since it seems to be a talent for undoing things. For unbinding. You've been so sheltered. Dora, are you aware that possessing even a touch of the Gift makes you more vulnerable to the supernatural?"

Now she was really frightened. "I thought my parents kept

me away from all that so I wouldn't be tempted.''

"Temptation, vulnerability—they're pretty much the same thing. Especially now. I don't think ignorance is going to help, though. Dammit, you don't know *anything,* and I don't know enough. We've got to find out more. My great-uncle collected arcane books. You can at least familiarize yourself with some of the basics.''

He tried to drop her hand, but she held on too tightly. She felt small and cold and afraid. "John?''

His mobile brows were drawn together in a frown. "What is it? We don't have much time, Dora. Halloween is tomorrow.''

"Does this change how you feel about me?''

His expression changed, softening into something between tenderness and despair. "No. No, I don't think anything could. But it may change how you feel about me.''

"I don't understand.''

"I know.''

At last he did what she needed him to do. He put his arms around her and held her close. *How odd,* she thought fuzzily. John's kisses left her with a nagging feeling that something was missing, but his embrace didn't. In his arms she felt whole and comforted and complete.

At least, she did until he spoke.

"I'm sorry. I told you there was no danger in this for you, but now I'm not sure.'' He stopped, swallowed. "Dora, I think you should leave me.''

Four

She tried. Dora didn't want to leave John, but she did want rather badly to find out if she *could* leave this place. The magical constraints binding them were supposed to keep her from leaving until she went through this mysterious choosing, but John thought that the existence of her long-suppressed Gift might have affected that. So at three that afternoon, after spending two hours locating and then loading a reluctant Mitzi back in her carrier, Dora got in John's car and tried to drive away.

The car wouldn't start. Nor was she able to walk away from Century's End when John insisted she try that. Her feet simply disregarded her instructions, turning her around and walking her back to him.

John expected her to panic. He was used to the oddities of magical compulsion, having lived with the bargain his ancestor had made all his life, so he was more frustrated than frightened by magical restrictions. But Dora's parents and her early experience of her own Gift had left her deeply frightened of magic, so he expected her to be badly shaken when first the car and then her own legs betrayed her.

Instead, she'd taken a deep, steadying breath and reacted with her usual good sense. "So what do we try next?"

They tried reading. For the rest of the day they skimmed through his great-uncle's collection. Dora approached the task as a distasteful necessity at first, but she seemed to get caught up in the subject as afternoon bled into evening.

Three hours after sharing one of Mrs. Millrow's excellent meals, they were still reading. John sat in one of the armchairs warmed by the fire he'd built in the living room fireplace. Dora was curled up in the other, her cat snuggled up to her, an old edition of Mandelson's *Dictionary of the Arcane* open in her lap, a pad and paper on the table beside her. She'd been making notes as she read.

John had a more advanced text in his lap—Blake's *Comparisons of Eastern and Western Traditions in Magickal Lore*—but as bedtime drew near, he wasn't looking at it anymore. He was looking at Dora, thinking of the small jeweler's box still in his pocket . . . and aching.

This was what he wanted, what he longed for: the two of them together, sharing the quiet time at the end of the day. But it wasn't all he wanted. He wanted mornings with her, too. And nights. Every night, all night, in his bed. But Dora obviously wasn't planning on joining him in his bed tonight. The clothes Mrs. Millrow had so helpfully unpacked for her were still in one of the spare bedrooms. John didn't want them there. He wanted to ask her to move them to his room, where they belonged. Hell, he wanted to grab her and drag her up those stairs right now, push her down on his bed, and prove to her how good they could be together.

It was hard to remember his father's warning when he watched Dora by firelight. The urge to make her his, to put her beyond the claim of any rival, was strong and primitive. But John had had a lifetime of training in resisting the pull of his baser urges, resisting all the wildness that tugged at him— not from inside himself, but from that damned bottle.

He could do this. He could behave like the civilized man that Dora deserved.

He sighed. It was hell being civilized.

She looked up. "Frustrating, isn't it? This is the most imprecise dictionary I've ever seen. Does everything connected with magic have to be so blasted cryptic?"

"Apparently." The ruddy glow of the fire skimmed the curve of her cheek like a lover, making it glow the way he wanted to make her glow. "But there are rules. Sometimes they're couched in obscure language, but they exist, and rules can be approached logically."

"I did notice one rule that was mentioned several times." She hesitated, then closed her book. "Several of these books mention a rebound effect. They say that if a witch uses her Gift to ill-wish someone, the bad luck rebounds on her. Do you think that's what happened with me at that pep rally? That because I tried to do, harm came back on me tenfold?"

"It's possible," he said gently.

She looked troubled. "If so, then the real cause for everything that went wrong wasn't magic. That was just the mechanism, but the underlying cause was my own spite."

"You were only twelve. You didn't know what you were doing."

"That's for sure. If I'd known—" She broke off, shaking her head. "I think my parents were wrong. They wanted to protect me by keeping me from learning anything about magic, but there's no safety in ignorance, is there?"

"Your parents were right about one thing. Magic is dangerous. Unruly. It causes more problems that it solves."

To his alarm, she didn't immediately agree. Instead, her eyebrows drew together thoughtfully, as if she were weighing his statement against some private thoughts. After a moment, she spoke briskly. "My past experiences with magic aren't going to help us much now. Have you had any luck?"

"Not much." None of the experts dealt with the problem

at hand. Probably, he thought wryly, no one had ever wondered what the consequences might be if an untutored witch became involved with the geas-bound descendent of a demagicked djinn.

"I just wish I knew what I was looking for. I don't even know what questions to ask, and certainly none of the books deal with this mysterious choosing. How will we know when it happens?"

"I'll know." Once she chose, truly chose, he wouldn't feel that nagging tug, the link that drew him, at times, into dreams of other times, other places—times and places no mortal man could know. If there was one thing John wanted as much as he wanted Dora, it was to be free of the infernal tie that bound him to what was in the bottle.

"But you can't tell me."

Slowly, he shook his head.

Obviously unhappy, she stood, dislodging her cat. Mitzi meowed a protest. "I guess I'll head upstairs and read in bed awhile."

"Dora—" He stood, too, wanting to tell her everything he wasn't allowed to say. He longed to tell her what she faced— or at least to stop her from going upstairs. Up to bed, where she would dream. John didn't know what form her dreams would take. But he could guess.

She looked at him, waiting.

John tried with all his strength to say what was literally unspeakable because of the binding, but it was hopeless. He shook his head. "Never mind."

Watching her go upstairs without him was the hardest thing he'd ever done. He reminded himself that she hadn't felt any pull from the bottle earlier, when she was standing right next to it. Maybe her long rejection of her Gift would protect her. Maybe she wouldn't dream.

•　•　•

In a place whose curving walls weren't exactly walls, a place linked to the curved sides of a bottle—though what truly bound it was not the simple, earthly porcelain of the bottle—a green-eyed man lounged on embroidered cushions. His head was tilted as if he were listening. After a moment, he shook his head. He could almost bring himself to feel sorry for his rival. John was obviously desperate for reassurance. He must be, to console himself with the idea that Dora wasn't susceptible because she hadn't felt any pull from the bottle.

Jack's smile was slow and wicked. Pandora was definitely susceptible. But he wasn't stupid enough to play any of his tricks on her while she was awake and John was in the room. He didn't want her figuring out what was going on before it was time.

He stood restlessly. It wouldn't be long now. He'd waited for years, waited through three heirs while each found safe, pleasant women to wed. Women who might be tempted—women he had enjoyed tempting—but they had lacked the spark. The hunger. The taste for daring, for risks.

For magic.

But this one was different. He felt it, knew it in his bones—or what passed for bones in this place. She was the one who would set him free. Knowing that the end to his captivity was drawing near made him impatient, his old restlessness a wild, primitive force urging him to act now.

Just a little longer, he counseled himself. Patience was a hard lesson, but not one he could afford to abandon. Not when he was so close. Soon she would sleep. His eyes glowed with anticipation, their spring-bright color unseen in the solitary place where he waited.

Soon.

He came to her in darkness, as he had before, slipping through shifting shades of night to reach her. Though her eyes were closed, she saw him. Knew him. He wore a desert nomad's robe over his beautiful, dusky skin, and his hair was blacker than the night. He stood beside her bed, smiling down at her, his lips curved with silent, laughing promises, his eyes alight with wickedness.

Green eyes, as green as the knowing eyes of a cat.

Heat, thick and drugging, held Dora still for a moment, but there was anticipation, too, for hadn't he come to her like this before? Many times now. Memory held no details of his other visits, only a drift of sensual excitement that slipped through her body just as he had slipped through the darkness to come to her. The covers she'd snuggled under so comfortably when she went to bed were suddenly a burden, hot and stifling. She shifted restlessly.

Some part of Dora knew that she dreamed, so she wasn't surprised when those covers disappeared at the restless movement of her body. She wasn't surprised when her nightgown, too, was suddenly gone, leaving her bare to his gaze.

His smile widened. He liked what he saw, oh yes he did, and the excitement glowing in those odd green eyes excited her in turn. As graceful as a cat, he went to his knees beside her bed. His hands reached for her but didn't touch. Instead they passed over her, stroking only the air above her naked body—yet with that nontouch, her body came alive. Aching. Craving.

She gasped. "I need you," she said, her voice blurry with sleep and hunger. "I need . . ."

"I know, beautiful one," he whispered. "Soon." The small, distant part of her that knew she dreamed was disturbed by his voice. He didn't sound quite like he should. Confused, she shook her head and reached for him. Though he was there, clear to her dreaming eyes, his body calling to her own, her hands couldn't find him. She made a sound of distress.

"Shh." He bent over her. She felt his lips on hers, soft as a whisper: one feathery taste, a breath of spices too exotic for her to name. Just as lightly, the tips of his fingers brushed her breast. Her body contracted around a hard knot of need. "John!" she cried out.

His eyes were still laughing, still hungry, as he stood. "Call me Jack." He winked, and gave her nipple an impudent tweak.

Dora's eyes flew open.

It was still dark. She was still in bed, but she was alone. And her covers still covered her. So did her nightgown. She checked to be sure, running her hands over herself quickly.

It had been a dream, then. Oh, of course it had been a dream! Silly of her to think otherwise, even for a moment. But what a dream! She drew a deep, shuddery breath. Her body throbbed, still caught by the promises of a thoroughly earthly joy that had glowed in his unearthly eyes.

No way was she going back to sleep now. Dora tossed back the covers and sat up, eliciting a sleepy mew from Mitzi, who'd been curled up near her feet. She stroked the cat in apology and felt with her feet for her slippers. The chilly air made her shiver. Her nightgown was a smooth sweep of ivory silk and lace rather than the flannel she usually wore once the weather turned cool. She'd bought it especially for this trip. Now here she sat, alone in bed with her pretty nightgown going totally unappreciated.

Dora sighed and reached for her robe. Her dream confirmed her feelings, but it didn't surprise her. She'd wondered sometimes if there was another side to John, a more playful, adventurous side he kept sternly hidden away, just as she had always suppressed the part of her that was drawn to magic. Certainly there was no surprise about dreaming of him coming to her, then leaving her aching and alone. That was exactly how she felt: aching, alone, and confused. Definitely confused.

She'd had such hopes for this trip, but nothing had happened the way she'd expected. Not all of her emotional muddle stemmed from the bombshell John had dropped about his heritage, either. Some of it involved herself. And magic.

She padded over to the window, thinking about what she'd

learned that day, and twitched back the curtain to look out.

The night wasn't pitch dark the way she'd expected a night in the country to be, not with the moon so nearly full, flooding the land around Century's End with its clear, witchy light. But the nearby woods were dark, steeped in shadows and mystery. Kind of like the books she'd been reading about magic, she thought—clear in some places, spooky and strange elsewhere. But the woods weren't evil simply because they were dark. Dangerous, maybe, because what you couldn't see might hurt you. But not inherently bad.

Maybe magic wasn't bad, either. Maybe it simply *was*.

She wrapped her arms more tightly around herself, unsettled by her thoughts. Her body was still unsettled, too. Aching. Making her think of her dream.

It was odd that she hadn't remembered dreaming of John before. Odd, too, that his eyes were green in her dream. She loved his dark, mysterious eyes. Was there some psychological significance to the color green?

Oh, never mind about his eyes. What mattered was the way the dream had clarified her feelings. Maybe she was a big, fat emotional mess in some ways, but she knew she loved John. She wanted him. He loved and wanted her, too. She was sure of that, even if he was being awfully blasted considerate about not pressing her for intimacy.

Or maybe . . . maybe he wasn't *able* to speak of sexual matters to her, just as he wasn't able to speak of other things.

Things connected to the binding and the choosing.

Excitement kindled in her as she followed that thought to its logical conclusion. John couldn't tell her what form her choosing would take. He also hadn't made any effort to take their relationship to the next stage, to physical intimacy, though he must know she was expecting it. What if there was a connection between these two things? What if making love was the choice she was supposed to make?

It made sense, she thought, her excitement rising. Oh, yes,

it made excellent sense. What more important choice did a woman make, after all, than whether to trust a man with the intimacy of her body? Surely such an act would unite them in a way that no amount of magical hocus-pocus could undo.

And maybe that was the reason for all this choosing nonsense. To create a lasting bond. One that would withstand—well, whatever supernatural test it was supposed to withstand.

She glanced at the travel clock she'd set on the table by her bed. It was very late, almost four in the morning. *Halloween* morning. They had very little time left, and if she was right about what her choice needed to be, John couldn't come to her, couldn't touch her or kiss her. No, if she was right, this was up to her. Dora bit her lip. It would be terribly bold of her to go knocking on his door at this hour in order to invite herself into his room. Into his bed. But it would be exciting, too.

Yes, she realized, the idea of seducing her man made her feel every bit as deliciously restless as her dream had. And even if she were wrong about lovemaking being the choice demanded of her, what was the worst thing that could happen? They might spend a few hours wrapped up in each other, instead of in their problems.

What could be the harm in that? Dora was smiling as she started for her bedroom door.

Five

John was dreaming. Part of him—a small and remote part—was aware that the dream wasn't entirely his, that it drew on experiences he'd never had, images he knew only from other, similar dreams. But the heat and the longing were his own. He dreamed of soft, silken cushions and soft, silken skin, warm skin that heated as it slid over his own flesh in a long, tangled embrace on those cushions. When he pressed a kiss to the rapid pulse in a smooth throat, he smelled musk and exotic spices. John couldn't see the face of the woman he held, but he knew what she was—a houri, a female being with only one purpose: to give a man pleasure.

She was obviously willing to fulfill her purpose, and he was achingly ready for her to do so. He lifted his head, feeling a vague need to see her face.

She was veiled. A light skimming of blue silk covered the lower half of her face, a nearly transparent tease of silk that pretended to hide what it meant to reveal. The eyes above that flirty veil were large, a clear gray in color.

Dora's eyes.

He smiled and reached out to move the veil aside so he could kiss her.

A sharp rapping disturbed his concentration. He blinked, and she seemed to fade, becoming less substantial. Another rap, another blink, and he was alone in bed, staring at a darkened ceiling while someone knocked on his door.

He was still hard. Painfully so.

There was another knock, and he tossed back the covers and stood. "Coming," he said, and wished it were true. He was wearing pajama bottoms, enough covering to greet any visitor rude enough to wake him at—he glanced at the clock. Good God, who could be knocking on his bedroom door at four in the morning? And why? Alarm cleared the last fuzziness of sleep from his head, though it didn't do much to rid him of his lingering arousal as he hurried to the door.

He flipped on the light switch and stood blinking in the sudden brightness when he opened the door.

Dora stood there. She wore a fuzzy blue robe that hung open, revealing a long slice of pale colors—silk the color of moonlight next to soft, fair skin. The glimpse of cool silk and warm flesh sent a renewed surge of heat through him, fogging up his brain again. He frowned. "What is it? What's wrong?"

"Nothing. At least, nothing that wasn't wrong already. I've decided it's time to do something about that."

She didn't look frightened. Nervous, maybe. Her hands twisted together in front of her and she was staring at his chest, not his face.

"I don't understand."

"May I come in?"

Feeling foolish, he stood aside. She walked to the center of the room—which happened to be quite near his bed—stopped, and took a deep breath. Then she turned to face him and shrugged out of her robe, which fell in a fuzzy blue puddle at her feet.

His breath caught. He saw a *lot* of skin now, and not all that much silk. Especially around her breasts. Very little silk there. Plenty of smooth, perfect flesh on display above the lace that edged a brief bodice. He could also see the hard little bumps her nipples made beneath the thin silk.

Dora wasn't as full-breasted as the houri he'd been dreaming about. No, she was, quite simply, perfect. All the blood in his body went south. "You're beautiful," he said, then stopped. That wasn't what he was supposed to say.

She smiled, delighted. "Thank you. I bought the nightgown especially for this trip."

"Yes, but—" With an effort, he dragged his gaze up from her breasts to her face. "But you aren't supposed to be here. Now. In my bedroom."

"Yes, I am." She started for him, and when she moved, he noticed the slit in the long skirt of her gown. He couldn't keep from noticing that slit, since it went all the way up, stopping a thread short of scandal. "This is exactly where I'm supposed to be," she whispered when she reached him, and she put her arms around his neck.

That brought her body into contact with his, and his poor, blood-deprived brain quit working. His hands worked fine, though. They skimmed along her sides, relishing the slide of silk over skin. Her face was tilted up to him. He managed, barely, to avoid the ripe temptation of her mouth and pressed a kiss to her temple. "You don't understand. I'm not supposed to do this," he muttered, skimming another kiss along her cheek.

"Yes, you are."

Her back was almost entirely bare, his hands discovered. Delightfully bare. When he slid his hands up and down all that naked skin, she wiggled all over.

He groaned. "My father said . . ." What had his father said? When she wiggled like that he couldn't think. "We're supposed to wait."

"That's sweet." She pressed a kiss to his jaw. "Unnecessary and rather irritating, but sweet." Another kiss, this one dangerously near his mouth. "Trust me, we do not need to wait any longer."

"He warned me not to . . ." But his hands weren't listening to him any more than Dora was. They were enjoying the feel of her too much. And somehow one of them ended up in her hair so he could tip her head back. Somehow his other hand slipped below her waist to the round, warm curve of her bottom, where it cupped her and pulled her more tightly to him.

Somehow his mouth ended up on hers.

She had such soft lips, slightly parted to welcome him. Such soft breasts that pressed against his chest as she fitted herself up against him. She was a perfect fit. Perfect. Hunger exploded in his belly and went prowling through his body, a hot and hasty beast urging him to take, taste, plunder. Longing woke in his heart, breaking down his control. He thought of the bed only a few steps away, and he deepened the kiss. She had come to him. She wanted this, wanted him. Dora had come to his room to—seduce him?

A shred of sanity remained, enough for that thought to bother him. Dora was a practical woman, sensible and cautious. She wasn't the sort of woman who knocked on a man's door at four a.m. with carnal intentions. What if this wasn't really her idea? He broke the kiss but couldn't pull away completely. Instead, he skimmed his lips along her neck, unable to give up the smell and taste of her. "Dora . . . why did you come to my room?"

"Just keep doing what you're doing," she murmured, her breath catching when his hand slid up to tease the side of her breast. "You'll figure it out in a minute."

Oh, he was getting the idea, all right. He licked the hollow of her throat. No alien spices here. She smelled like the peach-scented lotion he'd given her last month, and he wanted to make love to her with every aching fiber of his body. But . . . "We have to talk about this."

"John, there is a time for talking, but this isn't it!"

She sounded frustrated. And maybe a little hurt. He straightened so he could look at her and sternly ordered his unruly hands to relatively safe positions on her shoulders. Needs pulled at him, muddling his mind. He managed to find enough words to explain. "I'm not supposed to make love to you until after you've chosen."

"But I am choosing. Now. This is my choice." She smiled, but it wobbled uncertainly when he didn't respond. "That's why I'm here. I'm choosing you now, in the most important way a woman can choose a man."

He opened his mouth to tell her this wasn't what was meant by *choosing*—and closed it again. How did he know? He didn't. Sure, his father had warned him against taking the love of his life to bed before she made her choice, but maybe, while that had been true for him, it wasn't true for John. Though the essential choice remained the same, the manner of choosing was different for each bride.

Maybe, he thought, dizzy with the heated demands of lust, Dora was right. Maybe the way to keep his rival out of her head was to take her to bed. Maybe—

"John? You do *want* me, don't you?"

Maybe he needed to stop thinking. "Oh, I want you." And this time when he pulled her to him, his mind, body, and heart all acted together.

Heat met need as their bodies and mouths met. Hunger brimmed, dark and rich, overflowing from his body to hers, from hers to his. The taste of her intoxicated him, sweet and ripe with promises. Her hands were eager, hasty, a little shy as they sped over his chest, his shoulders, one of them clenching in his hair as he deepened the kiss.

And for the first time in his life, John felt free. Truly free. Free to touch her in the ways he had wanted to touch her for so long. Free to forget caution and plunge into the heady river that flowed deep inside him, the river of feelings he'd never dared release—a wild, furious flood that filled him with the hot delight of passion.

John was kissing her as he swept her up into his arms. He kissed her while he carried her the few necessary steps, and he kept kissing her as he followed her down onto the bed where he'd dreamed of a houri with Dora's face.

That dream was forgotten, burned away by the brightness of her reality.

Always, Dora had felt the draw, the physical pull John had for her. Always, she had sensed he was holding back, controlling his passion.

Not any more.

Had she thought something was missing when John kissed her? Not now. Now he held nothing back, and it was more wonderful than she had dreamed it could be, so good it was almost scary, but good-scary, like a roller coaster ride. The wild outpouring of passion from such a careful man thrilled her. His body was big and hard and overwhelmingly male as he sprawled half on top of her, capturing her restless legs with his, his hands everywhere—her hair, her hip, her thigh. She was trapped, pinned, enthralled by his urgency and on fire with her own.

Dora had sometimes thought her cautious John had a hidden reckless streak, but she'd never dreamed he could be so wildly passionate. "John," she gasped as he caressed her breast. "John, this is *much* better than talking."

His chuckle was low and wicked. He didn't speak. His mouth was too busy sliding down her throat, pausing to tease the hollow at its base, then taking a racing trip along her shoulder where his teeth closed over the narrow strap of her gown.

He used his teeth to tug the strap down, pulling ivory silk so low that only lace covered the tip of one breast. He took that lace-covered nipple in his mouth, using his tongue to rasp the lace over the sensitive flesh, and she cried out. Her fingers kneaded his shoulders, then moved lower. When she pulled at his pajama bottoms, he rolled suddenly, carrying her with him. Her nightgown rode up. They tangled—lips, legs, flesh-hungry hands finding heat and building it. She bent, twisted, tugged, and finally got him naked. He pulled on her nightgown. One of the straps broke. He pulled again, and she was naked, too.

Bodies met, rolled, and in a flurry of haste and need, they came together.

Dora's breath caught. He was big and hot and so very *real* inside her. Her mind paused along with her breath, time stopping as her world tilted and reshaped itself, all the pieces of her flowing into a new shape that included him inside her body, inside her being.

John groaned. He didn't move, his beautiful face tense with need, his eyes burning into hers. Black eyes. Gloriously dark, full of passion and love and—a spark of green? Had she truly seen a green as bright as new leaves flash over those dark eyes for a second? "John?" she said uncertainly.

"I'm here." He groaned again. "I'm right here, and I'm not . . ." He punctuated his words with a long, smooth stroke that made her shiver in wonder. "I'm not going anywhere I don't take you."

Downstairs, in a darkened library with no one to see, a lock came undone. A box shook, giving a strange, almost-living shiver, then toppled off its pedestal, one side falling open to spill its contents onto the carpeted floor.

A very old bottle rolled out of the box, coming to a stop against the leg of a table with a dull *thunk*. It was pottery, not glass, that bottle, pottery painted in faded patterns and runes the dusky reds, yellows, and ochers of the earth. Yet for a second it glowed green. Brilliant, soul-piercing green.

Then it shattered.
Free!!! I'm free!

At four-forty that morning, John lay in the darkness of his bedroom with the woman he loved snuggled up against him, sleeping peacefully. His own body was tired and sated, but he couldn't sleep. Not yet.

She was his. Dora was his now, and nothing and no one could take her away. The joy of that was enough to keep him awake, savoring the feel of her in his arms. And the tugging, the endless, terrible temptation of his infernal connection to what was in the bottle, was gone.

He was free at last.

There was no reason to feel sad. He *didn't* feel sad. Oh, maybe there was a twinge or two, but that was perfectly normal. Anyone would feel somewhat disoriented when something that had always been part of him—however unwanted it might have been—was suddenly gone forever.

Dora woke slowly. She wasn't startled by the presence of the large, male body in in bed with her. Waking next to John felt entirely right. He had thrown his arm over her waist; it rested there heavily. One of his legs was snuggled between hers, and his breath stirred her hair. She felt the presence of morning on the other side of her closed eyes, a gentle light summoning her from sleep, and she smiled.

"It's about time you woke up," a cheerful voice said from somewhere near her feet.

Her eyes snapped open. Beside her, John sat bolt upright, taking the covers with him. She had to sit up quickly, too, in order to grab the sheet and yank it up over her bare breasts. She blushed furiously, staring in appalled fascination at the man who stood at the foot of the bed, smiling benevolently at them. It was John—beside her, but also standing there—no, the second man *looked* like John, impossibly so, except for his eyes.

Green eyes, alight with laughter. "You needn't fear for your modesty. I've already seen everything. Quite a glorious sight, too."

Already seen everything? Green eyes?

John was rigid beside her. "Get out! No. You can't get out because you aren't here. You can't be here. You—"

"But I am," the other said gently. "In the flesh. And, oh, but it does feel good to be in the flesh again!" He ran a hand along his other arm, holding it out so he could look admiringly at bare skin and firm muscles.

The gesture drew Dora's gaze from his impossible face to the bare arm he appreciated so much. His shoulders were bare, too, she realized with a jolt. And so was his chest, which looked exactly like John's chest. His lower body was covered, thank goodness, but in a most unusual garment: silk pantaloons cut very full and dyed the brilliant orange of an autumn sunset. They were cinched at the waist with an elaborately worked gold belt.

"I'm sure you have some questions, pretty Pandora," the oddly dressed apparition said. "There are a few things our dear John hasn't told you, aren't there?"

"John?" she whispered. "Do you have a—a brother?" One who is not quite right in the head, perhaps?

"*No.*"

He loaded that one word with such loathing that Dora glanced at him, more startled at that moment by her always-reasonable John than by their weird visitor. His expression of barely controlled fury made her eyes widen.

John's green-eyed unbrother chuckled. "No, we're not brothers, but we are *very* close."

"Then who are you?" she cried. "What are you doing here?"

He gave her a sweet, caressing look—a familiar look. "Have you forgotten, sweetheart? I did introduce myself. I'm Jack."

Jack? Jack, like in her dream? Her eyes widened. Her hand tightened on the sheet.

"You can't be here," John said flatly. "Dammit, I felt it when you were . . . when you left. The tugging vanished."

"As to that," Jack said, sitting on the bed near her feet, "you really should know better. Of course the 'tugging,' as you put it, went away. It was bound to, once I was set free."

"Set *free?*" John's voice was horrified.

"John, what's going on?" Dora's voice rose. "Who is he? Why is he here?"

"This," John said grimly, "is—or was—your choice. Which apparently wasn't what I thought it was, or he wouldn't be here." He turned that look of tightly leashed fury on her. "*This* is what was in the bottle. What I couldn't talk about. But apparently now I can say anything I want. Because you've chosen. You've chosen *him.*"

She shook her head, utterly confused. "No, I didn't. I mean—he was just a dream, and I thought he was you, and dreams don't count! And what do you mean, *this* is what was in the bottle?" The hand that wasn't clutching the sheet gestured in the general direction of their unwanted visitor. "John, this isn't bunch of bad impulses and leftover magic! This is a *he!*"

Jack chuckled. "So glad you noticed, sweetheart. Now, we three have some things to discuss, and we don't have much time. It's already the middle of the morning on All Hallow's Eve."

"What the hell does that have to do with anything?" John said, his voice low and bitter. "You're here. You're free. She chose you."

But the other—Jack—was shaking his head. "No," he said softly. "That's not why I'm free. She hasn't chosen yet."

"Yes, I have!" Dora grabbed John's arm, willing him to look at her—but he didn't acknowledge her touch. "I chose John."

Those impossibly green eyes flicked to her face. "I'm afraid you haven't, sweetheart. Not entirely. If you had truly chosen him exactly as he is now, I wouldn't be here. John is right about that. Now, about what's going to happen today—"

John interrupted him. "If she hasn't chosen you, how can you be free?"

"Ah, that was your doing, mostly. You lost control, didn't you? That always lets me slip out for a little while. Of course, you couldn't have done it without Pandora. It was the combination that did the trick. Your loss of control let me out, and her witchy undoing abilities broke the binding completely." He brought both legs up on the bed with him so that he sat cross-legged. The new position made his thigh brush Dora's foot beneath the covers, proving that he was, indeed, there in the flesh.

Her body shocked her by tingling. She snatched her foot away.

"Quite a thorough job the two of did, too," he went on affably. "Pandora is a delightfully passionate creature."

He didn't mean—*surely* he didn't mean what she thought he meant. She thought of the instant when she and John had joined their bodies and his eyes had seemed to flash green, and she shivered. Maybe none of this was really happening. Maybe she was having the most bizarre dream of her life. "I want to wake up," she said plaintively.

Both men ignored her. "You weren't here earlier," John said flatly. "I felt you leave, dammit."

"John, John." He shook his head. "You should know that I'm always around. I haven't much choice, after all, although I can wander a bit farther now that the bottle is broken. As far as Boynton, at least, even without your escort." He grinned. "I can hardly wait to find out what all I can do now, assuming I don't wink out of existence in a few hours. Pandora, my love—"

"You leave her out of this!" John lunged at him.

Dora grabbed John's arm with both hands, then had to grab for the sheet again. Darn him, they were both entirely too naked for him to start jumping around trying to start a fight.

Before John could reach the other man, Jack reacted. There was a tiny *poof* of air, and in the blink of an eye—literally— he was standing on the floor next to the bed instead of sitting on it.

Dora stared. "How did you do that?"

He spoke to John. "I can't very well leave Pandora out of the discussion. She's rather central to whatever happens."

"You intend to use her. You don't care what happens to her."

Dora blinked. "Um . . . John? What exactly could happen to me?"

But John wasn't listening. He was too busy accusing Jack of trickery and evil intentions, and Jack was too busy baiting John, for them to pay any attention to her. While they argued, Dora sat motionless, hugging the sheet to her chest, as naked as she had been a few hours earlier when John had made such fabulous love to her.

Then, she'd been happier than ever before in her life. Now she was miserable. Her lips quivered, but she tightened them. She couldn't do much about her misery. Not yet. Everything had gone wrong this morning, and she didn't know why, and neither her lover nor her—well, whatever Jack was—wanted to do anything reasonable like explain. No, they were too caught up in some male rivalry thing to even remember she was there.

But she could do something about being naked.

"That's enough," she said firmly. When they didn't seem to hear, she said it louder. Much louder. "That's *enough!*"

John stopped talking. Jack stopped smiling. Both stared at her in surprise, as if *she* were the one who had suddenly appeared out of nowhere. "I've had it with both of you! I don't know what's going on, and I intend to find out." She fixed

John with a firm stare. "Soon. But not now. Right now, I am not dressed, and I want to be."

"Listen," John said, "you don't understand what you've done—"

"That's right, I don't. But you're going to explain. Later. Right now, *you*"—she said as she jabbed her finger in Jack's direction—"are going to get out of here and let me get dressed. And I don't want any comments about what you've seen or haven't seen."

Jack's lips twitched. "Yes, ma'am. I'll, ah, find something to occupy myself for a while. But I'll be back." He winked. Then he did that *poof* thing again. One second he was there. The next he wasn't.

"I hate it when he does that," Dora muttered.

John said something under his breath. It sounded like a comment on what Jack might have done that she *did* like.

Not now, she thought. Soon she'd have to deal with John's anger, find out what was going on, and deal with that, too. But right now all she really wanted was her clothes. She glanced around and saw her nightgown on the floor, a pale spill of silk on the dark blue carpet. She thought of the broken strap and how it had gotten broken, and she almost cried.

"It's a little late to worry about covering up," John said coldly. "Jack isn't the only one who's seen everything you've got. Though I suppose he did get a sneak preview, didn't he?"

Dora bit her lip against the sudden hurt and scrambled off the bed, blinking back the gathering tears. Her robe lay on the floor, too, and that's what she grabbed. She pulled it around her, tying the belt tightly. She didn't look at John as she headed for the closed door, afraid the tears would spill over if she saw the same coldness on his face she heard in his voice.

John didn't try to keep her from leaving, and that hurt as much as anything else. "We have to talk," he told her. "Meet me in the breakfast room off the kitchen once you're dressed."

She nodded without turning around, and opened the door.

Mitzi sat right there, looking up at Dora. As if she'd been waiting for her.

Dora looked at her cat's calm, bright eyes—eyes as green as the ones in her dream. The dream that had become all too real. She shivered and hurried into the hall, leaving her pretty nightgown on the floor of John's bedroom, tattered testimony to everything that had gone right a few hours ago. And everything that had gone wrong this morning.

Six

As mornings-after went, John thought grimly as he stared down at the shards of pottery on the floor of the library, this one sucked.

His conscience bit at him over the way he'd spoken to Dora. But conscience alone wasn't enough to stanch the anger that flowed from deep inside, the acid anger of betrayal. Especially when that anger was joined by fear.

He turned and left the broken bottle where it had fallen. It was too late to put the pieces together again. He wondered if it was too late to put back together the pieces of what he and Dora had shared.

To reach the breakfast room he had to pass through the kitchen, where Mrs. Millrow puttered around, putting together a big breakfast he doubted they would eat. He answered her cheery greeting curtly.

In the doorway that opened into the breakfast room, he paused. Normally this was one of his favorite spots. The two tall, east-facing windows made it a pleasant place to sit on a summer morning and watch dawn creep shyly over the estate's well-tended grounds and the untamed woodlands that surrounded them. But it was fall now, not summer. Here and there a maple splashed its crimson against the brooding green of the conifers, but many of the trees were balding, their branches thinly covered as the oncoming cold slowly stripped their color from them.

Dawn was over. It was full day now. Halloween day.

Dora was staring out one of those windows when John paused in the doorway. She wore a sweater the color of sunshine, but there was nothing sunny about the expression on her face when he joined her at the small, square table. She didn't speak, just looked at him, unsmiling. Unhappy, he guessed from the worried crease between her brows. And angry, according to her tightly held lips.

What right did she have to be angry? *She* wasn't the one who'd been betrayed—if not physically, then in the privacy of the heart, where it counted most. Was he supposed to charm her out of her temper? That was his rival's specialty, he thought bitterly. Charm. "I'm not going to apologize," he said abruptly.

Those pretty lips tightened further. "Well, that sets the tone for this discussion nicely, doesn't it? Maybe you don't think you owe me an apology, but you do owe me some explanations."

He ran a hand over the top of his head. "Dammit, Dora, how do you expect me to react? I'm only human. It's obvious now that coming to my room last night wasn't really your idea, but knowing that doesn't do a damned thing to make me feel better."

Her chin tipped up haughtily. "It most certainly *was* my idea."

"Are you telling me you didn't come to my bed after dreaming about *him?*"

She didn't answer right away, but her guilty flush told him how true his guess had been. "I thought it was you."

"Try again," he said coldly.

"So now you think I'm a liar."

He shrugged. "Maybe you fooled yourself. But you had to know the difference, deep inside. My mother did. Right from the first, she knew that whoever she was dreaming about, it wasn't my father."

Her eyes widened. "Your mother? John, are you telling me that your mother dreamed about Jack? And your grandmother, too, I suppose?" She shook her head. "That's . . . well, when I think about what *kind* of dreams——but never mind. Of course your mother didn't mistake Jack for your father. He looks just like you. I've seen a picture of your father. His jaw was longer, and his eyes weren't shaped like yours at all, and——"

"Jack always looks like the heir. Whoever the heir is. He's not exactly fixed, if you know what I mean."

"No, I *don't* know what you mean!"

Poof!

"He means that I'm a changeable sort," Jack said helpfully from where he now sat in the chair next to Dora. "Not constant at all, I'm afraid. Are you feeling better now that you're covered up, sweetheart? You do look delectable in yellow."

Dora's mouth opened, but whatever she would have said was lost when Mrs. Millrow bustled into the room carrying an enormous tray that only a woman of her size could have managed. When she saw Jack, she stopped dead. "Lordamighty!"

The tray teetered, threatening them all with an impromptu presentation of scrambled eggs. Jack leaped to his feet and took it from her. "Careful, darling! I'd hate for anything to happen to this. I can't tell you how much I'm looking forward to your cooking."

"My heavens, but you startled me." The woman patted her chest. "Master John, why didn't you tell me he was back?"

"Back?" Dora's eyes were huge. "You mean you know Jack?"

"Well, of course I do, though it's been years since the last time this rascal showed up, causing all sorts of riot and rumpus. Now, sir, you just put that tray down and have a seat. Try to behave yourself while I set things out.''

Her hands worked as quickly as her mouth and much more efficiently. "I've got some nice bacon here, and the jam is homemade. You'll want to try some of it on your biscuits, Miss Dora. The eggs are fresh. Nice brown eggs—I do think they have more flavor—from the Johnsons' farm down the road, and—Master Jack! Quit snatching bacon like a mannerless child! You can wait long enough for me to get you a place setting.'' So saying, she refilled Dora's coffee, turned, and left.

It was very quiet in the wake of Mrs. Millrow's departure, as if she had sucked up all the words and drawn them with her out the door. But there were words aplenty jumping around in Dora's head. It just took her a minute to string some together in a coherent thought.

She looked at Jack. The baggy orange pantaloons were gone. He wore jeans now, and a blue silk shirt with pirate sleeves, flamboyantly full. She frowned. "Mrs. Millrow knows about you. You've been out of the bottle before.''

"Oh, yes.'' Jack helped himself to Dora's knife and a biscuit, using one to slather the other with butter. "John used to let me out every so often when he was younger. Accidentally, of course.'' He gave John a mischievous glance.

John scowled at him. "You always caused trouble.''

"And you always regretted letting me out.'' The expression that crossed Jack's face then was so fleeting, Dora wasn't sure what it was. Wistfulness? Or hurt? He brightened again immediately. "But we did have fun while it lasted, didn't we?'' He took a huge bite of biscuit and closed his eyes, an expression of bliss on his face.

"Um . . . no offense,'' Dora asked as soon as he'd swallowed, "but just what *are* you? Some sort of spirit?''

"You could say that. You'd be wrong, but you could say it. Mortals don't have the right frame of reference for the likes of me. You might say I'm the part of Hassan that didn't fit neatly into a mortal's threescore-and-ten, plus John's own bottled-up impulses.'' He grinned. ''Here's a recipe for you: Take a handful of immortal memories, stir in a cup of magic, wait a few decades, and voilà!'' He spread his arms. ''Here I am.''

Dora shook her head in disbelief. She was having breakfast with a being made out of a djinn's leftover magic and memories. Shouldn't she be frightened? Yet it was hard to take Jack seriously enough to be afraid of him. ''So you're immortal?''

He looked thoughtful. ''No . . . at least, I don't think I am.''

''Don't you know?''

''Nope. Say, if you aren't going to eat, would you mind if I used your plate?''

She slid her plate over to him, her brow pleating as she glanced from him to John. Nothing made sense, not even her own feelings. She sat there looking at the two of them and she could see how different they were, in spite of the physical sameness, yet she couldn't seem to separate them in her mind. She watched Jack gleefully piling eggs on his borrowed plate, and he felt like John to her. Another sort of John, a more fun and feckless version. Probably not as dependable as *her* John, but awfully easy to like.

Dora bit her lip. She had to stop thinking that way. No wonder John was angry and jealous. Jack wasn't John, and she'd better get her feelings for the two of him—the two of *them*—sorted out.

What would happen if she couldn't?

Mrs. Millrow's entrance cut short that unwelcome speculation.

''I should have known you couldn't behave for two seconds, Master Jack.'' She brought with her a plate, a glass of water, a coffee cup, and silverware, and distributed them briskly. ''Your kitty is in the kitchen, Miss Dora, enjoying a bite of eggs that I saved her. I do hope that's okay?'' she asked, sliding a clean plate in front of Dora.

The question must have been rhetorical, because she continued without a pause. ''Now, don't let this rascal talk you out of anything other than your plate. The last time he was here there was such a fuss! Poor Master John had to take the blame, since no one outside the family knows about Master Jack, of course. But then, that Harold Hopkins always was one to raise a ruckus. Your father put his finger on it, Master John, when he said Harold was more interested in getting his daughter off his hands than in what was best for everyone. Young Letty was something of a handful back then.''

She shook her head disapprovingly while she moved around the table refilling their coffee cups, though whether it was Harold Hopkins's motives or his daughter she disapproved of wasn't clear. ''But that's all water under the bridge, isn't it, now? Letty did settle down in the end. Married a nice young man from Appleton, I hear, an electrical contractor who does very well by her and their two lovely babies, so all's well that ends well.''

Dora listened to the monologue in growing fascination. ''This doesn't upset you at all, does it? I mean, some people would be a bit bothered by Jack and his, uh, unconventional connection to the family.''

''It's not my place to approve or disapprove of the family,'' Mrs. Millrow said firmly. ''Live and let live, that's what I say. Besides, if you'd seen what I've seen at *other* households where I've been employed! Take the Petersons, for example, where I worked before coming to the Ravens. The Edgar Petersons, you know, cousins to the earl. Not that I had anything against young Timothy. Where's the harm, I say, if a man likes to dress up in pretty, lacy things in the privacy of his home? Although he was very particular about his blouses— starch this one, don't starch that one—which was something of a trial. But a nice young man for all that, and I wouldn't have left their employ if it hadn't been for That Woman.'' She paused for breath, glowering at whatever memory That Woman conjured.

Dora wanted to know what That Woman had done to incur the wrath of a woman as placidly tolerant as Mrs. Millrow, but before she could ask, Mrs. Millrow had her breath back. ''Well, now, if that's all, I'll be taking myself off. You did say, Master John, that I might have the rest of the day off to visit my gentleman friend.''

It wasn't a question, and Dora wasn't surprised when John nodded mutely. She suspected very few people disagreed with Mrs. Millrow, if only because they couldn't shoehorn in enough words to do so.

''You be sure and load these dishes in the dishwasher when you're finished, Master John. I'll wash them up when I get back in the morning. There's a nice casserole in the refrigerator for your luncheon and some cold cuts for dinner if you like, but you'd do better to head into Boynton. The steakhouse serves up a nice rib eye, and they keep their kitchen cleaner than most.'' She nodded, having disposed of them as she thought best, and bustled out of the room.

Blessed silence returned. Dora shook her head. ''I wonder what her gentleman friend is like.''

Jack grinned and reached for another biscuit. ''I suspect he's the strong, silent type.''

''We've got things a little more pressing to discuss than Mrs. Millrow's love life.'' John pushed his untouched plate away and reached for his coffee. ''It's Halloween, and midnight is less than fourteen hours away.''

''So what happens at midnight?'' Dora asked.

''I don't know. I can guess, but I don't know.''

If his guesses were as dark and grim as his expression, she wasn't sure she wanted to hear them. ''You know,'' she said thoughtfully, leaning forward to prop her elbows on the table, ''maybe you've made too much out of all this. Apparently

Jack has been out before, and nothing terrible happened.''

John set his cup down. ''Something terrible always happens when he gets out. Usually to me.''

''Yet you kept letting him out.'' She thought of that fleeting expression she'd seen on Jack's face. The one that had seemed wistful, almost hurt.

''Children don't have a great deal of self-control,'' John said stiffly. ''When I was young, I sometimes let my irresponsible impulses get the better of me. When that happened, Jack showed up.''

''What did he look like when you were a child?''

''Just like I looked back then, except for the eyes. That's why I always got the blame for whatever trouble he stirred up.''

She couldn't keep from smiling. ''I can hear you now; 'I didn't do it, my evil twin did.' ''

Jack put down his fork, insulted. ''I am not evil!''

''It's a joke,'' she explained. Jack wore indignation exactly the way John did: The mobile eyebrows lifted slightly, the sexy mouth tight. She did love John's mouth . . . *stop that,* she told herself sternly. That wasn't John's mouth she was smiling at, it was Jack's. She had to focus on the ways these two were separate, not the ways they were the same.

Well, she thought, John would certainly never wear that shirt. ''Where did you get the clothes? Did you *poof* them?''

He grimaced. ''Do you have any idea how hard it is to materialize something out of nothing? Especially items as large and intricate as clothing, although once—but that was long ago. What's left of me since the split is too thin for that sort of showy magic. No, I'm afraid I bought these things.'' He held out an arm, studying the billowing sleeve. ''What do you think? What passes for style these days in men's clothing is pretty dull, though I like the jeans.''

''Where did you buy them?'' John demanded. ''None of

the stores in Boynton are open this early. And what did you use for money?''

"Don't worry. I left something of value in their place. Dora, sweetheart, if you don't want any of that bacon, would you mind passing it my way? I've built up quite an appetite in the past twenty-two years.''

Dora moved the plate of bacon closer to him. "You haven't been out of the bottle for twenty-two years?'' How had Mrs. Millrow recognized him, then?

"It's only been fifteen years or so since the last time I was out, but I didn't eat that time.'' He bit into a slice of bacon with relish. "Until now, when I got out, I couldn't stay long, and I wasn't fully here. I didn't get all the senses. The last couple of times it happened''—he smiled roguishly—"eating wasn't the sensual experience John and I were most interested in.''

Fifteen years ago, she thought, John would have been nineteen. Just the age for giving in to some of those "irresponsible impulses.'' She could make a pretty good guess as to what sort of sensual experience Jack was talking about, especially after Mrs. Millrow's comments about Letty and her irate father. She raised her eyebrows at John. "Sowed some wild oats, did you?''

John flushed. "Never mind about ancient history. We'd do better to focus on what's going to happen between now and midnight.''

Jack spoke between sips of coffee. "I have to admit that I'm curious about that, too. You know, as wonderful a cook as Mrs. Millrow is, I don't believe this coffee is quite as good as what I used to get at the bazaar.''

"Wait a minute,'' John said. "Don't *you* know how this works? What form the choosing will take, and what will happen . . . after she chooses?''

Jack set down his cup. The humor died from his face. When he and John met each other's eyes, their expressions were as eerily alike as their features. "No. I'm not Hassan. I don't know everything he knew, and I'm not sure he knew exactly what would happen once the binding was broken, either. I think you're wrong about one thing, though. The line on the bottle about 'day's end' refers to sunset, not midnight. Midnight is a matter of clocks. The end of the day arrives when darkness takes over from light."

John brought his palm down on the table with such sudden, startling force that the dishes jumped. He closed his hand into a fist. "Why couldn't you have stayed in the bottle? Why did you have to risk everything by using Dora to break the binding?"

"I wanted to be free," Jack said softly.

After a moment, John sighed. "I suppose you had the right to take that risk. Maybe . . ." He looked down at his fist, still resting on the table. "Maybe you had the right to make me take that risk, too. But, dammit all! You had no right to force this on Dora!"

"John?" Dread trickled up Dora's spine. For the first time that morning she reached for John, touching his clenched hand. "What exactly is this risk?"

When he didn't answer right away, Jack cocked his head to one side. "Are you going to tell her what was written on the bottle, or shall I?"

"I will." John looked at her, his eyes as dark as she'd ever seen them. His words came slowly, reluctantly. "There's a verse written on the bottle. Or there was, before it broke. I don't know if it was part of whatever spell or rite Hassan performed, or if he meant it as a warning."

"Just tell me what it said."

"I'll have to translate, because Hassan wrote it in Arabic." He took a deep breath and recited, " 'Where one has been, let there be two—one who waits in shadows, one with a mortal's span beneath the sun. But if on All Hallows' Eve this binding breaks and two stand separate in the sun, then the final choosing must be made—for at day's end there can be only one.' "

Seven

John saw the shiver that traveled over Dora. "Tell me that doesn't mean what it sounds like," she whispered.

Her eyes were huge and horrified, and the anger he'd felt ever since Jack's appearance cracked into pieces and fell away, leaving him hollow inside. Hollow and hurting—for himself, and for her. "It wasn't supposed to be like this," he said quietly. "The choosing—that was supposed to be between me and him, yes. But he was supposed to stay in the bottle, except for the dreams. I never thought it would be this . . . final."

"I'm still supposed to choose?"

The two men looked at each other. "That's what it sounds like," John said reluctantly.

Her voice rose. "And—whoever I *don't* choose—won't exist anymore?" She shoved back her chair and started to pace. "This isn't right. This just isn't right. I won't do it."

When she passed Jack's chair, he stood, too, and laid a hand on her shoulder, stopping her. "Maybe it won't be that bad. Who knows? Old Hassan might have been wrong. He was hardly infallible, or we wouldn't be in this fix. Or maybe the words mean something else."

John tensed. *It's up to Dora who touches her,* he told himself, ruthlessly suppressing the urge to knock Jack's hand away from his woman. *A civilized man doesn't pick a fight over a casual touch.*

"What else can it mean? 'At day's end there can be only one.'" She looked up at Jack, her eyes swimming with tears. "This is impossible. I can't choose you. I'm sorry, but I *can't.* But I can't choose John, either, if that would make you not *be!*"

"We don't know that would happen." His hand slid up along her neck. "And even though you don't think you can choose me, you feel something, don't you? When I touch you like this . . ." He stroked her cheek with his fingertips.

That was no longer a casual touch. John came up out of his chair.

"Or this," he whispered, and bent and brushed his lips across hers.

John heard Dora's soft gasp as he rounded the table. Her eyes were huge with distress, but she wasn't pushing Jack away. No, dammit, she was just standing there letting him kiss her. John's vision was blurry with rage when he grabbed Jack's arm and jerked him away from Dora, and a peculiar shock zinged from the fingers gripping Jack's arm all the way up to John's shoulder.

It was unnerving, but it wasn't enough to stop the fist already swinging toward that maddeningly identical face.

Poof!

John's fist swung through empty air. Jack stood on the other side of the room, shaking his head. "I'm surprised at you, John. I'm supposed to be the impulsive one, not you."

John's whole arm tingled. He scowled. "How did you do that?"

Jack's eyebrows went up. "I didn't think you were interested in that sort of thing. Displacing from one point to another isn't something I can explain, I'm afraid. Think of it as an innate ability, rather like geese flying south for the winter.''

John shook his head impatiently. "No, I meant that shock you gave me when I grabbed you. You never did that before.''

"You never touched me before.''

Never? Puzzlement edged out anger as John searched his memory. Had he never once touched Jack, in all of the times his nemesis had popped up to make his life miserable?

Dora looked from one of them to the other. "No fighting,'' she said. "And no more *poofing*. It makes me nervous. I do not need to be any more nervous than I already am.''

The tingles were fading. John shook his head, setting aside that puzzle in the face of much greater problems. "Dora, I need to talk to you." He glared at Jack. "Privately.''

"It's a deal," Jack said promptly.

"What's a deal?" John asked, suspicious.

"I'll let the two of you have some time alone, and you'll do the same for me. Fair's fair, after all.''

"Forget it. I'm not about to let you spend time with Dora alone.''

Dora frowned. "Um . . . John? Don't you think that's up to me, not you?''

"Good point," Jack said, nodding. "We do want to be civilized about this, don't we, John?" His eyes danced with merriment.

John gritted his teeth. "There's a big difference between civilized and stupid.''

"Is there? I hadn't noticed the—uh-oh.'' Jack tilted his head to one side as if he were listening to something. His eyebrows flew up. "You'd better get the door, Johnny boy. Mrs. Millrow has already left to visit her gentleman friend.'' He grinned at Dora. "I'll see you later, sweetheart.''

Poof!

Dora rubbed her arms as if she were chilled. "What was he talking about? I don't hear the—''

The doorbell rang.

Dora went with John to answer the door, mostly because she didn't want to be alone if Jack *poofed* himself back. Because, in spite of her protest to John, she didn't want to be alone with Jack.

She had let him kiss her. Just a brush of the lips, a quick, gentle kiss, but his mouth had felt familiar. Even welcome. And she'd tingled, damn it. Jack's mouth had made her feel the way she did when John kissed her. Exactly the same, down to that small, nagging sensation of something missing.

Except that she hadn't felt as if anything was missing when John made love to her, had she? Everything had felt entirely right. Perfect. She thought of the instant when John's eyes had flashed from black to green . . . almost as if Jack had been there, too.

Magic, she thought darkly as they reached the entry hall. How could she trust her feelings when magic was involved? And how could she be drawn to a being built out of magic? For that matter, how could she be drawn to anyone at all when she loved John? What kind of person was she?

The doorbell rang again just as John reached the door. He opened it, and a small black shape raced through the opening.

"Mitzi!" Dora called. But her cat was streaking for freedom. She started to go after her. And stopped when she saw who was standing at the door.

Behind her, John sighed and said, "Sheriff Potts. I haven't seen you in quite some time."

"May I come in, Mr. Raven? There have been a couple of complaints."

The sheriff was a tall man, about sixty years old, skinny as a broomstick and almost as wooden. He stepped into the entry hall, but, insisting his business would "just take a minute," declined proceeding into the living room. Dora hovered nearby, wanting to go find her cat but needing to know what had brought a sheriff to John's door.

"You've kept your nose clean a long time," Potts told

John, "at least around here. I don't know what made you pick today of all days to start playing your little tricks again, but you couldn't have timed it worse. After those marchers went through here yesterday, folks are are stirred up about most anything magical."

Dora and John exchanged glances. She could tell that the same thought went through his mind that flashed through hers: *Jack did it.* Whatever *it* was. "Just what did John do?" she asked.

He gave her a cop's slow, measuring stare. "I don't believe we've been introduced, ma'am."

"Sheriff Potts, this is my fiancée, Dora Kitlock."

The sheriff allowed that he was pleased to meet her, and asked John if he wouldn't rather discuss this privately.

"I don't have any secrets from Miss Kitlock, Sheriff."

Surprisingly, that brought a dry chuckle. "If not, you're the first man who could say that honestly. As to what Mr. Raven did, ma'am, nothing too serious. Stupid, but not serious. At least, it wouldn't be if we hadn't had a bunch of outsiders hanging around lately, stirring people up about those marchers. It's the ones with the least sense who get stirred up the worst, too. Mr. Raven picked a bad time to pull schoolboy pranks." He gave John a disapproving look. "I'd have thought you'd outgrown that sort of thing by now, sir."

John wisely didn't comment.

"Mrs. Crowley isn't happy about her chickens," Potts went on. "Not happy at all. She agreed not to press charges as long as you get them all back the way God intended them—though she did say she wouldn't mind if you left the pink ones alone."

"Pink?" Dora said faintly.

He nodded. "Minerva Crowley is partial to pink."

With a little questioning, the sheriff revealed what else John was supposed to have done. Jack had been a busy fellow, Dora thought. In addition to creating Technicolor chickens, he'd freed the animals at the local pound, turned several stop signs upside down, transformed a pit bull into a sheep, and tampered with a statue in the town square. The stone general now bore his horse's head on his shoulders, while the horse wore the general's gloomy face.

As Dora listened, a fascinating picture emerged of John's relationship to the little town of Boynton. Apparently the townspeople all knew about his great-grandfather, if not about Jack. The story of a mighty djinn giving up his powers for love of one of Boynton's daughters had become part of the town's folklore. The sheer romance of the tale might have been why most of the locals were unexpectedly tolerant of what they considered the little magical quirks of the current Raven son.

Potts told John there would be a fine for setting the impounded animals loose, but no charges would be pressed as long as John put everything back the way it had been, with the possible exception of the pink chickens. As he was leaving, though, he gave John a warning. "You'd better stay close to the house for the next few days. Arnie Marshall and a couple others in that crowd have been talking big, and if you show up in town, they'll feel obliged to put their words into action. You shouldn't have turned his dog into a sheep." He shook his head. "I'll admit the animal's a nasty brute—a lot like his owner. There's a few who wouldn't mind having the beast stay a sheep. But Arnie's pretty worked up about it."

John agreed to stay away from Boynton for a few days.

"Good. I'll tell Sue you'll pick up that bit of glass you left at her place later, after the worst hotheads have had time to cool down."

John nodded as if he knew what the man was talking about, and Potts wished them both a good day and left. As soon as the door closed behind him, Dora said, "Good grief. Pink chickens. Mixed-up statues. And what was that 'bit of glass' the sheriff was talking about?"

"Probably a ruby," John said glumly. "Jack likes rubies. Hassan did, too."

"A *what?* Why in the world would he leave a ruby with someone named Sue?" She broke off, her lips tightening on a dreadful suspicion.

John eyed her sardonically. "I ought to let you go on thinking the worst, but the fact is, Sue Jenkins owns a men's clothing store. No doubt Jack thought a small ruby would cover the cost of his jeans and shirt. He's got a child's sense of values."

"The sheriff thinks it's glass."

He shrugged. "The local shopkeepers think those 'bits of glass' are tokens I leave behind when I, uh, shop at unconventional hours. Since my father and grandfather had the same odd habit when they were young, and those tokens have always been redeemed with cash, they treat them as an eccentric sort of IOU. It wouldn't be a good idea for people to think I could zap up a handful of gemstones whenever I wanted."

The possible repercussion made Dora's eyes widen. Greedy criminals might try to make John conjure rubies for them. Then there was the IRS. They did not take a casual view of illicitly conjured wealth that went unreported. "No, that wouldn't be a good idea at all." A thought struck her. "Where did he get the rubies?"

Poof!

"I didn't steal them, if that's what you're thinking," Jack said reproachfully.

"But you said you couldn't materialize things."

He shrugged. "Nothing as large as clothing, but a teensy little ruby isn't that hard. Their crystalline structure has a certain magical simplicity."

John ran a hand over the top of his head. "You've got to put everything back the way it was."

"I knew you would say that. I can't fix the general's head or the pit bull right away."

"Why not?" John demanded.

"Transformation takes too much energy, and I'm all *poofed* out at the moment—as Pandora would say." He smiled at her. "I'm not used to being out this long, and I got a little carried away. I'll recharge overnight, so I can take care of it tomorrow. If I'm still here."

"Dammit," John said, starting to pace. "You see what it's like, having him around? I said he's got the values of a child. Well, he's got the sense of one, too. He'll do anything that comes into his head without a thought for the consequences."

"And you're so busy being an adult you haven't the least idea how to have fun."

"It's not fun to have the sheriff threatening me with jail time if I don't put everything back the way it was."

Jack sighed. "I suppose I can manage the stop signs and the chickens today, but it will leave me completely tapped out."

"You might leave a couple of the chickens pink," Dora said. "The sheriff said Mrs. Crowley liked the pink ones."

"She did?" He looked pleased. "It's nice to have your work appreciated once in a while."

John's mouth twisted scornfully. Dora spoke quickly, before he could say something cutting. "Maybe if you get the chickens and the stop signs back the way they were, the sheriff won't mind waiting until tomorrow for the rest." *If Jack is still around tomorrow to fix things.*

Her unspoken thought seemed to hover in the air. Jack's eyes were just as green as ever, but the laughter was gone. "I'll do that." He found a grin from somewhere. "And then I'll be back to claim a little time with you alone, sweetheart."

Poof.

Dora and John were alone in the entry hall.

Whatever John had wanted to say to her when they were alone, he wasn't saying it. He just looked at her, and meeting his dark, unreadable gaze made her ache. Was he still angry with her? If so, she couldn't blame him. She wasn't happy with herself. "I hope he does put the stop signs back right side up. I'd hate for someone to have an accident."

He shrugged. "Visitors pretty much stick to the main street, which has stoplights. The locals know where the stop signs are. Jack's a real pain sometimes, but he doesn't mean for anyone to be hurt. Inconvenienced a little, but not hurt."

Her eyebrows went up. "Are you defending him?"

"Hardly. He's childish, has no sense of responsibility, and has caused me all sorts of problems over the years. But to be fair, he thinks he has reason for the pranks he pulls. According to him, if the citizens of Boynton hadn't been so hidebound a hundred years ago, so set against everything magical, Hassan wouldn't have had to give up his abilities in order to marry my great-grandmother. And he wouldn't have had to spend all this time locked up."

Something in his face gave him away. "You feel guilty," she said softly, suddenly understanding another reason for John's hostility toward his alter ego. "You've been out, free to enjoy your life, while he's been trapped in that bottle."

"I haven't exactly been free. He's always been there, tugging at me." He sighed. "But you're right. Sometimes I do feel guilty. And now . . ."

Now there was a chance that instead of being locked away, Jack would simply not be. Unless it was John . . . Dora shook her head. She wouldn't choose. She didn't care how all this hocus pocus was supposed to work. If she refused to cooperate, how could it make her? "Do you think he's right about sunset being the deadline, not midnight?"

"Maybe." He ran a hand over the top of his head. "My father told me what he'd been told about the choosing, but he didn't know what would happen if the bottle was ever broken. Apparently Hassan didn't share that information with my grandfather."

"Except for what he wrote on the bottle."

"Yes."

They looked at each other for a long moment. John's mouth twisted. "Dora, I'm sorry. For everything. For putting you in the middle of this mess, and for what I said earlier, too. It wasn't your fault Jack got out, and I shouldn't have blamed you for your dreams. I was wrong."

"John." Her lip trembled. She took one step, then another, and then she was in his arms. They closed tightly around her. "I'm sorry, too," she whispered. "I should have told you about my great-aunt, and—and my Gift."

"It wouldn't have mattered." He rubbed his cheek against her hair. "I would still have fallen in love with you."

His words brought a lump to her throat. "But if I had only told you sooner, you would have been prepared. You might have been able to keep everything from going wrong."

He straightened and looked at her sternly. "Dora, whatever happens, I don't want you blaming yourself. None of this is your fault. Promise me you won't blame yourself."

Because she loved him and wanted to ease his mind however she could, she nodded. Even though she knew it was a promise she couldn't keep.

He smoothed her hair back from her face, looking at her as carefully as if he were memorizing her. Then he bent and kissed her. It started soft, but quickly turned hard and possessive. She clung to him, needing the comfort of his arms and the quick, hot burn of passion. And there was comfort. A deep sense of rightness filled her when he held her. There was passion, too, in the feel of his body, hard and taut with hunger, in the heat licking through her veins as he deepened the kiss.

There was also guilt, a horrid, sour taint of guilt that made her pull away after a moment.

Because once again, there was something missing in John's kiss.

Eight

Jack crouched by the pond at the edge of the Raven property, flexed his wrist just so, and sent the smooth rock he held skimming over its surface. Without magical assistance, the rock only managed a couple of skips before sinking. He grimaced. He shouldn't have used up the last of his reserves on something as meaningless as putting those chickens back to their usual, boring selves. How was he going to charm Pandora into choosing him over John if he couldn't show her a little magic? Dora didn't want to be drawn to magic, but she was. It was the one edge he had over his rival.

She and John were alone now. Completely alone. He hadn't peeked once to see what the two of them were saying . . . or doing. Since he knew what he would be doing if he were alone with her, that thought left a grinding ache of jealousy in his middle.

Jealousy was new to him. He didn't like it. But neither jealousy nor his depleted magic was responsible for stealing the pleasure from what should have been the most joyful day of his life—the day he was finally free.

John was right. He didn't think of consequences.

He straightened. Guilt was also new to him, and even more unwelcome than jealousy. It was such a mortal emotion. He didn't understand it, or why he was experiencing it so sharply now. Wasn't this what he'd wanted, what he'd dreamed of for so many long, captured years? Always before, he'd taken joy in competing with the heir, whoever that heir was. Always he'd enjoyed the challenge, never doubting that victory, when it finally came, would be sweet.

But the joy of competition was missing this time. Because this time the consequences of winning were almost as bad as the consequences of losing.

He didn't want John to die.

Of course, he didn't want to die either. He didn't even know if he could, or what would happen to him if he didn't win this final round in the competition. Would he be banished forever to the half-life of the shadows?

He started walking, having no destination and needing none. Just being in the world was enough. The crunch of leaves beneath his feet was deliciously real, as was the scent of the air, crisp with fall and rich with the humus of the surrounding woods. In spite of the guilt, he didn't want to give this up. He couldn't stand the thought of going back to the dimness of the shadow place, where his existence had been so dependent on the heir that he faded each time the choice was made against him, falling into something like sleep. But in real sleep the identity remained constant. Jack didn't. After each choosing, he would drift in a barely aware state until the new heir was born. Then he'd begin to re-form around the hot, bright flame of mortal life, the memories from before still part of him but vague, ill-defined, nowhere near as compelling as the hunger for new experiences and the crisp lines mortals drew between themselves and their world.

Jack walked through the wealth of sensual experiences brought him by the woods, his head down, and wished he'd paid more attention to those old memories. He could remember some things from before quite vividly—like the feel of a horse beneath him, or the feel of a woman; the kiss of the desert wind; the taste of the dark, bitter coffee served in the bazaar. He could remember the sensual experiences, but he couldn't remember what it was like to *be* Hassan, the thoughts that went with the memories, except as fleeting ghosts that visited from time to time but refused to be summoned or examined.

Maybe, he thought, if he'd worked at remembering more often over the years, he'd know more of what Hassan had known about the binding. Maybe he'd know what he was supposed to do now, and whether there was any way for him to remain in this rich, wonderful world without stealing John's life here away from him.

Maybe he'd know what it was he felt when he looked at Dora, the odd, piercing longing that had so little to do with winning or losing.

The moment he thought of Dora, he stopped, his head tilted to one side. Even without peeking, he could tell that Dora and John weren't together anymore, feeling it in a deep place inside him that had no words nor needed any. Funny. He'd never felt this connection to any of the other brides. But his knowledge that Dora had left John, left the house, came from her, not from his tie to John.

Had she left because she wanted to give him a chance? Was she trying to be fair, to give him some time alone with her—or did she want *him?*

It took no effort for Jack to displace himself from one point to another. Like he'd told John, the act was an innate part of him. It didn't depend on his store of magical energy. But the quick, hard flare of hope—and that other feeling—was so intense that he wavered for a second, flickering between *here* and *there* before he could focus enough to join her.

·   ·   ·

Dora was looking for her cat.

It was a stupid way to spend what remained of the morning. She knew that. Mitzi was important to her, but nowhere near as important as John. But she'd needed to get away, to have some time to herself to think.

Pity it wasn't doing any good. She shuffled through the fallen leaves just inside the woods, pausing now and again to call her cat, unable to sort a single, coherent thought from the muddle of her emotions.

Poof!

"Sweetheart," Jack said, grinning at her from a few feet away. "Were you waiting for me to join you?"

Dora shook her head. Her heart was pounding—from fear or startlement, certainly, not because she was glad to see him.

"Are you sure? I was hoping—" He looked away and shrugged. "It's a beautiful day, isn't it? The sunshine is so warm and bright. It reminds me of that picnic we went on."

"We never went on a picnic."

"Don't you remember?" He started toward her. "I fed you grapes, one at a time."

All at once, she did remember. She remembered *all* the times Jack had come to her in her dreams, not just the most recent one when he'd seduced her into going to John. She remembered a picnic with golden goblets, dark purple grapes, and no ants. She remembered flying on a carpet into the night sky, and looking down on the lights of a small town with nothing between her and the ground but air and a bit of cloth, nothing holding them both up but Jack's cocky grin.

And she remembered laughing. They had had fun in her dreams. Some of their play had been sexual, but not all of it. Not all of it. "You made me forget, didn't you?"

"You didn't want to remember." He placed his hands on her shoulders in a gesture so like John's her breath caught. "You were more free that way. Happier." His smile tilted, becoming crooked. "I liked it when you were happy, so I suppose I encouraged you to forget."

She felt dreamy now, when he touched her, when he smiled down at her like this, his eyes glowing with shared memories. "It wasn't real, though. It was all just dreams."

"Real enough." His hand slid up to stroke her face. "You owe me a kiss, Pandora."

"What?" Startled out of her dreamy state, she jerked her head back.

"You kissed John, didn't you? After I left. Not that I peeked," he said virtuously, "but you must have kissed him. It's only fair that I get a kiss, too."

She shook her head. "This isn't a matter of being fair or taking turns. It's not a game."

"No, it isn't." A shadow passed across his green eyes. "Whatever happens to me or John by day's end will be all too real. Don't I deserve whatever chance a kiss might give me? And . . ." His hand was back, the fingertips beneath her chin tilting her face up, and somehow she couldn't protest. "Don't you deserve one kiss from me, here in the real world, knowing it's me you're kissing?"

Was it his words that held her still, compliant, while his lips came closer? Was it the hint of a plea in his eyes, or the tingling path his fingers traced, or the way her traitorous heart refused to separate him from John that made her close her own eyes as his mouth touched hers again? Whatever the reason, she didn't stop him.

He tasted as sweet as the grapes he'd fed her at their dream picnic, and as crisp as the ozone bite of the air when a storm is ready to break. His mouth was clever and beguiling, waking her body from the pores out with a rush of sensation. But she needed more, needed something else from him, so she lifted her arms and put them around him, trying to find it. He pulled her snugly against him, and he felt hard and strong and right. So right.

His body felt exactly like John's.

She pushed away. "Oh, God." She raised a hand to her tingling lips. They were slightly swollen from his kiss, and she hated herself. "How could I do that? Unless—you made me, didn't you? You used magic."

But he was shaking his head. "No magic."

She believed him. She didn't want to, but deep inside she knew it was true. She'd responded to him all on her own. She turned away, hugging herself miserably.

"Dora?" He touched her shoulder lightly, and there was no seduction in it this time. "What's wrong? Is it so terrible to realize that you want me?"

"I just feel so guilty," she said. "So confused. I came out here to think, to be by myself so I could figure things out, and then you showed up and I—I kissed you. I'm in love with John, but I kissed you."

He was silent for so long she had to look at him again. He stood very close, his eyes shadowed by feelings she couldn't read. At last he spoke. "I didn't mean for you to feel guilty. I didn't realize . . . it's not a good feeling, is it?" he asked sadly. He touched her face—one soft, fleeting touch. "I'll go away and let you think, pretty Dora. Don't feel guilty. It was all my fault."

Poof.

Dora stood alone in the small clearing in the woods, her eyes filled with tears and her mind filled with confusion. How could she be so drawn to two men? Or to one man and one whatever Jack was. She loved John, loved him with everything in her.

No, she thought with sudden, painful honesty. No, not with everything in her. There was a part of her—a sneaking, buried part of her—that loved Jack. A treacherous voice inside that insisted she could have them both, both parts of the man she loved. Oh, she had to stop thinking like that! Jack wasn't another part of John. He was separate.

Wasn't he?

At day's end there can be only one.

Dora heard the words again as clearly as if they'd just been spoken. They seemed to reverberate inside her, shaking something loose, an idea that wasn't solid enough to grasp. She spoke them aloud, hoping to recapture that fleeting thought: "At day's end there can be only one."

There can be only one . . . but it didn't say what would happen to the other, did it? She scowled and tried to remember the rest of the verse. There was something about having to make the final choice when two stood separate beneath the sun . . .

The final choice. Not the bride's choice. She wasn't mentioned at all in that verse.

What if the final choice wasn't hers?

What if her heart was right, and there weren't *supposed* to be two of them, but only one, the man who would have existed if Hassan had never split part of himself off and bottled it up?

It was a wild notion. Ridiculous. She couldn't believe in it, yet it made sense in a way nothing else did. Heart-sense. Dora stood, locked in indecision for a long moment, then she nodded. She had to go back to the house. She had to at least tell John her idea. He needed to know. Even if she was wrong, he needed to know.

She started to turn.

A heavy hand landed on her shoulder. Not John's hand. Not Jack's. Fear froze the rest of her body while her mouth flew open to scream—and another hand, heavy and rough, sealed it shut.

"Got you," a deep voice growled. "Hey, Arnie, look what I found!"

John stacked the last of the breakfast dishes in the dishwasher, poured the soap, and started it running. He scowled at the humming machine. It was typical of him, he thought wearily, that on the most important day of his life—on what might even be the last day of his life—he was washing the dishes. Good old dependable John, who always takes care of what needs to be done.

But he'd needed to stay busy, and he hadn't been able to think of anything else that needed doing. He couldn't do what he wanted, since the only thing he wanted to do right now was to be with Dora, and she'd said she needed time alone to think. So naturally he'd let her go off to look for her blasted cat, even though they were running short on time. The day was half over.

Was Jack with her right now? Helping her think?

He was so busy scowling at the dishwasher that it took a moment before he noticed the soft, plaintive meow coming from the back door. He went to it and opened it, and sure enough, there was Dora's cat. "Well?" he said after holding the door open a moment for the motionless cat. "Are you coming in or not?"

But the cat just kept looking at him with those improbably green eyes, almost as if she were trying to tell him something. "I suppose you're hinting that you'd like some more of Mrs. Millrow's scrambled eggs," he said, bending to pick her up and bring her inside. Dora wouldn't like it if the silly animal went off again. "Sorry, but they're all—hey!" The cat backed up a couple feet, sat down just out of reach, and stared at him.

He stepped out onto the back porch and reached for her again. This time she moved several feet and then paused, looking back over her shoulder at him.

He sighed. The stupid cat thought they were playing some sort of game. He remembered what Dora had done when she wanted to get her cat into the carrier, and went back into the house to open the refrigerator. Mrs. Millrow's cold cuts ought to do the trick.

Nine

There were three of them, three loud, stupid men who were scaring her half to death. One was small and skinny and nervous. He wore glasses. The other two were big men with matching beer bellies and butts so flat it was a wonder their pants stayed up. Maybe they were brothers. There was a certain Neanderthal resemblance.

The biggest one, the one with the beefiest shoulders and plenty of real muscle beneath the fat, was called Arnie. Arnie had a shotgun, and he seemed to be in charge. He'd told the others to gag her so she couldn't cast a spell on them.

The idiots thought she was a sprite.

The one who'd caught her—one of the beer bellies—held her arms behind her back while the skinny one tied the gag at the back of her head. It tasted like old sweat and motor oil. "Are you sure she can't spell us with this in her mouth?" he asked nervously, moving away from her as soon as he'd finished with the gag.

"She can't do a damned thing if she can't talk or move her hands," Arnie said. "Long as Ned keeps a good grip on her, she can't do nuthin'. Ain't that right, honey?" He chucked her beneath the chin and grinned when she jerked her head back and glared at him.

"What're we gonna do with her, though?" the other beer belly asked. "I thought we came here to get that Raven guy. What do we want with her?"

Arnie gave an evil chuckle. "Well, if you can't think of nuthin' to do with a pretty thing like this, I sure can."

Dora's stomach turned over. Instinctively she tried to pull loose, but the one holding her jerked her arms up painfully high. Tears of pain and frustration sprang to her eyes.

"Are you sure she's a sprite?" the nervous one asked. "She looks kinda big for one. If she ain't a sprite, we could get in big trouble for this."

"What else would she be?" Arnie demanded. "She was with that Raven bastard earlier, wasn't she, Ned?"

Ned—the other beer belly—nodded. "They was all over each other, too."

"That proves it. No decent human woman would be fooling around with him."

"Maybe she's not decent. Maybe she's a witch. I don't want to mess with no witch, Arnie."

Arnie laughed. "You don't want to mess with anything but your own five fingers, Dennis, that's fine with me. You can watch."

"But what about Raven?" Ned insisted stubbornly. "I thought we were gonna make him turn poor old Blackie back into a dog."

"We will. He's gonna pay for messing with me. And this pretty thing is how we'll do it. He wants her, or he wouldn't have been screwin' with her in the woods. We'll make him come out of his big house to get her, and then we can get him." Arnie leaned closer to Dora. His breath smelled worse than the gag tasted. "No reason we can't have a little fun first, though."

Poof!

"You fellows are really dumb, you know that?" Jack

leaned against an old oak, smiling, his arms crossed negligently. "Dumb as sheep, in fact."

The nervous one squeaked. Ned cursed, and Arnie swung around, the shotgun lifting as he turned. "Hold it right there, Raven."

Jack made a funny, waggling gesture with his hand and intoned, "Men thou art, but won't remain. Four cloven hoofs to match thy sheeplike—"

Arnie brought the shotgun up to his shoulder.

Poof!

"Oh, God," Dennis said, his eyes huge behind his glasses. "Oh, God. Oh, God."

"Where'd he go? Dammit, Arnie, where did he—"

Poof!

Jack grinned at them from the other end of the small clearing. "Boo!"

Arnie jumped, swung around, shotgun still on his shoulder, and fired.

John crouched near the porch, a slice of roast beef in his hand, and glared at Dora's cat, who kept moving away every time he got close. Maybe the stupid animal didn't like roast beef as much as turkey, but dammit, he didn't have any turkey. Maybe the ham—

A shotgun blast shattered the quiet. His head jerked up in alarm.

It had come from the woods. Where Dora was.

He dropped the meat and started running.

Jack was driving the Neanderthal brothers crazy. Dora knew he was out of magic, but his *poofs* were faster than a speeding bullet—or shotgun shell—and the three men were loosing it. Ned kept spinning around with her, trying to keep her between himself and Jack, but Jack was too unpredictable. The third man, the one with glasses, stood in one spot and shrieked every time Jack popped up.

But Arnie kept hold of his weapon, and he had just enough sense not to keep firing, though he held the shotgun ready on his shoulder. He was cursing a lot, but he hadn't fired the second shell.

Dora's heart was going crazy, too, pounding like it wanted to jump right out of her chest.

Poof! Jack stood directly behind Arnie and tapped him on the shoulder. Arnie whirled, bellowing. Dora stumbled helplessly as the man holding her spun around again.

Poof! Jack stood beside Dora, grinned, and goosed Ned's big belly. "Gotcha!" Ned growled and let go of Dora with one hand to reach for him and—

Poof!

Dora didn't see where Jack went that time. As soon as Ned reach for Jack, she flung herself to one side with all her weight. She managed to pull free from his one-handed grip, but the impetus carried her to the ground. She rolled away. The awful gag came loose in the process, and she scrambled quickly to her feet.

The roar of a shotgun blast made her freeze in a second's heart-stopping terror. *Jack!*

That second was all Ned needed to grab her by the arm, wrenching her back toward him so suddenly she twisted her ankle. He wrapped both arms around her, pulling her tight against him. Her mouth was free now, but she couldn't move. Arnie had the shotgun broken open and was popping fresh shells into it with alarming speed, and Jack—where was Jack?

"That's enough," a cool, commanding voice said from one side of the clearing. "I've already called the sheriff, so you boys better be on your way. Fast."

Dora's head, the only part of her that could move, turned quickly. *John!* He was walking toward them, as calm and collected as if he were the one with the gun, his black eyes as cold as the deepest pit of hell—and Jack stood only a few yards away, grinning!

"Omigod!" the one with glasses shrieked. "There's two of him!" And he bolted in the other direction.

Ned had finally had too much. His grip on Dora slackened, and she pulled away, but when she tried to run, her ankle gave out beneath her. She stumbled, going to one knee.

Arnie was either made of sterner stuff than his brother or he was too mad to think. He slammed the shotgun shut and raised it to his shoulder as he turned, sighting down it and yelling obscenities.

He's going to shoot! Dora thought, terrified. *He's aiming right at John, and John can't poof himself out of the way!* And she opened her mouth and screamed words she hadn't used since a certain junior high pep rally—the words to the only spell she knew: "Bibbity-boo, undo his shoe!"

It worked exactly the way it had worked at that long-ago pep rally.

Every stitch Arnie was wearing came apart instantly. His clothes fell away, leaving him in all his fat, naked, hairy ugliness. Behind her, she heard a strange, gargled scream. She turned her head and saw way more than she wanted to of Ned, whose tiny little eyes were opened as wide as they would go.

A small black shape darted out of the underbrush and flung itself at Ned. Claws out, howling her battle cry, Mitzi landed on the man's bare bottom and clung. Ned howled louder than the cat and shook all over like a fleshly earthquake, dislodging Mitzi, then he took off running.

Arnie bellowed. Dora's head snapped back around. She watched in terror as the shotgun came around with him as he turned toward her. She tried to get to her feet, but her ankle wouldn't hold her up. "You witch, you bitch, you witch," he was yelling over and over, with both barrels pointed straight at her.

She heard John yell something a split second before she heard the deafening blast of the gun.

Poof!

Jack stood directly in front of her. For a second. Then his knees folded, and he sank slowly to the ground.

She screamed and scrambled to him. Out of the corner of her eye she saw John—running now, flat-out—and Arnie, who stood staring stupidly at the result of his violence, as if he'd never expected a shotgun blast to cause all that blood.

Oh, God. So much blood. All over Jack's chest, so much blood. His eyes, those wonderful green eyes, were dazed, hazy with shock and pain. She took his hand in both of hers. "Jack. Jack, I'm here."

His eyes focused slowly on her, and he smiled. "My fault," he said faintly. "Not . . . yours."

And her heart broke.

She heard a loud thud, jolted, and looked over her shoulder. John held the shotgun by the barrel like a club. Arnie was on the ground at his feet, unconscious or . . . probably unconscious, she thought. Not that she cared much at the moment which he was.

John looked at her. "Are you all right?"

"I'm fine, I'm fine, but Jack—" Her breath hitched. "Jack took the shotgun blast in his chest. He saved me, but he—he—" She couldn't say it.

Jack said it for her. "Looks like . . . I was right. Not . . . immortal."

In the aftermath of farce and violence, the birds were silent. So were the four people who remained in that small clearing in the woods. One of them was quiet because he was unconscious; another because she was crying, the tears streaming silently down her face.

The third was quiet because he was dying.

And the fourth stood in helpless silence, looking at Dora's

tears and Jack's blood and feeling a terrible, yawning emptiness open up inside him. He knelt on the other side of Jack.
"Hold on," he said tersely. "We'll have a doctor here soon."

Jack's head moved slightly in a negative. "No . . . point.
Just confuse people. Damn." His eyes closed. "Hurts."

"If you think I'm going to let you die a hero's death,"
John started to say roughly—and Jack flickered, going from
there to not-there and back again so quickly John's eyes
couldn't quite follow. "Dammit!"

"John!" Dora cried. "John, he's going away! Can you feel
it?"

He could, and it felt worse than he would have dreamed
possible. As if someone were reaching inside him to scoop
something out, leaving an angry, empty place. "What can I
do?" He ran a hand over his hair. "Dammit, Jack, don't you
have any magic left? Just a little, even a little would help."

Jack's eyes opened again. The green was dull now, but one
corner of his mouth turned up irrepressibly. "Fixed the chickens. Can't fix . . . this. Have to deal . . . with the sheriff . . . by
yourself . . . tomorrow. Dora, do you . . . ."

He flickered and she cried out, her knuckles going white
as she held onto his hand tightly.

". . . think you might . . . have chosen me?"

She nodded, swallowed, and managed to speak. "I—I
might. If I'd had to choose. Because I realized that I love you
both."

Jack was smiling slightly as his eyes closed again. "Think
I . . . love you, too. Funny feeling."

Dora gulped back a sob. "Then you can't leave me. You
can't. I don't think this was my choice, not anymore. I'd just
figured that out and was going to the house to tell John when
they grabbed me. The verse wasn't talking about my choice.
It was your choice, and John's."

"What do you mean?" John asked hoarsely. "The bride's
choice. That's you. Not me. Not him."

She looked up at him, her eyes shiny with tears. "But this wasn't about the bride's choice, not anymore. The verse on the bottle talked about the final choice, not the bride's choice. I wondered—what if the two of you weren't supposed to be separate? What if you were supposed to somehow be one again?"

The words from the verse echoed in John's mind. *If on All Hallows' Eve this binding breaks and two stand separate in the sun, then the final choosing must be made—for at day's end there can be only one.* The damned thing seemed to be coming true. Soon there would be only one. And John didn't want it to happen. He didn't want—

Jack flickered.

John felt it deep inside him, but not like the tugging. This feeling wasn't a pull or a temptation. It was loss. Dreadful, permanent loss.

"Why don't you touch him?" Dora cried. "Even now, you don't touch him!"

Something deep inside John cracked open, and he *knew*. He'd never touched Jack. Never dared, because . . . because something huge and irrevocable would happen if he did. If he touched Jack, if he accepted the other even that much . . . but Jack was dying. Dying because he'd saved Dora. He had put himself in the path of that shotgun blast for her sake.

Slowly, John reached out his hand.

Jack's eyes came open. For a second they burned green again, bright, hot green. His fingers twitched as if he wanted to reach for John.

John took Jack's hand in his.

The shock was stronger this time, a rolling, reverberating current that belled through him from fingers to arm to shoulders, until everything inside him seemed to be shaking loose. But he didn't let go. He held on with everything in him, even when it felt like he was being shaken loose, shaken *free*—

Jack flickered. And was gone.

Darkness grabbed John in two fists and dragged him down.

Dora knelt in the fallen leaves and held John's hand. There was blood on her own hand, closed tightly around his. Jack's blood. More blood soaked the leaves in front of her.

But Jack's body wasn't there. Just John's. And he was unconscious.

Mitzi came out from wherever she'd hidden herself after Ned shook her off and rubbed up against Dora, purring. The warmth of her furry body was small consolation, but it was all Dora had at the moment. With her free hand, she stroked her cat, silently thanking her for her assistance and her company.

John's eyes flickered open. Black eyes, dark as a moonless night.

Dora cried out and flung herself down on him, kissing his cheek, his forehead, everywhere. "Oh, John, I was so afraid I'd lost you, too."

"Careful." He took her arms and pushed her gently off him. He sat up, looking dazed and rubbing his chest. "I'm still sore there."

Dora's heart stopped—and started again. "Still? John, it *is* you, isn't it?"

"Oh, yes. I'm John." He stopped rubbing his chest to look at her. There was a strange glint in his eyes. "Mostly."

"Mostly?"

He held out an arm and studied it. "My chest is sore, but it's not bad. The rest of me feels pretty good. Damned good, in fact." He looked back at her. "I had the translation wrong."

"You—you did?"

He nodded seriously. "Instead of 'there can be only one,' I should have said something like, 'there *may* be only one.' It was never meant as a warning. More like a guide, when the time was right. The split wasn't supposed to be permanent. It was only supposed to last until the hostility toward magic had eased." His eyes turned tender. "Especially in the heart of the woman the heir found to love. You were right. The final choice was mine."

It was one thing to contemplate two beings becoming one. It was another to sit and talk with someone who wasn't quite either of the men she'd loved. Dora swallowed. "You know everything now?"

"Not everything. But when I put together what I knew with what he knew, I can figure most of it out."

"Uh—which *I* are you?"

"Both. Which sounds confusing—hell, it *is* confusing—but it feels . . . not bad." He grinned suddenly. "Not bad at all."

There was something about his grin. Something cocky and distinctly un-John-like. "Jack?" she whispered.

"Yes and no. Here," he said, his voice lowering as he raised his hand to sift gently through her hair. "Let me show you." And he kissed her.

He tasted as sweet as dream-grapes and as faithful as the slow, rich promises of midnight. His hands slid over her, teasing her, easing her onto her back in the dry autumn leaves. Dora's head spun with a dizzying mixture of lust, love, and pure joy.

There was nothing missing in John's kiss anymore. It held everything she'd ever wanted.

After a long moment, he lifted his head. She thought she saw those dark eyes flash a bright, merry green, though the color was there and gone too quickly for her to be sure. "Shall we go back to Century's End to finish this?" he asked softly.

"No." She threaded her hands behind his neck, her heart full to bursting. "I think we're fine just like we are."

If you enjoyed **Charmed**,
turn the page for an excerpt from

Infinity

by MAGGIE SHAYNE

Available now from Jove Books

I rode my faithful Black, and he stepped high, as though he knew the man he bore to be of an utterly different breed than those others who surrounded us. Beside me rode an old friend . . . a mortal, chieftain of his clan, and laird as well. Joseph Lachlan welcomed my visit. He called me his cousin because I claimed to be. But though I supposed I might be some distant relative of his, the link was too old to trace now. I used the name and claimed the clan Lachlan only when it suited me.

Joseph didn't doubt me, nor did he ask why I might need to retreat here for a time. And that was just as well, for I couldn't have told him the answers had he questioned me. The truth was that resting from the constant battle was only one of the reasons I'd come.

Another was the skulking, dark robed pair who'd been following me on and off over the previous seven centuries. Always silent, always faceless within the caves of their hoods. But I didn't need to look upon their faces to know. I'd avoided them sometimes. On other occasions, they had vanished without explanation. But more often than not, I'd fought them. Sometimes one at a time, frequently both together. Once I had nearly bested Kohl, but he fled before I could finish the job. And once—this last time—the two immortal brothers had done the same to me, and *I* had fled. To Stonehaven—my sanctuary.

I feared very little, almost nothing. But there was a cold dread in the pit of my stomach where my oldest and most bitter enemies were concerned. And it came, I believe, of knowing exactly why they had stalked me so doggedly, and for so long.

They blamed me for the deaths of their sister and their nephews . . . my wife and my sons. And they would never stop until they had taken my heart.

Or I theirs.

So I had come here to rest from the endless fighting. I put it from my thoughts in order to focus on the other reason I had returned to Stonehaven—the more important one. Her. The girl who had drawn me back here time and time again over the past seventeen years.

"You never age, Nicodimus," Joseph remarked. "You look to be the same fair lad I last saw five years past."

I sent a cocky grin his way. "And you've grown wrinkles about your eyes, Joseph. Soon I'll mistake you for my father." Joseph was perfectly bald, his pale head as shiny as his cheeks and his bulbous nose. He did have brows and lashes, but of a hue so pale it seemed as if he were entirely hairless. When he smiled, as he often did, it seemed even his bald head smiled along.

"No hope of that, lad. Your father was twice the man I'll ever be." Joseph lowered his chin. "I do miss him. But havin' you here on occasion is almost like havin' my dear cousin back with me again."

I had to avert my eyes. Joseph had never known my father. He had known only me. But when he'd seen me die at his side on a field of battle, I'd had no choice but to stay away for many years. And when I returned—as I had been compelled to do—I had simply claimed to be my own son. He had believed me.

"My father often spoke similarly of you, Joseph," I said after a pause. I nudged Black's sides with my heels. The stallion trotted forward along the narrow, twisting paths of the village, chickens scattering in his wake. A fat man rolled a barrel of ale from a rickety wagon into the daub-and-wattle hovel that passed as the village tavern, while across the way a woman hurled wash water from a window hole where no glass had ever stood.

I'd seen London and Rome, Paris and Constantinople, great cities all around the world. Yet I marveled at how this tiny hamlet had grown. For when I had lived there it had borne no name. My home had been a thatched straw hut, cured hides stretched over the walls had served to keep out the cold. The meat I killed, my wife had cooked over a fire on the dirt floor.

Anya. Beautiful Anya. Meek, gentle, fragile. I could see her still, in my mind. Soft brown hair and eyes like the palest winter sky, her belly swelling with our third child as she watched over the other two. And I could see our boys. Jaymes, growing taller by the day and too skinny to stand up to a windstorm, though he ate more than his brother and I together. He had his mother's coloring, Jaymes did. And Will, a head shorter, but strong, already looking more man than boy. Hunting at my side, and outdoing me now and again. Begging to fight beside me as well.

The old pain trembled and howled and threatened to break free. I caught it with a will of forged steel, and forced it still and silent.

"The village hasna' changed since last you were here," Joseph said, pulling me out of my thoughts.

Ahead of me, the crofters' cottages leaned crookedly, their thatched roofs showing wear. I caught myself studying the villagers we passed, with their well worn kilts and haggard faces, and realized I was seeking the golden child as I did on each visit. But I did not see her there. And it occurred to me then that I might not even recognize her at first glance, after so long.

I nearly smiled at the unlikelihood of that.

She stood out from the rest of the villagers the way a diamond stands out among bits of coal; her dark brown eyes gleaming against ivory skin. Her corn-yellow hair. Her upturned bit of a nose, and the gleam of life in her little girl eyes. And more. A spirit, a fire, undefinable, yet all but gleaming in its brilliance.

She had been a child, barely twelve years of age, when last I had seen her. She would be . . . seven and ten now. Quite possibly wed—though people here now married later than they used to. I'd made Anya my wife when I'd been but four and ten. But things changed a great deal in seven long centuries. And wedded or not, this girl, Arianna, was likely still unaware of what she truly was.

"Is that saddle maker still in the village, Joseph?" I asked abruptly. "Sinclair, wasn't it?"

"Aye. Is your saddle in need of repair?" Joseph eyed it, likely seeing that it was perfectly fine. Likely thinking that I never paid him a visit but that I needed repairs done to my saddle.

"Only a bit of loose stitching at the girth," I told him. "But I ought have it checked before I leave again."

Joseph nodded. "'Twas a cursed bad year for poor Sinclair. Cursed bad."

My head swung toward him. "Was it?"

"Aye." Joseph's lips thinned, and his bald head joined his brow in a frown. "Lost a daughter, he did."

At those words, my heart seemed to ice over. I had been

watching the girl all her life, awaiting the time when I would explain her own nature to her. When she was old enough, and mature enough to understand and deal with the truth. Perhaps I had waited too long. I tried to speak, but couldn't.

Joseph never seemed to notice the force of my reactions. He was involved now in the telling of his tale. "Nearly lost the both of his girls, that sad day. Over a year ago, 'twas. They'd been up to no good, playin' in the loch when their father had forbidden it. My lads were about, heard the shoutin'. Kenyon pulled the one to safety, an' Lud went back for her sister. But 'twas no use . . . she drowned in the muddy waters of Loch Haven."

"Drowned?" I asked, nearly holding my breath.

"Aye. And young Arianna has ne'er been right since the day the loch claimed her sister."

I lowered my head and released my breath all at once. So Arianna was alive . . . Not that she could have died by drowning. She'd have revived . . . but to what?

Joseph nodded toward some distant point. "See for yourself, Nicodimus. She's there now, at the grave. 'Tis no place for a lass of ten and seven to be spendin' all her time. An' alone, no less! She's forever walkin' about alone." He ran a hand over his head, and slowly shook it.

I frowned, knowing exactly what Joseph implied. It was said that only a Witch walked about all alone. Only a Witch. And Arianna *was* one. But she couldn't know that. Not yet.

"Perhaps if I were to have a word with her," I suggested.

Joseph drew his mount to a halt, frowning at me. "Do you think it wise?"

"Why not? I've lost loved ones myself. I know a bit of what she's feeling." I knew, I realized, far too much of what she was feeling. It was a feeling she would have to get used to, for in time she would lose everyone and everything she knew. I sighed as I looked at her. Slight, so slight. Barely larger than she'd been at twelve. A golden wisp of a girl, the picture of innocence. She would have to learn to be hard. To close herself off. She would have to learn to stop caring, as I had done.

Looking worried, Joseph nodded all the same. "Take care, my friend. Dinna spend too long with her. She's promised to the cobbler's son, but even he's beginning to shy away. There's been some talk. . . ."

"What sort of talk?"

Joseph shrugged. "Ah, I pay it no mind, nor will I tolerate anyone persecutin' the poor lassie. We must make allowances, after all. Grief can twist a mind in all manner of—"

"*What sort of talk,* Joseph?"

Joseph cleared his throat. "Some claim she slips out alone in the dead of night. An' she's been seen speakin' to The Crones more than once. What people will make of it . . . well, you can guess as well as I."

The Crones . . . the outcasts. The word "Witch" was never spoken aloud here. The people were too superstitious to dare it. Everyone in the village knew what the three old women were, yet The Crones were tolerated. Their shack outside the village at the edge of the forest was left alone. That happy state would likely continue, so long as only good fortune smiled down upon the flocks and the crops and the crofters here. As for the blue-blooded Christians of Stonehaven, most would no more exchange a public greeting with The Crones than eat from the trough of a pig. But they visited the old women every now and then, for a potion to cure the croup or a charm for good luck. In secrecy. In hypocrisy.

I turned again to stare at the girl. She knelt beside the grave of her sister off in the distance. Perhaps she knew more than I'd thought she possibly could. It would explain her visits to the village Witches. But who was there to tell her? I'd never met another High Witch, Dark nor Light, in this part of Scotland. Never. And our secrets were seldom shared with anyone else. I'd ascertained years ago that The Crones were mere mortals, and knew nothing of our existence.

"I'll speak with her," I said. "Before she lets the gossips ruin her."

Joseph nodded. "Perhaps 'twill do some good at that. Shall I wait at the tavern, then?"

"If the owner still brews that secret recipe of his."

"Heather Ale?" Joseph asked with a crook of his invisible brow that resulted in new wrinkles appearing in his forehead. "That he does, Nic. That he does." Joseph gave a wink, and wheeled his horse about, heading away.

I turned my attention toward the cemetery once more, and nudged Black's sides until he leapt into a spirited trot. Stopping him a short distance away from the girl, I tied him to a scraggly tree, then walked to where Arianna Sinclair knelt. For a moment, I only stood still and silent, looking at her.

Arianna had changed. In five short years she'd grown from a waif into a woman. And that aura of vitality that had always surrounded her seemed stronger than ever before. Her golden hair draped about her shoulders like a shawl of spun sunlight, moving in the breeze every now and again. And I'd been wrong when I'd concluded she had not grown, for she had. Her breasts swelled now, a woman's breasts, straining the fabric of her homespun dress. Her hips had also taken on a sweet roundness, while her waist remained small.

Kneeling, spine straight, chin high, she lifted a fist, and let some herb or other spill from it atop her sister's grave, as she muttered soft words under her breath.

A spell. For the love of the Gods, had the girl no sense? In full daylight?

"What is it you're doing?" I called. I expected her to stiffen with surprise and perhaps fear at being caught. The lesson would do her good.

She didn't start, didn't turn to face me. "Should anyone

else ask, I'm plantin' wild heather upon my sister's burial site.''

"And if *I* ask."

"I think, Nicodimus, you know better than to ask."

I blinked in surprise. Just how much *did* she know? And the familiarity of her tone with me . . . as if she knew me far better than she did. We'd spoken only a handful of words to one another in the past. Polite greetings at most, though my interest in her had always been more than that of a stranger. She was my kind. A rarity in itself. She was without a teacher, and . . . and something about her spoke to me on a level I had never understood.

The herbs gone, she pounded her fist thrice on the ground; a time-honored method for releasing the energy raised in spell-work. Then she lowered her head for but an instant. Finally, she rose, brushing her hands on her skirts and facing me. Her velvet brown eyes hadn't been so large before . . . nor so haunted. "It has been a long while since your last visit here," she said.

"Long enough so I must wonder how you could have recognized my voice."

"'Twas nay your voice, Nicodimus. Although 'tis true, you speak distinctly enough."

"Do I?"

"Aye," she said. "Almost like a Sassenach, rather than a true Scot. Careful, an' slow, without a hint of an accent, so a body could never guess where you truly come from."

"I come from right here," I told her.

She shrugged, and I wasn't sure whether she believed me or not. "Regardless of *how* you speak," she went on, "I knew you were there long afore you did."

Her words gave me pause. If that were true, her natural powers were incredibly advanced—particularly for one so young. "How?" I asked her.

She shrugged again. "I always know when you're near. Have since . . . why since I was a wee bairn toddlin' along and clingin' to my mam's skirts . . an' you came ridin' into the village alongside Laird Lachlan. Do you recall?"

I did. It had been then I had first set eyes on her, and I'd known—even before I'd seen the crescent shaped birthmark on her chubby right flank—that she was one of us. "I remember it well."

Arms crossed over her middle, she sent me a steady look, and I studied her in return. Her small, upturned nose was the same as before. But her face had thinned. No babe's plumpness to her cheeks. Not now. It was a woman's face, touched by sorrow.

"I always wanted to ask you about it—that feelin' I get when you're near. But it seemed I should remember my place, and be neither impertinent nor disrespectful."

"But you've changed your mind about those things now?"

She glanced toward her sister's grave and her eyes grew darker, her voice softer. "They seem less important to me now than the dust in the highland wind, Nicodimus." Her eyes were round and filled with pain—and something else: rebellion. A dangerous wildness flashed from somewhere deep within her, and seemed to fit with the way her hair snapped whiplike with the wind, while her skirts flew about her ankles and bare, dirty feet.

"Propriety has its place, Arianna."

"Propriety," she whispered, looking directly at me again. "Society. Lairds and chieftains and crofters and slaves. What good is it, I ask you? What does any of it truly mean? Who cares whether a woman wears her hair unbound until she bears her first child, and bound up tight thereafter? Or if she walks about alone, or if she addresses a laird by his given name? What arrogant fool made up all these ridiculous rules that have us all hoppin' and scurryin' to obey?"

"You're angry," I said softly. "I understand that, Arianna . . ."

"Aye," she replied. "I am angry. 'Tis meaningless, all of it!"

Her voice had grown louder with every word, until I gripped her hands gently in my own and felt the jolt of awareness that occurs when one of our kind touches another. She looked at me quickly, shocked by that heat, wondering at it, I knew, but I said only, "Keep your voice low." And I inclined my head toward the village nearby, where already several sets of speculative eyes were turned our way. Hands shielding careworn faces from the morning sun. Squinting, searching gazes trying to see who dared raise her voice in the cemetery, of all places.

Arianna followed my gaze and saw her curious neighbors. She sent them a defiant glare with a toss of her head that reminded me of Black when he is agitated and smelling a battle; the way he shakes his mane almost in challenge. I moved to take my hands from hers, but she closed hers tight and clung with a strength that surprised me.

I looked down at our joined hands, and for the first time a ripple of alarm zigzagged up my spine to tap at my brain. For this was no child clinging to my hands. This was a woman, young and beautiful and full of fire. And her hands were slender and strong and warm.

'You *want* to make them gossip about you. Is that it?'' I asked her.

"Let them gossip. I dinna care."

I took my hands away. "Do you care what pain you cause others, Arianna?" I asked, in a second attempt to put her firmly in her place, to let her know that what she might have been thinking just now when our hands were locked together, could never, never be. She was hurting, full of anger, confused and lonely for her sister. That was all it was. "You're promised to the cobbler's son," I reminded her.

She tilted her head to one side and shrugged. But it seemed her rant had ended, for her face no longer seemed like that of a warrioress about to do battle. "*I* never made any such promise to Angus MacClennan. Nor do I intend to abide by it. An' believe me, that clod has no tender feelin's where I'm concerned."

"No? Why, then, do you suppose he's asked for your hand, Arianna?"

She smiled slowly, eyes sparkling now with mischief. "You can guess as well as I. He wants a servant. Someone to cook an' clean an' mend for him. But mostly, he wants someone to lift her skirts when he demands it. Someone to relieve his manly needs with so he'll nay have to hide in his da's woodshed an' do it himself—"

"*Arianna!*"

"What?"

She was all wide-eyed innocence, but I saw the gleam beyond it. I only scowled at her.

"A tender young girl isna supposed to ken such things, I suppose!" Again that expressive toss of her golden locks. "Nay, we're to blindly agree to be some man's slave an' his whore in exchange for our room and board. Well, it willna be me, Nicodimus. Not ever."

I had to bite back a smile. So bold and outspoken, and so damned determined. "A wife should be none of those things, Arianna."

"Name one who isna *all* of those things," she challenged me, leaning slightly forward, hands on her hips, legs shoulder width apart in a cocky stance.

"Your mother," I said.

She lost a bit of her cockiness. "'Tis different with my mam."

"Why?"

"Because my da loves her, I suppose."

"And are you so certain your cobbler's son doesn't love you?"

She peered up at me from beneath her dark lashes. "Not so much as he loves his hand on certain nights in his da's woodshed."

I had to look away. To laugh aloud would only encourage her. And she needed no encouragement.

For a moment I thought about how seldom it was that I found myself inclined toward laughter. Genuine laughter. "I like you, Arianna," I said. "Just take care to bite your tongue from time to time. Not everyone appreciates a sharp wit and bold talk from a young woman the way I do."

She smiled up at me, all but glowing. And I thought I would enjoy spending a bit of time with Arianna while at Stonehaven this time, getting to know the astounding young woman she had become. And then I was shaken out of my thoughts, for she suddenly grabbed my hands and held them, and her thumbs caressed the hollows of my palms in slow circles. She stared up at me, her inquisitive eyes probing mine.

"You're different from other men, Nicodimus. I've sensed it always. You pay no more mind to the world and its silly conventions than I do. You . . . you're like me, somehow."

I averted my eyes. "I don't know what you mean."

"Dinna you? You're supposed to be Laird Lachlan's kin, yet you dinna live in his keep. You bathe just as often as you like, without a care that the church calls it vanity."

"And just how would you know how often I bathe?"

Her smile was slow, and it stirred something to life deep within me. "You smell good, Nicodimus. Clean. I like the way you smell." I looked away from the heat in her eyes. Her palm came to my cheek, turning my head until I faced her again, and then it remained there. "An' what's more, you dare to talk openly and all alone to the girl half the clan thinks is crazy—"

"And the other half thinks is dabbling in Witchcraft," I interjected, hoping to shock her into silence. She saw too much, this girl. And she was looking far too closely, tampering with parts of me that no one had dared come near in a very long time. Her touch . . . rattled me. Relief sighed through my chest when her hand fell away from my cheek at last.

"An' what if I am a Witch?" she shot back, undaunted.

I stared at her in surprise. She was all fire and life and utter defiance, boldly blurting words that could easily get her killed. "'Tis no business of mine what you are, Arianna," I told her. "And no business of theirs, either. Do as you will."

She rolled her eyes. "I intend to do just that!"

I gripped her shoulders to make her listen. "But keep it to yourself, for the love of heaven! If you can't conform, then *pretend* to conform. And never, ever again must you say something so foolish aloud! For your own sake, girl, take the advice of one older and wiser. One who would like to see you live to grow into womanhood."

"I'm a woman already," she told me, chin high, hair sailing in the breeze. "A woman like no other woman you've ever known." She swayed slightly closer to me, gaze locked on my lips.

I dropped my hands from her shoulders and staggered backward as her bold, enticing eyes flashed fire at me. I'd come to her to try to help her. Instead, I felt as if I were under attack. Her forces battered my innermost tower, and I had a feeling they could bring it to rubble with minimal effort.

"An' since you've mentioned it," she went on, "just *how much* older and wiser are you, Nicodimus?" She smoothed the front of her dress as she spoke, her fingers brushing very near to her breasts, but her eyes never left my face.

I saw her meaning in those eyes. Saw it clear, for she didn't seem the least bit inclined to hide it from me. It unsettled me, shook me to my bones. I'd never thought of her in that way . . . not until this very moment—or perhaps a few moments ago, when I'd seen her again, a woman grown.

"Too old for what you have in mind," I said, hoping I sounded mildly amused and sardonic. "Go find your cobbler's son now, and torment him in my stead."

But even as I turned to leave her, my mind spun its arguments. She would be eighteen in a fortnight. Oh, yes, I knew the date of her birth. I knew more about her than she knew about herself. I was over seven centuries old . . . and yet at the time of my first death, I'd been twenty and eight. Physically . . . I still was. And never more aware of it.

"You're meant for me, Nicodimus," she called as I walked away. "You must ken that as well as I."

I froze where I stood. She came toward me, but didn't stop when she reached my side. Instead she kept walking, brushing past me, and dropping a kiss upon my cheek as she did. The touch of her lips sent heat through me all the way to my toes. "You'll be mine one day," she whispered. "An' then, Nicodimus, I will know all the secrets you hide behind your sapphire eyes."

A shiver raced up my spine as I watched Arianna walk away, golden hair dancing in the wind. She walked proudly right up to where a crowd of crofters stood pretending not to watch her antics. Her chin jutting high, she nodded hello to each of them, her entire stance oozing defiance—as if she were silently daring anyone to chide her for going about alone. Or for kissing a guest of their laird so boldly.

Or for muttering incantations over her dead sister—and in the daylight at that.

Daring them.

No one took the challenge.

She was right when she said she was a woman like no other. For there had never been another who touched my soul the way she did.